"If you've ever sensed, deep down, that the world you think you inhabit is a screen between you and divine reality, you are already primed for what David Bentley Hart has lovingly prepared for us in *Kenogaia*. What have we lost, to be born into this world? And what might be required of each of us to awaken from our dream of life in this shadow of reality? Plashing about in this thrill of a tale, I rediscovered, bit by bit, just what I have had to sacrifice in order to grow up."

— CRAIG LUCAS, author of *The Light in the Piazza* and *Reckless and Other Plays*

"David Hart's *Kenogaia* is many things — gnostic fairytale, satire of ecclesial hierarchy, anarchist comedy of terrors. But mostly, it is a rollicking good story, replete with shapeshifting wolves, heretical astronomers, nightmarish river journeys, scheming sorcerers, and ten thousand other magical tricks and treats. Hart is as erudite and mellifluous as ever, but make no mistake: this is a classic fantasy novel, to be shelved alongside those of Ursula Le Guin and David Lindsay."

— MICHAEL ROBBINS, author of *Walkman* and *Alien vs. Predator*

"David Bentley Hart is the most significant living theologian, and he's also certainly the most deft at turning a phrase and crafting a narrative. Contra Plato, Hart knows that there is no wisdom without poetry; contra Calvin, he understands that without beauty we can never ascend to God. His new book *Kenogaia* (A Gnostic Tale) is the *opus* of a thinker at the height of his abilities, a masterful embodiment of the philosophical novel, and a perfect synthesis of fiction and metaphysics. *Kenogaia*, as both gnostic conjuration and orphic incantation, is an initiation into the mysteries for our present moment."

— ED SIMON, author of *Binding the Ghost: Theology, Mystery, and the Transcendence of Literature* (forthcoming)

"When Aristotle wrote that the soul never thinks without images, could he have been anticipating the phantasmata of David Bentley Hart's brilliant Gnostic fantasy? What flickers through this gripping tale of awakening and coming very quickly of age casts its sublunary light on adolescent anxiety, celestial visitation, institutional mendacity, and a thoroughgoing demiurgical wickedness that dwells in the hearts of men (and wolves). But there is light in darkness. And the Pleroma beyond the spheres (we are assured) contains everything. What a book! I raise my phosphorion in salute to *Kenogaia*."

— PETER O'LEARY, author of *The Sampo* and *Phosphorescence of Thought*

"There are few philosophical-theological genres to which David Bentley Hart has not put his hand: always with gusto, characteristic brilliance, and spectacular results. His latest effort, a novel — and a Gnostic one at that — is no exception: *Kenogaia* is a work of outstanding literary craftsmanship, exuberant imagination, and rare religious insight. Hart brings forth a world at once alien (as any Gnostic universe should be) and frighteningly familiar, which makes his book such a compelling read. Inspired by *Hymn of the Pearl*, one of the finest Gnostic texts to have come down to us, Hart's novel breathes new life and meaning into the ancient art of mythmaking."

— **COSTICA BRADATAN**, author of *Dying for Ideas: The Dangerous Lives of the Philosophers*

"Written in evocative prose that wears its learning lightly and combines fairy tale simplicity with the author's inimitable flashes of verbal flair, *Kenogaia* is an enchanting work. It delights also in its surprising play with genres and familiar allusions to Gnostic myth and classical cosmology. Like a telescope, it opens out onto a cosmic vision; but, not stopping there, takes us on a journey full of adventure, beauty, and terror, while wisely subverting aspects of its setting, in a conclusion that exceeds, even while redeeming, our expectations."

— **JAKOB ZIGURAS**, author of *Chains of Snow* and *The Sepia Carousel*

Kenogaia

KENOGAIA
(A Gnostic Tale)

DAVID BENTLEY HART

Angelico Press

For information, address:
Angelico Press, Ltd.
169 Monitor St.
Brooklyn, NY 11222
www.angelicopress.com

ppr 978-1-62138-794-7
cloth 978-1-62138-795-4
ebook 978-1-62138-796-1

Cover art by Jerome Atherholt
Book and cover design
by Michael Schrauzer

For Patrick

C'est nous qui fabriquons la machine,
et nous qui créons son Dieu.

CONTENTS

ἐν τῷ κόσμῳ θλῖψιν ἔχετε·
ἀλλὰ θαρσεῖτε,
ἐγὼ νενίκηκα τὸν κόσμον.

PART ONE
Wolves in the Night

When I was a child in my father's kingdom,
I dwelt in a palace of gold and jade,
And roamed its shining halls in guileless freedom,
Unmindful of its splendors. There I played
In perfect innocence of lands beyond
My garden walls and gleaming marble pools;
I knew each flower and each bending frond —
Blue fountains, songs, the frolics of our fools.

But, while yet young, I was provisioned for
A journey to a distant land, then made
To leave my palace by a secret door
Of silver with pale chrysoprase inlaid.
In terror, trembling, I was led outside
The western courtyard's seventh crystal gate.
I clutched a vagrant's bundle, which belied
The riches that I bore from our estate.

— from "The Hymn of the Pearl"

I

IDWAY IN HIS ASCENT TO THE TOP OF HIS father's observation tower, Michael Ambrosius paused on the landing that separated the lower spiral flight of forty stairs from the higher—not, as he would usually have done, to look out through its large oval window at the forest canopy surging grandly away to the east in countless wind-stirred billows of shimmering green and blue, but because he had been startled by the sight of the strange bird perched on the outside sill, peering in at him. He had never before seen such a creature. It was of only average size, slightly smaller than a pigeon, but was of so pure and perfect and sleek a white—not only its feathers, but its delicate legs and small triangular beak as well—that it appeared almost to glow with a light of its own, and the soft rainbow sheen that played about the edges of its plumage seemed to color the surrounding air with a pale prismatic radiance. Only its eyes, which were intently fixed on him, differed in hue: they were like two small gleaming gems, of an azure so deep and yet so bright that it scarcely appeared natural. "Oh, my . . ." Michael whispered, because nothing else occurred to him. Cautiously, he stepped toward the window, wanting a closer view but fearing he might frighten the bird away. It seemed utterly unperturbed at his approach, however. Even when he drew within a few inches of the glass and laid his fingertips among the elaborately carved vines and flowers of the frame, it remained still, and merely continued to survey him with what to Michael seemed an almost haughtily reserved gaze of appraisal. For several moments, the two of them—boy and bird—stared directly at one another, and Michael could not help but feel that behind the uncanny blue of the eyes that met his own there lurked a penetrating intelligence that had made him the object of its scrutiny. Then at last, quite casually, the bird disengaged its gaze from his, turned its head, and then its body, spread its wings, and gracefully dropped from the ledge. Michael pressed his forehead against the glass to follow its flight, but could see it for only a few seconds as it sank toward the trees below, like a falling star flashing over an evening sea, then stretched its wings wide and glided swiftly out of view around the far side of the tower. "Beautiful," Michael said, again in a whisper. He waited several moments to see whether the bird would reappear, but when it failed to do so he resumed his ascent.

When he had reached the low door of dark red wood on the upper landing, and had briefly returned the jovial leer of the elfin, leaf-enwreathed face carved in it, Michael took hold of the knob of red cut-glass, entered the observatory, and found his father standing at the center of the room in precisely the pose he had expected: both shoulders slightly hunched under the shapeless cope of his large gray sweater, one eye pressed against the eyepiece of his enormous bronze telescope, both hands clasping one of the brass rails encircling its conical, rose-marble base. The angle of the telescope was steep, directed through the ceiling's glass dome at some point high in the eastern sky; and, set off against the lustrous leather spines of books and the amber wooden bookcases arranged around the room's walls, it gave the impression of some fabulous magical tree in a dark forest that the wind had partly uprooted and left at a precarious tilt. The illusion was enhanced by the delicate moldings that rose along the fourteen feet of its cylinder, designed to look like a copse of slender tree trunks, culminating at the copper casing of the great lens in a glittering cloud of silver and aquamarine enamel leaves, lavishly fruited with polished stones of green and purple.

"Father," began Michael, "I've just seen the most amazing . . ."

But Mr. Ambrosius, without turning his head, raised a hand and said, "Wait, wait, son. I need to concentrate." Then, with the same hand and with great care, he slightly adjusted the small knob of the eyepiece. For several seconds thereafter, until he seemed satisfied with the result, he did not move; then he reluctantly detached himself from the telescope and turned to Michael, smoothing his rather unkempt black and gray beard with one hand and donning his wire-rimmed spectacles with the other. "Are you back from school already?" he asked, blinking hazily.

"School doesn't begin again for another twenty-three days," said Michael.

Mr. Ambrosius stared at him for a moment, as if not entirely certain whether to believe this. "You haven't been down in the village then?"

"No. I haven't gone down the mountain all week."

"Why not?"

"Because school doesn't start again for twenty-three days."

"Really?" Mr. Ambrosius sighed and tugged pensively at one of his earlobes. "Are you quite sure?"

"Yes, quite."

Mr. Ambrosius shook his head gently. "I see," he said. "Well, well. Well indeed. And, so then . . . when does school resume?"

"In twenty-three days," Michael said, patiently. "Father"— he took several steps forward —"you've seemed a bit distracted lately. I mean, more than normal."

"Have I?" Mr. Ambrosius removed his spectacles again and laid his hand across his eyes. "Tired, I'm afraid. I should probably go to bed at a seemlier hour."

For some seconds, neither of them said anything. Then, perceiving that his father had already begun to forget that anyone beside himself was there, Michael idly remarked, "That really is a very beautiful telescope. Mr. Snout would hate it, but I love it."

"Mr. Snout?" his father murmured.

"He's the school's tutor in 'The History of Design: Organic, Mechanical, and Decorative.' He's opposed to the 'vegetal style' in art. That's what he calls it."

Mr. Ambrosius sighed, removed his hand from his eyes, and replaced his spectacles; he turned his gaze not toward Michael, however, but upward and away, as though contemplating something hovering in the air overhead. "Why, pray tell?" he said quietly, almost as if talking to himself. "Doesn't that style come from this part of the world originally?"

"I think that's one of the things he dislikes about it," said Michael. "He's not from Oreiotopia originally. He's from the city, like us."

"Seems a paltry reason for the prejudice."

"It's not just that, I don't think. He says that that whole approach to design comes from the arts and crafts movement of the last century, which he thinks is horrible and calls"— here Michael imitated his teacher's sternly pompous tone —"*one of those very lamentable periodic backward steps in cultural history.*"

"Backward from what?" asked Mr. Ambrosius with an air of indifference.

"From all the progress mankind has made ever since the Age of Illumination."

"Ah."

"He's very serious about it," said Michael when his father failed to elaborate on this. "He says it's a '*degenerate*' style and that it's polluted with a '*comically rustic sentimentality,*' and . . ." Michael's voice wavered back and forth between its natural intonations and his caricature of his teacher.

"Goodness."

"And," Michael continued, "he absolutely detests it because it's just, he says, 'a great heap of dainty, dreamy mannerisms, all pastels and plummy twilights and glimmery gossamers,' and that we're so fortunate that art has since turned back to 'the serene, supremely rational, unpretentious barrenness of the industrial-mechanistic style,' and away from 'a morbid nostalgia for nature's disorder,' and . . ."

"My," Mr. Ambrosius interrupted, still half lost in thought, "he does say a great deal, doesn't he? And you always remember things so precisely and . . ." — he coughed — ". . . exhaustively. But enough of the mockery now. He's still your tutor."

"According to him," Michael continued, scarcely noticing the rebuke, "the technical name of that particular kind of design there is either 'arborescent,' which comes from the Virtuous Tongue and means 'becoming a tree,' or 'dendrogonic,' which comes from the Noble Tongue and means nearly the same thing, and that . . ."

"Yes, yes," said Mr. Ambrosius with a feeble smile. "You really do have a lush vocabulary for a lad of twelve."

"I'm thirteen, father. Remember? My birthday was two months ago."

"I remember the event, just not the arithmetic. I especially remember you and Laura Magian devouring an enormous number of cakes." He stroked his beard again. "Thirteen, though — are you sure?"

"Yes," said Michael earnestly. "I keep a close account of those things."

Mr. Ambrosius nodded slightly, still staring into space. "Well, Mr. Snout wouldn't like our house at all, I suppose, since it's all in that style, and I don't think our house would like him very much either. For what it's worth, though, you're absolutely right. It is a lovely telescope, in every way."

Michael waited a moment, hoping for some further comment; when none came, he said, "Father, why are you always looking at the same place in the sky?"

This roused Mr. Ambrosius from his reveries; he looked at Michael with an expression of mild surprise, or perhaps embarrassment. "What makes you think I am?"

"The telescope has been at the same inclination for weeks now."

"Oh, that." Mr. Ambrosius glanced up at the glass dome above and vaguely waved his hand in the general direction of the sky. "Yes, of course. Well, you know . . ." He smiled again, more nonchalantly this time. "Sometimes something takes my interest."

"One small patch of stars?" Michael asked. "Weeks on end?"

"No, not precisely. Not . . ." Mr. Ambrosius smiled again, this time in gentle resignation, and nodded. "Yes. But, no, not a patch of stars. A single star . . . if that's what it is. To be precise, a *stella nova* — a new star."

Michael's eyes grew wide. "A . . . *new* star?" he said. "New?"

His father did not reply except to raise his eyebrows meaningfully.

"How can that be?"

Mr. Ambrosius pursed his lips.

"But Mr. Choiros says that's completely impossible."

Mr. Ambrosius breathed in deeply and again looked up at the dome. "So it's generally believed. So we say, at least. But who" — he turned again to Michael — "who exactly is Mr. Choiros again?"

"He's our ouranonomy tutor. He's talked about this many times — why there can't be any such things as celestial novelties. He says there can't be any new stars, because the . . . the eternal harmony of the heavens can't be violated . . . and because the sphere of the fixed stars is the uppermost heaven, except for the primary motile sphere, the Great Engine, and that there's nothing beyond the Engine from which anything new can come, and so the heavens are unalterable, and . . ."

"Yes, well, all right," said Mr. Ambrosius, clapping his hands together, "that's all very . . . true. I mean, that's the standard scientific and . . . and doctrinal view of the matter. And I'm sure Mr. Choiros is a very sound fellow, and not to be quibbled with. But it's just that . . ." He paused and gazed at Michael for a long moment, clearly uncertain whether to say more. But then he continued, in a more subdued voice: "It's just that something's amiss. Mine's a very powerful telescope, you know. Confidentially, a little more powerful than is strictly legal, at least since the anti-speculative laws were published. Well, considerably more powerful, as it happens. A decade and a half ago, perhaps, it would have been a bit suspect, but not regarded as seditious. But now . . . well, that's why we don't tell anyone about it, not even Paichnidia. Not that she'd be interested." He rubbed the back of his neck wearily. "Anyway, several months ago I caught a glimpse of something that was . . . as I say, something amiss."

"Amiss?"

"Something that wasn't there before, and shouldn't have been there at all, to be frank. A small, brightly shining, very blue, very new *star*."

"But that's wonderful," said Michael, his voice rising, "incredible. You should tell the . . ."

"Oh, no, no, no," said Mr. Ambrosius hastily and emphatically. "That we

7

most absolutely mustn't do. We mustn't mention it to anyone. In fact, I shouldn't have told you." A look of genuine alarm had come into his eyes. "Do you understand me, Michael? No one."

"Yes," said Michael, lowering his head. "But surely someone should know."

"It might all be a mistake, anyway" said Mr. Ambrosius, still shaking his head vigorously, "some sort of optical illusion. Or some ordinary object I've mistaken for . . . for something else. But, whatever the case, it's not the sort of thing one can talk openly about. It could be misconstrued as heresy, or as a psychotic disorder, both of which are very, very illegal. And the penalties for defamation of the heavens are, you know, quite persuasive — quite *therapeutic*. No. You're very young, so you might not entirely grasp the danger, but believe me."

"All right, father," said Michael in a rather abashed tone, "I won't say anything."

"It was quite irresponsible of me to tell you. I can't imagine what possesses me sometimes."

"It's all right, really."

For several moments both were silent. Evening was drawing near, and the sky above the dome was beginning to dim. The single cloud visible from Michael's vantage, floating high above, was already pervaded by faint hints of a gauzy violet. The light that entered the room from the dome and the windows all around (those not obscured by bookshelves, at least) was now an ashy silver. Mr. Ambrosius walked over to his octagonal writing table, where a phosphorion on a bronze, lotus-shaped base sat amid the sprawl of papers. He passed his hand lightly over the surface of its clear glass globe and at once the vapors within it flickered into undulations of transparent luminescence and began to cast a warm golden glow upon everything in the room. Then, turning back to Michael with an expression of pained hesitancy, he clapped his hands together again and, in a hushed voice, said, "There's something stranger still."

"What?" asked Michael.

"It *is* a star, you see — I mean, to all appearances a star — and yet it's not actually situated up in the astral sphere where a star should be. It's in the lower lunar sphere."

Michael could think of nothing to say, or anything to do other than furl his brow.

"I'm quite serious," Mr. Ambrosius continued. "It's located in the aether of the lowest heaven. I've made quite sure of that. It's not a trick of perspective

8

or anything of that sort. All the higher heavens visibly pass behind it as they turn. What's more . . ." He fell silent again.

"Yes?" said Michael when many seconds had elapsed. "'What's more . . . ?'"

"It's moving, but not in concert with the rest of the celestial orbits. It's as if it's in the lowest heaven, but independent of its rotation."

"It's rotating . . . differently?" Michael asked. "Is it turning in a . . . is it what Mr. Choiros calls an 'epicycle' maybe? You know, a kind of miniature orbit of its own within the sphere? Or . . ."

"No," said Mr. Ambrosius in a tone of surprise, as if he too were hearing of it for only the first time. "That's just it: it isn't revolving at all. It stays fixed in one quarter of the sky all the time, in a stationary relation to the surface of Kenogaia, with the exception of a very small, ever so gradual, continuous change in the angle of incidence, or the distance from the celestial equator, or whatever the right way of putting it is. I wish I were a proper ouranonomer."

"I think you mean its declination," offered Michael.

"Yes," said Mr. Ambrosius, "you're probably right. Whatever the term, what I want to say is that it's . . . you see, it's . . . getting closer."

"Closer?" said Michael, his voice growing at once softer and more anxious. "I don't understand. You mean it's falling?"

"No, I wouldn't say that." Mr. Ambrosius shook his head distractedly. "There's nothing precipitate about its motion. It's more like it's approaching . . . furtively, so to speak. As if it's sneaking up on us."

"I don't understand at all," said Michael, looking up to the dome and down again to his father in bewilderment. "How can that happen? Are you sure you're right?"

"Oh," said his father with a tired shrug, "that's the easiest thing of all to verify. You see, the star's located along the lower lunar ecliptic — I think that's the right term — and when I first discovered it some months ago Aurea screened it from view as she passed by in her orbit. And the same thing happened again and again for the first three months that the star was visible. Then one night, two months ago, Aurea began passing by without obscuring the star, because now the star was stationed between her and Kenogaia — just at or just above the sublunary air. So I can see both that it's a very small star, hardly a small blue spark against the moon, and that it's a star in . . . transit."

Michael all at once became aware that what he was feeling was a kind of fear, but also a kind of eager curiosity. "Can I . . ." he said softly, "can

I look at it?"

Mr. Ambrosius drew himself up stiffly and with a mild grimace. "I'm not really sure that would be . . ."

"Please, father," said Michael. "You've already told me about it. What harm can seeing it do?"

"A great deal, perhaps," said Mr. Ambrosius. "If you've never seen it, no one can accuse you of delusions, except perhaps the delusion of taking your mad father seriously. So, no, I don't think . . ."

"But we won't tell anyone," said Michael, "and I'll believe you whether you show me or not. Please."

"You might disturb the balance of the telescope."

"I never have before," said Michael. "Anyway, you have it locked in place."

"It's not dark enough out to see it very well just now."

"Weren't you just looking at it?"

Mr. Ambrosius closed his eyes, breathed deeply once more, frowned, and — after several moments of obvious indecision — slackened his shoulders and nodded. "I'm a fool," he said. He opened his eyes again and looked at Michael almost imploringly. "I'm so desperate to talk to you sometimes that I don't think of the risk at which I put you."

"Please, father."

"Oh, don't worry, I'll let you look. I only wish I could hold my tongue."

When Mr. Ambrosius had fetched a set of library stairs from his closet and unfolded them — three steps in a small, elegant frame of copper filigree, all in the local "vegetal" style — he placed them below the telescope and, with a limply ceremonious wave of his hand, invited Michael to ascend.

"You know, I don't really need these anymore," said Michael; but he mounted the lowest step nonetheless, placed his hands on the telescope rails, and — with a feeling of strange apprehension that was also somehow pleasantly exciting — pressed his eye against the eyepiece. There was always a kind of magic in this moment for him, which he had felt more intensely when he was smaller, but which still had the power to captivate him now: to peer into the minuscule, mysterious, crystal world of that tiny lens, only to find himself all at once plunged into the immense, far more mysterious crystal world of the turning heavens — it never failed to seem like sorcery to him, a dazzling enchantment, no matter how often he experienced it. And so it was now: the momentary sheen and sparkle of glass, the brief misty gleam, and then suddenly he was immersed in the luminous blue depths of the early evening sky. He allowed himself an instant to luxuriate in the tingling sensation that passed over him, and then for many instants he simply floated there.

"If you look to the upper right"— his father's now disembodied voice somehow reached him from the lower world he had just escaped —"you should be able to make out part of one of the gears of the rotary mechanism that joins the spheres of Aurea and Argentea. It's the one with a missing tooth, and the break is visible at the moment."

Michael had already made out the figure of the gear wheel's lower quarter. Perhaps no other telescope now in use would have been able to bring it so lucidly into view. Seen through the deepening blue of the rising twilight, it seemed a pallid, almost translucent green; and a section of its circular rim and spokes and serried teeth was perfectly discernible, as was the jagged gap where apparently one tooth had broken away.

"I know all about that," said Michael without removing his eye from the telescope. "Mr. Choiros says that it looks like a flaw in the heavenly machinery, but it's actually not a flaw at all, and that the tooth never really broke off, but that it's all part of the miraculous harmony of the spheres, and the Great Artisan designed it that way so that there'd be a . . . I can't recall which thing it is . . . a 'deferent,' or an 'equant,' or something . . . or maybe an 'eccentric' . . . one of those. Anyway, it keeps the two lunar orbits synchronous by allowing Argentea to slip back a little once every day . . ."

"Yes," his father interrupted, "that's at least one way of explaining it, I suppose. But don't bother with that. Just look down and to the left a bit, slowly, and you should be able to find the star. It's small, but . . ."

"Oh," Michael gasped, for he had seen it now: very small and very bright, like a hard brilliant sapphire shining out from a sea of liquid turquoise. "It's beautiful."

"It's terrifying," Mr. Ambrosius half whispered.

For fully five minutes, neither of them said anything. Michael continued to gaze at the exquisite bright blue splinter of light that should not have been there, unable to imagine what it might portend, simply caught up in the marvel of it. Finally, he drew back from the telescope, his mind quietly but quickly drifting down again into the world of tangible things; then he turned about, sat down upon the second of the portable steps, and looked up at his father. Mr. Ambrosius returned his gaze with a hapless expression.

"What does it mean, father?" Michael asked after a few moments. "What is it? It makes no sense."

"Oh, I don't know about that," replied Mr. Ambrosius, looking away to his right, evidently at nothing in particular. "Maybe it's not really so unexpected as all that."

Michael parted his lips to ask what this meant, but before he could speak a flash of something startlingly bright, high over his father's head, caught his eye: there, at the edge of the dome above, the same bird Michael had seen from the landing below had just glimmeringly alighted on the outer casement rim, drawn in its wings, and started staring down at them. Even in the falling dark its plumage seemed to shed a soft rainbow glow on the air.

"Ah," said Michael softly; then, suddenly and eagerly: "What's a good word for 'rainbow-colored?'"

"What?" Mr. Ambrosius turned his eyes back to his son. "Why?"

"I'd just like to know."

Mr. Ambrosius arched his eyebrows and weakly raised his hands, palms upward. "I see. Well, all right. What's a new star after all? Just a flake of aethereal tinsel, I suppose." Letting his hands drop, he gently smiled. "But haven't we established that you're thirteen years old?"

"Yes."

"Which is quite old enough to look such things up for yourself. We have a good synonymicon downstairs, which you may consult whenever you like. Is that why you came up here — to ask me that?"

"No. But I'd like to know."

"Well . . ." Mr. Ambrosius shrugged. "I suppose the best word would be 'iridescent,' since that's literally its meaning. 'Iris' is simply an ancient word for rainbow, in both the Noble and Virtuous Tongues, and was also the name of the goddess of the rainbow in the days before the, um, the Age of Illumination." Mr. Ambrosius pronounced this last phrase, as he always did, with an inflection precisely poised between morose distaste and acid irony. "There are other quite lovely words for it as well — 'opalescent,' for instance, which refers to the sheen of an opal, or 'cymophanous,' which refers to the sheen of chrysoberyl, which can have a kind of polychromatic sparkle, or . . ."

"I like 'iridescent' well enough," said Michael. "And I know who Iris was."

"Very well. But I'm not sure why you had to . . ."

"It's just that I saw a strange bird at the window of the lower landing," said Michael, "as white as anything I'd ever seen, and the way the light . . . seemed to flow over and spill off its feathers, and . . ."

"What's that?" Mr. Ambrosius interrupted curtly, his eyes all at once narrowing, his voice all at once urgent. "A white bird, you say?"

"Yes," said Michael, "and there it is again." He pointed upward.

Mr. Ambrosius turned his head around almost violently and looked upward. He did not move at all for several seconds. Neither did the bird.

"Father . . ."

"Hold on," Mr. Ambrosius said without turning about. "Wait a moment."

"What's wrong?"

"Michael, I . . ." Mr. Ambrosius fell silent.

"Father?"

"Michael . . ." — now he did turn, slowly, with so obvious an expression of anxiety on his face that Michael quickly rose to his feet — "You should go back down right now. I'll be along in a few moments."

"What is it, father?"

"Tell Paichnidia. . . . I imagine she's beginning to prepare dinner. Just . . ." He returned his gaze to the dome. "Just don't tell her about any of this — about the star or the bird. Don't mention the bird. No need to confuse her with such . . ." His voice drained away into silence.

"Father," Michael said, his own voice now rising with unease, "what's the matter?"

"Please, son," said Mr. Ambrosius, turning back to Michael, "just do as I say for now. We can talk later. I really must . . ."

This time, his words were curtailed by a long, high, bitter moan coming from outside the tower to the east, one that was soon joined by another of the same kind coming from the west, and only a moment later by yet another from somewhere else. Michael shivered.

"The wolves are gathering for their nightly prowl," said Mr. Ambrosius. "Listen" — he stared into Michael's eyes with a look that clearly forbade any further delay — "please go down into the house *now*. Wait for me. We can talk later. And do me a favor — lock all the windows and draw the curtains and . . . and please lock and bolt the front door."

II

ON HIS WAY DOWN, MICHAEL PAUSED AGAIN on the lower landing and looked out of the window, over the darkening forest canopy and into the deepening purple dusk. The bleak, ghostly keening of the wolves was now rising out of the shadows beneath the trees in constant waves: swelling, receding, overlapping. He wrapped his arms about himself, as though he were cold (though he was not). Four months earlier, the sight or sound of any wolves at all had still been a rare event in these woods; they had never been numerous in the region, and had always been wary of human habitations. For most of the first five years since the family had come to live here, Michael had not seen even one, and only three times had he heard one howling, very far away. Now, though, they came out every night, in every quarter of the forest and on the low mountain ridges to the south, calling to one another from every direction, at times coursing through the darkness in packs large enough to raise a clamor as loud as waterfalls, and sometimes coming so near to homes that their great shaggy shapes could be glimpsed slinking past porches or beneath windows. And those who had seen them had said they did not even resemble the region's native wolves, which were slighter, silvery gray, and really rather handsome creatures; these new arrivals were altogether more terrible in form, and far more audacious. No one could account for the change, and soon practically no one was willing to venture out of doors after dark (though as yet no one, apart from two goats and a few domestic fowl, had been harmed by them). Nor could anyone in the village or any of the local forestry authorities recommend a solution, either to the mystery or to the problem it presented. Two "official" surveillances had been undertaken, which had consisted in a few of the Wilderness Ministry's aerial barges hovering over the treetops in a rather vagrant manner for three or four hours and then wafting away again in a low drone of rotary thrust motors; and three representatives from the Ministry of Public Safety and Sanctity had arrived one morning by train in Brightrill, the village in the valley below, had lingered through the afternoon, had spoken to a few locals, and then had departed again before nightfall. But nothing more had been done.

As disturbing as the new nocturnal peril was, however, and as hauntingly sad as those desolate howls often were, Michael would have felt less disquiet over the wolves had their sudden appearance in the area not coincided — ominously, it seemed to him — with certain other odd events. For two or three weeks before the evening when that terrifying chorus had first broken out in the forest, he had awakened each night from deeply troubling dreams of being lost in the darkness, in the woods, pursued by something dreadful (though he could not quite recall what), occasionally catching sight of spectral figures — sometimes human, sometimes animal — passing fleetingly through shafts of golden or silver moonlight, or silently moving at the edges of small clearings, or quickly darting into the open from behind one tree's bole and out of sight behind another; and each time the dream had left a feeling of fear in its wake that made it impossible for him to sleep again till dawn came. Also during those weeks, and then ever since, Mr. Ambrosius had insisted on taking Michael out for expeditions every third day or so to a secluded glade roughly three miles from the house, one ringed about by bushes of a kind that Michael had never seen before and that seemed to be perpetually in full, overflowing, brightly golden blossom. No path led to it, and he and his father could reach it only by going through several thickets (some tangled with thorns), then in and out of a narrow but steep defile filled with bracken, and finally around the edges of a small but deep mire; and, while refusing to explain why, Mr. Ambrosius had required Michael to commit every detail of the tortuous route to memory, as though it were a matter of the direst consequence, while charging Michael to mention it to no one, not even Paichnidia. And then there had been that fragment of a hushed and uneasy conversation between his father and Mr. Magian, on the very day before the wolves' arrival, that Michael had accidentally overheard from an adjacent room: "But, goodness me, we know it's true now," Mr. Magian had said in an urgent rasp, his usually mild voice suddenly vibrant with worry, "and we know it will be soon." And to Mr. Ambrosius's impatient hiss of "We also know it will be dangerous," Mr. Magian had replied, "But, ah, dear me, dear me, it will open the way for us, at last, and . . ." Just then, though, Paichnidia had fluttered into the room chirruping elatedly, "I've just made tea, darlings, and cakes and toast, and I have plenty of fresh butter and honey and . . ."

Yes — *Paichnidia*. "Paiky," as she demanded Mr. Ambrosius call her. Michael sighed resignedly and resumed his descent to the main house below, where she would surely sweep down on him from her little private paradise of tireless cheer, burbling and babbling and menacing him with cakes and biscuits, and where he would be submerged beneath the torrents of all that insufferable cheerfulness; but he knew he had no choice but to submit. Even so, when he arrived at the bottom of the stairs he was briefly but powerfully tempted not to go through the door into the house, but instead to steal around the stairway to the door leading to the cellar; for down there — as his father had shown him but had, predictably, never told Paichnidia — there was an old emergency escape exit hidden behind a cumbersome set of shelves, and this led to a brickwork passage, which in turn, after a few hundred yards, opened into the access tunnel of an old, long-abandoned mine; and this in its turn opened out into the woods another hundred yards along. It would have been so pleasant quietly to vanish for a few hours. But the night was falling, and the wolves were singing, and his father had been so worried and had so clearly thought it imperative for him to seal their home against . . . something. He opened the door to the main house and entered the large room that served as both atrium and parlor, already awash in the soft yellow light of six phosphoria ensconced on the walls' tawny wooden paneling.

Immediately his ears were assailed by a noise part squeal, part giggle, part articulate speech: "Oh, there you are!" Paichnidia trotted excitedly toward him, almost as if she had been lying in wait, her gait reduced by the tapering tightness of her bright pink, knee-length skirt to tiny mincing steps and a rapid clatter of high heels on the hardwood floor. "I was just thinking you might want a little snack before dinner. Don't tell your father, but maybe something sweet." She came within a foot of him, her wide blue eyes and scintillating grin and glistening blond hair and vividly pink lipstick all conspiring to make her abnormally perfect prettiness seem a little shrill and unnerving. "Oh, you always look so adorable in that red shirt and those blue trousers. If you were one of my dolls I think I'd dress you like that every day." And she actually pinched his cheek with her small, cold, soapily perfumed hand.

"No thanks, Paichnidia," said Michael, trying to drive from his mind the ghastly image of himself as one of the dolls in her terrifyingly huge collection. "I'll just wait till dinner."

Her grin, almost impossibly, became broader. "Call me 'Mother,' dear," she told him, as she had been doing for six years now without seeming to notice that he had never complied. "Are you sure? Boys have such lovely appetites."

"Yes," he said, stepping around her and crossing to the door. "Excuse me. Father wants me to lock up."

"He worries so," she said, shaking her head indulgently. "Well, maybe you're right not to spoil your dinner. I'm making a lovely provincial stew, with rabbits and woodcocks and snails and fresh herbs, and I've baked such lovely bread, and there's such a lovely custard for dessert, with lovely fresh morphinium berries — very good for sleeplessness or bad dreams or low spirits, you know."

Michael glanced back at her with a labored smile. "Oh," he said, "that all sounds very . . . lovely." He turned the key in the lock and slid the bolt into place, and was just attempting to think of some pleasantry that might bring the conversation to a quick conclusion, when a loud, long, especially miserable howl broke out from the other side of the door, very near the house. He involuntarily jumped back, shaking.

"Oh how cute they are!" Paichnidia cried out in delight. "I wonder if they can be kept as pets." Then, as Michael stared at her, trying to control the tremors of his limbs, she turned about and set off for the kitchen with her quick minuscule strides, swinging her round hips from side to side and emitting small, wordless twitters of effervescent happiness.

Michael breathed deeply, calmed himself as best he could, and diffidently but resolutely went to each of the room's five windows to make sure it was shuttered without and locked within before closing its curtains. "Perhaps she's actually insane," he whispered to himself when he was done.

Once, about a year ago, in a moment of frustration, Michael had asked his father why he had ever married Paichnidia. Rather than reprimanding him for temerity, Mr. Ambrosius had acknowledged that it was a reasonable question, but had added that she was ultimately harmless and meant well. "And, you know," he had said, "after your mother . . . after we lost her, and then after I had to leave the city, I was in no fit state to make wise decisions, or to look after myself, and men have needs, and you were young and I needed help . . . and there she was. And she *did* help."

This Michael could not deny. Back then, even though he had been only seven, he had been able to grasp just how broken his father had been by the events of the previous three years: his wife's removal from her senior research post and her extended "therapeutic detention," her unexpected death soon after her release as a result of (so the official report declared) "complications of acute psycho-spiritual trauma," his own protracted investigation by the Psychical Adjustment Commission for suspected "unhealthy cognitive practices," the diagnosis of his "obsessive suspicion disorder," his compulsory retirement from the Academy in Kenopolis, and his "compassionate exile" with disability pension. Paichnidia had been his departmental secretary at the Academy, and she had looked after him so indefatigably in the months leading up to his final dismissal from his post that, shortly before he left for his new home, he had more or less simply found himself married to her. At first, her vapid merriness had clearly been comforting to him, if only as a distraction from his thoughts; and perhaps her constant attentions — the pear-broth soups, the herbal infusions of morphinium and fruit-of-forgetfulness for "soothing the distempers," the sumptuous meals, the frenetic and perpetual housecleaning, the ceaseless cascades of inane chatter — had forced him to rouse himself from his depression, if only to escape the sheer relentlessness of her care. So yes, Michael knew, she had truly helped when it was most needed.

Still, there was something unsettling about her. Her ability to be simultaneously excited by everything but curious about nothing was positively bizarre. Her enthusiasm for any reality within her reach — a quaint saucer, a hair ribbon, a morsel of gossip, a flower, a bar of fragrant soap, a red shirt paired with blue trousers — was boundless; but she showed no desire to discover anything new. When the three of them had first moved into this house and Mr. Ambrosius had proposed the tower annex as his study and private retreat, not only had she accepted the arrangement with voluble approval; she had never once, as far as Michael could tell, bothered to visit the tower at all, even to see what it looked like. Mr. Ambrosius, moreover, clearly confided nothing to her; but she did not notice, because it apparently never occurred to her to ask any question whose answer she did not already know.

Of course, this had often proved convenient. It allowed Michael's father to hide many things from her effortlessly, and there was clearly much he wished to hide. When Mr. Ambrosius first chose this district of Oreiotopia for his exile, near Brightrill, the reason he had given the Office of Public Health and Piety was simply that it was where his childhood friend Mr. Magian lived, and that the company would be good for his state of mind. But after they had arrived Michael soon realized that his father and Mr. Magian were united not only by friendship, but by some sort of secret common purpose. Not only had Mr. Magian found this disused forester's house, with its fire watchtower, for the three of them to live in; even before they had taken up residence, he had arranged for a roofer, a carpenter, and a glazier to install a glass dome in the tower, doing the work only very late at night; and on one occasion Michael had heard Mr. Magian assure Mr. Ambrosius that all three craftsmen were members of "our circle." It was also Mr. Magian who had arranged for his wife to take Paichnidia away to a dinner and a musical entertainment down in the village on the night that these same three men, along with four others, had brought the disassembled telescope to the house by cart and carried it in pieces to the top of the tower. Fashioned by a local master of the craft half a century earlier, it had once been the pride of the small village ouranorium, but it had been ordered dismantled and its lenses crushed in compliance with the new state ordinances five years earlier. And, as far as the authorities knew, such had been its fate. In fact, it had been discreetly stored away in the basement of the village library, from which Mr. Magian had procured it with the connivance of the head librarian, Mrs. Philon, who also apparently belonged to "our circle." And, when it was reassembled and in place, Mr. Ambrosius had said to Mr. Magian, "Now our vigil begins." Then, though, noticing Michael standing nearby, he had smiled enigmatically and suggested a cup of tea before bedtime.

The wolf howled outside the door again, just as forlornly but at a somewhat greater distance from the house. Michael retreated agitatedly to the green velvet armchair in the corner, where he had left a book earlier in the day, paused long enough to note that the intricately carved clock on the wall was nearly at eighteen, and began trying to read. But, after only a few moments, he found he could not. His mind soon drifted back to what his father had just shown him. A new star — a *moving* star. But how could that possibly be? It made no sense. From earliest childhood, he had been taught what the shape of reality was, and had described and sketched it out at school for more exams than he could remember: There were nine turning heavens above, each of which was a flawless sphere of impenetrable crystal aether and all of which were arranged concentrically around Kenogaia. Each heaven was contained by another higher up, except for the uppermost of all, the Engine that moved all things, which was contained by nothing. No object could enter or leave any of the spheres, or pass between them, or impede their orbits. Everything there above was eternal and changeless. And everything was accounted for. Each of the seven great celestial bodies — the two moons, the sun, the four planets — was embedded in a sphere of its own, which bore it around the unmoving globe. And between the highest planetary sphere and the Engine was the sphere of the fixed stars. It was only beneath the lower moon, in the sky of fire and air and on Kenogaia itself, that anything ever altered.

And then, for some seconds, Michael's thoughts drifted much further back still, to the Dominion Oranorium to which his parents had taken him so many times when they had all still lived in the city and his mother had still been alive. He thought especially of the wonderful Grand Orrery, a whole room devoted to an enormous mechanical model of the kenocosm. How often, as a small child, he had stood at the center of the room, right at the middle of a large circle of blue and green marble set in the white marble of the floor, representing the world's northern hemisphere and ringed in golden letters: "*Kenogaia: Terra Firma et Immobilis.*" Stationed there, atop the world as it were, he could gaze up into a succession of nine silver-fretted crystal domes overhead, each slowly turning at its own pace. Each of the lower seven contained a brightly polished orb — gold and then silver for the two moons, glowing phosphoric crystal for the sun, and blue, green, red, or yellow quartz for each of the planets — while the sphere of the stars was brilliantly studded with countless semi-precious stones of every color and shade. The beauty and the mystery of it all had always held him in thrall.

The wolf outside now made a sound like an impatient moan, followed by a deep snarl. Michael shivered. He tried again to begin reading, with no better success.

HALF AN HOUR LATER, MR. AMBROSIUS ENTERED THE room from the annex, the expression on his face still as apprehensive as it had been when Michael had last seen him.

"Father, really, what's wrong?"

Mr. Ambrosius turned, stared vacantly at Michael for a moment, and parted his lips to speak. But Paichnidia had heard him come in and rushed out through the swinging door of the kitchen, ecstatically trilling, "There you are! Oh, I've missed you! It's been hours!" Taking hold of his sweater with both hands, she rose up on her toes and offered him her nose to kiss; and he, with a taxed but kindly smile, obliged.

"Hello . . . Paiky," he said, pausing awkwardly, as he always did, before uttering the diminutive.

"He's so affectionate, isn't he?" she said to Michael, detaching herself from Mr. Ambrosius. "I feel just like a new bride every day. Well, come on then." She buoyantly gestured with both hands for them to follow her. "Let's eat, even if it is a little early." And off she set again for the kitchen, while Michael and Mr. Ambrosius ambled in silence to the alcove where the dining table stood.

The meal was, as always, lovely — and very plentiful. Michael and Mr. Ambrosius scarcely spoke as they ate, however. Not that there was any need: even while somehow still contriving to devour her food, Paichnidia refused to let a second slip past her in silence. And yet, by the time he had finished his custard, Michael could recall almost nothing she had said (something about Miss Frogthistle the postmistress, something about fresh cream, something . . . else . . .). He had been so absorbed in his own thoughts that he had even failed to notice that, behind the sound of Paichnidia's voice, other sounds had been growing gradually but persistently more audible over the course of the meal; so it came as a surprise to him when his father abruptly broke his silence to say, in a portentously soft voice, "The wolves seem to be all around us now."

"They're so adorable," said Paichnidia. "Would you like some more?"

It was true, Michael realized all at once. The baying outside was not only distinctly louder than usual, but was coming from close by, on every side of the house; and as he listened he could now hear other noises as well: the rustle of large animal bodies moving about outside in the bushes and across the leaf-strewn lawn, a soft low snarl from somewhere just beyond the nearest window, an indignant canine yelp slightly farther away, followed by a meek whimper. Michael was about to ask his father what was happening, but a sound that was unquestionably a sudden brisk scraping of claws on the front doorposts caused him to catch his breath.

"Another dish of custard, Michael love?" asked Paichnidia, more insistently and even more sweetly.

"No thanks," said Michael, barely above a whisper. "Father, they're at the door."

"Yes," said Mr. Ambrosius, turning his eyes toward the front of the house. "They've grown so bold . . ."

"It's such a lovely custard," said Paichnidia. "It would be a pity to waste it."

"Father . . ."

And then the noises outside ceased — the scratching at the doorposts, the snarls and whimpers, the rustling of bushes and shifting of fallen leaves, even the howls — but the quiet was so unnaturally sudden that it was even more disconcerting.

"Father . . ."

Mr. Ambrosius turned back to Michael with an expression of deep dismay. "I don't know," he said.

"The berries are all gone, of course, but the custard . . ."

Then five loud knocks rang out from the door.

"Company!" Paichnidia almost shouted in exultation.

"Who in the world could that be?" said Mr. Ambrosius with a start. "Who'd be out at this hour, with all these . . . ?" But he did not complete the question.

"Wolves?" Michael suggested helpfully, unable to control the quaver in his voice.

"You just see who it is," said Paichnidia ebulliently, rising and beginning to gather up the dishes. "I'll make things presentable."

"Did you hear an aerial car?" asked Mr. Ambrosius as he pushed his chair away from the table and stood.

"No," said Michael.

"Be out in a moment," Paichnidia called over her shoulder as she bustled away toward the kitchen. "I'll put the kettle on."

Five more knocks rang out, and after a moment a man's low voice, at once rather piercing and oddly sing-song, called out from the other side of the door: "Hello, hello . . . are you in there, please?" Then, after several seconds: "Hello, my silents. I believe you've finished your dinner now. May we come in?"

"'We' who?" said Mr. Ambrosius so only Michael could hear. Then, slowly, he walked to the door.

Michael rose and followed at a distance of about ten feet.

"Who's there?" Mr. Ambrosius called out.

"Only a humble priest and psychologist, among other things," the voice called back. "And I've brought a few friends."

"But why?" answered Mr. Ambrosius. "It's nighttime, and it's not safe out. There are wolves about."

"Oh, nonsense," the voice replied. "It's an official visit, a visit by the state, so you've nothing at all to worry about."

Mr. Ambrosius said nothing, but simply bowed his head.

"Please open the door. We're here to be of help."

Mr. Ambrosius's voice was quieter now, hardly loud enough for someone on the other side of the door to hear him: "Can't you come back in the morning? We're not really ready to receive you."

"I'm afraid time is of the essence," the voice replied firmly. "And the law allows for no delay — not when someone's social, spiritual, and psychic welfare is at stake. Please open up. This is a very prettily decorated door and it would be such a shame to leave it in splinters."

Mr. Ambrosius momentarily leaned his forehead against the jamb; then, with a deep breath, he straightened himself, turned the key in the lock, slid the bolt free, and opened the door, stepping back as he did so.

"The problem with all these vines and flowers and curlicues that they carve on everything around here," said the man who entered, "and especially these elaborate tree carvings on all the doors, is that they do tend to bruise one's knuckles when one knocks on them." He was tall and very slender, though with broad shoulders; his face was pale and narrow, his chin sharp, his nose prominent, and his lips thin; and his distinctly unpleasant smile revealed teeth of exceptional whiteness. He was clad entirely in black: a suit dapperly tailored in some opulently glossy fabric, a silk shirt, a black silk cravat, brightly polished boots with pointed toes, a neatly blocked, narrow-brimmed velvet hat with a deep, elegant crease down its crown. "So very good to meet you, Prof. Ambrosius," he said in a tone of flaccid cordiality, "and my blessing on you and your home." He did not bother to remove his hat, however.

Michael immediately felt a strong emotion welling up within him, but it was a few moments before he realized that it was terror.

"With your leave," said the man, his smile widening, "or without it I suppose, I'll just invite two of my colleagues to come in as well. Others are here with me too — quite a few, I confess — but they can wait outside to make sure everything's safe. They're well-armed and I believe you were worried about wolves, or something of the sort."

Mr. Ambrosius stepped farther away from the door and reluctantly nodded his consent. The man turned his head and beckoned with an upraised hand to the two figures standing behind him in the light of the porch's phosphorion, both of whom were as tall, pale, and unattractive as he, if somewhat broader in build, and both of whom wore the same black attire (which was evidently some kind of uniform). They too neglected to remove their hats on entering the house, but the second of them did have enough manners to close the door behind him.

"Thank-you, my gracious, for admitting us," said the first man, with a slightly sinister grin.

"I had little choice," Mr. Ambrosius replied.

"Who are your friends, sweetheart?" Paichnidia suddenly sang out as she came careening from the kitchen and into the atrium. "What a lovely surprise to have visitors."

"Madame," the man replied with a slight but courtly bow, "allow me. I've come from the Secretariat for Spiritual Sanity, in pursuance of what has been officially warranted as a compassionate medical and sacral intervention, and I'm certified as both a priest and a psychologist. No, no"— he threw up his hands before him as if warding off an approaching crowd — "don't abase yourselves, my dear Ambrosii. I entreat you, don't grovel. I require no displays of deference, however spontaneous." He lowered his hands again. "My name is Fr. Lucius, or Dr. Lucius if you prefer, or Deputy Minister Lucius, or — let's be informal — just plain Mr. Lucius. I like that best. My clerical order is the Lupine Brethren; my altar is that of the *Mallei Sancti Aedes*, the Demiourgeion of the Holy Hammer, where I serve as a canon; and my area of medical expertise is psychometry. As for my two colleagues" — he gestured over his shoulder with an open hand at the two men behind him, each of whom was frowning sullenly and rather stupidly — "they also have names, one of which is Pallidus and the other Stultus, but I'm not sure which name belongs to which, and neither frankly are they, and it really doesn't matter."

"Well," said Paichnidia with a glittery grin, "you're all very welcome. Such eminent guests. My. Would you care for some tea and biscuits?"

Before Mr. Lucius could reply, however, Mr. Ambrosius said, "I'd like to know why you're here, please."

"To be of help," replied Mr. Lucius with a suave smile, "as I've said. But I'm getting ahead of myself." He removed a folded sheet of light green paper from his jacket's inner breast pocket and opened it. His fingers, Michael now noticed, were abnormally long and slender. "Let me, if I may, confirm your identities according to proper form." He glanced at Mr. Ambrosius, then looked at the sheet of paper. "Yes, this seems right. Valentine Adamantius Ambrosius, professor emeritus of the Great Academy of Kenopolis, currently retired on disability pension, diagnosed with incurable crepusculitis, a rare condition whose chief symptom, it seems, is debilitating and morbid melancholy during twilight hours, in this case aggravated by a nyctohemeral dysphoric dementia, also incurable . . ."

"Oh, it's so true, the poor darling," Paichnidia sighed tenderly.

Mr. Lucius took no notice of her. "Eyes glaucous gray, hair a blend of black and gray, bearded and bespectacled, height slightly above average, lean, age fifty-four, early second stage of senile decay; classification: cognitive convalescent. Yes." He looked up, now at Michael, then down again. "Master Michael Clement Ambrosius, child and legal minor; eyes blue, hair a color often floridly described as 'auburn,' height within the standard range of a healthy puerile build, age thirteen, late pupal stage of development; classification: precocious urchin." He glanced at Paichnidia and then continued reading. "Mrs. Valentine Adamantius Ambrosius, official personal name in the Dominion marital register Valentina Adamantia Ambrosia, private name Paichnidia Athyrma Ambrosius née Marioneta; eyes periwinkle blue, hair stridently blond, height diminutively average, of a build often preciously described as 'pert' and 'shapely,' age thirty-five, early final flush of youth; classification: inconsequential domestic poppet." He raised his eyes from the page, folded it again, and returned it to his jacket pocket. "Now, then, that all seems to be in order."

"You did that wonderfully," said Paichnidia. She turned and winked at Michael. "Poppets are dolls, you know."

"So, then," said Mr. Ambrosius dourly, "*now* can you tell us why you've come?"

Mr. Lucius closed his eyes and a somewhat stertorous laugh issued from his throat. "Of course, my impatient." He opened his eyes again and looked intently at Mr. Ambrosius, his expression becoming all at once gravely solicitous and shatteringly sincere. "I know it's been a difficult several years for you, professor, very difficult, and in your time up here in the mountains in exile — in compassionate exile, that is — you've probably come to believe that you've been forgotten by those responsible for your wellbeing. You feel abandoned by God and the state. But you aren't, my son. I have very encouraging news for you — very encouraging. We've kept a watch on your progress, and have determined that the time for a benevolent intervention has arrived, to aid you in your recovery at a rather . . . precarious moment. I've come here with a warrant for your remedial custody and spiritual repair. So you can rest assured that we're still looking after you. You'll be absolutely delighted to learn that you're under arrest."

"Oh, how lovely," said Paichnidia with a radiant smile.

III

MICHAEL'S EYES WERE ALREADY FILLING with tears as he flung himself forward, past his father, to seize hold of Mr. Lucius's lapels. "No, go away! Leave him alone! Why can't you leave him. . . ?"

His father caught his arms from behind and began pulling him away. "Michael, don't."

But Michael would not relax his grip. "Leave him alone!"

Mr. Lucius looked down at the boy, his dark eyes utterly impassive but his thin lips fixed in a faint smile that somehow seemed at once affable and malevolent. "Really, young Master Ambrosius," he said, his voice sinking to a mellow growl, "we mustn't become frantic, my impetuous, and we absolutely mustn't" — and he took hold of Michael's hands in his long sinewy fingers with a grip that instantly suggested untapped reserves of considerable physical strength — "put creases in other people's very fine bespoke suits." He pulled Michael's hands forcibly away, released them, and stepped back, smoothing his lapels.

"Please leave him alone," Michael said, more feebly now, striving to hold back his tears.

"Michael," said his father gently, drawing him back and enfolding him from behind in a protective embrace, "be calm. Everything will be all right."

"Father," said Michael, closing his eyes and shaking, feeling the tears sliding down his cheeks, "don't go with them . . . hire an advocate . . ."

"What's the matter, Michael dear?" asked Paichnidia from somewhere beyond his father's shoulder.

"Truly, Master Ambrosius," said Mr. Lucius, a menacing tenderness insinuating itself into his voice, "you mustn't upset yourself so. One might suspect you of being in need of some emotional correction yourself."

"Pull yourself together, Michael," Mr. Ambrosius said, more softly but more commandingly, pressing his fingers into Michael's arms. "Do as I say. Don't provoke them."

Michael opened his eyes and, through the molten film of his tears, looked up at Mr. Lucius. "Please," he said more quietly, "my father's perfectly well. Really. You don't need to take him away."

Mr. Lucius resumed his broader smile. "Now, now, I understand. You'll miss your father while he's away. That's only natural. But we won't detain him long — no longer than it takes to correct a few small but dangerously volatile maladjustments."

"Please listen . . ."

"And he'll be treated with the utmost care. It's for his own good, I assure you, and we'll lavish every attention on him."

"Listen . . ."

"We can provide you a receipt if you like."

Paichnidia's glistening blond hair and glaringly bright smile suddenly rose up in front of Michael like an eruption of fireworks. "Darling, sweetie, don't worry so. You're just like your father, such a worrier. They're just going to take him for a nice rest, and we'll have him back right away, I'm sure. And you and I can have a lovely time together while he's gone. We can play games, and I could teach you to bake — would you like that? — and . . ."

"Please . . ."

"I knew you'd like that," said Paichnidia. "Oh my goodness, the kettle will be boiling." And she vanished amid a staccato diminuendo of clattering high heels.

"Michael," Mr. Ambrosius said quietly in his ear, "I'm going to let go of you now, but you must promise to remain calm and to say nothing more. Yes? Do you understand?"

"Yes," said Michael after a moment.

Mr. Ambrosius gently relaxed his embrace, briefly pressed his lips against the back of Michael's head, and stepped away.

"You know, my pathetic," said Mr. Lucius, now adopting a tone of chilling fondness, "your distress genuinely affects me. It strikes a pastoral cord in my heart. A son's devoted love for his ailing father . . ."

"Now," Paichnidia called out as she gushed in again from the kitchen, "what was the answer on tea?"

"It truly touches me," Mr. Lucius continued. "It makes me . . ."

But he was suddenly interrupted by a hoarse, thick voice: "I'd like to try some tea, please," said one of the two men who were either Pallidus or Stultus, this one bearing a thin livid scar on his right cheek. "Is it nice?"

"I'd like some tea too," said the other of them — this one with a nose

27

slightly askew to the left — in an almost identical voice, "so long as it isn't too chewy."

"Ah, no, gentlemen," said Mr. Lucius, composed but obviously irritated, "we haven't the time. Forgive me, dear lady — forgive us, my attentive — but we simply can't avail ourselves of your hospitality this night. When we return with Prof. Ambrosius, perhaps we shall."

"If you're sure," said Paichnidia.

"Alas," said Mr. Lucius, "I am. But, before I go, just let me, so to speak, slip into my clerical habit for a moment. As I say, the boy's plight moves me. May I offer a few edifying counsels on parting?"

Paichnidia clasped her hands together. "Oh, that would be . . ."

"Lovely," interjected Mr. Lucius. "Yes, it will be. Most lovely." He cleared his throat, stretched his arms out to either side with open hands as if pre-paring to address a multitude, and turned a horridly benign countenance upon Michael. "My son, my bliss, my precious soul" — his voice had all at once become rich, sonorous, and grandiose — "recall if you will a few famous lines from the celebrated twelfth homily of the *Therapeutikon*. 'Sor-row,' it tells us, 'is a prison we have builded unto ourselves; we are our own wardens therein, and are bound fast in chains of our own forging. Cast off thy fetters, therefore, throw open the iron doors, and look out upon the boundless wonder of creation. Raise thine eyes, O my ghostly child, look to the heaven of the fixed stars, glistering with ten millions of gems of every hue; gaze upward to the imperishable crystalline spheres and pellucid aethers of the planetary heavens — the realms of Flavescens and Rudescens, of Viridiana and Caerulea, of Hyperion the royal Daystar, of Argentea and Aurea the celestial sisters — grandly pursuing the stately measures of their eternal concentric dance, turning upon the immovable axletree of this our world, Kenogaia, this fiery gleed, this brilliant, burning jewel at the heart of the whole great and shining Kenocosm. Look on all this glorious spectacle, this marvelous divine invention, this perfect harmony of every splendor, which the poet Ludibrius hath called "the great machine of earth and sky," and which . . .'"

"Oh, Ludibrius!" Paichnidia cried out. "We studied him in school!"

Mr. Lucius barely glanced at her. "'. . . is so exquisitely calibrated in all its parts: all its springs and levers, gears and pistons; all that shines and sparkles, glitters and glints. Know thyself, who art the most superb machine of all, to be a veritable mirror and epitome and microcosm of the whole, and of its limitless mystery. Think thou also upon the sheer grandeur it compriseth;

contemplate the prodigious beauties of Kenogaia herself: the mountains and the oceans, the forests and the plains, the valleys and the denes, the deserts and the dells, the gorgeous gulfs of twilight and the blazing seas of dawn, all the glories and delights — all the daedal delicacies and stupendous sublimities — that bedizen every portion of the whole terraqueous globe in all its faceted, imbricated, and diamond-bright magnificence. Consider simply her vastness. Why, even if paths were opened through the deeps and bridges cast across the canyons, a man could not circumambulate this world in fewer than sixty-two days! See how everything declares the power, providence, and pride of the Great Artisan, how every . . .'"

"Should I pack anything for the journey?" Mr. Ambrosius suddenly asked.

Mr. Lucius stopped abruptly, clenched his jaw and then his fists, lowered his arms, and slowly turned to Mr. Ambrosius with a baleful scowl. After a few seconds, however, his unpleasant smile returned, he unfurled his long pale fingers, and in a voice of purling mildness said, "All your wants will be provided. You need bring only yourself, good professor. And, of course, you're right: it's time we were going."

Michael stepped forward again. "Not yet," he said pleadingly. "You don't need to . . ."

"Michael," his father said, laying a hand upon his shoulder from behind, "these aren't men we can resist. Please, I don't want to have to worry about you too."

"Yes, let's not become tiresome," said Mr. Lucius. "Stultus," he said, without turning around. Neither of the men behind him answered. He dropped his head, heaved an exasperated sigh, and again said, more loudly, "Stultus."

After an awkward silence of some several seconds, the man with the crooked nose turned to the one with the scar and said, "I think you're Stultus."

"No," replied the man with the scar, "I believe that's you."

"One of you," Mr. Lucius snapped angrily, still not turning, "let's say the one to my left" — and he pointed to his left, obviously to assure there would be no confusion on this score either — "conduct Prof. Ambrosius outside and leave him with the officer of the watch. Tell them I shall join them presently to escort our patient personally. When you've done that, come back here."

"Yes, your eminence," said the man with the crooked nose, positively slouching forward. "Which one is that?"

"May I say goodbye to my family before going?" asked Mr. Ambrosius in a tired voice.

Mr. Lucius, who was just then glowering at his subordinate contemptuously, waved an indifferent hand and said, "Yes, of course."

"Bye-bye, sweetie," said Paichnidia serenely, walking over to her husband and again offering him her nose to kiss. "Don't forget to eat regularly."

"I won't, dear," said Mr. Ambrosius.

"I don't believe you," she replied with a playful smirk, then spun about and traipsed away toward the kitchen again. "I have to deal with the rest of the dishes," she called over her shoulder. "Dress warmly, and take your spectacles."

Mr. Ambrosius watched her go, then turned and extended a hand toward his son, who took it firmly in his own hands. "Take care of yourself, lad, and don't fret." Then, quite suddenly, he leaned forward and drew Michael into his arms.

"Father," Michael said, "don't go with them. We can . . ."

But Mr. Ambrosius now had his lips pressed close to Michael's ear and was whispering into it: "Hush, hush, listen to me. Wait and watch — every night. Watch the star, with the telescope if you can. And listen to the bird."

"Listen. . . ?" Michael was whispering too.

"To the white bird, yes. You don't need to understand right now. And go to Mr. and Mrs. Magian if there's an emergency, but not otherwise. The Magians won't come here unless they must."

"Father, how. . . ?"

"But keep watch. I love you." Mr. Ambrosius briefly tightened his embrace, kissed Michael upon the forehead, and then released him. "All right, then," he said aloud, and walked over to the man with the crooked nose. "I'm ready."

The man with the crooked nose stared at him curiously. "Ready for what?"

Mr. Ambrosius hesitated a moment. "To go, I think. I'm . . . Prof. Ambrosius. And you . . ."

"Oh, are you?" said the man with the crooked nose in a tone of surprise. Then, narrowing his eyes and assuming a severer expression, he added, "You shouldn't have tried to hide that fact. I'm supposed to take you outside, you know."

"So I believe," said Mr. Ambrosius. "My apologies."

"Yes," Mr. Lucius nearly barked. "Take him."

With a sudden twitch of fear, the man with the crooked nose took his charge by the arm and started for the door, "Right away, your eminence."

Mr. Ambrosius glanced once at Michael, smiled, and then allowed himself to be led away. A moment later he was gone, the front door now standing open but revealing nothing beyond the porch's light except the darkness. And then a great swell of despair rose up in Michael. "No, please!" he yelled out in anguish and began to rush after his father.

But Mr. Lucius caught him by the arm and held him still with an inescapable grip. "Really, young Master Ambrosius, really," he said, "such a commotion. He'll be back in no time, better than new. Why don't you sit down and relax? That red divan by the fireplace looks quite comfortable."

When the man with the crooked nose returned five minutes later, however, Michael was still in the middle of the atrium, fiercely staring through the open door into the night. By then, Mr. Lucius had lost interest in him and was standing a little apart with his hands clasped behind his back and his head bowed in thought.

"Sir, the prisoner has been delivered to the officer of . . ."

"The patient," Mr. Lucius snarled, "not the prisoner." He glanced at Michael with his most appalling smile yet and then turned to his two subordinates. "I'll be going now to take the professor to the transport. But the warrant also enjoins confiscation of the telescope."

A dismal shiver ran through Michael, but he made no sound.

"You're to see to that," Mr. Lucius continued. "Find it and call on as many of the men outside as you need to carry it out and cart it down to the barge. It's much too large for a car, I imagine. Understood? Good." In fact, neither Pallidus nor Stultus — whichever was which — had indicated that he understood anything at all, but Mr. Lucius was now clearly in no mood to tarry. "Master Michael," he said, lightly touching a long, thin forefinger to the brim of his hat, "until I return with your father and we meet again, I invoke every blessing upon you and your house." And quickly but noiselessly he strode through the front door, down the steps of the porch, and out of sight.

"Right, then," said the man with the scar, "we have to find this telescope then."

"Yes," said the man with the crooked nose, nodding sagely, "but they're not easy things to find."

"Aren't they?"

"No, I shouldn't think so. Very slippery sorts of things, I've heard."

The man with the scar pursed his lips, looking down, and shook his head in consternation. "That's a shame." Then, lifting his head and noticing Michael, he said, "You, sir . . . boy, I mean . . . there's a telescope around here, isn't there? Where is it?"

Michael, still struggling to control his shaking limbs, looked up with innocent eyes. "A telescope? Here?"

"Oh, now," said the man with the crooked nose, "don't play that game. We always work with good intelligence, and Lord Lucius doesn't make mistakes like that. Just you tell us where it is. Is it something in this room? Have you got it about your person, perhaps?"

"About my person?" It took Michael a few moments to grasp that neither of them had any idea what he was looking for. "Have you ever confiscated one before?" he asked, trying to sound as casual as he could.

"Can't say we have," replied the man with the crooked nose. "Hey, madam," he called out at Paichnidia, who was just emerging from the kitchen, "Mrs. Professor."

"Yes?" she asked sweetly, advancing into the room.

"Do you know where the telescope is?"

"Yes, of course," she said. "It's under the stairs, in the cupboard."

"Under the stairs?" asked the man with the scar.

"Yes," she said, pointing away behind her, "over there. Those stairs to the left of the kitchen door go up to the bedrooms, and it's just there" — she moved her finger slightly sideways — "behind that little green door. It's lovely. Our friends the Magians gave it to Michael for his birthday."

"Ah, I see," said the man with the crooked nose significantly. "And precisely why did they give him this door?"

"No, no," Michael interjected, all at once feeling a flood of sincere affection for his stepmother, "it's the *telescope* that they gave me. And she's right, it's behind the door."

"Ah ha," said the man with a scar, "now the truth comes out. You should have told us right away."

"Yes, I expect I should have," Michael conceded in a penitent tone.

"Exactly so," said the man with the crooked nose, strolling to the cupboard with an air of triumphant nonchalance. "Now then" — he threw the door open, reached in, and withdrew a long red rake — "here, I believe, it is."

"Oh, no, silly," said Paichnidia with a shrill squeak of mirth. "The telescope is that steel tube thing, the one with the collapsible legs. Oh, you darling!" She laughed again.

The man with the crooked nose glanced at Paichnidia a little peevishly, stared resentfully at the rake for a moment, and then set it aside. "This?" he asked in a doubtful tone, withdrawing a small portable telescope — roughly three feet long — with a folded tripod limply hanging from it. "Well," he added, "could be, I suppose." He brought it back to the atrium and held it up for his companion to examine.

"I don't know," said the man with the scar. "It might be. It might be something else, though."

"Like what?" asked the man with the crooked nose.

"I don't know. A soup dish of some kind. Or maybe a shellfish."

The man with the crooked nose narrowed his eyes and, leaning forward, sniffed at it diffidently. "No, it's not any kind of fish," he said, "and it's never held soup."

"Perhaps a subversive idea, then," suggested the man with the scar. "I've heard that those are particularly dangerous."

"Yes, I know they are," the man with the crooked nose replied testily. "You're not the only one with an education. But, for your information, those always have sharp quills. Do you see any quills on this?"

"A telescope is for seeing things far away," Paichnidia said. "You look in the small end of the tube and see out the large end."

"Ah ha!" said the man with the scar again, as if he had elicited this information through great cunning. "Now things are becoming very clear indeed!"

"I'm not really sure we'll need the barge to carry it, though," said the man with the crooked nose.

"Now, now," said the man with the scar, "Lord Lucius knows as of what he's talking about. These telescopes are tricky things."

The man with the crooked nose nodded gravely. "Yes. So they are, I reckon. Well, then. Yes. All right." And, resting the telescope upon his shoulder, he walked through the door, passed beneath the porch's phosphorion, and also disappeared in the darkness.

"Well, we'll be on our way, then," said the man with the scar. "Will you require a receipt?"

"No, no," said Michael hastily, "not at all."

Touching the brim of his hat with his forefinger, obviously in an inept imitation of Mr. Lucius, the man with the scar walked out through the door, and Michael rushed forward to close it behind him.

"Bye, then," Paichnidia sang out. "Come back whenever . . ."

Just then, however, Michael uttered a cry of perfect fear, slammed the door resoundingly shut, frantically locked and bolted it, and leapt away violently. "I . . . I . . ." he began to say in a faltering voice, pointing toward the door, but then dropped his hand and fell silent.

"Dear me," said Paichnidia. "Gently, love."

Michael, however, could only shake uncontrollably for several seconds; for though what he had seen walk shufflingly from the house onto the porch was a graceless man dressed in black, what he had glimpsed lithely diving out of the phosphorion's light and into the darkness beyond was a black, bristling, quite monstrous wolf. "Oh, father, father . . ." he finally succeeded in saying, but in a voice now so weak that he himself could barely hear it.

PART TWO
The Child from Beyond the Stars

From our deep treasure vaults they gave me gold
Brought from the Most High's house, and jacinth stone,
Bright Indian rubies, gems of worth untold,
Chalcedony, sky-blue and white as bone,
Great Gazzak's silver, sapphires, emeralds,
High Kushan's agates, topaz, amethysts —
Then, garbing me in adamant and folds
Of some poor pilgrim's cloak as gray as mists,

They took from me my lovely, precious robe
Of deathless glory, pure and opaline,
In whose fair weave rich seas of color flowed,
And which at night would variously shine
With lights as soft as evening stars; they took
As well my purple mantle — to my shame —
That none might know from but an idle look
Whose child I was or from what land I came.

— from "The Hymn of the Pearl"

I

THREE WEEKS PASSED, AND IN THAT TIME NO word came to the house concerning Michael's father. Now and then, as the days went by, Paichnidia declared that she missed her husband frightfully, and could not wait till he returned, and no doubt she meant what she said, but her demeanor remained one of invincible cheer. She continued to prepare meals, to keep house, to chatter and chirp and laugh, to tell Michael to call her "mother," to fail to notice his refusal to do so, and to float through the days on clouds of inexhaustible bliss. Michael, however, spent much of his time in a state of despair and fear. It was terrible enough to have had his father taken away, and to have heard nothing since; but the memory of that brief glimpse of a man instantaneously transformed into a wolf had cast a deep shadow of inexpressible horror over everything. How was it possible? And how could he bear to go on thinking of his father in the power of such creatures? But he scarcely had the luxury of allowing himself to sink into passive sadness. His father had charged him with a task, however mysterious it still seemed to him. On five or six occasions, he pored over his father's papers and notebooks, which were scattered among various shelves in the tower observatory; but all he found there of any relevance were mathematical notations, in Mr. Ambrosius's minute handwriting, of the great telescope's angles of inclination on certain dates, a few intentionally cryptic records of the new star's position from night to night, and the odd stray fragment of a thought, such as "The question is: *from where?*" or "Do we presume too much regarding his benign intentions?" or "To a prisoner in his cell, the mere sight of a bird in flight must be precious."

Otherwise, the days were endless and empty, the nights frequently sleepless. When, moreover, Michael did succeed for short intervals in shedding waking consciousness, he had disturbing dreams: sometimes a reprise of the those that had visited him before the wolves had first arrived in the forest, sometimes others, equally awful. He tried to read, but found he was too agitated to concentrate on the words before him. There were several days of rain, sometimes a chilly, early autumn downpour, whispering and pattering among the leaves of the surrounding forest and on the wooden rooftiles of the house, sometimes more of a falling mist from clouds that had settled on the mountaintop, enveloping everything in drifting veils of gray and silver, glazing the grass with a soft bright sheen, coalescing in gleaming droplets at the tips of leaves and needles, turning the nearer trees into ghostly shadows, and hiding the deeper woods from view entirely. Whatever the weather, however, wet or dry, he went for walks during the day, though never far from home, and he was always back well before dark — even though the wolves no longer came near the house at night, and he now heard them howling only at a considerable distance, in other parts of the forest. But nothing could relieve his sense of imminent catastrophe.

Occasionally the wind chimes of the anemophone on the wall by the stairs rang out, but the voice borne in on the wind's subtle currents and emerging from the device's small silver trumpet was almost always that of the village grocer, asking (somewhat hesitantly) what supplies should be sent up the mountain from Brightrill on the next delivery. Three times, however, Mr. Magian called, anxiously inquiring whether anything new had happened. And on the third occasion, when two weeks had elapsed since the night of Mr. Ambrosius's arrest, rather than wishing Michael well and signing off he asked whether anyone else was within earshot at Michael's end. When Michael replied that he was quite alone, Mr. Magian — after a long pause and then obviously against his own inclinations — said, "Laura wants to talk to you."

Michael found it difficult to contain his emotion. "Oh, yes, please!" he practically gushed.

"But only a moment, now," Mr. Magian said. "You understand. We mustn't . . . say too much. You . . . ?"

"Yes, please," said Michael. "I understand."

There was another pause of some seconds on the other end; and then Michael heard Mr. Magian saying. "Only a few words, dear."

Then, blessedly, Laura's voice came gusting in through the whispers of the wind: "Yes, Father, I promise. I know." And then more loudly: "Michael, are you there?"

Michael was surprised to feel how forcefully he was shaking. "Yes, Laura. Yes. I'm here."

"Are you all right?" The note of warm concern in her voice was conspicuous. It was also somewhat unnervingly novel.

"Yes," said Michael. "I . . ." He swallowed. "Yes. I wish you could visit. Or I could come to you."

After another moment of silence had passed, Laura said, "I wish you could too. Or we could. My father..."

"I know, I know," Michael interrupted, and then was immediately embarrassed by the hint of sulking irritability he heard in his own voice.

"I wish..." Laura began. Apparently thinking better of whatever she was about to say, however, she changed her tone entirely. "I certainly hope you're not moping around too much," she remarked dryly. "You do sometimes, you know."

Michael felt himself almost beginning to smile. "Well, it's hard not to."

"It's no use to your father if you behave stupidly," she added; and, in his mind's eye, Michael could see an extremely pretty face, framed by vividly lovely if somewhat disordered red locks, peering sternly at him from forest-green eyes.

"I know," he said, feeling momentarily less miserable. "I'm trying not to, honestly."

"Really?" She sounded unconvinced. "I know you. You can work yourself up into a depression and make yourself useless for days."

Michael felt his smile, weak as it was, widen slightly, quite against his will. "It's good to be chided by you. I was beginning to forget what it felt like."

Laura did not reply for some seconds. When she did, all she said was, "Don't be absurd." But her voice was much quieter now, and not at all severe.

"I miss my father horribly," said Michael.

Again it was several seconds before she replied. "I know," she said at last, and now her voice had grown gentle again. "I know. You're not alone — really."

"I miss you too," he added.

"Oh, Michael..." Her voice trailed off.

Mr. Magian, clearly only a few feet away from the anemophone, said, "Hurry now, darling."

Laura's long frustrated sigh mingled with the wind currents in an almost ghostly way. "Yes, Father," she said sullenly. Then Michael heard her clear her throat, and a moment later, in her most commanding voice, she said, "Do be sensible. I miss you too. Take care of yourself, and try not to... cry or anything."

"I wasn't..." Michael began.

But then, evidently, Mr. Magian had decided to bring the conversation to a close. "It's time to say goodbye," he interjected. "I'm sorry, Michael, but we really must go now."

Michael gazed down at the floorboards. "I understand," he said.

Then Laura's voice wound its way through the soft hiss of the wind currents one last time, but from farther away: "Goodbye, Michael. Be brave."

"I'll try," Michael said, but he could tell that the connection had already been severed.

AS MUCH MOMENTARY COMFORT AS THOSE BRIEF exchanges had brought him, it was not long before their rushed and fragmentary brevity, as well as the achingly disembodied remoteness of Laura's voice—almost to the point, in that last fading moment, of seeming to reach him from some other world—all began to add to his feeling of helpless loneliness. And so, three days later, on a morning that was dry but dreary with heavy clouds, Michael ventured farther away from home than usual, more out of aimless desperation than anything else. Even then, he went only down to Brightrill. He descended the road from his home to the wayside post where the public coach stopped four times a day. The wooden sign hanging there was illustrated with the bright blue silhouette of a splendidly erect, energetically striding, elegantly proportioned horse. The actual stallion drawing the rustic, open calash, however, proved on arrival to be a stout, placid, and somewhat elderly sorrel swayback, moving at a leisurely pace. Michael paid his silver penny to the old, thickly mustached driver, who glanced at him in obvious distress before looking away. The only other passenger in the carriage, seated opposite him with her back to the driver, was a dark-haired, gaunt woman in her late middle years whom Michael had seen in the village before, but whose name he did not know. She too seemed uncomfortable at the sight of him and quickly drew her black, oversized woolen coat more tightly about herself and turned her eyes off to her left, toward nothing in particular. Michael sighed and watched the woods and mountain ridges flowing by without any interest. Twenty minutes later, the village came into view in the broad shallow bowl of Brightrill Vale: the loose flock of modest clapboard structures in dark red, bright yellow, soft green, and softer blue; the high street (such as it was) of chalk-white dust and pink pebbles; the somewhat larger public buildings rising up on the opposite side of town—school, domed ouranorium, library, village hall, the local temple with its gold-leaf spire—all of which had doors and window casements ornamented with traditional Oreiotopian carvings of fruit-laden trees and lushly flowered vines; the brightly glittering, icy ribbon of the railway just visible to the southern side of the town, out past the far end of the raised boardwalks of the shopping plaza (again, such as it was) and a low palisade of white pickets. Farther to the south, past the rails, the valley's narrow stream was a pale glassy glitter at the base of that gradually ascending terraced slope that, in less than a mile, rose suddenly into the steeper incline of Mount Titan, whose ice-capped peak was lost for the moment among low clouds. In every other direction, the village was immured within the less imposing elevations of the nearer mountains, great frozen waves of dark green interrupted by occasional splashes of vivid turquoise and a few flamboyant sprays of the early season's yellow and scarlet.

Michael stepped down from the carriage in front of the small postal office and entered, setting off the bell at the door's lintel. Miss Frogthistle the postmistress — stationed behind the counter on her high stool, knitting what appeared to be a scarf from lavender yarn — looked up at Michael from under a downy haze of white, disordered hair, peered at him through dense, watery spectacles, dropped her knitting-needles with a start, and abruptly exclaimed in an excited, reedy voice, "No, Michael dear, no need to come here. There's nothing here for you, no mail. I'll certainly call up to your house if there is, and have it sent straight up. All right?" Michael paused in his stride, grasping at once that he was not welcome and would gain no information here. For a moment, he stared idly at the painting hanging on the wall behind her — the large official oil portrait of Lord Cosmas Theoplast, presiding minister of the World Dominion, looking quite grand in his snowy beard, red military tunic, and heliotrope sash of office — and then thanked her and left again. He walked to the other end of the village, only ten minutes distant, noticing with indifference that the few villagers who passed him on the way all looked quickly in some other direction and, without fail, crossed to the other side of the street. Among them was Fr. Nebulus, the exuberantly corpulent village priest, in his cassock of bright cerise and powder-blue, the tiny cut crystals and silver foil of his sacerdotal chaplet twinkling amid the thick shining ringlets of his sea-green wig; on seeing Michael, the priest's smooth, pleasant, babyish features were immediately disfigured by an especially scandalized frown and an indignantly porcine squint of the eyes, and he immediately pretended to be examining his own fingernails.

Michael came to the library and entered. The building's high windows filled the interior with the day's bleak light, which here — reflected from the golden wood of the ornate bookcases lining the walls and standing in rows in the middle of the room — seemed to become warm and rich. At first, no one was present on the main floor, but a moment after Michael had closed the door behind him Mrs. Philon — a small woman, somewhere just short of forty years old, brunette, very pretty, with a delicate face — emerged from the back office in her typical dress of sober black, paused with parted lips, and then hurried across the room to put her arms around Michael. "Oh, it's good to see you!" she said, somehow managing simultaneously to cry aloud and to remain quiet. She held him fast for a moment immersed in the florid fragrance of her perfume, then released him and, placing him at arm's length, looked him up and down as if expecting to find part of him missing.

"I'm all right," said Michael.

Then Mr. Philon also entered. He was a tall, black man with a hint of silver at his temples (coming, as he did, from the Southern Islands, he was the only person Michael had met since moving to Oreiotopia not of northern extraction). "Michael!" he said, in his infallibly kindly voice. "We've been worrying about you." He crossed the room and laid a gentle hand on Michael's shoulder. And Michael, with considerable difficulty, refrained from breaking down in tears.

They led him back into the library office, seated him beside the old wooden desk there, made him accept a cup of hot fruit tea and a dish of biscuits made with nuts and honey and flower petals, and asked him to recount what had happened the night of his father's arrest and to tell them what word he had received since. When he morosely informed them that he had been told nothing, and that he had come to them in the hope that they might have heard something, they confessed that they were as ignorant as he.

"The men in black suits did visit us," said Mr. Philon, "about two weeks ago, and their leader asked us any number of questions. He seemed to know something of . . . well, of our circle, though he didn't say so, but they left after an hour, and we told them nothing."

"About what?" asked Michael, in an almost anguished tone. "What is 'our circle?' What did they want to know?"

"What has your father told you, dear?" asked Mrs. Philon.

"Almost nothing." Michael told them of the conversation in the observatory the night of Mr. Ambrosius's arrest, of what he had seen through the telescope, and of his father's hastily whispered instructions just before being taken away. But, when he asked them if they could explain what all of it meant, they both shook their heads and looked downward, avoiding his gaze.

"We can't," said Mr. Philon.

"Please."

Then that gentle hand was on his shoulder again, and Mr. Philon's dark, almost obsidian eyes were looking directly into his. "Michael, it's not to hide anything from you. It's a matter of safety — yours and your father's."

"And the safety of a few others," added Mrs. Philon, "including your friend Laura and her parents."

"Yes," said Mr. Philon, still staring into Michael's eyes, "that's right. Remember, they have methods — very therapeutic methods — for discovering the things we know. And, if we aren't prepared — and you aren't, not yet — we have very little defense against them. Remember, there's no legal defense against a charge of heresy or insanity, or any appeal of conviction. Anything we tell you could endanger those you love, and so for now it's better to wait."

This was worse, Michael felt, than being told nothing whatsoever. He had known that his father and "our circle" constituted some kind of secret association, but until very recently he had thought of it more or less as a slightly subversive social club with a taste for daring conversation. At least, he had made himself believe it was essentially unthreatening. Now Mr. and Mrs. Philon were clearly intimating to him that it was something of far greater consequence, attended by far greater peril, while still disclosing nothing about it that might give him some clue to why his father had been taken. He tried for a few minutes, fruitlessly, to persuade them that they could confide more in him. But he was unable to do so with much conviction, since it seemed to him that they must be right about the dangers. He even briefly attempted, even more fruitlessly, to resent them for their discretion; but their kindness easily extinguished whatever brief, feeble flicker of anger he succeeded in summoning up within himself. Their company made him feel, as nothing else had since that dreadful night, somewhat safer; and so he stayed as long as he felt he could, drinking a second and then third cup of tea and eating too many biscuits before thanking them, and assuring them he would remain silent about everything, and submitting to their parting embraces. Then he returned to the coach stop. Somber premonitions of dusk, ashen and dimly purple, were collecting in the gray western sky when the carriage — manned by the same nervous driver but this time without any other passenger — deposited him once more at the wayside post near his home, and he returned to the house no more at peace than when he had set out.

OTHER THAN HIS DAILY WALKS AND THAT SINGLE
excursion, Michael's days were devoted to the anxious, barren routine of
waiting for a word that did not come. Principally, and faithfully, he continued to keep watch as his father had commanded. Early each evening,
starting from the second day after his father's arrest, he had gone up to the
observatory, stood upon the lowest of the portable library steps, and peered
through the telescope, still fixed on the same quarter of the sky that Mr.
Ambrosius had been surveying for months. Each time, except when clouds
intervened, he oriented himself by looking first at the celestial gear wheel
that joined the lunar spheres, imperceptibly turning in the deepening azure,
and then shifted his gaze to the new star; and as night fell, while the wheel
faded away to a phantom tracery of greenish gray and finally disappeared
altogether, the star became clearer and more brilliant and more exquisitely
blue. It also, over the course of the three weeks, became larger. At first,
Michael had not noticed this, and later had not been certain of it, but at last
there could be no doubt. By the twentieth night of his vigil, the star had
come close enough that—set against the night sky or against the glowing,
richly golden surface of Aurea—it now possessed a clear circular shape; and
it was also casting a corona of bright blue out into the aether of the lowest
heaven. Had it not been for his father's arrest, Michael might no doubt
have found the star's gradual approach a little frightening, but would have
been much more caught up in his own excited anticipation of something
unimaginable and wondrous; now, though, it merely made his tormenting
sense of uncertainty all the more intense. Then, on the twenty-first night. . .

II

A DREAM WOKE MICHAEL ONLY AN HOUR AFTER night had fallen. On completing his celestial observations, he had retired early, as had become his habit over the past several days. More and more, he was seeking refuge from his depression in sleep, even though he could never quite find it. And this time, it proved more unattainable than ever. He sat up abruptly with a gasp, the sheet and counterpane falling away from his chest, his mouth dry. and his heart beating rapidly. It had not been a merely terrifying dream, like those that had been waking him these past three weeks, but something more overwhelming, and somehow much more real. He had been standing in a field at night, looking up into a cloudless sky at the new star, which now loomed overhead as large as a moon; and it was no longer only a star, but a great, shining, beautiful gate as well, like the gate of a fortress or a city but with doors entirely fashioned from sparkling sapphire; and these were slowly opening even as he looked up, and a light of the purest white was increasingly pouring out from between them; and then the heavens were not the heavens, but a face, larger than the sky: a young boy's face, extraordinarily handsome, even beautiful, with eyes as blue as those sapphire doors and hair as golden as the light of Aurea, though lighter; and the boy was looking down at Michael, meeting his gaze with an expression, it seemed, of expectation; and then the wind was rising, bitterly cold across the field where Michael stood, and the sound of the wind was also a voice, deep as thunder and unutterably sad, speaking no words, but desolately and furiously wailing; and it continued to grow louder, and the ground beneath Michael's feet seemed to be quaking, and. . . . Then he had wakened.

Michael threw his covers aside and went quickly to his window, pulled the curtains apart, and looked out. The night was clear, calm, and — since both moons were halfway up the sky and nearly full — exceedingly bright. The narrow lawn separating this side of the house from the forest was like an unrolled bolt of bright green silk, glistening with the mingled incandescences of Argentea's silver and Aurea's gold; in the treetops the moonlight was like tens of thousands of burning tapers; the gentle swells of the distant mountain crests were a soft smoldering purple; and the fixed stars above were an ocean of rubies, emeralds, sapphires, garnets, topazes, diamonds, amethysts... But Michael was looking *at* none of it; he was trying to see beyond it or even through it, searching the whole expanse of sky, from horizon to zenith and from zenith to horizon, for something else, though he did not know precisely what. After a few minutes, he left the window, put on his dressing gown and slippers, poured and drank a glass of water from the carafe by his bed, quietly opened his bedroom door, and slipped out into the corridor. Treading lightly past Paichnidia's door, he descended to the ground floor, took a phosphorion by its stalk from a wall sconce, lit its glass globe with a brush of his fingertips, and hastened to the annex. He was so consumed with a feeling of nameless urgency that he scarcely noticed the long ascent of the tower, and when he reached the observatory he was so impatient to get to the telescope that he nearly broke the phosphorion by carelessly tossing it onto the writing table.

The star had changed. The star was changing. Since the early evening, when it had not discernibly differed in aspect from its appearance of the preceding five days, it had grown larger in the sky: not as in his dream, but enough that Michael wondered whether it might be visible to the naked eye if one knew where to look for it. He raised his head from the telescope and peered upward through the tower's dome to see if in fact it was, and for a moment he fancied that he could indeed just make it out: an elusive shimmer, a glint of diamantine blue. But it was only through the telescope — to which he soon returned his eye — that he could see it clearly, and also see that it was obviously moving. Its corona now seemed to be wheeling slowly around it, and was no longer purely blue, but fluidly varicolored at its edges; and the star itself was steadily, if gradually, sinking downward in the sky. It must now, Michael thought, be at the very boundary between the aether of the lowest celestial sphere and the air of the sublunary region, or even past the boundary by this point, somewhere in the upper aerial sky. He could see also that, at the center of the star, the brilliant sapphire blue had a small, sharp, clear heart of equally brilliant white. For several minutes — he could not tell how many — he simply gazed at it, not knowing what to do or feel; and then he realized that the angle of the star's descent had brought it very near the lowest part of the area captured by the telescope at its present inclination, and that he would have to adjust the angle if he was to continue keeping watch in nights to come. He was just trying to recall whether he knew how to do this, and was about to lift his head from the eyepiece to look for the correct knobs or levers, when a sudden flash of bright white light erupted from the center of the star and flared out in every direction.

Michael drew back so abruptly that he nearly fell from the step, but steadied himself and looked upward to the dome again. Now the naked eye was more than adequate: where only the faintest spark of blue had been visible moments before, there was now a tiny but conspicuous gleam of piercing white, shining more intensely than the moons above it. "Father," Michael whispered, "if only you were . . ." But, before he could complete the sentence, the star flared out again, becoming momentarily even brighter. And then a single ray, or rather something more on the order of a thin but solid strand of milky light, was descending from it, perfectly vertically, straight down toward the earth, rapidly growing longer by degrees, like a cord being lowered from a high window. For perhaps twenty seconds it unraveled itself, appearing to grow thicker as it grew nearer, and Michael had to run to one of the windows to see it plunge into the treetops as a slender but impossibly tall column of pure white radiance, extending from the floor of the world to the ceiling of the sky, casting a blanket of splendid, almost satiny white over a vast portion of the whole forest canopy. "Everyone can see," Michael said, talking to himself as if to someone else. "Everyone." But then, suddenly, the column was gone, first dissolving into the colors of the rainbow and then, in only a few seconds, melting away altogether; a mild golden glow briefly lingered above the trees at the point where the ray of light had reached the earth, but it soon sank away into the forest.

At once, before Michael could compose his thoughts well enough to tell whether what he felt was horror or hope, a truly terrible clamor broke out from every direction: the wolves, all of them it seemed, had begun howling at the same time, more raucously than they ever had, and from every part of the wood. It was as loud as a thunderstorm and like nothing Michael had ever heard or even imagined: a sound of utter, desperate, inconsolable misery — and of rage. And it seemed to go on and on interminably, wave after wave, rising and falling and then rising higher, until it had become so oppressive in its sheer wretchedness that he doubted he could bear it much longer. Five minutes, perhaps . . . ten? Maybe only three? However long it lasted, he remained immobile and unable to think the entire time. Finally, though, it subsided, becoming gradually feebler and more diffuse, dispersing into isolated moans and whimpers, until it had died away altogether. He did not stir for several moments, afraid that the wolves might resume their lament. At last, however, he felt able to move, and began to step back from the window.

But the step at once became a jump and then a stagger, as well as an alarmed gasp, because there was yet another flash of white, this one just on the other side of the glass. Only after steadying himself against the back of a nearby chair did he realize that it was the bird he had seen the day of his father's arrest, suddenly arriving in a spangled flare of beating wings. And no sooner had it settled on the ledge than it gave the window three sharp sudden pecks of its beak; and then, a moment later, three more; and then, a moment later still, three more, so hard this time that the third left a thin crack in the pane. At that, Michael recalled his father's hastily whispered, inscrutable instructions; he hesitated briefly, but then went to the window and began to raise the sash. In an instant, the bird was past him, rushing into the room along with a gust of cool night air filled with the scents of the forest. It immediately soared to the top of the telescope and perched on one of the silver leaves rimming the lens. And, before Michael even had a chance to be properly startled, the bird opened its small beak and a loud, mellifluous, urgent, bell-like, and very clear voice came out: "Go! Go at once! Find the child! Protect him!"

Michael now truly could not move, or think, or even remember how to think. It was not dread that he felt, but an entirely new and nameless emotion. He felt uncannily cold, and could only stare up at the bird mutely.

"Go!" its voice rang out again, "Quickly! The wolves will gather, the child will not be spared! He does not know the way, he is lost here!"

"Child?" Michael at last gasped. "Go...?"

"Quickly!"

Michael wondered if this was what it was like to be fainting. He felt as though the tower itself were swaying.

"Go to the place your father showed you"—suddenly the voice was gentler, but just as impatient—"the clearing in the woods, and do not delay. He is there, waiting for you. Rouse yourself, boy. If the Brethren find him, all is lost." And then the bird spread its wings and flew down from the telescope, coming so near Michael's head that its eyes were briefly only inches from his; and then it was swiftly gliding through the window and back out into the night.

"What child?" Michael was finally able to whisper. "Why...?"

Then the bird soared back into the room again, as if it had neglected to say something. It circled three times in the dome, calling out, "Take clothes, some of your own. His raiment is woven of moonlight; it is evanescent; it will not last till dawn. Quickly!" And then it was gone again, disappearing in the darkness outside like a candle's flame suddenly blown out.

Michael did go, as the bird had commanded, but moved at first as if in a dream. And perhaps he was in a dream, he thought, or in a reality that was becoming a dream. What was real, anyway? Apparently he inhabited a world he had never known, where men became wolves, where stars descended through the heavens and pillars of light descended from the sky, where birds spoke. And, for some reason, it seemed especially strange to him that the bird should have used the word "evanescent," as if that were more fantastic than the very fact of a bird speaking at all. But it was important now, he resolved, not to let himself pause to think about any of it, since nothing made sense to begin with, and there was clearly no time to waste. He retrieved the phosphorion, left the observatory and tower, returned to his room, dressed and wrapped himself in a light fabric jacket of dark blue, packed some clothes and a pair of walking boots in his knapsack, strapped the knapsack on, and set out, phosphorion in hand. Every now and again, whenever he sensed some kind of question or hesitation rising in his mind, he whispered, "Don't think!" to himself and continued on with all the more haste. He should have been terrified at the prospect of venturing out into the wolf-haunted darkness — perhaps he was, as far as he could tell, since the difference between calm and panic seemed to have been erased — but he went all the same, intent upon not thinking about anything. When he reached the ground floor he returned to the annex, went to the cellar door, and descended the stairs.

The cellar was large and dark, cold and full of dust; his father kept very little there apart from some paintings, some disused pieces of furniture, an old folding ladder, a collection of tools and oil-cans (mostly for maintenance of the telescope), and the single large empty bookcase hiding the fire escape door, all of which seemed particularly stark and threatening in the honey-dim light and moving shadows cast by his phosphorion. He went directly to the bookcase, wedged his shoulder into the slight gap between it and the brick wall, and pushed; it was difficult but not impossible to move, and it groaned somewhat resentfully against the concrete floor, but he had soon shifted it enough to allow him to reach the low red metal door, to pull the lever that released its latch, and to slip into the narrow, chilly brick corridor beyond. The way was easy, the smooth stone floor sloping gently downward and turning to the right in a large lethargic bend, and in less than five minutes he reached the corridor's end, where it issued at a right angle into the broad, damp access tunnel of the abandoned phosphoric crystal mine. To the left, the tunnel led downward into the depths of the earth, or so his father had told him; to the right it led to the outside world; and directly ahead, opposite where he now stood, a low aperture opened into another tunnel that, according to his father, continued on for two miles till it reached another of the mine's entrances, not far from where the Magians lived. He briefly considered continuing on straight ahead, to see if he could find Mr. Magian and ask him for help; but, remembering the urgency of the bird's commands, he went to the right instead.

Everything still seemed quite unreal, as though he were floating slightly above or behind himself. When, however, he drew within twenty yards of the tunnel's mouth and could see a slender crescent of moon-bright sky framed in its upper arch, he at last recovered the sense of being actually present to himself, and with it a sense of fear, because a faint sound of voices was coming from outside. Hastily he bent his head over the phosphorion and blew on it and its light flickered out. For a moment he considered turning back, but only a moment. Instead, taking a deep breath and whispering, "Be brave," he pressed himself to one side of the tunnel and crept forward until he could see what was out there. The cool, slightly moist night air roused him a little more out of his distracted state. He at once understood why he had never noticed this tunnel entrance before, even though it could not be very far from his house. There was a high row of pyrokarpos bushes concealing it, about eight feet from where he was now standing. And this told him precisely where he was, as he had seen those bushes often enough from the other side, at the upper edge of a clearing that he and his father had frequently crossed when out for walks. He could still hear the voices, moreover, coming from somewhere farther away, though he could not yet make out any of the words. "Be brave," he repeated and, laying aside the knapsack and phosphorion, he approached the row of bushes as stealthily as he possibly could, crouched at one end, and listened. Now intelligible words became audible, though still from something of a distance.

"Wherever he is, of course!" The voice was harsh, curt, and almost frantically angry. "Didn't any of you see where it came down?"

"Well, sir, over there . . . somewhere in the woods . . ." This voice was sullen, low, and somewhat cowed.

"Yes, of course it's in the woods. Everything around here is in the woods. We're in the middle of a gigantic forest, you imbecile. But what part of the woods? It was only a few minutes ago!"

"Well, yes, sir, but it was all very fast, and through all these trees, and with it all up and down and such, it's so hard to tell . . ."

Michael leaned forward on his hands and cautiously looked around the edge of the bushes. Then he became very still, chewing his lower lip and digging his fingernails into the grass beneath him. On the other side of the bushes lay the wide clearing he knew so well, on a treeless slope from which there were occasional small outcroppings of granite, descending toward a narrow stream with sandy banks, beyond which the forest resumed; and at the clearing's middle — maybe twenty yards from Michael — six tall figures stood in the glassy moonlight, in something roughly like a circle, all anxiously shifting about on their feet and all dressed, from hats to boots, in the same black costume worn by the three men who had taken his father away.

The tallest of them, the one with the harsh voice, was doing most of the talking: "I'm quite sure that there was no ambiguity in your instructions. The moment any sign was seen of the invader, you were to make for it with all speed. I'm also quite sure that what we all saw just a little while ago most definitely qualifies as such a sign. Why then do I find you here?"

"Sir," said the figure standing directly opposite him in a surprisingly high, querulous voice, "it's rather hard to get one's bearings. It was all very confusing . . ."

"Nonsense, man, utter nonsense! The truth is that you're all frightened."

"Oh, sir . . ."

"There's absolutely nothing to fear, you miserable curs, and even if there were it wouldn't excuse insubordination. The Brethren serve God and their masters, not their own hides. Those large bright lights in the sky may have all been very impressive, and intimidating too, but our quarry is neither. The invader is a child, nothing more, a young adolescent at most, who doesn't even know where he is. Now run. Spread out. Find him at once."

"We're not frightened," said the one with the sullen voice from somewhere else in the circle.

"At once."

"We're a bit hungry is all. We'd do much better with a bit of a . . ."

"At once!" And the tall figure flung both his hands high in the air, as if striving to summon down lightning. "Go! And you're to capture him, not devour him."

After a few final moments of reluctance and two or three murmurs of complaint, all five turned toward the trees below, and even in turning were no longer men but rather enormous black wolves, who raced down the slope and leapt over the stream with extraordinary grace and disappeared into the woods on the other side amid a crashing of undergrowth. Only the one who had been issuing commands lingered in the clearing, first lifting his face upward, as if either consulting the stars or sniffing at the air, and then for a horrible moment shifting his gaze toward the bushes where Michael was hiding. At this distance, Michael could not tell if that scowling face was turned toward him or merely toward the mountain slope above him, and he pressed his fingers more fiercely into the earth and bit his lip more painfully. After a few ominously silent moments, however, the man turned about, was all at once a wolf, and charged away after the others with an ecstatic yelp.

Michael was quivering. The transformation of these Brethren was an eerie and dreadful sight. But he had been quivering at intervals for weeks, especially during the past hour, and had become accustomed to going on nonetheless. He rose, retrieved his knapsack and phosphorion, and took several deep breaths. And this much was encouraging, he thought, as he set off on a path not down towards — but rather parallel to — the streambed: though the wolves had dashed off in what was undoubtedly the general direction of the glade where he was heading, he knew they would never be able to reach it by the route they had taken, because a sheer forty foot granite escarpment, an impenetrable wall of thorns, and a deep broad mire all lay in their path. And, if they did not know the way, then perhaps none of their comrades knew it either, despite their four months roving these woodlands, and perhaps all of them would be bearing away from the path he intended to take. It would be easy for him to get from here to the way his father had shown him, which was the only one affording access to the glade, but which swung around first to its south, along the near side of the Plegethon, the great river that separated this mountain from the next.

Not that this route was any less difficult than it had been when his father had led him along it repeatedly for months, and he had never followed it at night before; but the moons were bright and pierced the forest canopy everywhere with brilliant shafts and sharp darts of cold light, and he required the phosphorion only now and then, for no more than a few minutes at a time. As he had hoped, no wolves were anywhere near, and in a little less than an hour — weary, bearing a few thorn scratches on his legs and hands, but otherwise unharmed — he came to the boundary of the glade. He made his way between two of the strange bushes ringing it about, with their copious golden blossoms — extravagant, sweetly aromatic flowers, each with five great, languidly drooping petals surrounding a misty spray of tenuous stamens — and pressed through into the open.

There, perhaps twelve yards away, in the center of the moonlit clearing all by himself and not moving, with his eyes turned upward to the sky, stood a boy of about Michael's height, with striking golden hair, clothed in a thin robe that reached nearly to his ankles and that seemed indeed to be woven from shimmering moonlight.

III

SLOWLY, CAUTIOUSLY, YET WITHOUT ANY CON-
scious feeling of fear, Michael approached; and, as he drew near,
the shining boy lowered his eyes and looked directly at him, with
an unthreatening but impassive expression. As Michael had known would
be the case, the boy's face was the one he had seen in his dream, in all
its uncanny beauty. Even the eyes were the same luminous sapphire
blue, vividly visible despite the darkness, and he found them so entrancing that he came to a halt a few yards from where the boy stood and
simply stared.

The boy stared back, now with a very faintly inquisitive look on his
face perhaps, tilting his head slightly to one side. Then he spoke, slowly
at first, as though finding it difficult to make his lips form the words:
"I . . . am . . . here. . . . I . . . have . . . been waiting . . . for someone. . . .
Are you . . . the one I . . . am waiting for?"

Michael did not reply. He could not: the boy's voice had a disarming,
musical, almost glassy clarity to it that Michael found just as captivating
as the color of his eyes.

The boy tilted his head the other way, a little more quizzically perhaps.
"Is this the . . . place of . . . golden flowers?" he asked, the words already
coming somewhat more easily. "Are you . . . Ambrosius?"

At this, Michael came out of his daze. "What? Oh. Well, yes, but I believe
it was my father you were expecting."

"I was to meet . . . *Ambrosius*, in the place of the golden flowers — the
flowers whose breath . . . makes it hard for my . . . my enemies to find me."

"I didn't know you were coming until tonight," said Michael. "There are
certainly golden flowers all around us. I'm not sure how long they'll keep
anyone away, though."

"Can you show me the way to my sister?" asked the boy. His words were
beginning to flow with less impediment.

"Your . . . sister?" said Michael, taken aback. "No, I'm sorry, I can't. I
don't know who she is."

54

"Can your father show me?" His voice was oddly devoid of inflection, even cold.

Michael bowed his head. "No. Or yes, maybe. I don't know if he could have done." He raised his eyes again. "They took him away, many days ago. Your enemies, that is."

The boy's expression did not change. "Will he be harmed?"

"I don't . . . I don't know."

The boy did not reply, and still his face betrayed no emotion.

Michael was beginning to feel somewhat unsettled by this. He looked at the boy, from head to feet (which were unshod), and brought his gaze to rest for several moments upon the radiant fabric of the boy's robe — or, perhaps more accurately, the fabric that was pure radiance. It certainly seemed to be woven from nothing less fine than strands of golden light: it gleamed and glimmered and shone, and even its folds seemed to be only ripples of softer brightness. "Your clothing . . ." he said, then fell silent.

"I brought this raiment from above," said the boy, "from the sphere of the lower moon."

"Yes, well . . ." Michael could think of no response to this; he knew, moreover, that there was no time for further questions. "You'll need to change," he said, removing his knapsack, kneeling in the grass, and extracting the clothes and boots. "I've brought these."

The boy looked down at them almost with an air of indifference. "Please show me how they are worn," he said after a moment.

Michael explained as quickly as he could, pointing to his own clothing to demonstrate his meaning, and the boy soon tersely remarked that he understood. "Please hurry," said Michael. "There are men out looking for you. Or not men, really — something worse. Your . . . your enemies."

"Yes," said the boy, loosing the strings at his throat and chest and letting the robe fall from his shoulders. Michael went apart a few steps and began looking from one end to the other of the glade. A minute later, the boy asked for assistance with the boots, and Michael crouched down and tied the laces.

"My thanks," said the boy with a tone of rigid formality. "These are strange fabrics. So shadowy, so rough."

Michael stood up straight again and examined the boy. He now wore dark trousers and a darker shirt, as well as a light, loose brown sweater with large wooden buttons. But for his hair and eyes he might have looked little different from any other (impossibly handsome) boy. "What's your name?" Michael asked, with a definite hint of awe in his voice.

"I am called Oriens," the boy replied with a slight but rather courtly bow of the head.

"Oriens," Michael repeated. "I see. I . . . my name is Michael . . . Michael Ambrosius."

"Michael Michael Ambrosius," said Oriens with another bow.

"Just one 'Michael,' actually. And where do you come from?"

"From above."

"From . . . ?"

A wolf's howl, prolonged and melancholy, rose from somewhere far away in the forest; and then another howl answered it, considerably nearer.

"We have to go," said Michael. "It isn't safe out. They'll find you. I have to take you to my home."

Oriens looked about the glade, almost casually. "Is it far?"

"Not very, but the way is difficult."

"I shall try not to delay you," said Oriens. "I am not yet accustomed to this body."

"This . . ." — Michael was gazing at the robe that Oriens had cast aside, which was even now melting away in the grass in small, shrinking pools of luminescence — "this . . . body?" He looked at Oriens in bewilderment. "I don't understand."

"I am not accustomed to it," said Oriens, just then examining his own hands. "It is coarse . . . awkward . . . opaque."

"Opaque?"

Another howl broke in upon them, and to Michael it seemed to come from nearer still.

"This flesh," said Oriens. "It is heavy . . . difficult to master." He stretched his jaws, as if speaking were still something of a labor.

"Well," said Michael, hurriedly taking up his phosphorion but leaving the knapsack, "please try. If we don't go soon, we may be cut off. Your enemies move very fast, and there are many of them, and I'm somewhat tired already."

"Too tired to elude them?" asked Oriens.

"I hope not," said Michael. "I'm afraid I forgot to bring water. But it isn't very far." He reached out, hesitating for a moment but then taking Oriens gently by the arm (and he was relieved to discover that it felt like any other arm), and led the way toward the edge of the glade. "There isn't a path, but I know where we're going." They passed between two of the encircling bushes, and would have proceeded directly into the woods had not Michael recalled what Oriens had said about the golden blossoms;

instead, he paused to pluck several of them from the bushes and to thrust them into the pockets of his jacket and the sweater he had provided Oriens. "In case their fragrance really can confuse your enemies," he said.

As Oriens had warned, he was slow, at least at first: his gait was stiff, he held his back so straight that he seemed to be balancing his torso precariously upon his hips, and he repeatedly tripped in places where the ground was uneven or where roots or broken branches or tangles of undergrowth obstructed his progress, and would have fallen once or twice had Michael not been there to support him. But as they made their way through the darkness, through high leaf-vaulted halls of trees and shattered colonnades of moonlight, he soon began to grow more adept at moving his limbs and bending his body in conformity with the world around him, and after about thirty minutes, when they reached the bracken-thronged defile that lay between two minor but impassable forest scarps, he was able to descend into it, thread his way through its weeds and thickets and thorn brakes, and scrabble out again at the other end with no less agility and poise than Michael.

"The thorns seem to have torn my flesh," said Oriens in a detached tone. "There is some blood on my hands. And there is pain."

"Yes," said Michael, "I'm sorry, but this is the only way we . . ." But then something large moved in the darkness, maybe thirty yards ahead of them, crossing their path from left to right just at the verge of a large sprawl of moonlight. Michael took hold of his companion's arm and whispered, "Wait. Be silent." Then another shape, equally large, followed in the other's path. It took only a moment for Michael to recognize the second as a wolf. "They're here," he said, drawing Oriens behind a tree. "The ones looking for you. They're finding the way."

"Can we go forward?" asked Oriens, hesitating ever so slightly as he clearly strove to imitate Michael's whisper.

Michael waited to answer until he was sure the wolves had entirely passed by. "I don't know how we can."

"Is there no other way?"

"No. To the left, it all sinks down into thick thorns and we'd be caught. On the right, around that rock wall we just passed, the ground goes up to the edge of the mountain where there's a ridge, but . . . but we can't swing back around to the path because there's a high rockface, and the ground also slants down into a gully below it, and there's just no way to climb . . ." But he paused. For several seconds, he said nothing, trying simultaneously to think clearly and to calm his heart's rapid beating. "Of course, if we went to the other side of the ridge at the top . . ." He fell silent as yet another wolf passed along the edge of the moonlight, on the same bearing as its fellows. Then he resumed: "On the other side, the ridge drops down to the river, the largest river around here, the Phlegethon. It's terribly steep. If we lost our footing we'd be killed. But there are ledges, and there's a kind of gap in the ridge farther along, past the scarp, where we could come back to the way we're going . . . if we could get there without falling." One wolf called out, three high barks resolving into a despondent whine; another replied in kind; both were very near. "It's extremely dangerous," Michael added.

"Is it more dangerous than my enemies?" Oriens asked.

They did not hesitate long. Turning to the right, they made their way up a moderate incline and, after a minute, passed through a dense covert of bushes with broad leaves that parted before them fairly easily but that also obliged them to move with great care so as not to make much noise. After another five minutes they emerged into an area of fuller moonlight, where the ground briefly dipped into a shallow trench and then began to rise again; and, a few moments later, they entered a part of the forest composed entirely of tall pines, where the ground started to rise more steeply, where the needle-strewn forest floor was devoid of any undergrowth or shrubs, and where countless sprays of moonlight descended from the high branches that sighed and hissed overhead in the moving air. Michael shook his head as he looked through the trees to a stretch of open ground rising to the dark line of the mountain ridge. He realized that here he and Oriens would become easily visible to any of their pursuers who might happen this way, and he was just wondering whether it had been wise after all to leave the deeper shadows of the forest when a sudden yelp and excited howl broke out behind them, followed by a tumult of snapping branches. He spun about violently, raising his phosphorion in a tremulous hand; but the sound was coming from the far side of the covert, and after a moment he could tell that the wolves were not breaking through it, but rather racing past it toward the defile, back along the way he and Oriens had been taking before they had elected this detour. "They nearly found us," said Michael, turning back around. But Oriens was several yards ahead, still striding onward through the trees. Michael hastened after him. Ten minutes later they emerged from the woods altogether, onto a bare, rocky, continuously rising glacis. The ridge above was a great frozen ocean wave rearing up against the moon-drenched sky. They could reach the top in perhaps ten minutes more, Michael thought, but would be wholly exposed to view the whole way. "We have to be quick," he said.

"I believe I am becoming tired," said Oriens, with such a tone of indifference that he hardly seemed to be speaking of himself. "This flesh is not very strong, is it?"

"We can make it," said Michael, trying not to feel his own weariness. "We must."

The ascent was more tedious than arduous, but Michael's fatigue was slowing his steps even so. Still, they were soon near the spine of the ridge, and Michael had begun to hope they would be able to rest for a while on its other side before attempting the ledges; but, when they were only a yard away, a loud, atrociously savage snarl, culminating in a high furious bark, sounded at their backs. Michael spun around again. This time, there truly was a wolf behind them, hurtling out from the trees with something horribly like a scream of jubilation and starting up the slope with terrific speed.

"Oh, fast!" Michael cried out, turning, and finding that Oriens was already at the top and calmly extending a hand to pull him up more quickly. Michael took it, yelling, "Be careful, don't slip!" Once alongside Oriens, on a granite ridge that was considerably narrower than he had expected, he looked briefly toward the opposite mountain ridge, and then down at the stony ledges and narrow terraces on this side, descending in a precipitous cascade toward the broad, deep, magnificently glittering Phlegethon, perhaps six-hundred feet below. It was a sight to inspire awe or induce dizziness, but Michael had time for neither. He could now hear the wolf's paws pounding up the slope behind them. "You have to get down to that ledge"— it was maybe seven feet beneath them and, at a generous estimate, two and a half feet wide —"as fast as you can, or . . ."

Oriens was already down upon it, however. Apparently, in the brief time since leaving the glade, he had progressed physically not only from ineptitude to competence, but to considerable nimbleness. "Come," he said, in a voice so clear and unperturbed it nearly tolled.

Taking the smooth metal stalk of the phosphorion in his teeth, Michael turned about, lay face-down, and lowered himself backwards with great care, inch by inch, clinging as securely as he could to the surface of the granite, until he felt Oriens guiding his legs into place and steadying him with a hand upon his back. And no sooner had he gained his balance and taken the phosphorion in his hand again than the wolf was there, thrusting its hideous face over the precipice above with a low, fierce growl; its eyes were red, its lips tautly pulled back from its teeth, its enormous fangs flashing, and even from there its hot, rank breath reached Michael. It was all he could do in his terror not to lean away from the cliff face and let himself fall, in the hope that the terrace directly below might miraculously reach out and catch him. Hardly able to breathe, he frantically gestured for Oriens to move on along the ledge, and the two of them began to make their way forward, sidling at first rather than walking, hands upon the mountain wall, progressing as swiftly as they could over the rough stone. But the wolf stayed with them, growling and snapping continuously, hovering on the ridge overhead, pacing back and forth, clearly looking for some point where it could leap down without risking a fall. Twice Michael looked up, only to look away again quickly from the great prowling shadow interposed between him and a disturbingly broad section of the moon-bright sky. And twice also he had to pause to gather his courage again after a particularly harsh growl had frozen him in place. For something like four dozen yards they continued on, keeping their footing despite the unevenness of the ledge, with the wolf still unable to reach them; but Michael knew that sooner or later it would find a way down. "Please," he whispered, though he did not know to whom.

"It is wider here," Oriens said, his voice still strangely tranquil.

And, indeed, the ground widened beneath them to four feet or more, and became somewhat smoother as well, and he and Oriens were able to turn forward and walk properly. They both quickened their steps.

But, while the ledge here allowed them to move more freely, it also afforded the wolf a way down. Bounding along the ridge, it reached a place about thirty feet ahead of them, where the angle of descent was more forgiving, and with an especially ferocious snarl it sprang down in an economically graceful arc, wheeling about even as it landed. Then it lowered its shoulders and began to stalk toward them, a continuous stream of deep growls issuing through what looked like a scornful and ravenous grin.

"Back, back . . ." Michael began to say to Oriens, who stood between him and the wolf.

"Can we go back?" Oriens asked, as if merely curious rather than frightened. "Will he not catch us easily where the ledge narrows?"

"Yes, I suppose so," said Michael. The wolf was drawing nearer, panting loudly, the deep incessant growl rising from its throat becoming continuously louder. "But we can't . . ." He fell silent. After a moment he lit the phosphorion's globe with his fingertips and thrust it forward, past Oriens, waving it in what he hoped was a threatening manner. The wolf was not intimidated, however; the yellow light did little more than make its grimace appear all the more ghastly — as well, perhaps, as a little amused. With a small, dejected groan of frustration, Michael raised the phosphorion and flung it as forcibly as he could at the beast, missing its head by several inches. The globe shattered against the cliff's side, its light quickly dissipating in a haze of glowing vapors, and the metal stalk went flying away into the chasm, where it could be heard glancing off one ledge after another for several disheartening seconds. The wolf continued to advance. "I'm sorry," Michael said in a quiet, hopeless voice. "I'm so very . . ." But he stopped and clutched at his own collar with both hands. He had suddenly realized that the wolf was not simply growling; it was also, horrifyingly, talking.

Not that the words were easy to understand; the sound coming from its rumbling throat and snapping jaws was so low, harsh, and guttural that distinct syllables seemed to detach themselves from it only grudgingly; but they were most definitely words nonetheless: "Enough, boy. The stranger is mine now . . . the one with the nasty eyes . . . aren't you, child?" Then it snorted.

"You must let us pass," replied Oriens in a mild, untroubled voice. "I shall not harm you if you step aside."

The wolf halted, now no more than twelve feet away, and to Michael it seemed as though it had winced. "Harm me?" it snarled. "What, with your wicked eyes?"

Oriens did not reply.

The wolf lifted its snout and sniffed at the air, then growled still more deeply. "You can't harm me," it said, its voice becoming even lower and more menacing, "even if I can't smell you. Your eyes don't scare me, child." It widened its jaws and ran a repulsively large purple tongue once around its lips. "You'll come with me."

"I shall not," said Oriens.

"Just as soon as I've eaten the boy," the wolf added, "or some of him." And, with a furious roar, it charged at them.

Michael stepped backward, lurching dangerously near the edge, turning his gaze down toward the river, and opening his lips to yell some pointless warning to Oriens. But then he stopped. Before any words could come out of his mouth he was aware of a bright, clear, altogether beautiful light all at once flooding over him and the cliff face and ledge, and also of an instant, unaccountable feeling of peace. He heard the wolf yelp again — but now as if in pain — then snarl, then whimper pitiably. He lifted his eyes. Oriens was standing quite still with his right arm extended before him, and from a small, sharp, exquisitely brilliant point of light at the center of his upturned palm a warm splendor of crystalline purity was pouring out all around him. In that light, everything was at once less terrible: the jagged stone face of the cliff on their left was now not a grim, overshadowing, unyielding barrier, but a lovely curtain full of delicate, fugitive gleams; the open air on their right was not a vertiginous plummet into the abyss, but an exhilarating open prospect, revealing a scene somehow simultaneously charming and sublime; even the wolf was not so much monstrous as pathetic, just a pitiable brute cringing low to the ground and meekly backing away and moaning beseechingly.

"What . . ." Michael asked softly, "what is that?"

"What is that?" the wolf suddenly, yelpingly shrieked. "Put it away, you horrid child!"

"Look at the light," Oriens said.

But the wolf began throwing its head violently from side to side, as if trying to avoid a series of blows. "Put it away," it growled desperately, "or I'll tear that arm off your shoulder."

"Look at it," said Oriens, almost imperiously now.

The wolf howled, miserably and furiously. "Put it away!" And now it began to lift its chest from the ground, as if gathering itself for another charge. "I've told you, child." Oriens said nothing, but the clear enveloping light continued to flow from his hand. "I've told you!" it roared once more, and then had overcome enough of its terror that it was able to leap forward again with another savage snarl. At this, Oriens did give way, not hurriedly, but stepping backward almost into Michael's arms even so. But, before the wolf had completed three bounding strides, a bright bolt of glistening white was descending toward its head with a high ringing cry. Michael gasped and clenched his fists. It was the white bird, and suddenly it was beating its wings just in front of the wolf's eyes, darting at them and drawing back and thrusting itself forward again, all the while emitting sweet, shrill cries. The wolf instantly stopped, flinched wildly, reared back up on its hind legs for a moment, retreated, snarled once more, snapped violently at the bird, then surged forward again, and then drew back again; and all the while the bird continued to hover before its eyes, singing out, repeatedly swinging back away from its jaws and then forward again. "Get away!" the wolf was howling. "Horrible wings! Horrible eyes!"

"You need not be harmed," Oriens replied coolly. "But my patience is not infinite."

"Get away or I'll tear you to shreds!"

"You need not be harmed," Oriens said again.

But the wolf was now in a frenzy, barking and yowling and slavering: "Horrible, hateful . . . !" And the bird did not desist from trying to drive it back and away from the two boys. Finally, the wolf could obviously endure it no longer. Crouching very low indeed, it curled its upper lip, bared its fangs, wailed madly, and then opened its jaws wide and lunged at its tormentor. The bird, however, merely retreated with three rapid wing strokes, out over the chasm, and the wolf — giving vent to one final howl of despair and fury — leapt after it recklessly, flew out from the ledge, and fell. Michael watched as it descended, wildly twisting and writhing until, two thirds of the way down, it struck the edge of a terrace in passing and instantly ceased struggling, its body becoming perfectly limp the rest of the way down; and in the bright moonlight, even from so great a height, Michael could see that the dark form that came to rest on the white sparkling sand of the riverbank far below was not a wolf's, but a man's.

"He did not listen," said Oriens blandly, closing his hand, and at once the beautiful crystalline light was extinguished.

The bird swept toward them, turning about in the air above their heads and calling out in its chiming voice: "Quickly! The Brethren are moving through the forest! If you do not make haste you will be found!" And then it was gone, like an arrow shot into the night.

IV

"WEREN'T YOU AT ALL AFRAID?" MICHAEL asked Oriens twenty minutes later. By this point, they had climbed up to the low breach in the mountain ridge on the far side of the scarp, reaching it sooner than Michael could have hoped, because the ledge where they had confronted the wolf had been wide enough the remainder of the way to permit them to move quickly.

"I felt fear," said Oriens blandly.

"You didn't seem to," said Michael.

"My apologies," said Oriens, "but I am not familiar with the proper way to express fear in your world."

"Ah . . . ," said Michael uncertainly.

"If I offended you, I ask your pardon."

"No," said Michael, "not at all. It's just that, usually, when one's afraid, the way one reacts is . . . it's not a matter of form. It's spontaneous."

"I was ignorant, then, of the proper customs for spontaneous reactions."

Michael could think of no answer to this. "But that wolf," he said after a moment, "that animal — it spoke . . . and turned into a man, you know. I mean, you saw. . . ?"

"Yes."

"You didn't even seem surprised."

"Should I have been?" asked Oriens.

"Well, yes," said Michael. "I was. To be honest, you . . . you don't seem to react to anything."

"I am not yet accustomed to this form," said Oriens. "In time, many things should come more naturally to me."

Michael wanted to ask what this meant, but somehow felt certain that the answer would be too much of a distraction just at this moment. A few minutes later, however, when they had regained the shadows of the forest and had begun moving back toward the path to the mine entrance, he did feel able to ask another question. "What was that light?" he said. "The one you held in your hand?"

"That was a jewel from my father's treasure house," said Oriens. "I brought several with me when I set out on my journey, very long ago."

"Several?" said Michael. "Do you have many?"

"Now only a small number. I keep them in a purse around my neck."

Michael, parting two pliant saplings before him, shook his head. The glimpse he had caught of Oriens removing his robe in the glade had been brief, but also clear. "I didn't see any purse on you," he said.

"Even so," said Oriens, "it is there. None but the one wearing it can touch it, or take anything from it, or lift its string from one's neck. It cannot acquire souls or a carnal body, so it is veiled, and has no common substance in these lower worlds."

Michael did not see, of course. "Souls?" he said. "Carnal body? Worlds?" A twig snapped sharply beneath his foot. "Veiled?"

"Yes," said Oriens simply, evidently failing to note Michael's confusion.

They came to a small rivulet that Michael knew to be only about half a mile from his house and they leapt easily across it, though Oriens with the greater gracefulness. "Where do you come from?" Michael asked again, in an extremely tentative voice.

"From above," Oriens again replied.

"Yes," said Michael. Then, after a moment's hesitation: "From the sphere of Aurea?"

"From far beyond that."

"Beyond the moons?"

"Beyond the sphere of stars," said Oriens; "from beyond all the spheres."

"But . . ." Michael paused in his steps for a moment, looking up at the sky out of the dark, narrow well of tall trees. "There's nothing beyond the spheres, I thought. The nothing, that is: the infinite solid nothing from which the Great Artisan hollowed out the Kenocosm in the Primal Excavation. At least, that's what I've always been taught."

"By whom?"

"Tutors . . . priests . . ."

"They are in error," said Oriens.

"Yes," said Michael after a moment. "Yes, I never really believed it, I don't think." Then, after another moment, he added, "What is beyond the spheres?"

"Everything," said Oriens.

THEY EXCHANGED NO FURTHER WORDS THE REST OF
the way; it occurred to Michael that it was foolish to make any unnecessary
noise, and he was too weary and thirsty to want to speak. The moons were halfway down the sky by the time they reached the mine entrance, having skirted
the now empty clearing and slipped behind the row of bushes. "It's very dark
in there," Michael said, "and I don't have a light now, so be careful. Or"—he
looked at Oriens hopefully—"could we use that jewel of yours as a lamp?"

"It is better to conserve the jewels," said Oriens, "unless you think it very
dangerous. In this world, their light can last only so long. And they are
very precious. The one you saw was already half spent when I used it, and
it melted away even as I closed my hand on it."

Michael nodded silently and then remarked that they could find their
way in the darkness if they each kept a hand upon the wall to their left until
they reached the brick corridor. When Oriens said nothing to this, they set
off down the tunnel, Michael leading the way. Twice he nearly tripped on
the uneven floor underfoot, and both times he felt himself caught from
behind by Oriens, who apparently was able to see better in the dark than
he. After several minutes, Michael felt the wall against his palm vanish.
"Here's the entrance," he said, turning into it and spreading out both arms
to touch the bricks on either side.

"Yes," said Oriens simply.

They proceeded on, a little more quickly now but still cautiously, until
Michael was certain they were very near the emergency door leading into
the cellar. But then he halted, because he realized that their surroundings
were all at once becoming visible, bricks emerging from the darkness on
either side as dim gray oblongs, then quickly taking on a tinge of dull red
or murky blue. A light was approaching from ahead, coming around the
broad bend of the corridor. He turned and waved his hands in the direction from which they had come, trying to make Oriens retreat; but Oriens
merely raised his own hands, as if returning some kind of salute. "No . . ."
Michael began to whisper.

But then another voice, high and full of grateful relief, rang out behind
him: "Oh, Michael, there you are. Thank goodness."

Michael turned back around. Hurrying toward him with slightly echoing
steps and bearing a small glowing phosphorion in her hand was a very pretty
girl about his own age, with dark but vivid red hair, clad in a neatly formal
blue dress with narrow lace cuffs and collar, and quite incongruously shod
in a pair of plain walking boots. "Laura," said Michael as she wrapped her

arms around him, "what are you doing here? When" — he gently extricated himself from her embrace — "did you come?"

"And you," she said abruptly, turning to Oriens, "you're the visitor. My father and mother told me about . . ." But then she paused and simply stared at his eyes.

"Yes," said Oriens.

"About you . . . you . . ." said Laura haltingly, as if in a small trance. Then, after a second, she remarked, "You're very . . . beautiful."

Oriens bowed his head. "Thank-you." Then he added, again perhaps repeating what he took to be a formal salutation, "You are very beautiful."

"Oh." This seemed to please her. "Your eyes, I mean . . . they're very . . ."

Michael caught the phosphorion as it began to slip from her fingers. "This is Oriens," he said to her. Then, when she failed to reply, he added, "That's his name: Oriens."

She turned to Michael. "Oriens?" she said.

"This is my friend Laura Magian," said Michael to Oriens.

"Laura Magian," said Oriens with another courteous bow.

"Laura," said Michael, "why are you here?"

"I . . . I . . . Why?" She was waking from her momentary stupor. "That's an idiotic question," she said, suddenly irate. "Didn't you see the lights in the sky?" And she raised a foot as if to kick him.

"Yes," said Michael, stepping back defensively. "That was Oriens. He . . ."

"I know, I know," said Laura impatiently, setting her foot down again. "There's no time for that now."

"How do you know?" asked Michael. "How can you possibly?"

"Oh, Michael," she interrupted, "please don't be so stupid." She threw up her arms in exasperation, and her shadow loomed up on the bricks behind her with such spectacular suddenness that Michael took another step back. "My mother and father told me. After your father was arrested . . . after . . ." But then she lowered her arms and her voice became somewhat kindlier. "Well, they told me he was coming. Sorry, I don't mean to be nasty." She looked at Oriens for a prolonged moment. "They told me you were coming," she said, her voice gentler still. Then she looked at Michael again. "They don't know much about him, but they knew someone would come."

"But how did they know?" Michael began.

"How did you get him here?" Laura asked.

"I went to find him," said Michael.

"You?" said Laura. "Alone?"

"Yes, I had . . ."

"In the dark?"

"Yes . . ."

"And you didn't get lost?"

Michael sighed. "Yes, Laura. I'm not as helpless as you think."

"How did you get here *really?*" she said, turning to Oriens.

"Michael Ambrosius led the way," said Oriens calmly. "We were pursued."

"Pursued? By the men . . . ?"

"Laura" — now Michael interrupted — "why are you here? What's going on?"

"The men," Laura said, "the ones in the black suits, like the ones who took your father?"

"Yes," said Michael.

"The men who're wolves?" Laura continued.

"You know, then," said Michael.

"Oh, hush," she said in vexation. "They came to our house, about an hour after the light in the sky. I saw them from the stairs, but they didn't see me. There was the one called Lucius . . ."

"Lucius? He's the one who . . ."

"I know," said Laura. "When my father showed him into the drawing room, my mother said she had to turn off a tap or something and came and told me to take some water and run as fast as I could to the mine entrance on the other side of the hill. She said she and my father would try to get away too and go in another direction, and we'd have to meet later at our other place if it was safe. Well, I couldn't even go to my wardrobe to change out of my nightclothes — I had to grab my temple dress from the laundry rack. I look like an idiot." She gave her skirt a contemptuous flick with the back of her hand, briefly glancing at Oriens sideways. "My mother said the visitor had come and I had to find you and tell you. And I looked for you. I sneaked into your room but you weren't there, and I went up to your father's observatory but you weren't there, and I was going to go back into the house and wake up Mrs. Ambrosius, but then I heard someone beating on your front door, over and over, and calling out, and then your . . ."

"Who was it?" Michael interrupted.

". . . and then your stepmother coming downstairs and letting them in, and I heard their voices, and I think one of them was Mr. Lucius again, and I sneaked back down into your cellar and waited and waited, and then I decided to come back this way, because my mother said that if it wasn't safe at your house . . . Oh, bother, I left my water back at your house."

"Are they still there?"

"I don't know," said Laura.

Michael looked at Oriens with an expression of something very near despair, which Oriens met with his usual expression of imperturbable calm. "I don't know what to do," said Michael. "I don't know where we can go."

"Will these men stay in your home?" asked Oriens.

Michael hesitated for a long time, pondering.

Finally, Laura became impatient, retrieved her phosphorion from his hand, and said, "Let's go see, then."

Michael began to demur, but she was already striding away purposefully, the light receding in a yellow nimbus about her retreating form. "We'll have to be very quiet," he said to Oriens as he began to follow her.

When they had reached the cellar and had made certain that no one else was there, they went in and Michael and Oriens sat down to rest on the cold concrete floor (though Oriens did so only after having secured Laura's formal assurance that she would not think it rude of him). Michael reminded Laura that she had said something about water and she took a full and rather heavy leather flask on a long strap down from the shelf in the bookcase where she had left it and gave it to Michael and Oriens, both of whom drank deeply (again, the latter only after having secured Laura's leave and having punctiliously thanked her). As they rested, Laura continued to stare at Oriens, a few times changing the angle of her phosphorion in order to throw some feature or other into sharper relief. "Where do you come from?" she finally asked.

"He comes from above," said Michael.

"I am not of your world," Oriens added.

"I know," she replied solemnly. "Your eyes and your hair couldn't be, at least. But where is . . . 'above?'"

"Beyond the fixed stars," said Oriens.

"And beyond the Great Engine too?"

"Yes," said Oriens.

"How is that possible?" Laura asked, not in amazement, but as if she already knew the answer. "What does it mean?"

"Laura," said Michael, "we can talk about this later, if we survive. But right now we have to find out whether Mr. Lucius or his . . . any other of the Brethren are still here. We can't stay here if they are, because they'll find us sooner or later."

Laura opened her mouth, clearly to issue some sort of rebuke, but then her expression changed to one of slight surprise. "Yes, you're . . . you're right," she said with a hint of bafflement in her voice. "I'll go look."

"No, let me," said Michael, rising to his feet before she could object or tell him he was too clumsy for the task. "It's my house and my . . . Paichnidia. Just please go back to the tunnel if you hear anything troubling."

Before Laura could object, Michael crept up the stairs, flinching at every slight creak of the wooden steps underfoot, and warily opened the door at the top. The ground floor of the tower annex was empty and none of its phosphoria were lit, but it was not entirely dark; a wan glow, coming from the front of the house, hung in the air — just bright enough to make the walls, though not their color, visible. Stealing around the staircase, he found the annex door standing half ajar, opened inward toward him, and he slowly approached it. There were voices in the next room, one a man's and one obviously — piercingly — Paichnidia's. When he pressed himself against the wall beside the door and peered around the jamb, he saw that both speakers were seated on the long red divan near the fireplace, one at either end; and fortunately the divan faced away from the annex. It seemed an oddly casual, even cozy, scene. The man, who was very still and appeared to be staring directly ahead of him into empty space, was wearing the glossy black suit jacket and black velvet hat of one of the Brethren, while Paichnidia, who was excitedly gesturing with her hands and buoyantly bobbing up and down in her seat, was wearing one of her innumerable frilly pink nightdresses.

"But, of course," she was piping animatedly, "some of the most adorable dolls come from right here in Oreiotopia. They make them by hand from the baked sap of milk-rushes, and they paint the most delightful lovely little faces on them, and dress them in lovely little traditional mountain costumes, and . . ."

The man, without turning his head, suddenly coughed in a transparently forced manner. "Yes, Mrs. Ambrosius, that's fascinating, but it takes us somewhat far afield — yet again." Michael at once recognized Mr. Lucius's voice, though not its intonation: rather than the tense, suave, malicious liveliness of three weeks earlier, he now spoke with what sounded like a deep and defeated listlessness. "I was only saying how surprised I was to discover the telescope at the top of the tower, since it had been reported to me that a telescope from this residence was duly received and destroyed by the Office of Contraband Regulation."

"How silly of me," Paichnidia replied with a shrill laugh, clapping her hands together merrily. "I had no idea there were *two* in the house."

"Yes," said Mr. Lucius lethargically, "I'm sure you didn't. It does make one wonder, though. How exactly is that possible? How could you not have known of something quite that large?"

"Now, now," said Paichnidia, "that's my husband's study, where I never intrude."

"Yes," said Mr. Lucius again. "Yes indeed. And about which you never ask questions." He heaved a bored sigh. "You're a very *compliant* woman, aren't you, my voluptuous?"

"Thank-you," said Paichnidia.

"It's our fault, I suppose. You wouldn't know this, but you were conditioned to be compliant . . . by us, that is — or by those I serve — over a period of some years, for much of your life really."

"Oh, that was kind of you."

"The idea, of course, was that you would comply *with us* when we sought information from you," he continued. "For just that reason, you were assigned — without knowing it, of course — to Professor Ambrosius."

"Imagine that," Paichnidia said in a contented murmur. "Well, it was very thoughtful of you. It's been such a deliciously happy marriage."

"We succeeded too well, it seems," Mr. Lucius continued, still staring away, not noting her interjections. "You're so compliant that you're apparently entirely devoid of all natural curiosity, and so don't actually have any information to impart."

"Don't forget what I told you about dolls."

"Oh, I couldn't, I assure you, my garrulous. But it occurs to me that, if only we'd instilled a little spitefulness in you, perhaps we'd have been better served. But there's something in you perversely resistant to that sort of thing, I suspect. Something not just vapid but incorrigibly . . . innocent . . . *sweet*. And that undetected congenital flaw, alas, seems to have thwarted our designs." He sighed again, this time with a touch of disgust.

"Are you sure you won't have some cake?" asked Paichnidia.

"No, madam, a thousand times no," said Mr. Lucius. "I eat only meat. What we Brethren call the 'repast of the righteous.' Anyway, the telescope doesn't matter any more. The story has moved on to another chapter. My chief concern is the seeming absence of your stepson from your house, on this of all nights."

"You know what boys are like."

"It all depends on how they're prepared," said Mr. Lucius absently. "In any event, if he's not here, he may soon wish he were."

"Don't worry," said Paichnidia with another laugh, "he'll be back soon. Where there's cake the boys will gather."

"Some of my subordinates have expressed a desire to feed here before going on, incidentally," Mr. Lucius remarked coolly. "They're famished. They've wreaked considerable havoc among the local livestock these past two nights. But I've explicitly ordered them to refrain from eating you."

"Oh, that's a relief," said Paichnidia. "I have so much housework to do."

At that moment, there was the sound of heavy boots upon floorboards, coming from outside Michael's field of vision, in the general direction of the front door. "Ah, lieutenant," said Mr. Lucius, at last turning his head and rising from the divan. Michael drew back from the door and now merely listened.

"My lord" — the voice was low but clear, and Michael was almost certain it belonged to the commander he had seen addressing his men in the clearing outside the mine — "the inspection party is assembled."

"Good," said Mr. Lucius without enthusiasm. "Conduct a thorough search of the premises, and this time I do mean *thorough*. Upstairs and down, in and out and around, in front of things and behind them, on top of them and underneath. Yes? But be quick, because if the boy isn't here, the invader certainly won't be either, and you must return to the chase. The packs must keep running."

"Yes, my lord." The voice's owner cleared his throat. "My lord, I'm sorry to say that we've received word that the Magian family has somehow . . . slipped away."

"Naturally," said Mr. Lucius impassively. "Two aging bipeds and one young girl left in the custody of eleven of the Brethren in perfect health and primed for the hunt — how could they fail to escape?"

"We never saw the girl at all. As for the parents, they're being pursued."

"I can't tell you how reassuring I find that," said Mr. Lucius. "Be about your work." But, a second later, he added, "Wait, don't go yet."

"My lord?"

"I've been on the anemophone and I've received instructions," said Mr. Lucius. "I had hoped to avoid the eventuality, but . . . well, yes, after months of scouting and reconnaissance, surveillance and spying, over five thousand of the Brethren roving these mountain forests, the invader announcing his arrival with a beacon from the sky that I imagine a quarter of the globe could see, somehow — *somehow* — he eludes us with apparently no effort, and with no assistance except perhaps that of a rather awkward, bookish child. Once again, I am utterly in awe of the skills of my den."

Michael scowled to himself.

"We couldn't anticipate that all our aerial vehicles would become inoperable when the great light appeared, my lord," the voice protested. "We'll find him, though. It's only a few hours since . . ."

"In fact," said Mr. Lucius, "every contingency was anticipated — except the contingency of epidemic incompetence. That's why our ground forces were out in such numbers. But it doesn't matter now. Our masters now have no greater confidence in my hunters than I do. They've decided that other, more dangerous predators must be loosed, ones adept at tracking the light of spirit, not merely the scent of flesh. I've been ordered to summon the Great Ones — to call up the Shadows of the Deep." He uttered this last phrase with a slight but definite quaver of trepidation.

"The . . . Great Ones . . . ? The Shadows . . . ?" And what had begun as a human moan of distress immediately dissolved into a distinctly canine whine of misery.

"Oh, how cute!" cried Paichnidia.

"Resume your human form at once!" Mr. Lucius snapped. "How dare you!"

The response was a curt currish cry of anguish, which instantly mutated into a human voice again: "Please, my lord, no, you mustn't! Please, we can't continue hunting if they're to be set loose. Don't make us, I beg you. They won't distinguish . . . They won't care . . . My lord . . ." The pure, unabashed terror vibrating in every syllable quickly communicated itself to Michael, who found himself all at once feeling something like incipient panic.

"Send out word to the Brethren and then conduct your search," said Mr. Lucius in a glacial voice. "If you find nothing, immediately return to the hunt. We serve God and our masters, not our fears. Now I must pray to my king and maker for the Great Ones to be roused. I must go down upon my knees with head bowed low, beneath the open stars, and invoke them. I'm going to that nearby clearing. I need solitude for my . . . devotions. And, of course, I'll need open ground to get away quickly. You'll know when my supplications have been answered. You'll shortly hear them rising from the deep."

"My lord, surely . . ." The voice dwindled away in a wretched whimper, but whether it was canine or human Michael could not now tell.

Nor did he wait to hear anything further. Hurrying back to the cellar door and closing it gingerly behind him, he began feeling his way down through the darkness, calling out in a loud whisper to Laura as he did so.

A second later, the light of her phosphorion flared out from below and he hastened his descent. "We have to go, quickly," he was saying even before he reached the bottom. "They're about to search the whole house." Within a few moments they were back in the corridor, the escape door shut behind them. "We can't stay here either," he said, urging Laura and Oriens ahead of him. "They're certain to find the door." And they began running, Laura leading the way, holding her phosphorion aloft with one hand and pressing her water flask against her hip with the other. When they reached the junction of the access tunnel, all three were out of breath (though Oriens seemingly less so than his companions), and they paused to rest. When his panting had somewhat subsided, Michael gave Laura the news of her parents' escape.

He had rarely ever seen Laura weep, and certainly not since she had been very little, so he did not know quite how to react when tears all at once filled her eyes, and she failed to repress three sobs, and briefly laid her head against his chest and shook so hard that the light from her phosphorion danced about them. "Sorry," she said, after only a few moments, standing up straight again, regaining her composure, wiping her eyes, and turning away to make certain the access tunnel was empty. "I don't mean to be an idiot."

"There's another thing," said Michael, but then hesitated.

"Well, what is it?" said Laura impatiently, her brusqueness already restored. "Go on."

Michael told them of what he had heard just before returning to the cellar, and of the terror that Mr. Lucius's words had inspired in his own lieutenant.

"Great Ones?" said Laura. "Shadows of the Deep?" And her voice suggested that some of the nameless dread that had infected Michael as he listened by the annex door had now been passed on to her.

"Are these a greater threat than our pursuers?" asked Oriens calmly.

"We don't know what they are," said Michael, "but our pursuers themselves seem terrified by them."

For several seconds, none of them said anything. Then Oriens broke the silence: "I have brought you great danger. I regret this."

"Oh, no," said Laura.

"No," Michael concurred. "Your enemies were persecuting my father for years before you came."

"I have brought you greater danger, then," Oriens replied. "It grieves me."

Michael still found the tone of unnatural equanimity in Oriens's voice somewhat disconcerting, but this time it seemed to him that he may also heard an extremely faint note of feeling.

V

"WE SHOULD GO BACK," SAID LAURA. "I MEAN, back the way I came. My parents won't come here—my mother was clear. We're supposed to meet at our other place, if it's safe."

"You mentioned that before," said Michael. "What other place?"

"My parents' fishing cabin," said Laura. "It's where I'm supposed to go if it's not safe at your house, and I'm supposed to take you there if I can, and the . . . and Oriens too. It's a sort of secret place. There's a hidden sort of . . . I don't know, a little closed off bay beside the Glitterglass, and you get to it through a hidden pass, and it's all under the cover of a sort of small forest of marmoreans." She turned to Oriens. "Whitewoods. Huge trees with bright white wood, right through to the core, and with bright blue leaves. Beautiful trees."

"Well, let's go there then," said Michael sharply, it now being his turn to grow impatient.

"We'll still have to go through forest to get there," said Laura uncertainly. "And with the wolves out, and whatever these . . . Shadows are."

Michael looked at her, then at Oriens, and then at her again. "If we stay here, they'll find us," he said, "and we can't go down into the mine without getting lost forever, or without them trapping us."

"And if we go out into the woods," said Laura grimly, "we might be eaten . . . or worse. Shadows of the Deep . . ." She suddenly, visibly shivered. "Here, hold this." And she thrust the light into Michael's hand.

"What other choice . . . ?" Michael began.

But he was immediately silenced by an immensely loud noise, resembling nothing he had ever before heard or could ever have imagined. It was like a vast, atrocious, ruinous groan that seemed to come from outside the mine but also from everywhere at once, as though it were soaking through the stone around them: something like thunder, something like an impossibly deep cry of anger, something like the very foundations of the mountains grinding against one another. And, as it continued, it became still more horrible. Somehow, it seemed to be full of voices, or the echoes of voices, screaming and weeping and pleading, in fear and utter loneliness and terror heaped upon terror. Michael saw the horror on Laura's face, and was sure her expression was a mirror of his own; and he saw that Oriens too, for the first time that night, had a look of unease in his eyes. The noise seemed to go on interminably, though it probably lasted only a few minutes; and, even when at last it passed, it left behind an almost palpable atmosphere of desolation. Then, drifting down to them from far beyond the tunnel entrance, came the howling of the wolves, frenzied and forlorn and (as if all of them were madly flying away) rapidly fading.

"Do you know what that was?" asked Oriens, and for the first time his voice sounded subdued.

"Shadows?" Laura weakly whispered.

"Go, go, let's go," said Michael frantically.

They went, Michael now in front and lighting the way through the broad, iron-gray tunnel that led to the Magians' side of the mountain. They paused only twice, neither time for much longer than it took to drink from Laura's flask, and midway along Laura took back the phosphorion and the lead. They were all three very weary (though, again, Oriens seemingly less so than the other two), but the memory of that terrible sound drove them on; and, though they now heard nothing but the echoes of their own footsteps, Michael continually glanced back apprehensively. When, however, they reached the tunnel's end, where it issued into another access tunnel at a point only a dozen yards from the second mine entrance, Laura extinguished her light and they rested, sitting on the cool stone floor in silence for fully ten minutes.

Michael was the first to speak: "It can't be long till dawn. If we want to get out of these tunnels, we should go now, while we still can't be seen."

"Seen by what?" Laura murmured. "What's out there?"

Michael did not reply, but merely asked, "How far is this fishing cabin? Is it hard to get to?"

"It's not even a mile and a half from here, and it's easy if you know the way. You have to know where the cleft in the hills is, because everything is hidden by those trees." She paused. "But what's out there?" she said again.

When they were refreshed enough to will themselves on, they rose and went to look outside. The mine entrance was sheltered under a low, somewhat decayed wooden awning, crowded in on either side by high, concealing shrubs, and was separated from the trees beyond by only a few yards of clearing. The moons were low in the sky now, behind the treetops, but the night was still bright.

"We should go then," said Michael.

"Yes," said Laura, "all right."

Neither of them moved though. After several moments Oriens asked, "Are we waiting for a sign? A good omen?" But then a distant voice, calling out something unintelligible but obviously urgent, came faintly reverberating along the tunnels at their backs.

"They've found the way," Michael said. "We have to go."

"Yes," said Laura firmly. "Right. Stay near me, because I'm not going to use the light." She took a deep breath and set out, adopting as vigorous a pace as her tired legs would allow, and Michael and Oriens followed close behind. "Through these trees," she said in a loud whisper, "then across a little meadow under Mount Woodbine, then into the trees in front of the pass. It's easy." But her voice was not as confident as her words.

The ground was mostly level, the shadows of the trees were deep but not impenetrable, the way was largely unobstructed, and they moved quickly. Occasionally a sudden sound, perhaps a falling branch or a small animal dashing away, caused them a momentary pause, but after ten minutes Michael had begun to hope that this night of relentless flight would soon be at an end. After another five, the meadow had become visible through the trees ahead, softly luminous in the slanting rays of the moons. "Are we nearly there?" he asked quietly.

"Yes," said Laura, just as quietly.

At that moment, something moved deep in the forest to their right — or, rather, it was as if part of the forest itself had moved. Michael saw it but did not see it, or at least could not make sense of what he saw: something immense and dark passing noiselessly through the trees, entirely obscuring an enormous span of moonlit trunks and branches and leaves as it did so, but reflecting absolutely no light from itself. He could not tell how far away it was — fifty yards? a hundred? — and its shape was impossible to make out; but he could see that it was at least as tall as many of the fully grown trees it briefly hid from view. He halted and reached out to either side, catching Laura and Oriens each by an arm; but they had already stopped walking, obviously having seen it as well. None of them spoke as it went by, vast and slow, or for a long time after it had sunk away into the forest again, a giant shadow disappearing in an immense well of shadows.

"I don't want to stay here," whispered Laura.

"Do we absolutely have to cross that meadow?" asked Michael.

"There's no other way," said Laura. "It runs right along the mountainside in both directions for miles. There's no way around. You'll have to be brave." Then she sighed glumly, as if hearing her own last remark had annoyed her.

Michael bowed his head and, for the first time that night, was truly conscious of the aching of his legs. "We'd better run across, then."

They continued on till they reached the meadow's edge, but then lingered for some moments under the trees. In the blended light of Aurea and Argentea, the uncropped grasses shone the color of jade, the scattered white wildflowers glittered like frost, and the tall white trunks and blue crowns of the marmorean trees on the far side, under the low ridge of the mountain, were like bright columns of alabaster rising into a huge enameled blue vault. They could be across in only a few minutes, but they would be bathed in light and wholly exposed to view every step of the way.

"Do you see anything moving?" Michael asked.

"No," said Laura.

"I do not," said Oriens.

Michael and Laura exchanged glances and then, each wordlessly prompting and prompted by the other, they both nodded at Oriens and all three of them simultaneously began to run. Michael felt the weariness in his legs and the long grass catching at his feet, and every step was toil and jolted him painfully, and he was practically out of breath as soon as he was in the open, but his fear sustained him. Laura was at his side and keeping pace, while Oriens was slowly drawing ahead of them, and the only sounds Michael heard were his own footfalls, his own and Laura's labored breaths, the soft flapping of Laura's water flask against her hip, and the fluttering of her skirt. Everything was awash in lunar light, nothing gave cover, every moment was dread; but when they were more than halfway across the field, it seemed to him that they might actually reach the marmorean trees undetected, and hide beneath those great sheltering pavilions of turquoise.

Just then, however, the whole world was thrown out of joint. A tremendous and horrid sound rang out at their backs, like the one they had heard in the mine, but more acute, more limited in range, nearer at hand — a wail of fury, a storm-wracked ocean beating against a cliff, a clash of iron against iron, a savage shout of triumph and a cry of immeasurable suffering all at once — and Michael saw Oriens stagger before him and fall to his hands and knees, and realized that the earth was shuddering beneath his own feet and that he too was losing his balance and falling, and then felt

Laura falling also, careening into him and bearing him to the ground more violently. He instantly turned over and sat up, Laura rolling away from him to do the same, while Oriens tried to stand but fell again when a second shock ran through the ground beneath them. And then behind them, in the woods from which they had just come, trees were falling — groaning, cracking, crashing to the ground — and they all three turned their heads and raised their eyes. A moment later they saw for themselves what a Shadow of the Deep was. Something outlandishly huge and abysmally black had separated itself from the darkness of the forest, perhaps a hundred yards farther along its edge than where they had emerged into the meadow, and was now quickly advancing into the open with gigantic strides that struck the earth like peals of thunder. It was too large to believe at first, too dark to seem real. Michael reached out to Laura wildly and met her hand as it reached out to take his own, and they held tightly to one another. And then the giant came to a sudden halt, midway across the meadow, between them and the western horizon, and simply towered above the world, hiding the moons from their view and casting a great lead-colored shadow over them and the grass all around. It was unimaginable, unbearable. Was it sixty feet high? Higher? A hundred feet away? Nearer? They could see it outlined against the moon-bright sky now, hiding the stars, and see also that it had the form of a man, at least crudely so — its limbs monstrously thick, its shoulders and head misshapen and hideously enormous — but it had no features they could make out. It was not merely dark, but darkness itself; none of the light through which it moved could find a place of rest upon it; it was like a great fissure rent open in the fabric of reality, revealing nothing behind. Michael tried to cry out, but could not. He let go of Laura's hand and tried to rise, but found his legs would not support him. And, turning his head desperately from side to side, he saw that Laura and Oriens were both also struggling and failing to regain their feet. Somehow, from outside themselves or from within, the Shadow was holding them all in place.

Michael shook; he had felt terror many times already tonight, but this was something more unendurable, more paralyzing. It was a freezing flood of despair, overwhelming his will, a sense that nothing in the world could protect them from this horrifying vision, that there was nowhere to run, and that only pain lay ahead. And again that terrific noise rang out, nearly deafening now — that cry or groan of anger and cruel exultation and sheer devastating power — and he felt himself pressed further down to the earth by its force. "Please," he barely succeeded in rasping as the din faded away once more, and again he attempted to rise, and again found he could not. Then, slowly — colossally — the Shadow raised one of its massive arms and extended it toward them, as if stretching out an inviting hand. And, as it did, the darkness within it was changing, and something was slowly becoming visible in its depths: at first only a phantom glow welling up out of the vacant blackness where its chest should have been, small and pallid and dim, but soon beginning to expand and turn, ever so gradually, like a mist caught in a sluggish whirlwind, and then continuing to become larger and to revolve more quickly, until it was a great wheeling spiral of gray and ghastly white. And Michael could only stare into it, all his thoughts dissolving in wave after wave of overflowing fear. "Laura," he hissed, "run . . . you, Oriens . . ." But he could say no more.

Laura choked out a single sob, and was just able to whisper, "You go. I can't move."

Michael wanted to look away, but could not. A sound like a rushing wind was rising about them, though no wind was blowing; the Shadow's entire torso was now a spinning miasma of hoary light, and Michael was all at once aware of feeling an incomprehensible, chilling, but almost overwhelming desire to reach out to it, even to touch it. In fact, he could not bear not to touch it. And the sound was also the sound of voices, moaning, lamenting, full of hopelessness and loss, full of fear; and the spectral lights in the giant's chest were also dreary clouds floating over and parting before some cold, gray, barren waste, visible in fleeting glimpses deep in the abyss of that darkness. "I don't want to go there," Michael hissed. Then, though, he found himself rising to his feet, with no effort at all, not because he chose to do so but because he could not choose to do anything at all, and when he looked to one side he saw Laura rising as well — on her hands, then fully up on her feet, leaving the phosphorion in the grass — and when he looked to the other side he saw Oriens upon his knees but with his back straight, his hands pressed against his chest, his hitherto inexpressive face so distorted with anguish that even his unearthly beauty had become frightful to see. Then Michael was conscious that he was himself walking, though he had not been aware of taking a first step, forward toward the giant — slowly, with great difficulty, but inexorably. "Please," he whispered, "I don't want to go there."

Laura's voice reached him, weakly, under the sound of wind: "Michael, I can't . . . Michael, run . . ."

He continued to walk, one unsteady step, then another, then another, nearer and nearer to the Shadow, and to its gigantic darkness and swirling lights and outstretched hand, and with each step his fear grew deeper, and his horrible desire to touch the lights grew more intense, and he could not halt, and could not cry out. "Please . . ." he whispered once more, "please." But he felt no hope.

And then he did. It was an instant change, a sudden release: the compulsion forcing his limbs to move against his will ceased, his fear was still immense but now not utterly crushing, and he realized at once that all around him there was a gentle brightness, the same limpid crystalline light he had seen driving back the wolf on the ledge above the Phlegethon, and he knew what had happened. He turned his head and saw that Oriens was now on his feet, his arm outstretched as before, that peaceful radiance flowing from his open palm. And when Michael turned again to Laura he saw that she also was no longer advancing. Then he looked at the Shadow, hoping to see it retreat as the wolf had done; but it did not. Instead, it merely leaned slightly to one side, then to the other, like a vast cloud of smoke shifting in the wind. Once more the shattering cry rang out, though this time, as if the light from the jewel had weakened it, it failed to drive Michael to the ground. Then the giant stepped forward, the earth thundering under its foot again. But now Michael found himself able to turn around and to shout out: "Run, Laura, go!"

Laura, however, was already turning, and was calling out to him at the same time: "Come on!"

Then they were both dashing toward Oriens, and then around him, and he too was giving way, stepping back, still holding the jewel before him for a moment, and then closing his hand around it and running along with them, his fist shining like a scarlet lantern. They heard a second pounding footstep from the giant behind them, another cry of rage, and the earth shook again, but this time they were all able to stay on their feet. The sound of the wind, however, was now no longer only a sound; Michael felt it, not so much blowing against him as dragging upon him, trying to draw him back toward their pursuer, and it was growing stronger as he ran. The thick grass beneath his feet sometimes seemed to be tripping him, but he flung himself onward, and Laura was there beside him, and when he glanced back he saw Oriens only a pace behind. The footsteps of the Shadow continued to crash to earth behind them, gradually, at long intervals, but Michael knew that those titanic strides were covering the distance quickly. And now the wind was pulling at him fiercely, slowing his steps, and the grasses around him were bending and whipping at him, surging wildly like a sea in a storm, and slender turquoise leaves from the grove ahead were flying through the air above them. He saw Laura flinging her water flask behind her, and saw also that it never struck the ground but was instead caught up and carried away in the wind. Then he began to feel that he might himself be lifted from his feet, the pull was becoming so powerful, and he saw that Laura was struggling even harder to move forward, her skirt dragging back against her legs like a thrashing sail. They were very near the white trees, however, and Oriens had caught up to them, and had linked his arms with theirs — Michael on his left, Laura on his right — and he was stronger than they were. They drove themselves onward, struggling to advance, leaning forward as they did so, moving with agonizing slowness toward those towering, gleaming white trunks and the misty blue light that hovered beneath their boughs. When the next footstep of the giant hammered the ground behind them it sounded as if it could be no more than a few yards away. Without detaching his arm from Laura's, Oriens turned over his right hand and momentarily opened it, and the clear bright light poured out over them again. It seemed to Michael that the force of the wind was diminished for an instant, or at least that his own strength was increased, and he pressed forward and felt Oriens and Laura pressing forward with him.

And then they were among the trees, immersed in the mysterious white and blue glow of the grove, and the light sank again as Oriens closed his fist, and they all let go of one another and ran ahead as best they could, the wind still dragging at them. After a dozen steps, Michael threw his arms around the slender white bole of a young marmorean, with its silkily smooth bark, and clung to it desperately. The wind was roaring in his ears, the leaves of the trees were rattling overhead with a sound like rain lashing against a million window panes. Exerting all the strength he had, he pulled himself around the tree until he could brace his chest against its trunk and look back. Oriens was nearby, a little behind, like himself holding fast to a tree trunk and staring toward the meadow; Laura, however, was farther behind, having evidently tripped over something, and was lying face down on the ground clutching the low sinuous arch of a protruding white marmorean root with both hands; and beyond her, visible through the trees, was the massive form of the Shadow, its upper body still a writhing spiral of those dismal lights. It was no longer advancing toward them, however, and Michael somehow sensed that it was unwilling — even unable — to follow them into the grove. Perhaps it did not need to, though: as it stood there, the wind continued to grow stronger and louder, and streams of blue leaves and silvery green grass and dark woodland debris were flowing through the air toward and into the Shadow and simply vanishing in its seething darkness.

And then a high, frantic scream from Laura, piercing right through the clamor of the wind, recalled his attention to her, and with a shock of utter misery he saw that her whole body had been raised from the earth, her skirt drawn taut against her legs, her hair coursing in whipping waves along her neck and shoulders; only the root to which she still clung prevented her from being borne off entirely, and she certainly could not hold on much longer. Scarcely thinking about what he was doing, he twisted himself around the tree trunk again, into the draft of the wind, and let go. He tried to keep to his feet as he turned about and sent himself staggering toward Laura, simultaneously surrendering to the wind and struggling to resist it, but after seven rapid reeling steps his feet were seized out from under him, he fell down painfully among a mass of white roots, and immediately he felt himself being dragged onward. Laura was only a few yards from him, and he could see the expression of pain and fear on her face, and he wanted only to get to her. He could also see her hands beginning slightly but surely to loosen their hold and hear her scream again right through the blast of the wind and, thinking he would never reach her in time, he yelled in desperation.

But then all at once Oriens was there between them, falling to the ground in front of Laura, taking hold of her wrist with his free hand, and raising the hand in which he held the jewel high above his head. Once more, the Shadow's cry broke in upon them, louder than the wind, sounding and resounding among the trees, and Michael opened his mouth to shout to Laura, to tell her to continue to hold on. But Oriens shouted first, his melodious voice suddenly ringingly strident: "Find its heart!" And he flung the burning jewel from his hand. It rose up into the wind, but swifter than the wind, flying away in a streak of beautiful clear flame, shedding its serene brilliance on everything around it as it passed by, momentarily creating a splendid dome of shining turquoise and alabaster as it soared up just below the treetops and out into the open; and then it sped directly at the giant like a blazing arrow and plunged into the wheeling morass of tarry darkness and bleak light at its center.

At once the wind fell, its roar dying away with a frail whistle among the trees. The terrific stress of the blast ceased to drag at them, Laura's body dropped to the ground, and she coughed roughly as the breath was forced from her lungs. For a moment, the massive figure beyond the trees was silent and perfectly still; even the spiral of lights within it had all at once vanished; but then it swayed and lurched away, steadying itself with one thundering backward step, as though it had nearly fallen. Then it raised its arms to its breast, like a man clutching at a wound, and its monstrous cry rang out one more time; now, however, it sounded far feebler, and far more like a cry of startled indignation and fear. Suddenly light burst out in its chest again — and again and again, like flashes of lightning in quick succession — but this time it was the bright, lucid, shimmering light of the jewel. It threw its arms up above its head and turned violently away, as if trying to escape a tormentor; but before it could take a single step its entire form began shaking and wavering, and suddenly it was simply folding up into itself, and the fissure in reality seemed as though it were being forcibly closed, and it continued rapidly collapsing into the flashing light at its core until the whole vast shape had contracted to no more than a minuscule point of flickering gray hovering perhaps forty feet above the ground; and then it entirely disappeared in a final burst of that beautiful splendor.

MICHAEL, LAURA, AND ORIENS REMAINED WHERE they were for a long time. Michael was so weak he could hardly raise his arms, and he heard Laura coughing and trying to take deep breaths as she continued to lie face down among the bone-white roots of the marmorean tree, and he knew that she had been no more than a few seconds from losing her grip when Oriens had reached her. Dawn came now, first as a pearly glow in the sky beyond the trees, then as a fiery crimson flush in the east, and then as the mild silver brightness of waking day. The last trace of the moons—the almost transparently waxen upper edge of Argentea on the mountainous western horizon—was visible through the tree trunks as it melted away among the peaks. Finally, Oriens reached into his shirt and withdrew another of his jewels; assisting Laura to sit up, and even gently brushing a tangled tress of copper-red hair from before her eyes— the first apparently genuinely human gesture, Michael realized, that their visitor had exhibited—he opened his palm, and the three of them stared for many minutes into its peaceful light. When this had calmed them and restored enough of their strength, he put the jewel away again and they all three rose and began slowly—wearily but also almost floatingly—to journey on, deeper into the wood. Laura led the way through the trees and into and along an extremely narrow grassy pass, a deep crevice in the mountain wholly covered overhead by the intertwined treetops of two low forested cliffs.

As they walked among the blue, softly lustrous shadows descending from the canopy, they did not speak. The only sounds were the quiet treading of their feet on grass and moss and fallen leaves and a few birds singing above with particular delicacy. And all the while the encompassing peacefulness of this place continued to deepen around them. Occasionally, Michael's mind fixed itself upon some small detail of his surroundings — how, for instance, a small white twig and two turquoise leaves caught in Laura's hair looked almost like a jeweled clip — but for the most part he was aware only of an overwhelming calm, as well as of a peculiarly sweet freshness in the air. At one point, two small birds with emerald plumage and ruby beaks flew past them, only a few feet above their heads, emitting small trills. At another, a sleek golden fox trotted across their path far ahead, glancing at them as it did so, but with no sign of concern. Then they emerged from the pass and the small fishing cabin came into view at the end of a gentle downward slope where the land met the river: more an elegant cottage, really, constructed from bright milk-white marmorean wood, with a wide, girdling covered porch, blue shutters, a low roof with blue shingles, and a door with the typical lavish carvings of the region. It stood entirely sheltered under the spreading boughs of the white and turquoise trees, next to the bank of cream-colored pebbles that rimmed the sweetly splashing, softly gleaming, blue and silver waters of the Glitterglass.

PART THREE
Prince Oriens

And then their covenant with me they wrote
In mystic letters on my inmost heart:
"Go down to Egypt in your pauper's coat;
From there bring back the pearl that lies apart
Amid the waters of the sea, kept by
The crimson serpent of the western sun;
And then return, and thou wilt reign on high
And wear the mantle of the Blessed One."

I journeyed from the East, escorted by
Two royal envoys, for the way was harsh
And full of perils, and so young was I
They feared to leave. But when at length the march
Had taken us past Maishan's bounds and brought
Our feet to Babylon, to Sarbak's keep,
They took their leave, and all alone I sought
Bright Egypt's shores, and saw the shining deep.

— from "The Hymn of the Pearl"

I

WHEN, A LITTLE PAST NOON, MICHAEL ROSE from the small but generously yielding featherbed in the cabin's rear bedroom, still wearing his clothes of the previous night, he thought he must have been the first to awaken, as he could hear no one else in the cabin. On looking out of his window, however, he saw Oriens standing not far off, beside the river bank, dressed all in black, with one bent arm raised before him and the strange white bird perched upon the back of his hand. The picture lasted only a moment: before Michael could even properly take it in, the bird spread its wings, sprang into the air, and rose swiftly into the treetops, a fragment of rainbow vanishing in the blue, white-fretted vault of the canopy. And when he went to the front of the cabin, intending to join Oriens outside, he found Laura standing by a window and staring out toward the river. She wore a light green blouse and red hiker's trousers, and from her smoothly brushed and neatly tied locks it was obvious that she had already had time to bathe, dry her hair, and make herself presentable. When Michael spoke her name, she turned to him with a distracted expression. "We're about to eat," she said. "My father left some provisions here the day before yesterday. I've put some clean clothes and a towel out for you by the bath. We . . . we still keep some of Rafe's clothes here."

"Oh," said Michael, nodding awkwardly. "Thanks."

"I gave some to Oriens too," she remarked, looking away to the window. "He thanked me and was about to undress and go to the river to wash, and I had to stop him and explain about not going about naked, especially with . . . with a girl around." She looked at Michael again. "He just apologized and said he didn't know it was bad manners. I had to show him the bath and how to run the water and . . . *everything.*"

Michael nodded again. "It must be very different where he's from."

"And it's very hard to . . . to read him. He seems so . . . " But some other thought seemed to have distracted her.

"Reserved?" Michael offered after a few seconds. "Cold? I know. Apparently he has to get used . . . "

"Michael," Laura interrupted, folding her arms tightly against herself. "Yes?"

"There's no sign of my mother and father." She was obviously straining to control her emotions. "I'm so. . . . They could be dead, or captured, or . . ."

"They will be here soon," said Oriens, who was just then opening the front door and entering.

Laura, dropping her arms, practically ran across the room to him, around the dining table. "What do you mean? Why do you say that?"

"My pneumatagogue has told me," said Oriens, closing the door behind him. "He would have come to tell me sooner, but for some hours before dawn he was leading one of the Shadows away from where we were. He did not know about the one that had found us. He came back through another grove of the white trees, and he found your father and mother there. He knows them."

Laura was standing directly in front of him now, her hands clasped together before her throat, her expression simultaneously impatient, dubious, and grateful. "He knows my. . . ?" Then all the contending impulses in her eyes resolved into a single look of perplexity. "Your what? Your *pneumat-*. . . ?"

"My guide," said Oriens, "and guardian, and emissary. He can fly far and see many things, and he discovers many secrets."

"The white bird," said Michael quietly.

"Your father is injured," said Oriens.

"Oh!" Laura moaned and stretched out a hand to Oriens.

He hesitated a moment, then took it in his own. "It is not a mortal wound, but he cannot move quickly. You must not go to find them. They are near." He looked down at Laura's hand, turning it from side to side and then gently releasing it. "It is so strange," he said. "It is so difficult to feel another person through this shell — this flesh. There is no . . . immediate contact, is there? It feels so dull . . . so numb. It is like the shadow of the echo of a touch."

Laura shook her head uncomprehendingly. "How do you expect it to feel to touch someone?"

Oriens was looking down at his own hands. "It is different where I come from . . . came from, long ago. Bodies are subtler, more luminous. There the touch of another is . . . delight. A brightness, a warmth flows between us. A thrill of joy. Communion." He raised his eyes to hers. "Bliss."

Laura drew in her breath sharply, as if the word had stung her.

There was a small mirror in a plain wooden frame hanging by the door, and Oriens now turned to look into it. Tentatively, he raised his fingertips to his jaw and cheek. "It seems so unreal," he said quietly. "Like a statue, or a toy . . ."

"What?" said Laura in a subdued tone, her eyes wide. "Your face?"

"Yes," said Oriens, still staring into the glass with an expression of cool fascination but also, perhaps, of faint revulsion. "It is as if a puppet were to come to life . . . so stiff and . . . mechanical . . ."

"Haven't you seen your face before?" she asked, her voice quavering slightly.

"Not until this morning," said Oriens. Then he turned to her again. "In this form, that is. I do recognize my face through this mask, but it becomes harder each time." He looked into the glass again and stared pensively for several seconds. "It is more like an image of my face than the real thing, molded from something . . . I cannot say . . . something coarse and lifeless . . . dead." Then, oddly at first, a look of discomfort or disorientation — or something else altogether — came over his features. After a moment, it became obvious that he was struggling to make them assume some particular configuration. He squinted, seemed to grimace, drew his lips taut, loosened them again, parted them, closed them; and then, all at once, his expression relaxed, his eyes widened, and his lips curved slightly upward; it was stiff at first, even pained, but within a few moments it seemed to be quite a natural, if somewhat restrained, smile. "Yes," he said, turning to the other two, "I am learning to make this form respond to me."

Laura's voice was nearly a whisper now: "I don't understand."

Oriens continued to smile, kindly but enigmatically. "I shall explain when I can."

A silent but obviously deep uneasiness, which until this moment Michael had not realized was oppressing him, all at once vanished. He now smiled as well.

WHEN MICHAEL HAD BATHED, CLEANED HIS TEETH with the brush and powder Laura had left him, and changed into the dark gray clothes she had set out for him, he joined the other two at the table, which was laid with simple platters of smoked fish, woodland berries, pears, and cakes of oat and honey, as well as coarse seed-bread, butter, milk, and fresh cider. Oriens refused the fish, graciously, explaining that he must eat no flesh, but he took a portion of everything else, lingering inquisitively over every mouthful. And, as they ate, Michael related to Laura as briefly as he could all that had happened to him and Oriens before they had met her in the mine. She registered some degree of amazement at a few junctures — the talking bird, the garment of moonlight, the wolf on the mountain ledge — but the night had apparently largely exhausted her stores of incredulity, and she was in any event so preoccupied with glancing at the door and listening for her parents that she could not become fully absorbed in the tale.

"I did not know whether the jewel would have any effect against that creature," said Oriens when Michael asked him. "It did not draw back before the light. In all the worlds I have passed through, I have never met an adversary who did not retreat from it, at least a little. And, if the jewel had failed to find its heart, perhaps it would not have been driven away. But when I saw that the giant did not want to follow us in among the trees I thought it might be vulnerable after all."

"What difference did that make?" asked Michael.

"These trees around us," said Oriens, lightly gesturing with both hands in all directions, "I know them. They come from my home. They spring up from seeds of light, the same light that is captured in the jewels, and they were sown in your world by countrymen of mine who descended in the past, to help prepare a place for me here."

"Oh, no, there've always been whitewood trees in Oreiotopia," said Laura. "It's the only place they grow naturally."

"It's even an old adage," said Michael: "Oreiotopia, land of marmoreans and heresies."

"It was long ago by your reckoning," said Oriens, "but they do come from my home — though there they are far larger. The greatest and most ancient of them are called the Pillars of Heaven, so high that the blue of their leaves is sometimes indistinguishable from the blue of the sky. The golden blossoms where you found me in the forest are also from my home. They are called chrysastra." He lowered his eyes to his plate for a moment. "Many of those who brought the seeds here never returned."

"Where is your. . . ?" Michael began.

But Laura spoke over him: "Where was it taking me? Taking us? The Shadow, I mean."

Oriens looked at her blankly. "I do not know this world. I only glimpsed something in its darkness — as though the giant were itself a doorway leading to some place very dark and empty."

"And full of pain," said Laura, closing her eyes. "I saw it too. I think . . ." — a violent shiver ran through her — "I think it was the Land of Hel. I think that's where it was taking us."

"What is that?" asked Oriens.

"The land below," said Laura, still not opening her eyes, "the place of perpetual torment."

"Perpetual torment?" said Oriens, the usual calm of his voice acquiring a small but definite nuance of surprise. "Is there really such a place?"

Laura lowered her head further. "Supposedly. It's 'for the wicked, the dissident, and the maladjusted.' That's how it's described in the Book of Disciplines."

"But why?"

Michael shrugged. "The Book of Disciplines says that the Great Artisan created it to reveal his love and justice."

"Love and justice?" said Oriens with a hint of vehemence. "That makes no sense. It is a cruel and evil notion." His brow furrowed and he looked away to one of the windows. "And I do not think it can be true. I was told that, in order to keep the spirits of this world imprisoned in forgetfulness, they must be made to be reborn over and over again, so that they will forget again and again, and never awaken. Every death must be followed at some point by another birth. No death can be final. Those who slay other living spirits may imagine that they truly slay, and those who are being slain may even imagine themselves truly slain, but it is an illusion. All of them return, over and over again. It is a cycle of oblivion."

"Return?" said Michael. "Return how?"

"And he certainly would not be powerful enough to imprison any spirit eternally," Oriens continued, too immersed in his own thoughts to notice Michael's question.

"He?" said Michael. "Who? Who wouldn't be powerful enough?"

Oriens raised his eyes to Michael's but, before he could answer, sounds came from the porch outside: sudden, uneven footsteps on the wooden stairs and boards, a man's loud groan, a woman's voice saying something in a soothing tone. Laura opened her eyes with an anxious cry, sprang up from her chair, and ran to the door. But it was opening before she reached it, and Mr. and Mrs. Magian were entering: a tall, somewhat heavy man with a round face, bald head, and thick spectacles, and a small woman, slender to the point of angularity, with a rather lovely face and dark silver hair. Both of them were obviously haggard and very unkempt: his charcoal suit jacket was badly torn at both shoulders, her yellow blouse was stained with grass and soil, and her hair hung down in limp tangles. Mr. Magian was also pressing his right hand to a bloodstained bandage bound around his thigh, and Mrs. Magian was helping to support him, his left arm over her shoulders and her right arm wrapped as far as possible about his broad torso. In a moment, though, Mrs. Magian had detached herself from her husband and she and Laura were embracing one another with tears and exclamations of joy; and then Mr. Magian was drawing Laura into his arms so fiercely that he began to lose his balance and had to steady himself on his wounded leg, which caused him to utter a sharp grunt. Oriens and Michael rose to come to his assistance, but at their approach Laura's parents drew slightly back, both of them staring at Oriens with undisguised wonder.

"Oh, my," said Mrs. Magian, in a tone that seemed almost despairing in its tenderness.

And, when Oriens reached out to Mr. Magian, the latter raised both of his hands and said, in his mild voice, "Oh, no, please, you shouldn't trouble yourself with me." And then he added a characteristic "Dear me" in a whisper.

"Why not?" asked Oriens.

"I'm not . . . worthy."

"We knew you were coming," said Mrs. Magian in a hushed voice and with wide eyes, "even if we didn't know how . . . or why. But, even so, truly to see you . . ."

"Yes, to see you," said Mr. Magian, removing his spectacles and wiping away a tear with a dusty hand, "at last. It's . . . dear me, I can't think . . . my goodness . . ."

"Oh," said Mrs. Magian, looking at Oriens even more intently, "your eyes . . ."

"I shall assist you," said Oriens with a gentle but curiously peremptory firmness, reaching out taking Mr. Magian's arm. "You are very tired."

After a few moments, Mr. Magian consented, and Oriens and Michael, one under each of his arms, guided him to a red upholstered chair near the small granite fireplace. Laura knelt to remove the dressing from his leg — a strip torn from the hem of Mrs. Magian's skirt — but he reached down and took both of her hands in one of his. "Not yet, darling. Let your mother deal with it."

"What happened?" asked Laura.

"A wolf," said her mother, raising her by her shoulders and drawing her away. "It's a bad wound and it needs to be cleaned."

"A wolf?" said Laura with a fretful moan. "How did you get away from it?"

94

"From *them*," corrected Mr. Magian, running his hand over his scalp. "There were three, and they'd run us down in the forest and were circling us. But then there was that . . . that absolutely horrendous noise — you must have heard it — and they all started whining and cringing, and ran off yelling in terror. We didn't come here right away because we were sure they'd be hunting us again, and we didn't want to lead them here; but they never came back. And then there was that noise again, several times, not as loud, but . . ." His voice died away and he closed his eyes. "Oh, dear, I'm very . . ."

"I had a hard time stopping the bleeding," said Mrs. Magian. "We hid west of here, in the whitewood grove under the mountain ridge. Your father lost consciousness for a little while. I need to clean that wound. Sweetheart," — she bent over and kissed Laura on the forehead — "get the bandages and antiseptic from the cupboard. I'll get some water and soap."

When Laura had gone, Michael was about to ask if he might assist; but he paused when he saw that both Mr. and Mrs. Magian were continually glancing at Oriens with expressions of unconcealed but somehow bashful awe. Then, however, Mrs. Magian asked Michael to help her husband to bed, and he did so, accompanied by Oriens — despite more self-effacing protests from Mr. Magian. For half an hour, Mr. and Mrs. Magian were closed away in the master bedroom, with Mr. Magian occasionally giving reluctant voice to his pain, and a few times crying out "Dear me" or "My goodness" or something similar, and then Mrs. Magian emerged to ask Laura to bring them something to eat. Laura, Michael, and Oriens brought plates of food and glasses of cider into the bedroom, and found Mr. Magian sitting up in bed in a plain linen nightshirt, his face fatigued and pale and grim but also washed. Mrs. Magian too had washed and had changed into a plain dark blue linen dress. And, while they ate, Michael and Laura told them the tale of the previous night, eliciting occasional looks of surprise from both of them, but rarely luring their eyes away from Oriens, who sat quietly in the window seat the whole time. But at two points the story captured their complete attention: first when Michael told of finding Oriens in the forest glade (which provoked an expression of wonder from each of them, in Mr. Magian's case almost dreamy), and then when Michael and Laura together told of the encounter with the Shadow (which caused both of them to stare in horror and then, when they both grasped how near Laura had come to being lost, to call their daughter over to submit to their anxious caresses, despite her embarrassed protests).

"The Great Ones," said Mr. Magian after several moments, in a somber voice. "So they really exist."

"What are they?" asked Michael.

"Oh dear, your father could tell you better than I can." Mr. Magian's hand shook as he removed his spectacles and laid them on a bedside table. "He's the one who knew most about the old lore and the prohibited books. But there are local legends too. The Shadows of the Deep were supposedly called up in the days of the Purist heresy, almost eight hundred years ago, and before that, I think, when the Escapist heresy was spreading."

"What are they?" Michael repeated.

"Oh, goodness me, I don't know," said Mr. Magian, a note of quiet horror audible below his voice's natural gentleness. "Pure darkness. Terrible dark fays from the underworld — from the Land of Hel. I don't know. Gracious. They supposedly carry their victims away, machine and ghost alike, to the deep places. Or to terrible prisons from which there's no escape." He swallowed laboriously and shook his head. "Valentine knew — your father knew better — knows better — than I. I know that marmoreans are supposedly a charm against them. At least, your father thought . . . thinks that's why there are all those local folk legends about whitewood amulets and necklaces and bracelets keeping away evil spirits, and why mountain people still keep marmorean leaves on their windowsills, and why marmoreans are carved on doors."

"Are they gone now?" Laura asked.

Mr. Magian shrugged. "Darling, I just don't know. Goodness. I think they stay for seven days when they're called up. Valentine told me that once. But they hunt only at night. They don't go about in the sunlight. I mean, assuming that all of that isn't just so much rustic superstition."

"It didn't follow us into the grove," Michael said. "I think it couldn't. At least, it wouldn't."

"I wish the same could be said of the wolves," said Mrs. Magian. "Or, I suppose I should say, the Lupine Brethren. They followed us right into the whitewoods. We may be protected from these Shadow things here, at least for now, but not from them."

"If they come back," said Mr. Magian, "or dare to hunt at night with the Shadows out, which I doubt. And, dear, how likely would they be to find us? They're so enormously stupid."

"They very stupidly nearly killed you last night, dear," said Mrs. Magian with a touch of asperity in her voice. "Sooner or later they could find their way here."

"I must go," said Oriens suddenly, though quietly. "My enemies are seeking me, and they may leave you in peace if I part from you."

"No . . ." Laura began.

"And I must find my sister," he said simply, "before I am found."

"Your sister?" said Mrs. Magian. "You have a sister here?"

"Who is she?" asked Laura.

"It is for her that I have come," he said.

Mr. Magian retrieved his spectacles, put them back on, and gazed at Oriens. "We didn't know," he said. "My goodness. We know so little, really. We've been told you were coming . . . we've waited so long . . . but, really, we know so little."

At this point, Michael found that he could not contain himself. "Oriens," he said forcefully, pleadingly, "I know even less than that. Everything has happened so quickly, and I don't know what any of it means. I don't know why my father was taken away, or why we're being chased, or how anyone knows about you. I don't know who you are, or who your sister is, or why you're here. Please, please, tell me what's going on."

Oriens looked about him, at each of them in turn, briefly smiled the serene smile he had mastered earlier in the day, and said, "Yes, I should." He lowered his eyes for a moment, evidently pondering how he ought to proceed, then looked up again. "It is a long story. But it is not mine only. It is yours as well."

Michael and Laura exchanged perplexed looks, as did Mr. and Mrs. Magian, but none of them said anything.

"I shall explain," Oriens continued. He took a deep breath and sat up slightly straighter. Then — framed there, with his golden hair and shining sapphire eyes, against the window and the mild blue splendor pouring in through it — he began: "I am from above . . ."

II

"MY HOME IS BEYOND YOUR WORLD," SAID Oriens, "beyond even the uttermost spheres of its heavens. It is a kingdom, and we who live in it call it Pleroma—which is to say, of course, the Fullness, the All—and the king my father and the queen my mother reign over it."

"You're a prince, then," said Laura hesitantly.

"Yes," said Oriens. "My house's name is Enteles. That is of no consequence just now. I do not think I could describe the place I come from to you, since this world of yours is so . . . shadowy by comparison, so vague. I could tell you of the air filled with the floating lights of many colors, day and night, or of the great gardens and blossoming woodlands and fragrant breezes, the shining seas and countless islands, the rose and blue mountain peaks, the great city, its palaces and temples, its fountains and avenues and squares — but I do not know how to make you see it. My father does not keep his high seat in the city; he dwells with my mother far to the north, beyond the Golden Ocean, which is also called the Sea of Spirits, and beyond the Azure Mountains and beyond the meres in the valleys and the tarns in the mountains and the streams that flow down to the ocean. To the east of the city lies the great Forest of Dawn, where many beautiful trees grow, including those you call marmoreans. To the south are flowered meadows and green hills, the Fields of Paradise, stretching away to the shores of the distant Crystal Sea. And to the west is the Forest of Dreams, a darker place, more mysterious, but still beautiful, and beyond that, far away, lies a land simply called the fallows, and beyond that another called only the barrens, and beyond that, very far away indeed, the great western desert. There no one from my country ever goes, or ever had gone, and at its heart is another realm — if that is the right word — a very ancient place, of which there had always been legends, but nothing else: Kenoma, the Emptiness . . . the Void. We knew no other name for it.

"There was a time I never thought of those places, however — the fallows or barrens or desert or Kenoma. I had heard a few stories, but I had always dwelt in the royal palace, along with my sister, Aurora. We were innocent of everything but our lessons and our games, the beauties of our home, the garden courtyards, the shores of the Golden Ocean under the rose-quartz cliffs, the eastern woodlands, the southern meadows — we knew only joys. And my sister was my greatest delight. She was everyone's delight, loved by the whole city, and throughout the kingdom. She was the child of the entire realm, and she loved to sing, to dance, to play, to listen to stories and songs, to gather flowers from the meadows and pebbles from the shore. And, because she was so greatly loved, everyone wanted to indulge her in everything, even when it was not wise to do so. She was even made keeper of the vessels of light when she was much too young for the office, because everyone longed to see her in her ceremonial gown in the great processions on high holy days. As she was a daughter of the royal house, it was her place; but, as she was still a little girl, it was not yet her appointed time. Still, there seemed no harm."

"What does that mean?" asked Michael. "What are vessels of light?"

"The Sea of Spirits," said Oriens, "is called golden not because that is the color of its waters — though sometimes it is — but because it is from there, at the turning of the great year, that the sparks of glory come, which are life, and which are gathered in two vessels that rest upon the altar of the city's greatest temple. The temple is consecrated to my father's secret name, which is a mystery only my mother may know. And it is traditional for a daughter of the king and queen to bear the vessels through the city on certain days of the heavenly dance."

"Sparks of glory?" said Michael.

"Living spirits," said Oriens: "life and flame. We all of us come from the Sea of Spirits. We are born from that glory."

"Don't they . . ." Mrs. Magian began, then hesitated, then completed the question: "Don't they have babies where you come from?"

"Yes," said Oriens, "that too. And, as they do, the sparks depart from the vessels and become the children born into the kingdom, and thus the kingdom grows. At the end of the great year, the vessels are empty and must again be filled from the ocean."

"This sounds just like a fairytale," said Laura.

"Laura!" her mother admonished.

"Oh, I meant that in a good way," Laura protested. "I mean it's lovely, like the story of the celestial sisters or something like that."

"More than two years ago," Oriens continued, "my sister began to change, though at first no one — not even I, who was with her constantly — truly noticed how much. She spoke of having strange dreams but was unwilling to recount them, to me or to the royal counselors. She became secretive at times, but I could not imagine what secrets she could possibly have, so I was not much concerned. I was only a little older than she was, after all, and had not journeyed beyond the kingdom, and still thought like a small child. I was not prepared to see any danger. But then Aurora began to become restless, and to give voice to new, strange longings. At times, she said that she wished to sail over the Golden Ocean and to go up into the Azure Mountains, and even beyond them to our father's high seat, which no one but he and my mother has ever seen. At other times, she spoke of going to the dark fallows beyond the Forest of Dreams, and even of wishing to see the barrens and the western desert, and occasionally it seemed as if these held more fascination for her than did our father's palace in the north. We should have seen the danger then. We should have known that what was born in her longings would continue to grow if not checked. All that we are follows upon our thoughts, we are told — pain follows evil thoughts like a wheel following the horse that draws the chariot; happiness follows pure thoughts as the shadow follows the wanderer. And, we are also told, so long as evil bears no fruit, fools think it to be like honey. And yet we were fools. We had been warned.

"During the day, my sister began wandering farther from the city walls, toward the west, and ever more often roaming the forest's edge. The Forest of Dreams has always been filled with voices, singing, telling tales, laughing — coming, it is said, from the children of the forest, and the children of its unseen king, whose nature has always been a mystery to us — and she listened to the voices and spoke back to them; but there seemed no harm in this either, for the voices had always been gentle and kind and full of cheer. Young couples in love often walked along the forest's paths to listen for voices that might tell them of their years together ahead, or for the lovely songs the forest sings. Once, though, late at night, one of those couples came upon my sister as she was wandering into the trees, and they saw that she was sleeping even as she walked, and they roused her and brought her back to the palace. Thereafter sentinels were set outside her door and around the palace and even outside the city's western walls, for fear she might wander off again and this time become lost. Still, no one suspected that any real calamity would come of it. Only a few days later, she and I were by the shores of the Golden Ocean, visiting Nereids along the strand, and Aurora wandered away toward the rose quartz cliffs. After a time, when her absence became unusually prolonged, I went to look for her. I found her in the Cave of the Nymphs, bent above a pool of water in a well of limestone — the Mirror-Pool, it is called, for the purity and brightness and clarity of its reflections — and she seemed to be speaking to it, into it, in whispers. When I called to her, she turned to me with a happy smile, but she would not tell me what she had been doing, and we soon returned to our games.

"At about that time, the forest to the west was beginning to change. At first, it was just a rumor in the city, but soon it was beyond doubt. The voices were no longer the same: they still whispered in the swaying branches and soughing leaves, and sang out of hidden dells and grottoes, but often now they were harsher, and spoke of darker things — of pains and fears and dangers — and the songs were becoming sadder, more dissonant, broken. I heard of the changes in the palace, but did not go near the forest myself, and my sister was prevented from doing so by the royal counselors. Still, all of us were sure that whatever was amiss would soon be corrected and the old order of things restored. But then greater, more disturbing changes also began to occur. Strange figures began to be glimpsed walking in the Forest of Dreams, apparitions, pale or like walking shadows, vanishing when approached. And the voices were becoming still more melancholy, and sometimes even angry. At first, the figures were seen only rarely, but soon they became more numerous and more frequent in their appearances, and no one went down from the city to the forest any longer, and no young couples walked on the woodland paths. And at night, even from the city walls, one could see dim white and yellow lights moving among the trees. Sometimes one could even hear the voices from that far away, because now and then one would cry out, in tones of rage or sorrow, which had never happened in the past. And then the dark dreams came: throughout the city, throughout the kingdom, in every household, first to the children and then to their parents, strange and terrible dreams, unlike anything any of us had ever known before. They came to me as well, almost every night: I saw the shadowy figures from the forest walking in the city's streets, or found myself lost in the forest and surrounded by them, or by things more terrible than that, and a few times I saw a quite . . . malevolent face, bearded and with flame-yellow eyes, gazing at me . . . and for the first time in my life I knew what fear was.

"Finally the royal council determined that whatever was happening was becoming a graver threat than they had first imagined, and that it was coming from the western woodlands, so they began sending out parties of scouts into the forest, often along with many of the city's scholars in their brocaded cloaks, and these parties kept going deeper and deeper into the forest. At first, they were able to learn little, except that the voices of the forest were continuing to alter and that the spectral figures were multiplying and lingering longer in plain view. Then they began to return with troubling stories of something even more mysterious happening still deeper in the forest, and even beyond its far boundary. After many months, the scouts were able to approach some of the forest's wandering phantoms — that is what they had come to be called — without driving them away, and to speak to them, and finally to receive answers. They spoke in whispers, like the softest of the forest voices. They told us, incredibly, that they were our children — children of the kingdom — born from our dreams, out of secret places within us. They said that they had always dwelt in the forest, and had been able to see and hear us in the past, watching us out of our mirrors or out of reflections on the surface of water, and had sometimes thought that they were dreaming us as we were dreaming them. But they said also that they had now been summoned forth from our dreams, out into the open, to walk in the forest, and that the one who had summoned them commanded a great and irresistible magic. But they had no name for him. This was when we first learned that somehow a mighty sorcerer had appeared, had arisen deep in the forest, or in the fallows or barrens, or in the desert or Kenoma — it was impossible to say. The phantoms knew only that he had made himself their master, and had been gathering them to himself because he had need of them. He had spoken, they told our scholars, of founding a kingdom of his own, deep in the wastes, and of one day perhaps making war upon my father's kingdom with armies and great machines. Where this sorcerer had come from no one could at first imagine. But one scholar returned one day from a journey that had taken him to the very edge of the great desert, and he had spoken there to phantoms who were journeying into the waste, and one of them had told him that this sorcerer was also a child born of dreams — in his case, the dreams of my sister. I am sorry to tell it all so hastily . . ."

"No," said Mr. Magian, in a deferential tone, "we can follow you. Dear me, please don't worry about us."

"We did not know yet what to do. And even then we did not fully grasp how great the peril had become. And after a season the dark dreams began to depart, and we believed that the disorder was beginning to pass. We did not really fear talk of armies from another kingdom. We knew that no living things could be created without the lights gathered in the vessels from the Sea of Spirits, and that they were kept in the great temple, and were in my sister's keeping and would not go where she did not go. Only she could bear them from the temple; the vessels could not even be lifted from the altar by anyone but the royal daughter to whom the power had been given. As a small child I once tried to lift one — I was being mischievous — and I might as well have tried to move the entire kingdom. The scholars told us that the sorcerer had been able to give the phantoms shape and some kind of substance, but only of the slightest kind, by gathering up a faint light from pools in the forest, which were mirrors of our dreams — I do not know exactly what that means — but which could not impart the light of true life. The royal counselors continued to investigate, to collect reports, to try to think of ways of restoring order in the forest below the city; but still no one was prepared for what was about to come. My pneumatagogue says that we were all under the perilous enchantment of our own innocence — the fateful innocence of the gods, he calls it."

"What's a pneumatagogue?" asked Mr. Magian, a little timidly.

"It's that white bird," said Michael.

"He comes from the northern lands, beyond the Golden Ocean, where my father dwells," added Oriens.

"Oh," said Mr. Magian, with an expression of, if anything, deeper mystification. "Goodness."

"Our innocence was destroyed in one night, however. A thunderstorm arose in the west, just before midnight, with terrific bolts of lightning and great winds, far more violent than anything we had ever seen in the past. It lasted perhaps an hour, and most of the kingdom's folk retired to their beds afterward. But a slow, constant breeze continued to blow from the west, and after midnight a heavy, cold mist began to arise from the forest, and then to be blown toward the city, and then across it, through all the streets and houses and temples, and with it came confusion and drowsiness and finally very deep sleep. But there were some who, before falling asleep, saw my sister walking, as if entranced or dreaming — first through the palace, then into the great temple, then through the western gate. At last one sentinel outside the walls, lying in the grass and unable to move and sinking into sleep, saw her enter the Forest of Dreams, and saw also that she was bearing the vessels of light in her arms as she walked. Then she was gone.

"The next day, when we had all awakened and the confusion had cleared and the story of her departure was learned, word spread quickly, and there was panic, and there were lamentations in the city temples, and searches were dispatched into the forest — half the city's inhabitants perhaps. The voices of the searchers, calling her name, could be heard coming from every quarter of the woodlands. In fact, only their voices could be heard, as the voices of the forest, we soon found, had fallen silent, as though the forest itself had been abandoned by the hidden king and his children, or was slumbering. But there was no sign of her. Then, after four days, the vessels were found, beyond the forest and the fallows and the barrens, at the very edge of the desert — and they had been shattered, which seemed impossible, and the sparks of glory were no longer in them . . . scattered, it seemed, lost in the vast wastes . . . lost in the dark golden sands and dark golden skies. . . .

"The horror of this discovery — the loss of those spirits, of the vessels, of those . . . children — it cannot be described. All the houses of the city were in mourning, and liturgies of lamentation were sung every day in the temples. And the searches continued. Expeditions were sent again and again into the desert, but it is so huge and featureless, and no one had ever gone there before, and so for a long time they found nothing at all. Some of those who went far into the wasteland returned bewildered, others came back with fragments of information — things glimpsed in the distance, the whispers of wandering phantoms — and some never returned at all. The scholars believed that many had fallen under some spell of the nameless sorcerer.

"Throughout the Great Year, the searches went on, while the heavenly dance progressed across the sky. That is . . . our stars are not like yours, you see, fixed and lifeless lights, but have life of their own, vital intelligence; their fire is like the glory that arises from the Sea of Spirits, and they proceed across the heavens and exchange places in grand patterns, and as the year proceeds their dance unfolds, different each time; but by the end of the year they have returned to the stations from which they began. And the year was very near its end when word finally came back from an expedition that had penetrated deeper into the desert than any before, and that had at last reached the frontiers of Kenoma. No one was prepared for the news. The searchers had found a city, terrible, grim, and seemingly empty, at whose heart stood a giant citadel that was simply a great sphere of impenetrable black crystal, so large that it rose far higher than any tower of our city and took most of a day to walk around. There were gates into it, adorned with strange occult devices, but they were sealed, and at first we did not know how to open them. The royal counselors, however, were soon certain that what we sought could be found only within it — that my sister was hidden inside, that it was the dwelling of the sorcerer, that whatever had become of the sparks that were scattered in the breaking of the vessels could be discovered only there. And so the scholars and the searchers labored on it day and night, and a royal road was built to it, through the forest and the fallows and the barrens and the desert, to make the path there and back easier. After many days, one of the citadel's gates was finally unsealed — I do not know how, for I remained in the palace far away — and then we found out just how powerful a sorcerer my sister's captor truly was. As vast as the citadel was without, it was far, far vaster within: not only was it larger on the inside than on the outside; it was larger than many worlds and many heavens. To enter it was to be drawn into its own inner dimensions and amplitudes, its huge magic — it was to find oneself at the far reaches of a whole cosmos. I cannot describe the astonishment felt by those who first realized what they had discovered, and by all of us when word first reached us of this . . . this prodigy. And it took our finest instruments to peer deep enough into its mysteries truly to understand what it was. How he had done this, no one knew, but the sorcerer had created an immense machine, a whole universe of spheres within spheres, each of crystalline aether, each a heaven enclosing other heavens, each slowly revolving, and each with sealed gates. To reach its heart would take a very great and dangerous journey indeed. And surely that, the counselors concluded, was where Aurora had been imprisoned.

"After a long time, the first inner gate was breached, and even to get to that had required crossing a great abyss by a powerful exertion of magic and craft, the building of an immense bridge of light and brightwood — what you call marmoreans or whitewoods — and then new expeditions were sent into the immense inner distances of the great citadel, or great machine, or crystal labyrinth — it was called by many names by the scholars and engineers — sailing the aethers of the spheres in large ships fashioned from diamond and sapphire. But the way was harder than anyone could have imagined, and again and again the expeditions were turned back, having penetrated no farther than the outermost spheres, or they were lost entirely and never heard from again, and gradually we learned of how well guarded the citadel truly was. The crystal spheres — the turning heavens — contained worlds, and each was presided over by its own ruler, and defended by legions, and by aethereal fleets; and the farther our ships penetrated into the depths, the more difficult the elements became for our people, the more the increasing density of the aethers became oppressive to them. They suffered defeat after defeat, and when they returned, if they returned, they were weary and sad and confused. The regent's council finally determined that, rather than expeditionary forces, they would send individual agents, who by going singly might be better able to slip by the guardians of the spheres and to travel deeper into the labyrinth. And the council was correct in this. Many who were sent out were lost, many returned in defeat, but some found their ways deeper in and farther down and returned to tell what they had discovered.

"They also learned that they could hide themselves better, and survive the journey better, by garbing themselves in the aether proper to each of the spheres through which they journeyed — by wearing the body of that world, that is. The aethers, you see, are also a substance for which the only word the scholars thought appropriate was soul, psyche, a principle of vitality, a kind of animating . . . element, and the inhabitants of the heavenly worlds — many of whom were once the phantoms in the Forest of Dreams, we learned — inhabit forms composed from it. At long last, some of our agents reached the innermost, or lowermost, sphere, the world at the heart of the machine, and in time learned as best they could that my sister was somewhere there. But still they could not find her, or reach her. And they learned as well what had become of the lost sparks of glory: these had become that lower sphere's native life, the children of that world, though children who could know nothing of the kingdom from which they had originally come — from which they had been abducted, rather, wrapped as they were — imprisoned as they were — in many aethereal souls and in carnal bodies . . . forgetful of themselves, of their glory. And our agents discovered that it was by my sister, by her dreams, that the sorcerer had conjured up his great invention . . . his great machine. Those of them who were able to make the journey back to us told us so."

Here Oriens paused for several moments, staring before him as if contemplating something far away and long ago. After a while, Laura spoke, very quietly, almost fearfully: "It can't be. You're . . . you're talking about this world . . . the whole Kenocosm . . . us."

Oriens looked at her as if only half aware of her words, impassively, then looked away again and resumed his story: "Then one day, as the Great Year reached its midpoint, I was summoned into the royal council chamber and was told that word had come from the north, from my father's court beyond the Azure Mountains, that I must make the journey into the great machine to find my sister. I was told also that agents had been sent ahead of me already, and had been preparing the way, and that a wise guide and guardian sent from the north would also precede me when the day of my departure approached, and would be my advance scout and close companion all the way down to the world at the center of the machine. No one could accomplish the mission in my stead. Only I would be able to lead my sister out of her captivity, for the sorcerer had ensnared her in a dark enchanted sleep from which only my familiar voice could wake her, and only I would have the power to break the fetters that bound her. I was afraid. I was much too young for such an adventure, and I already knew how great the dangers of the journey were. But my love for my sister and my reverence for my father and mother made refusal impossible.

"When the day for my departure arrived, they took from me my royal robe, which shone with all the colors of the rainbow, and the purple mantle that I wore within the palace, and clothed me instead in a simple gray cloak. They brought me jewels from my father's treasury to carry in this purse I wear about my neck, and cautioned me to make use of them only when I must, for the deeper I penetrated into the machine, the briefer their light would be. They gave me provisions for the journey, and two court envoys conducted me along the royal road that led through the forest and the fallows and the barrens and the waste, until we came to the empty city and the great machine. The scholars and artisans exerted all their skill and knowledge to create a vessel of sapphire for me to voyage in upon the aethers, one that would listen to my voice and the voice of my guide, but which also could find its own way through the labyrinth, through the gates of the crystalline spheres that those who had gone ahead of me had discovered with so much effort and at such great cost. I was told that at each level of my descent into the depths of the machine I must array myself in the garment of that sphere — the element of vitality, the soul, the native aether — and wear it till I returned; thus, at each level, I would acquire a new layer of concealment, and would have to struggle each time to remember who I was and why I had come, or my new garment would become my prison. 'You must become the labyrinth in which you wander,' one of the royal envoys told me. And then, in each world I traveled through, I must disguise myself in the clothing and the manners of its inhabitants, though I must take care what I would eat and drink, so as not to taste of what they called 'the viands of oblivion' or 'food of forgetfulness' and be unable to remember who I was or to find my way out again. In crossing the heavens, I must also descend into each sphere's world, for there the ruler of the sphere kept his court, and guarded a gateway of cold aethereal flame, through which I must pass in order to be able to assume the soul of the next sphere — in order to temper my form for assuming a yet newer form. In almost every world, I would have allies — agents, wearing forms proper to that world — and I must let my guide go ahead of me, and lead me to them and them to me, and trust them to help me; but, in the end, I must pass through the gate alone, while my ship passed on its own through the aethereal boundaries to meet me on the far side, moving as secretly as I possibly could to avoid discovery and imprisonment in the dungeons of the heavens, where many of our agents already languished, and so never find Aurora. And I must remember that, though at first my mission would be a secret to the rulers of the spheres, as I descended deeper in it would become almost impossible for word of my coming not to reach my enemies in the lower worlds; so the way would surely become more difficult the nearer I came to the center of the machine.

"So I went, afraid, embarking in the great ship they had made for me. The two royal envoys accompanied me on the first stage of my journey, across the abyss and through the sphere you call the Great Engine, which contains no world and no ruler and whose aether is lifeless, but when we came to the uppermost of the heavens, the wall of stars, they departed from me and turned back in a diamond vessel of their own, and I had to venture on alone, following the pathways described by those who had gone before me and had found the gate through the fixed stars and the seven celestial gates between spheres. When the envoys left me, I gathered that strange starlight about me, that astral aether, and I grew darker. And in each sphere I drew about me another aethereal soul or body — it can be called either — like a thin veil, but always at first like iron: each time I had to strive to remember who I was, why I had come, where I was going. Sometimes it was torment. In every sphere I did as I had been instructed, and as my guide led me to do, and descended to its world and found my way through its royal gate of aethereal fire. There were many perils, many difficult and terrible adventures, wherever I went, whatever form I wore: that of the yellow world, the red world, the green, the blue . . . the fiery form of the solar sphere, the cold forms of the lunar worlds. And wherever I went I saw what monstrous legions guard the gates, and what hideous pomps and revelries and processions occupy the royal courts, and I saw why it was necessary for me to pass through the gates alone: we could never have forced a passage through such armies; we do not make war; the only possible way past was secrecy, stealth. And, as had been predicted, as I descended through the spheres word of my coming began to precede me, and in the lower worlds my enemies began to anticipate my arrival, and had it not been for our agents and for the vigilance of my guide I should never have come so far. And it was such a long journey.

"At last I reached the lowest of the heavens and could see the world below, immersed not in aether but in sublunary air. The way had been made ready, secret alliances had been forged by means of messages and dreams sent to those able to receive them, but my enemies were also now awaiting me. The sorcerer knows why I have come, and knows that I truly have the power to rouse my sister from her slumber. This he cannot allow. She sleeps in the deep places of Kenoma, and it is by her dreams that he creates and governs and sustains his world, and he will never let her go."

Again Oriens fell silent and turned his gaze to the window at his back.

"Where is this sorcerer?" asked Michael after many moments.

"Where?" repeated Oriens. "Somewhere here, I suppose. Or in many places. I do not know what form he wears or where he dwells or how. I do not have a name for him either." He turned his eyes back again and looked at Michael as if only half seeing him. "You call him the Great Artisan, king and maker, this world's God. I call him a monster of inscrutable malevolence, and I know only that his power is greatest here, on Kenogaia, for that is where my sister is, and where the sparks of glory lie . . . live . . . life upon life, reborn again and again . . . in all of you who, like me, come from above."

"Us?" said Michael. "We?" He felt a cold tingling run along his spine and over the surface of his skin.

"Yes, of course. There are others here also, phantoms, men and women only half alive as yet, as well as still others who are only puppets dangling upon invisible strings, but they are agents of the sorcerer, and their only task is to see that the glory within you never awakens — that it continues to sleep forever, and to dream and to forget its true home — like my sister. But you, all of you, have worn many bodies and lived many lives, been many men and women, and many other things beside . . . but each birth is a new forgetting."

Laura rose from her chair near the door, clearly agitated, and took a few steps toward Oriens. "I don't understand, though," she said. "You said your sister was lost about two years ago. I'm sure you did. But all the things you describe — I mean, planting trees here ages ago, and all those long expeditions, and . . . the creation of the Kenocosm . . . I mean, two years ago . . ." She lifted her hands helplessly before her.

"Two of our Great Years," said Oriens, "two heavenly dances ago. But, just as the machine is immeasurably more spacious inside than out, so its spans of time are different within — longer and more taxing. For each Great Year of the kingdom of Pleroma, more than five thousand years pass within the machine."

"Oh," said Laura. Then, after a moment, she added, "But, still, Kenogaia is older than that — much older."

"No," said Oriens, "it is not; but you have been made to believe it is."

"And you," Laura continued, before she could have quite grasped what he had said, "you're so young, and your sister is younger than you, and the world is so old."

"Beyond the stars, my journey began half a year ago," said Oriens, "and I have not aged greatly; but, within these spheres, I have been journeying for many, many centuries. At times I feel the full weight of this alien time I must traverse and these alien forms I must wear, but at other times I feel myself still a child, and at all times I try to remember my father's kingdom."

"But you're so young," Laura repeated. And then she gasped. "Oh, but then you're also . . . very old. How . . . how can that be? What's it like?"

Oriens gazed into her eyes for a moment with a calm expression and then, the faintest of smiles once more flickering on his lips and in his eyes, he turned his head slightly to one side. "I cannot describe it," he said. "It is very strange." He looked around him, at Laura and Michael and Laura's parents. "But, again, I am not the only one of whom that may be said, after all — that I am very young and very old . . . an ancient child. In another way, the same is true of all of you."

III

M R. MAGIAN SLEPT THROUGH THE LATER afternoon, with Mrs. Magian beside him for two of those hours. He had begun to grow somewhat feverish, and his wife (who was, as Michael well knew, always the more efficient and officious of the two) had given him a potent and soporific distillate of local roots and berries to bring his temperature down. In the evening he woke and, after the others had dined, sat up in bed to take food and drink. As darkness fell, they all listened for sounds from outside—the howling of wolves, the cries of Shadows—but they heard nothing other than the quiet flowing of the river, intermittent breezes among the branches overhead, and the occasional calls of the small white owls native to all marmorean groves. Once Mr. Magian had finished the small portion he felt able to eat, everyone gathered in his room, arranging themselves in the same pattern as earlier in the day, in order to make plans. Almost at once, Oriens repeated his assertion that he must soon leave them and go in search of his sister.

"It's safer here than anywhere else," replied Mr. Magian. "Dear me, I don't want to presume . . ." He cleared his throat uneasily. "In all these past several months, no matter how far they've ranged through these woods, the wolves seem not to have found their way here through the pass. They say predators can't pick up the scent of prey where whitewood are plentiful. And neither the pass nor this cabin is visible from the air, because the canopy is so thick. And even in winter marmoreans never lose their leaves, and these mountains are so hard to explore thoroughly that the Forestry Ministry has never produced a complete survey map. And the locals guard their secrets jealously."

"My sister is not here," replied Oriens, "and the longer I delay my search for her, the better my enemies can prepare for my coming. Everywhere I have journeyed, I have learned the need for haste."

"But do you even know where to go?" asked Mr. Magian. "Kenogaia's large."

"My guide has told me where she is," said Oriens. "She sleeps at the heart of your world, in the emptiness deep within it, and the entrance to her bedchamber lies beneath your great city to the east. There she dreams, age upon age, and from her dreams the sorcerer is forever weaving your world anew, and weaving the illusions that keep her — and you — imprisoned here. That is where I must now go."

Mr. and Mrs. Magian looked at one another for some moments, and then turned to Oriens again. "But where?" Mr. Magian asked. "Kenopolis is a large city."

"My guide has gone ahead already," said Oriens. "He is still seeking. But I cannot wait. I must start out upon my journey, if you can only tell me the way."

"Oh, but you can't go alone," said Laura.

"I'll be going with you, wherever you go," said Michael.

"Oh, no, Michael" said Mrs. Magian, "no you won't. Your father would forbid it."

"I don't think that's right," said Michael, politely but a little sullenly. "And he's not here to tell me."

"There are many dangers," said Oriens.

"If my father's still alive," said Michael with quiet grimness, "he'll be in Kenopolis. That's where all the government detention centers are, all the ministries and secretariats and offices and departments for this and that, and . . . that's where my father will be."

"Your father would . . ." Mrs. Magian began.

"And I'm not any safer here," Michael added. "None of us is. The wolves will be back, at least when the Shadows are gone, and they won't stop looking. And maybe the Shadows don't want to come in among these trees, but maybe they can . . . maybe they will . . . sooner or later."

"Yes," said Mrs. Magian in a faltering tone, "yes . . . but . . ."

"Can one walk there from here?" asked Oriens.

"Walk?" said Mr. Magian in surprise. "Through these mountains? Across the lowlands? It would take forever, and you'd never make it without being caught."

"No one will be safe here indefinitely," said Mrs. Magian, half to herself.

"But you couldn't go by train either," said Mr. Magian, "or by aerial transport, or by any open means, what with your conspicuous looks, and with police agents everywhere, and these Brethren . . ."

"Laura isn't safe here," said Mrs. Magian, even more quietly.

"No, the only way you can hope to get there, quickly and safely," said Mr. Magian, "is by water. You're well placed for that, at least. We have a fishing skiff and a river flatboat — it's like a raft but with a shallow hull under it, and with railing and a rudder — moored just around the bend; and the river here, the Glitterglass, is a tributary of the Phlegethon, and the mouth is just a few miles from here, and the Phlegethon's the great avenue from Oreiotopia down to Kenopolis. It's about a five or six day journey this time of year, all of it quite smooth. Before aerial barges, all the commerce between the mountains and the city went down the Phlegethon or came up along the river canals and locks on the other side of the southern range. Now there's not much traffic at all — just some large barges of timber and . . ."

"Basil," said Mrs. Magian suddenly.

"Yes, Eve?"

"It's not safe here . . . for anyone. It's not safe for Laura."

Mr. Magian removed his spectacles and began to clean them with the fringe of the counterpane. "Where else is safer?" he asked. "And where can I go on this leg? It's stiffening."

"We can't go yet, you and I," she replied, "but I think Laura must."

THE CONVERSATION BETWEEN LAURA'S PARENTS PER-sisted well into the night without resolution, and resumed in the morning without any prospect of a conclusion. Neither of them wanted to be parted from Laura, both feared what might become of her if she went with Oriens to Kenopolis, both granted that the supplies in the cabin would have to be replenished if all of them were to stay more than a few days, and both acknowledged that Mr. Magian would not be able to travel for some time, at least not without slowing the journey to a dangerous crawl. But, when Mr. Magian proposed that everyone but he should travel down the river, his wife told him she would not leave him to starve or be eaten by wolves. The conversation paused during lunch, and when it began again it soon became clear that, however reluctantly, the Magians were planning to send Laura along with Oriens and Michael, but only part of the way, and planned then to follow after her as soon as they could.

"There's an establishment, a tavern and inn, by the banks of the Phlege-thon," Mr. Magian told Laura, Michael, and Oriens, "twelve miles or so from here, on this side of the river, where boats and rafts can moor in a small bay. It's called the Silverwood and its sign can be seen from the water easily, even at night. Its proprietor is Marius Goldentoad, and he's one of our circle . . . one of our school . . ." — he looked at Oriens — "one of your friends. He and his wife live in a cottage behind the tavern and, if you can get to them undetected, they'll give you shelter and supplies. There's a village, Wildwind, two miles away or so — Laura's been there. The three of you can take the flatboat — Laura is an excellent pilot — and we'll take the skiff afterwards. Laura" — he looked at his daughter — "you must stay there until we come. The Goldentoads will hide you. They have friends in the village there too."

"What about Michael and Oriens?" said Laura. "I can't just . . . send them off."

"Our hope," said Mrs. Magian, sitting upright on the edge of the bed, wringing her hands fretfully but speaking very calmly, "is that the two of them — the two of you — will not go on ahead yet, but will stay at the tavern too. We know you're in a hurry . . ." — here she paused for a moment, clearly deferentially uncertain how she ought to address Oriens, but then simply resumed on the far side of the omitted name or title — ". . . and that you don't want to give your enemies too much time to recover themselves, but caution's needed too. With the help of the Goldentoads and other friends nearby, we may all be able to think of the best way — the most discreet way — to proceed. Really, a few more days of planning might make all the difference. If, however, the two of you choose not to wait, or can't, let the Goldentoads help you in any way they can, and listen if they suggest a better way of getting to the city."

Oriens turned halfway around in the window seat and gazed out at the river. "I wish my pneumatagogue were here to advise me. But he will find me on the way." He said nothing for a few seconds and then turned back to them. "If you wish it, and if everything seems safe, I shall wait a day or two; but do not think me ungrateful if I leave before you join us."

"We wouldn't," said Mr. Magian, "I assure you. My goodness, no. And, Michael, if you do finally go ahead without us, don't approach the city till after dark, and remember that the canal entrances in Kenopolis harbor are poorly lit and poorly watched — at least, that was true in the past — and so you're more likely to be able to slip into the city unobserved that way, especially at night. Laura can show you how to use the wind motor if you don't know, because you'll need it for the harbor and canals. I'll sketch a harbor map, as best I can. If you go up the canal called Red Clover, by the old Red Clover Company warehouses, you can moor at the stone docks under the bridge of Trifle Lane. There are two places there, not far apart, where you should be able to find shelter from allies of ours. One is the home of the Fravashi family, who're originally from around here. Well, Mr. Fravashi, Irya, is from the Eastern Prefecture originally, from Persis, but his family came here when he was a boy. Laura used to play with the daughter Persy — Persephone — when they were very small. And their boy Phane — Epiphanius, that is — is only a year older than you. The other place is a confectioner's shop four or so blocks on the other side of the canal. Its owner is Symeon Goëtus, and he lives over the shop. He's extremely resourceful and intelligent. Eve will write out both addresses for you before you go. But, again, this is just in case you have to go on without us. I implore you to wait as long as you can before risking that. I don't even have a map of the river to give you. I can tell you that there are very few places of cover along the way, particularly in the lowlands. There are some coves and a few whitewood groves in the mountains, and some tributary rivers that lead back up into the woods, but in the lowlands there's practically nothing." Then he gave an anxious start. "Oh, dear me, I nearly forgot. Remember, when you get near Ghostwood — you'll know it, because it's the only part of the river with an island, and there's a large bend in the river just upstream — make sure, if it's dark, that you wait till daylight to go forward. Even the old riverboat hands don't go through Ghostwood at night. They say the spirits of the rebels . . . the Purist heretics, that is . . . were sealed in the trees there."

"Stories . . ." Michael began to say.

"Much more than stories," Mr. Magian interrupted. "My goodness me, much more than stories. Your father knew . . . knows. In the old days, even river pirates stayed away from the Stone Forest after dark."

"Laura," said Mrs. Magian, rising from the edge of the bed and taking her daughter into her arms in one fluid, frantic movement, "please, please, be sensible, and very careful. I hate this, I hate everything about it. Don't — absolutely don't — think of going to Kenopolis, especially without us. Remember, we . . ."

"Mother," said Laura, trying not very vigorously to extricate herself from the embrace, "please don't say . . ."

"We lost Rafe," Mrs. Magian continued, tears now visible in her eyes. "We can't lose you too. We'd never survive it."

"Eve," said Mr. Magian softly.

Laura sighed and ceased to struggle. "Yes, mother."

IT WAS THE NEXT EVENING, HOWEVER, BEFORE THEY left. Even Oriens, perhaps feeling for the first time how fatigued his new body could become, was persuaded that he should rest another day while provisions were packed for the journey, clothes were washed at the river and dried on a line, plans were recited over and over, and various doubts were allowed to arise and then subside again in the hearts of Mr. and Mrs. Magian. While sorting clothes for the journey, Michael found the golden blossoms he and Oriens had carried with them, and discovered to his surprise that they were neither withered nor bruised, but came out of the pockets as if freshly plucked; and so, after some consideration, he separated them into heaps of detached petals and stamens and distributed them among the pockets of the clothes that he, Laura, and Oriens were to take with them, saving a few to give to Mr. and Mrs. Magian. "They may help keep danger away," he told them. At the very last moment, it seemed as if Mrs. Magian would change her mind and refuse to let Laura go; but, not long after darkness fell, the very distant but still utterly terrifying cry of one of the Shadows came echoing through the trees, and she instead began urging the three travelers along, enjoining them to change into their darkest travel clothing and coats and then helping to carry bedrolls and supplies down to the boats, which were moored at a short dock on the far side of a bend in the river. The farewells between Laura and her family were tense and tearful, the shared assurances that they would soon all be together again were ardent and numerous, but at last the journey began.

While Mrs. Magian stood on the dock in the first glow of the rising moons, her figure starkly erect and motionless, Michael, Laura, and Oriens boarded the boat — narrow but long, rectangular but for a semicircular prow, its deckhouse a simple low awning of oiled russet reed-cloth on four posts, its deck an even plane made from slender polished planks of deep red wood, its surrounding wooden parapet a luxuriant tangle of carved vines and flowers and fruiting trees in the old Oreiotopian style — and then Michael pushed out from the shore with one of the long barge poles, and Laura took the tiller as they swung out into the broad central current of the Glitterglass. Laura and Michael continually looked back from the stern as the river carried them away, smoothly but swiftly; even as the water bore them around another bend, about five minutes later, their last glimpses of the dock showed them Mrs. Magian still standing there watching.

Oriens, however, had been at the front of the boat and gazing forward this entire time, clearly lost in thoughts of his own. Only when they had traveled perhaps a mile downstream did he rise and — now so graceful in all his movements that the gentle rocking of the boat seemed to have no effect on his balance — join them. He sat down on the low bench along the rear of the parapet, on the other side of the tiller from Laura and across from Michael, who was sitting directly on the boards just at the back of the deckhouse. "Who is Rafe?" he asked.

"That's my brother," said Laura, looking away, out over the water. "Rafe — Raphael. You and Michael are wearing clothes of his."

"Where is he?" asked Oriens.

"He died," said Laura, "seven years ago, when he was as old as I am now."

"How did he die?" asked Oriens.

"He was sick for more than a year," said Laura, "and the physicians couldn't cure him."

Oriens lowered his eyes. "I am sorry," he said. "I have learned of death since leaving my palace, and have seen it on several worlds, and I have learned of disease and suffering, and I know that all of it is quite terrible."

It was a moment before the import of these words reached Michael's conscious mind, but when they did he stared at Oriens in wonder. "Don't you have death where you come from?" he asked.

"No," said Oriens, "not as you do. For you, death is the sundering of soul and flesh. Where I come from, there is no difference between body and soul, flesh and spirit, and so nothing to separate."

"Not even when people grow very old?" asked Laura.

Oriens shook his head. "People grow, but they do not grow old. They grow *onward*, so to speak. But they do go from the city ultimately, and even from the land, after many, many Great Years, to other parts of the kingdom. They become something . . . else . . . other. They move forward. But, as you mean it, no, they do not die. And certainly children do not."

Michael looked at Laura, but she was still gazing away, so he turned back to Oriens. "And no illness, no suffering?" he asked.

"No, not as you would understand suffering, though sadness is not unknown."

"I can't even imagine that," said Michael.

"This underworld they tell you of," said Oriens calmly, "this place of dark fays and endless suffering called the Land of Hel, it seems to me a strangely needless fable. What else is Kenogaia itself, after all, other than a place of continual suffering?"

Now Michael turned his eyes to the river as well. Aurea and Argentea were both full and gradually ascending the sky, their reflections spread upon the water in narrow fans of sparkling gold and silver; and, where the fans converged and their facets intermingled on the waves, their blended light became the color of electrum and rippled and glittered all about the boat like flaming glass. The mouth of the river, issuing through the gleaming white and turquoise of the marmorean grove's farthest southern margin, was now visible in the middle distance, and beyond it the broad shining breast of the Phlegethon, and beyond that the deep violet crest of the mountain that rose above the far shore and up toward the sable-blue sky and gem-bright stars. "No," he said after several seconds: "there's . . . so much beauty here too . . . so much goodness."

"Yes," said Oriens, "there truly is — and, like my sister, all of it stolen . . . all of it in bondage."

PART FOUR
Phlegethon

Upon the strand, near where the serpent lay
Coiled in the silver waves, a tavern stood,
And there I waited for the end of day,
When it would close its eyes so that I could
Steal on it as it slept. And there I met
Another of my kind, of noble birth;
He wore Egyptian raiment now, and yet
I saw he was no child of that base earth.

In secret we allied ourselves and spoke
In whispers — certain none could overhear —
Of how to strike before the serpent woke,
And how to still the counsels of our fear.
Then in my father's name we pledged our trust.
We knew the people of this land to be
Our enemies, who — if they thought they must —
Would rouse the serpent from the peaceful sea.

— from "The Hymn of the Pearl"

I

"**M**ICHAEL'S THE SCHOLARLY ONE," SAID Laura, "and he knows all those old books we're not supposed to read. I only mentioned the story because it's one of the few I've heard. Michael knows it better."

"Would you be so kind as to tell it to me?" Oriens asked Michael.

They were still seated in the stern of the boat, though Michael was now facing forward, constantly surveying the northern shore of the Phlegethon for the first sign of the tavern, which could not now be far away. "Well," he said, "there are different versions of the myth. My father knows all of them. But the basic tale is that Aurea and Argentea were sisters, daughters of King Hyperion, the god of the sun. Aurea was the elder, but they were very much alike, almost twins, though differently complected, and very much like their mother Queen Aetherea, and Aurea rode in a chariot of gold drawn by four golden chargers, and Argentea in a chariot of silver with four silver chargers. Sometimes they rode out of their palace together but sometimes went off on different journeys, with their retinues and postilions in gold or silver liveries, and so in those days they weren't always seen side by side. The sisters were devoted to one another, in any event. Aurea came of age first, and suitors began to vie for her attention, and all the royal courts of the higher heavens sent their unwed sons to ask for her hand. But the god of the underworld, who's called King Chthonos or King Hel, desired her for himself, and he hated the heavenly gods, and so he sent two of his magicians in secret to the Court of the Sun, and they cast an enchantment over Aurea as she slept, and late at night she fled away to his kingdom below the earth. King Hyperion's men discovered what had happened, but they couldn't free Aurea from the underworld, because they couldn't break through its gates and fortifications. Not even the greatest of heroes could win entry by force. She could be rescued only by someone willing to beg admission to the realm of Chthonos as a suppliant, unarmed and alone, to pay court to the king, and to answer three questions; and anyone who failed to answer all three questions correctly would also become a captive, imprisoned there so long as Aurea remained. The questions are slightly different in different versions of the myth, but they're all very simple. In the version I know, they're 'Who art thou?' and 'Whence hast thou come?' and 'Whither art thou tending?' But no one was able to answer them, because anyone who entered the Land of Hel fell under its spell and forgot nearly everything, even his own name, and so no one was able to set the princess free. In the end, it was Argentea, even though she was just a little girl, who slipped away on her own from her father's court, wearing a magic pearl that the god of the sea, King Thalassos or King Sæ, gave her — a pearl that had originally fallen from the heavens — which protected her from forgetting herself and her mission. She walked right into the king's presence, in the throne room of the Nether Court, and gave the right answers to all three questions. King Hel was furious, but he was honor-bound to release Aurea into Argentea's care and to let the sisters leave his kingdom, along with all the other prisoners he had taken." Michael fell silent for several seconds. "It's really a wonderful story when it's told properly," he finally added. "Oh, and I should have said: that's why the sisters are inseparable now — Argentea is afraid to let her sister out of her sight, because she couldn't bear to lose her again."

"You see?" said Laura.

"Yes," said Oriens, "you are right, the tale is very much like that of my sister and me, as you say."

"I really only meant that what you told us has that . . . that *feeling* about it . . . like a fairytale."

"Perhaps it is our tale, really," Oriens continued, in a reflective tone.

"I don't know how it could be," said Laura. "It's not true. It didn't really happen."

"I do not see how that matters," said Oriens. "It is only a story, yes, and perhaps did not happen, at least not in that way, but I do not know why that means it cannot be true. Just as there is no reason that something may be real, like this world, while not being true. Since this world exists only because of my sister's dreams, and lives because of the glory that sleeps captive here, in all of you, it may be — I do not know — that something from her dreams shines through into your dreams, into your stories. And maybe the glory that sleeps and dreams within you recalls something of how it came into this darkness." He stared upward to the stars. "It is merely a thought."

"Well, anyway," said Laura, "we don't tell those stories any more. We're not even really supposed to know about them. They aren't taught in school and the old books aren't supposed to be kept. That's all from before the Age of Illumination."

"What is that?" asked Oriens.

"It's when everything changed," said Laura, "when . . . well, it's when reason and progress and things like that were . . . discovered."

"Discovered?"

"It was . . . oh, ages ago," said Laura. "Michael could tell you better."

"It began four-hundred and seventy-nine years ago," said Michael, in a suddenly somewhat pedantic tone. "It's also called the Great Advance. It started when Talos Archytas Metrontes invented modern science and published two books called *Cosmomechanema* and *Psychomechanema*, all about how all nature and life is a system of machines, and how we're machines too, and how the soul is a kind of energy pattern that lives in the machine of the body, which he called the 'cogitative ghost.' But it was more than that; it was a whole century and a half when science, and medicine, and technology, and politics, and art, and religion all started moving forward . . . supposedly."

"You have doubts?" prompted Oriens,

"My father says it's not that simple . . . that the story's full of distortions."

"It's also when all sorts of things were discovered," said Laura: "anemotechnics, phosphorology, chemical sarciatry, psychometrics, aerial thrust technology, therapeutic encephalotomy, rational deism, spiritual psychodynamics . . . oh, just about everything."

"That is a long list," said Oriens blandly.

"We have to memorize it in school," she said. "I think I've left some things out, though."

"Mechanical realism in the arts," Michael added, "biochemical hedonistics, and neurotechnics. I think that's everything."

"And all sorts of technological advances started then," said Laura: "phosphoric vapor engines, for trains and ships and aerial cars, and phosphoria, and anemophones, and psychotherapy, and photeinic eidolography, and on and on."

"And why did it change the stories you can tell?" asked Oriens.

"Well," said Michael, "the old tales supposedly misled people into thinking that behind nature there was a realm of invisible spirits and gods and fairies and such, and that there's such a thing as real magic, and so for a really rational understanding of the world we had to drive all of that out of how we think about nature . . . for the good of everyone's psychological and spiritual health and welfare, to prevent . . . inner conflicts and confusions, and an unhealthy view of reality, and dangerous fixations . . . that sort of thing. So there was something called the Great Catharsis, when the old books were destroyed for the most part, except in some government collections and in the Academy in Kenopolis, where they're used for Social Pathology Studies and Psychohistory and such. When the course of common studies was created, it became illegal to teach and read those sorts of stories, or any of the older philosophies either."

"May you tell no stories now?" asked Oriens.

"Yes, we can," said Michael. "The approved style is industrial mechanistic realist narrative. But there are fairytales people still tell also, especially in this region, though those aren't approved officially. And there are more of the old books around than the government realizes."

"It is all strange to me," said Oriens.

"It's all part of the Great Reform," said Michael, "the new religious awakening. . . . That is, the discovery that the one God is the Great Artisan, the sole supreme being, and that he designed and governs the Kenocosm according to . . . to what our tutor Mr. Choiros calls 'eternal rational principles of force and structure,' because he's a rational being. The old gods and spirits belong to an unenlightened religion. At least"— Michael rose to his knees —"that's what we're taught in our catechism courses. Look, I think I see the tavern."

He did see it, and so did Laura and Oriens a few seconds later, but only on account of the full moons overhead. It stood downstream, along the northern shore, three stories tall, with several high windows and gables, all under a steep roof of dark tiles; and in front of it there was a short inlet from the river and a nearly circular bay whose calm water shone like a great brilliant coin of moonlight; but not a single phosphorion was shining from within the tavern, or at its doors, or along the dock, or over the sign that stood upon the river bank, and there were no figures strolling around the grounds or lolling in the porches or sitting on the dock, and as the boat continued its approach no music or laughter or loud conversation came drifting out above the sound of the flowing river.

"It's deserted," said Laura. "No one's there."

"Maybe it's closed for some reason," said Michael. "Maybe that's for the best, if the Goldentoads are still here."

"It doesn't look like anyone's there at all," replied Laura.

"Your father said their cottage is around back. We should look." But Michael was unable to conceal the doubt in his voice.

Saying nothing more, but with a distinctly displeased expression on her face, Laura steered the boat toward the tavern and, as they drew near, guided it up the inlet and into the bay with the outboard anemokineton on its lowest setting. There were only two other small craft there, in their slips, one just a rowboat. The stillness was so profound that the quiet, foaming gush of the motor sounded atrociously loud, and Laura switched it off as soon as the boat was within reach of the dock and Michael could fasten its ropes to the moorings. They waited for a time before disembarking, listening intently to the silence, but eventually they climbed out onto the dock, each with an unlit phosphorion in hand, then crept over the pebbles and grass, and quickly dashed across the tavern's courtyard. Michael, however, stretched out his arms and stopped the other two several yards from the steps of the front porch and pointed up at the door. Even under the low roof of the porch the ambient moonlight was strong enough to illuminate the official quarantine seals — vividly puce paper bordered with silver foil — pasted to the door and jamb, as well as the white notice pasted over the large pane of frosted glass in the door's upper half.

"I'll just have a look," said Michael softly, cautiously ascending the four steps and bringing his face close to the door. When the light proved too weak to make the notice legible, however, he looked about a few times, lit his phosphorion, and quickly read out the words in a loud whisper: "These premises sealed by order of the Office of Spiritual Hygiene and Public Welfare, pending investigation for psychopathological contagion and gross violation of spiritual and material sanitation statutes. Entry strictly prohibited, under penalty of fine and detention." He extinguished his phosphorion and slipped down to the courtyard again.

After a moment, Laura said, "We'd better leave."

"And go where?" asked Michael.

"Oh, Michael," Laura replied in exasperation, "to Kenopolis, of course."

"But your parents . . ."

"Please," Laura said, waving one hand impatiently before her, "don't be idiotic. They didn't know anything like this had happened."

"And if they come here in a few days," said Michael, "do you want them to find us gone? Look, let's at least see if the Goldentoads are at home."

"Yes, all right," said Laura irascibly.

But the Goldentoads were not at home. The small white stone cottage with its low thatched roof, set behind the tavern and on the opposite side of a gravel yard, was also unlit, inside and out, and also sealed in puce and silver, and a large notice was also pasted to its door. This time Michael needed only the moonlight to read it: "This property sealed by order of the Department of Domestic Chattels and Domiciliary Law, and its occupants placed in protective therapeutic custody, pending investigation for psychodynamic irregularities and for abuse of a mercantile license. Entry forbidden, under penalty of detention and punitive orthodonture."

"You see," said Laura, "we're too late. They're looking everywhere in the area . . . maybe everywhere in Oreiotopia. There've probably been arrests all over the place."

"Yes," said Michael quietly, "I . . . I imagine so." He looked past the cottage and away to the north, where some of the lights of the nearby village were distantly visible. They glittered in the darkness at the base of a forested mountain whose bare ridge was a stark black against the sky. "Perhaps Wildwind?"

"We'd be arrested immediately," said Laura. "You can't hide the way Oriens looks."

"I meant just you," said Michael. "Your parents begged you not to go farther down river. Do you know anyone at all in the village?"

"No," Laura practically growled in her pique, "and even if I did I wouldn't go there." Then her voice became gentler. "I'm sure there are government police agents and, oh, Brethren and such all over the place. It's just not safe here. We have to keep going."

Michael was silent, still gazing toward the lights. He could think of no further argument to make. And a moment later he felt no desire for one. There was a movement upon the ridge, something large enough to stand out quite clearly against the satiny night sky. It was instantly recognizable as a Shadow of the Deep, its misshapen form as tall as any mountain pine and somehow darker than the mountain's silhouette, and it was moving across the skyline with slow, gigantic strides. Exerting all his strength of will to prevent himself from crying out, Michael lifted a hand and pointed toward it, and Laura and Oriens turned to look. Even at this great distance, miles away, it was a terrifying sight, and for a moment Michael could not move; but Oriens laid a hand on his shoulder and drew him back into the shade of the cottage. From there he could see that the giant had come to a pause and now seemed to be surveying the valley and river — if, that is, it was facing in this direction.

"We need to go now," Laura hissed. "Now."

"I don't know if we should," said Michael. "I feel as if it could see us from there."

"We aren't safe here," said Laura.

"Won't it be able to see the boat from there," asked Michael, "if we go back out onto the water?"

"I don't know," said Laura. She momentarily glanced away toward the river. "Probably," she admitted in a disheartened voice.

So they remained where they were, Michael fearing even to breathe too loudly, and the Shadow remained where it was for what seemed an extremely long time. Then, slowly, it turned and began to descend from the ridge. At first, it was difficult to tell whether it was coming down the near side of the mountain, toward the village, or going down the far side, into the deep forest; but, as its head and shoulders sank away into the darkness, they could tell that it was the latter. All three exhaled audibly.

"If they walk only at night," said Michael, shaking but maintaining his composure, "maybe we should wait for dawn before we put out on the water again. I'd rather risk being seen by police agents in the daylight than by one of those things in the dark."

"That seems wise," said Oriens.

"And all three of us are going to Kenopolis," said Laura firmly.

"I suppose we are," Michael replied.

BEYOND THE EASTERN END OF THE TAVERN'S REAR courtyard, near the narrow paved road leading to the village, stood a barn and stable in which they found only five clean, empty stalls and, at the back, bales of fresh hay and a loft, and they decided after some deliberation that they should stay there until daybreak. They brought their bedrolls and knapsacks from the boat, as well as food and water, glancing about in every direction the whole way. In the barn, they ate some dried fruit, nuts, and oatcakes, lay down under their covers and generous heaps of straw, and—despite their anxiety, and despite Michael's and Laura's resolve to keep watch in turns—were all three asleep within the hour. The first light of dawn woke them, seeping in through the gaps in the weathered clapboard walls. A pump at the drinking trough across from the stalls allowed them to wash their faces and clean their teeth, and they changed into fresher clothes in turns behind the stalls, and afterward breakfasted on the rest of the food they had brought with them. Then they made their way back to the boat, keeping as close to the buildings as they could. Michael pushed them away from the dock with one of the boat's poles and Laura turned on the anemokineton, switching it off again as soon as they had passed through the inlet and into the river's currents once more. The Phlegethon was as deserted as the tavern, and at first Michael and Laura assumed that this was because of the early hour; but, as the morning progressed and they still saw no other craft on the water, they could not help but begin to grow apprehensive. It was true that there was only sparse merchant traffic on the Phlegethon these days, but normally they could have expected to see one or two barges carrying timber, or boats carrying fish from the mountain streams down to the city; and certainly fishermen still went out on the river as a rule, as did local long-boat and sail enthusiasts, and at this time of year river journeys were a popular amusement.

"Everyone around here must know about the Shadows by now," Laura opined, "and the wolves and the arrests, and no one wants to go out."

"It makes us very, very conspicuous," says Michael. "Maybe travelling by day isn't a good idea after all."

But they continued on for several miles, cleaving closer to the northern side than to the southern, borne by the even flow of the gleaming waters between green and blue mountain slopes, along sandy or palely pebbled shores, and past occasional fishing piers or boat docks, all quite devoid of human life. Only when they saw a large grove of marmoreans on the southern shore, stretching from the foot of the mountain all the way down to the water's edge, and Laura abruptly chose to steer the boat toward it, did they halt their journey. It was a fortunate decision. Under the thick cover of the turquoise canopy, there was a natural shallow lagoon, carved into the shore in a deep crescent, where the water was tranquil and where there was also an old wooden pier, obviously disused and in considerable disrepair but sufficiently intact for mooring the boat; and no sooner had they disembarked than a low, loud, monotonous, immediately recognizable drone began to arise from the west. "An aerial barge," Michael told Oriens, then bit his lower lip. The noise continued to grow in volume until, after several minutes, it sounded much louder than any barge Michael had ever before heard, and the surface of the water in the lagoon began quivering in small but increasingly rapid vibrations, and the leaves above began shaking and rattling and finally thrashing, and all at once an enormous shroud of shadow was spreading over the water beyond the reflections of the marmoreans, and was darkening the blue ceiling of leaves overhead. Exchanging looks of alarm, Michael and Laura crept down to the water's edge, cautiously peered out from under the fringe of the leaves, and saw the huge oblong shape of the barge passing overhead at a surprisingly low altitude, barely a dozen yards above the treetops, and with almost monstrous slowness. They also saw that, rather than the familiar green and red of a Wilderness Ministry vehicle, its hull sported the gleaming black varnish and dark blue trim of a police transport. They backed away from the water's edge and waited with Oriens in silence until the barge had passed downriver and the sound of its rotors had — with a deeply unpleasant graduality — died away in the distance.

After a long while, Michael said, "No more traveling by daylight. We'll never make it all the way to the city except at night."

II

ICHAEL SAT AT THE END OF THE PIER, HIS bare feet submerged in the chilly, marmorean-blue water, his eyes all but entirely closed so that they took in the wimpling sheen of the river as only shifting silvery patterns of floating lights and melting shadows. He had been asleep only thirty minutes earlier and when he had left Oriens and Laura they were still under the covers of their bedrolls, the one on the sand where the bank began to rise into the woods, the other under the boat's awning. He was thinking of many things, in no particular order. He remembered, for instance, Mr. Lucius's lieutenant mentioning that aerial vehicles had been disabled when Oriens had arrived, and he wondered whether more barges and cars would have been searching for them before now had those in the vicinity been operable, and whether then they really should have started out on their journey a day earlier. Oriens was probably right that haste was paramount. Michael was also thinking of the miles that still lay between them and the city, and whether they would be able to find enough cover in the mountains and hills to continue to elude the notice of aerial patrols, or be able to find any cover at all in the lowlands, and whether the night alone would veil them adequately. And then a kind of hopeless sense of the sheer vastness of everything began to oppress him, as he wondered what would await them even if they got as far as the river harbor and canals of Kenopolis. He was also thinking, however, more sporadically, of the story Oriens had told of his glorious kingdom beyond the world: a tale so fantastic that it seemed beyond Michael's power of either belief or disbelief, but which he chose to accept because of all the seemingly impossible things he had seen since his father had been arrested—these past three days especially—and because he found himself unable to suspect Oriens of falsehood, and because he had scarcely had a moment in which to allow himself the luxury of doubt. He even briefly thought about Paichnidia, and wondered whether his prolonged absence had yet begun to cast a few shadows of doubt over the incessant glare of her cheerfulness; and, at this, he felt a small spasm of pity. At one juncture, a memory of his mother came unbidden to his mind, one that occasionally visited him but that he could not place in time: the image of her bending above a book she was reading aloud to him, laughing at something there, a spray of sunlight from a window across the room glistering in a single loose lock of her dark, honey-golden hair, her light brown eyes full of happiness. Principally, though, he was thinking about his father: how fiercely he missed his father, how deeply fearful he was for his father's safety, how hopeless any search for his father seemed. He had never felt himself to be especially brave, and had always thought himself more studious than adventurous; but he had done things of late he could never have previously imagined doing, and now he was proceeding relentlessly onward into yet greater danger rather than fleeing from it, and he was quite certain that nothing would deter him. This was in part because circumstances had overtaken him, obviously, and in part because his choices had become so few, and in part because he felt somehow responsible for this tremendous child from beyond the stars for whom his father had apparently been waiting in secret for years; chiefly, though, it was because he longed to see his father again, however implausible that hope now seemed, and this longing was far more powerful than all his fears.

"School started again the day before yesterday, I think," said Laura.

Michael turned his head, startled. He had not heard her approaching, even on the weathered boards of the pier, because her feet were bare. "I expect we're not the only ones who failed to turn up for lessons," he said.

She sat beside him and also, after a few hesitant dips of her toes, immersed her feet in the water. "Who knows? I can't imagine what's been happening while we've been running and hiding."

Michael nodded. "Shadows and wolves and police," he said.

"Michael," said Laura in a tone that suggested a reluctance to ask what she was about to ask, "what do you think would have happened if that Shadow we saw last night had gone down into Wildwind and not into the forest?"

"I don't know," said Michael. "I don't like to think about it. Perhaps it would have taken everyone away."

"What if these Shadows *have* gone into villages?" said Laura. "What about Brightrill?"

"Maybe they don't, though," said Michael. "Maybe . . . maybe that's not what they do. Maybe they just search out in the darkness, in the woods, and the police agents deal with the villages."

"Do you really think so?"

"I don't know. My father never told me anything about them. But he did talk about Oreiotopian charms and all those whitewood amulets and such, and he used to say they were originally meant to keep away forest demons and 'nightwalkers,' whatever that meant. At least, that was how people thought before the Age of Illumination. Maybe that's what Shadows are — forest demons . . . out there in the darkness, in the woods . . . never seen out in the open, or where people live. I mean, otherwise they'd be more than just legends in people's minds, right?" He shrugged.

"But maybe they aren't only that," said Laura, her voice sinking down to a whisper. "Maybe they *can* go into villages, and carry people away — men and women and children . . ."

"I don't know," said Michael again, "but if they were that uncontrollable, that unpredictable, that destructive — I mean, who would be foolish enough to call them up? Wouldn't they be too dangerous?"

Laura stirred the water with one of her feet. "It all depends on just how badly they want to catch Oriens," she said after a moment.

"Well," said Michael, "I don't think there's anything they'd be unwilling to do to capture him. Anything at all."

ANOTHER POLICE PATROL PASSED OVERHEAD TWO hours before twilight, not quite as low as before but closer to the southern shore, near enough to send down a flickering blue shower of spinning and tumbling leaves on their moored boat. Half an hour after that, Oriens asked whether it might be possible to bathe before they departed. Michael joined him in the cool liquid sky of the leaf-strewn lagoon while Laura went apart to the eastern end of the grove; and then the two of them went apart in their turn while she bathed. They washed clothes in a basin and with soap they had brought from the cabin, hung them to dry on a line strung diagonally under the deckhouse awning, ate from their provisions, and prepared to resume their journey at nightfall. Just before twilight, the white bird arrived, suddenly descending out of the spreading treetops; Oriens, who had apparently seen it coming before either Michael or Laura had, was already on his feet by the pier, waiting to receive it on his upraised forearm. Laura and Michael, deciding together to allow Oriens his privacy, moved away up the shore. After several minutes, the bird rose into the air again and sped away, out over the river and toward the west, and Oriens came to them.

"My pneumatagogue knows where a way to my sister's prison house lies," he told them simply, "but it will not be easy to reach. And it is not certain where it leads." He looked at Laura. "He has gone to tell your mother and father of what we found at the tavern and assure them that you are with us now."

"Oh, yes," said Laura with a deep sigh of gratitude, "thank-you so much."

"He also says that ahead of us there are more places of cover to be found on this side of the river than on the other, and more brightwood groves, and that no other boats are out here in these parts of the mountains. In the hills and plains below, however, there are vessels on the water."

"I suppose no news is going down the mountains," said Michael. "The anemophone links to the lowlands have probably had their funnels battened."

"The police have probably stopped all the trains too," said Laura, "and all the horse coaches."

"Probably, yes," said Michael.

"It will be dark soon," said Oriens, looking away eastward, beyond the trees and down the river to where the sky was becoming a deep transparent blue, and then to the west where the daylight was dissolving in layers of rose and violet. "My pneumatagogue says that there is another place like this on this side of the river, under a still deeper brightwood cover, seven hours and sixteen minutes downstream."

"That's very precise," said Michael.

Oriens apparently saw no need to reply.

"Do you think," continued Michael after a moment, "that next time he flies west to Laura's parents he might have time to go to my stepmother? To tell her I'm well? A talking bird would be a shock to most people, of course, but somehow I think Paichnidia would just take it in stride."

"I shall ask him," said Oriens.

THEY EASED BACK INTO THE RIVER'S FLOW IN THE last of the twilight, keeping as near the southern shore as they could, and were nearly four hours farther along downstream, steering by the weak, brittle starlight, before the moons began to rise. Laura refused Michael's offers to relieve her at the tiller, even when Aurea and Argentea were lighting the path ahead, and when he reminded her that he had been out on the river in boats in the past she merely looked at him with an expression of affectionate scorn and told him that she knew this boat better than anyone else. No aerial cars passed overhead the entire time, or were even audible in the distance, and at one point Michael wondered aloud whether anyone among their pursuers was willing to venture out after dark so long as the Shadows were known to be walking. "Surely they'd be searching the river in the darkness too if they weren't afraid," he said.

"Yes," said Laura, "that makes sense." She shook her head, seemingly a little astonished at having to admit it. "So maybe if we can get to the city before . . . How long do they stay? Seven nights?"

"Supposedly," said Michael. "At least, that's what your father said my father said. But who knows?"

"And how many nights would that leave?"

"After tonight," said Michael, "two, I think. But who knows if that's right?"

Laura became silent for several moments. "It just doesn't seem to make sense," she remarked at last, seemingly as much to herself as to her companions. "Why would they call on these Shadows if they're so dangerous they scare off even the police agents?"

"Maybe they're so powerful," said Michael, "that they think it worth the risk."

"Or perhaps," said Oriens, gazing over Laura's head and off to the west, as if transfixed by something he saw, "they have not thought clearly at all. Everywhere I have gone, every world within the machine, I have found that my enemies are not as a rule extremely wise. Some have been quite intelligent — very much so — but most have not. My pneumatagogue says that, in many cases, their wits tend to lack liveliness because the golden light — the spark — does not burn in them."

Michael also looked westward, but saw only the bright night sky, the shining river, the sylvan shadows, and the distant peaks. "What does burn in them?" he asked.

"If anything, the pale light of phantoms," said Oriens simply. "The ghost light that was born in the Forest of Dreams. A faint glow of awareness, of life."

"It sounds horrible," said Laura. "They're . . . they're monsters, then."

"No," said Oriens firmly. "They are prisoners here too. They were called forth from our dreams, stolen from their home and made to serve the sorcerer. They too are slaves . . . captives . . . lost . . . part of the plunder of my father's kingdom. They are to be pitied."

"They wouldn't pity us," said Michael. "They've never shown my father any pity . . . or my mother."

"They do not know how," said Oriens somberly. "They have been deprived of the ability. That also is to be pitied."

"Who are you talking about exactly?" said Laura. "The police, the priests, the psychologists, the government officials — who?"

"The ones in charge," said Michael bitterly, "all of them."

"I am speaking of those who serve your Great Artisan," said Oriens, "those who do his bidding, who labor to prevent you from awaking — from knowing yourselves. But I do not know your world. I cannot tell you who they are."

"I can," said Michael. "I've seen them take both of my parents . . . torment both of my parents. They drove my mother to her death."

Oriens gazed at Michael in silence for some moments, his uncanny eyes shining like small blue flames in the light of the moons. "I did not know this," he said at last. "I am sorry. Still" — he looked away again to the west — "I have learned a great deal about hatred in my travels. It has been very long . . . within this machine. I might have hated the sorcerer who stole my sister. Perhaps I did for some time. But now I believe I pity even him."

"You pity God?" said Laura with a small laugh.

Oriens looked at her. "The God of this world, yes," he said. "The God of this terrible machine, of this cosmos and its . . . inner worlds, inner ages . . . yes, I do. Such a God must be as much a prisoner of his creation as its lord. What spite, what envy, what cruelty must dwell in him — to cling so fiercely to what he has stolen, to use such violence and terror to preserve his power, to marshal armies and build prisons, to tell lies and threaten eternal torments. *Eternal* torments — how hideous, how vile that idea is, how cruel. He has made himself a pompous, malevolent, jealous tyrant, one who calls his vindictiveness love, calls it justice. I do not understand him at all. But I do know that he is pitiable."

"Our catechism tutor," said Michael, "Mr. Talion, says there has to be a Land of Hel, and its punishments have to be unending, because the Great Artisan allows us . . . It has something to do with our being free to make choices, to reject his love, and with how he respects our freedom . . . and how . . ."

But Oriens, quite uncharacteristically, interrupted, and with a hint of even more uncharacteristic impatience: "No good creator could allow such an end, even for the sake of freedom. And how could it be freedom anyway? No creature could truly be free whose choices could lead to such an end. They would be choices made in the darkness of ignorance and fear . . . delusion. Eternal suffering could never be anything but a work of vengeful cruelty — especially from a creator whose world is so flawed that its children die of incurable diseases." He had turned his eyes away from both Michael and Laura now and was staring upward at the stars. "I have traveled far through this cosmos, and in every world I have found shelter for a time. In each there is beauty, and in each there is horror. In the red world, for instance, the peoples make perpetual war upon one another, and say they are serving God in doing so. Every battlefield, one of their priests told me, is an altar of sacrifice, of holy slaughter, well-pleasing to the maker of all things." His voice was growing weary, almost despondent. "In all the worlds above this world, I have heard the ways of your Great Artisan extolled and explained, and have heard even the cruelest of teachings described as counsels of mercy or goodness or justice. But all the arguments always prove false and fruitless — attempts to make evil sound good. I have descended too far, seen too much of this machine, this . . . this cosmos to be able to listen in peace to such words anymore." He smiled weakly, recovering his composure. "Forgive me. I do not mean to be discourteous."

"I never . . . I never really believed it," said Michael meekly; then, after a few seconds: "The explanation is in the Book of Disciplines and in the Catechism of Rational Orthodoxy."

"What is orthodoxy?" asked Oriens, his voice having regained its normal smooth placidity.

"Correct belief," said Laura dryly. "I mean, that's what it means."

Oriens nodded. "The word I understood. What I do not know is what it signifies in this world."

"My father," said Michael, "liked to say, 'Orthodoxy is a humble half-truth exalted to the majesty of a total falsehood.'" A small wistful smile came to his lips at the memory. "But he always says not to repeat that, especially not to my tutors."

"Mr. Talion also says that creatures can't reproach their creator," Laura remarked.

"Why not?" asked Oriens. "If the creator is inferior in goodness to his creatures, why should they not reproach him?" His eyes passed from Laura to Michael; then, when he received no answer, he looked up to the sky again. "It does not matter in any event, since you were never his creatures to begin with. You are his captives. He cannot create spirits. He can only imprison them."

"I never really believed it, either," said Laura after a moment. "At least, I don't think I did."

"Some of the sorcerer's servants are not even phantoms, of course," Oriens casually added. "Some are only mechanisms, as I told you before: puppets or toys or dolls. Nothing at all burns within them. No light of awareness, however dim."

"How does that work?" asked Laura. "Everyone seems . . . alive. I mean, I've never seen anyone who . . . wasn't obviously alive."

"Machines can move," said Oriens. "Puppets can be made to dance. They can even be made to speak and act, if the maker is cunning enough. But they cannot live. Everything in your world that has any true life in it — you, those you love, the animals and birds and blossoming trees, all of it — has its life from beyond. It is a stolen fire. Life is eternal, and no machine can produce it."

"That's the opposite of what Metrontes taught," remarked Michael.

"He was mistaken," said Oriens. "It would be a great marvel indeed if this flesh" — he lifted a hand and turned it before his own eyes — "came about by virtue of the spirit; but, if the spirit came about by virtue of this carnal body" — he lowered his hand again — "that would be a marvel among marvels. In truth, it amazes me that such extraordinary fullness can inhabit such dearth . . . such squalor. If you could only see your own spirit unveiled."

Michael breathed deeply and looked upward at the stars. "Do you think that Paichnidia could be one? I mean, my stepmother. Could she be a phantom, or just a puppet? Sometimes she seems so . . . so only half there."

"That I cannot know," replied Oriens. "I have never met her, and would not be able to tell you even if I had. In some of you, the light of the spirit has been bound fast, deep in the dungeons of your bodies and souls, down where it can illuminate nearly nothing. He who has imprisoned you has many skills, many powers, many methods of enchantment, many glamors and illusions at his command. Most of you are asleep throughout your lives, I should think, if this world resembles those above. Only a few at any time are awake, or struggling to awaken. So you cannot easily tell from someone's manner, I would imagine, whether the light burns within. Someone may seem to you a fool or a puppet, but in his or her deepest self may be a god. It is a mystery till the end."

All at once, Laura rose to her feet, and the boat lurched slightly to the left as she jarred the tiller. "Fire," she said, pointing over their heads to the northern shore: "something's on fire, I think."

Michael and Oriens turned, and both soon stood as well, the boat rocking gently beneath them. It did seem as though something were burning on the far shore, well downstream from them, casting a clear yellow light upon the air and over a distant stretch of the normally bone-white sand

and out upon the river's sparkling margin. But it was not fire. There was no smoke and the light wavered and swayed rather than flickered and leapt; and as the boat drew nearer it gradually became clear that what they were seeing was actually a tall vertical jet of ignited phosphoric vapor, streaming upward from the cracked engine of an aerial barge that was lying shattered in two enormous sections along the shore, like a fallen tower, splinters of deck and twisted shards of metal scattered all about it and the cylinder of one great rotary thrust motor rising up from the wreck at a disjointedly perpendicular tilt with its propeller still quietly spinning. And, by the time their boat was opposite the scene, they could see from its glossy black finish that it was a police transport. The crash could not have occurred many hours before, or the engine would have exhausted its fuel by now; but there were no human figures anywhere to be seen: no corpses on the sand, no injured police agents lying apart, no one walking around the broken hull. The only sound apart from the water lapping against the boat's hull was the faint hiss of the engine's escaping vapors. Set against the smoky purple of the mountain slope only a few hundred yards beyond, the entire scene was altogether eerie. They stared at the broken hull as they passed by in silence, and at the gushing fountain of golden light and at its scintillating reflections on the water, and continued to watch the vapors shimmering and effervescing and dissipating in the air — with only Laura turning her head at intervals, so that she could steer — until the current had carried them around a broad bend downriver and the barge's remains were hidden behind the low granite spur of the next mountain.

"I didn't even know those things *could* crash," said Laura after several moments.

"Maybe our question's been answered," said Michael, his brows knitted. "Maybe they came across one of the Shadows. Maybe they stayed out too long, till it was night, and . . . got in the way or something."

"Could something else have caused them to fall from the sky?" asked Oriens.

"I've never heard of such a thing," said Michael. "I don't know what could bring down an aerial barge, especially a thirty-rotors barge, let alone what could tear it in half like that. The hulls are built from something — a kind of alloy called lamina inruptibilis — that's absolutely unbreakable. You can't even dent it, not even with an aeroballistic cannon." He swept his hair back from his forehead and realized as he did so that his hand felt abnormally cold. "And where is everyone? Where are the police agents? *Someone* must have been injured . . . or killed."

"Perhaps they fled because dark was falling," said Oriens, "and they feared the Shadows."

"But there's no sign of anyone at all," said Michael. "Could they all have escaped unharmed from a crash like that, or carried away the injured and dead already?"

"They aren't there because they were taken by the Shadows," said Laura, quietly and grimly: "all of them."

JUST AS DAWN WAS RISING IN THE EAST, AND THE birds had begun singing in the trees along the river, they reached the next large marmorean grove on the southern shore. It overshadowed the mouth of a small tributary and—to one side of it—a small ovoid bay no more than five feet deep at its center. There was no pier here, but they moored the boat to two saplings near the water and, in a low covert, ate and then slept through the better part of the day in a haze of blue light and blue shade. When they awoke they bathed again, first Laura and then Michael and Oriens, each of them lingering for some time in the cool shallow bay, with its calm surface like blue marble from the reflected leaves overhead and with its fine sand underfoot; then they washed and hung out more clothes, and then ate again. They only once heard an aerial barge passing by, but this time higher up in the air than those of the previous day, moving much more quickly and flying much nearer the northern shore. The white bird came to Oriens again not long before twilight, and when it had departed Oriens told Michael and Laura that they could hide the boat a little more than six hours downstream by going about a quarter mile up another tributary into a smaller area of marmorean cover, and that they would know the mouth of the tributary was near when they passed a large white boulder on the river bank. They could then reach the lowlands in little more than a day, before the second dawn. He also told Laura that her father and mother were as yet still safe in their fishing cabin, and that her father's fevers had diminished, but that they were anxious over her and intended to follow as soon as they were able. He also told Michael that the bird would visit his stepmother at some point after dawn.

"Thank-you," said Michael; and then added, "If there's still traffic down river, I suppose we can just try to merge in with it, once the fishing boats are out."

"But," said Laura, "we'd better do something to make this look like a fishing boat to the patrols, and less like a boat from Oreiotopia."

"True," said Michael. He looked about somewhat aimlessly. "Do you, by any chance, know what the proper kind of fishing boat would, you know, look like?"

Laura smiled a little triumphantly. "The bench in the stern is a storage chest, and there are nets and lines in it."

"Do you know how to put them out, though?"

"Yes, of course," she said impatiently. "I've been fishing before. I didn't grow up in Kenopolis like you. But I thought we should just hang them over the railing, to hide all that carving. Even from the air, it'll be obvious we came down from the mountains."

"You know," said Michael distractedly, "I'm not sure I like the idea of going upstream into the woods, even only a quarter mile, at least in the darkness. If another Shadow comes, I want to be able to get out into the middle of the river as quickly as possible."

"Why?" asked Oriens. "Do you believe we could possibly move quickly enough wherever we are?"

"Well . . ." Michael began; but, having no answer, he said nothing more.

"I believe," said Oriens after a moment, "that the chrysastra blossoms we have about us give us some protection — somehow shield us from their eyes, or whatever they see with. It seems to me they must."

"How much protection?" asked Laura.

"Enough to make it hard for them to find us over great distances. Perhaps."

"Perhaps," Michael repeated in a hollow voice.

They set out upon the water again as night fell, and for the first part of the journey Michael and Oriens occupied themselves by disentangling the seven fishing lines and the three large, light, coarse fishing nets they had extracted from below the tiller bench, coiling the lines and carefully folding the nets when they had finished, and then laying all of them out in the prow. The night would have been otherwise uneventful had the distant cry of a Shadow, prolonged and furious, not come drifting down to them from the west just after both moons had cleared the eastern horizon, each now a little more than three-quarters full. Michael instantly felt a shock of terror radiating out from his spine and rose to his feet; Laura turned to look behind her with a small shrill gasp; Oriens gazed away into the west but betrayed no alarm. For only a moment, at the farthest visible reaches of the moonlight shining on the waves, something like a pillar of smoke seemed to be hovering above the river, faintly outlined against a dim, shimmering, velvet-gray wedge of sky in the cleft between the two lower slopes flanking the water. Then it was gone.

"It was a Shadow," said Oriens.

Laura moaned softly and Michael, finding he could not swallow, still managed to say, "Yes . . . we heard. But could you make it out that far away?"

"I saw it," said Oriens simply. "It was walking across the river's surface, from the southern to the northern shore, toward the trees."

"Walking?" said Laura. "On the river?"

"But he didn't see us?" asked Michael.

"It seems not," Oriens replied. "As I said, I believe it was wise of you to bring the chrysastra blossoms with us."

"Walking on the river," said Laura again, with a shudder. "If my parents follow us, how can they get past?"

"Perhaps only one night more," Michael said. "Perhaps they'll be gone then."

"Perhaps," said Laura. "Perhaps not."

A FEW HOURS LATER, AND FOR THE FIRST TIME IN several nights, clouds began to gather in the sky, drawing a soft and shifting veil across the moons, dimming the light on the waves. The air grew cooler, and then began gently to gust, and finally a light rain—at times little more than a swirling spray—began to fall. Michael and Oriens retreated beneath the awning, but only after Laura had refused to relinquish the tiller to either of them and they had brought her two blankets to cover her head and wrap about her. Just before dawn, as Oriens had said they would, they passed a milk-white boulder standing on the southern shore, right at the water's edge, and a little beyond that they came upon the mouth of a tributary; and Laura, turning on the anemokineton, steered the boat upstream against the current and into the grove of marmoreans. By then the rain had ceased, but the ground was wet and they slept on the boat, under the awning, a few feet apart from one another. They woke in the early afternoon, washed but did not bathe, ate, spoke, and waited. Michael observed that they had heard no wolves since the night when Oriens had arrived; Laura attributed this to the Shadows; Michael and Oriens concurred, though Michael wondered aloud whether those who had chosen to summon the Shadows had also imagined the Brethren would continue hunting at night; Oriens again remarked that, in his experience, his enemies were often a little foolish. Three times, they heard an aerial vehicle go by, out over the river, each time from west to east, moving at considerable speed. The white bird came late in the afternoon and, when it had gone, Oriens told Michael and Laura that the boat could reach the lowlands by the morning of the day after tomorrow, that they would encounter other craft there, and that the great bay of Kenopolis lay only a little more than ten hours beyond those foothills. There was another place of rest ahead, he said, on the southern shore again, a grove not of marmoreans, but heavily shaded. He also told Laura that the bird would now go to her mother and father to tell them all they and it had seen upon the waterways. As evening rose in the west, they returned to the river and, under a starry sky once again perfectly clear, continued their journey to the city.

III

T WAS AN HOUR BEFORE MIDNIGHT, THE MOONS
in their diminished aspects were well up in the sky, and the waters
of the Phlegethon were a riot of flashing silver and gold when the
boat rounded a particularly broad bend in the river and, about two hundred yards ahead, an area of peculiarly deep murkiness came all at once
into view. It stood out in sharp contrast from the surrounding brilliancies, almost like something solid. A long stretch of the river looked as it
were composed not of water, but of liquid tar; in place of the glitter of
capering waves there was only a dull sleekness and a gluey sheen. Even
the trees along the shorelines there were curiously lackluster, seeming
to swallow rather than reflect the moonlight. It was as if the shadow of
some colossal but otherwise invisible tower had fallen across the boat's
path. Oriens, who had been sitting beside Laura in the stern, rose to his
feet; Michael, in the bow, did the same. Farther downstream, beyond the
dark waters, the waves clearly resumed their coruscating dance; but this
strange interval of obscurity seemed to extend for something like a mile
ahead of them, and as far on both sides of the river as the lower mountain
slopes. There was, moreover, a narrow wooded island—scarcely more
than two dozen yards wide at its broadest and about forty yards from
either shore—running the entire length of the darkened waters like the
protruding, jaggedly serrated spine of some immense sea-monster resting
just below the surface.

"Is there something in the water here?" asked Oriens, with no
sound of alarm in his voice. "Are these trees dead or living? They seem
stunted . . . twisted."

Michael was now walking toward the stern along the boat's starboard
side, steadying himself on the railing but obviously agitated. "They're
petrified," he said. "At least, I think so. What an idiot I am. We've reached
Silva Larvarum — Ghostwood, I mean. The Stone Forest." As he reached
the stern, he looked at Laura with a hopeless expression. "And after your
father warned us."

Laura moaned in frustration. "Of course. How could we be so stupid?"

"We've had other things to worry about," said Michael, but so feebly that it was obvious he himself found the excuse wanting.

"I recall the name," said Oriens calmly, "but I do not grasp its significance."

"Normally water-traffic doesn't pass along this part of the river by night," said Michael. "There's something in the soil that comes down from the mountains, some kind of poison mineral or something, and it petrifies the vegetation, and gets into the water supposedly. But, that's not why it's . . . why they avoid it, really. Barges and such coming down from Oreiotopia, if they get near here as night is coming on, will moor or drop anchor at least a few miles upstream. And fishing-boats never . . ."

"I think I can get near the shore before we reach it," Laura interrupted, shifting the tiller so abruptly that Michael lost his balance and fell against the starboard railing, while Oriens had to steady himself with an uncharacteristically graceless lurch.

"I don't think you can," said Michael, quickly extricating himself from the meshes of a fishing-net and regaining his feet. "And what's the point? There's nowhere here to hide when the sun rises."

"Why must this Ghostwood be avoided at night?" asked Oriens, still without any hint of worry in his voice. "My guide made no mention of any particular peril at this point of the river."

"I don't know, really," said Michael in a distracted and anxious voice. "I mean . . ." His voice trailed off into silence.

"It's haunted," said Laura with a sudden urgency. "Like my father said, the souls of heretics are sealed in the trees."

"That's one story," said Michael, turning to look forward again. "Maybe it's just hard to navigate. A shelf of rock, or reefs, maybe . . . treacherous currents . . . or maybe the roots of those petrified trees reach out into the water. Maybe you need to see where you're going to get through safely . . ."

"Oh, I can't do it," said Laura angrily. "The flow here is too strong. I can't get to the shore in time."

Michael moved forward, with a few reels, into the bow again. "We've a very shallow hull, after all," he called back. "Maybe we'll go right over any obstacles." Then, after staring ahead for several seconds more: "Try to stay on this side, midway between the island and the bank. It looks a little broader here than on the other side . . . I think."

"I hope you're right," Laura called out as she eased the tiller into position, first shifting back to the left, then bringing the rudder into alignment with the keel, and then beginning to maneuver the boat gently toward the middle passage between the island and the southern shore.

As they entered the area of darkness, Michael was immediately aware that the night had grown considerably chillier, and a sudden dimness in the air made it seem as if they were passing through a diffuse but stagnant fog. The trees on either bank and along the island had a markedly ghastly appearance to them: leafless boughs warped and truncated in oddly jagged ways, bark dark as coal but without any of coal's soft glossiness, trunks stark and bent as if doubling over in pain, twisted branches massed in tangled silhouettes against the starry sky. And the river's surface seemed oddly slick and dismal, almost viscous. The boat slowed, as though it were making its way through something denser than mere water.

"What's there?" called Laura from the stern.

"Nothing," Michael called back. "Nothing at all."

Yet something seemed to be gripping at the hull — if not to hold it fast, at least to detain it — and this caused the boat constantly to veer from side to side in the suddenly leadenly sluggish current, now toward the island, now toward the shore, but never straight onward.

"What are you doing, Laura?" Michael yelled, more loudly than he had intended. "Can't you keep it straight?"

"No, I can't," came back a distinctly irate reply. "Something keeps pulling us left or right."

"I don't even see any movement in the water," Michael answered.

"Do you . . . want to take the . . . tiller?" Laura's voice was straining along with her body as she fought to hold a steady course.

"Let me help you," said Oriens.

"I can't even see any ripples," Michael continued, scarcely audibly. And, indeed, when he bent forward to look downward from the bow, nothing at all was visible: no glassy moonlight along the folds of displaced water, no reflections of moons or stars; it was as if the boat was floating above an abyss. Several yards ahead, there was an oily pallor visible, spread over the river's surface like a mildew stain; but directly below him he could see only this dizzying emptiness. He stepped back, stood erect, and looked about. The trees here were not only withered and contorted, but much shorter than the living trees of the forest; and this made them seem all the more threatening as the boat swung to port or starboard and drew near them. Again and again, the prow came within ten yards or so either of the island or of the shore and then pulled away only with agonizing slowness, accompanied by Laura's labored groans. Michael considered for a moment joining the other two at the back of the boat and lending his strength to theirs, but he was afraid to take his eyes from the way ahead. Now the air was growing positively icy. He drew up his collar and breathed into his cupped hands. There was also a peculiarly dank, stale fragrance rising from the water. The area of darkness seemed to be unfurling before them — and the shimmer of the open water beyond to be growing no nearer — as they advanced.

And then, before he was aware that he heard it, Michael realized that he was listening to a strange hissing and whispering among the branches, and in the air all around the boat. Really, it seemed to be coming from nowhere in particular, but as he listened it grew noisier and rasped and sighed and even softly whistled around his head.

"What's that?" said Laura, just loudly enough for Michael to hear her. "What's that sound?"

There was no breeze. Nothing stirred the boughs of the trees — not that anything in all likelihood could have. There were no leaves on the branches to rattle together. And yet in every direction the air was now filled with this strange, sibilant noise. And, after several moments, Michael realized that it was not a single sound, but a combination of many sounds at once, in differing registers, high and low and everything in between, intermingling but still mostly distinct from one another.

"It sounds like voices," said Oriens.

It *was* the sound of voices — of many voices — Michael was certain of it. And they were coming from both the shore and the narrow island, as if emerging from the petrified trees themselves.

"Oh, that's horrible," Laura said. "It can't be."

But Michael said nothing. He merely listened. Yes, it sounded like spoken words — distant or near at hand, whispered or groaned out, interweaving, blending — but it was all too confused to make out. Perhaps it was an illusion, he thought, a purely natural phenomenon, produced by some sort of steam vent or fissure nearby, hidden among the trees and echoing off their stony trunks. It might be no more than a kind of sonic mirage, precisely the sort of thing, he mused, that would excite the superstitious natures of river-folk or boatmen, and make them believe the woods here were haunted. He listened more intently. Perhaps . . .

But then he heard it, quite clearly — one voice emerging from the welter of voices, small and querulous but ringingly clear among the contending whispers:

— I remember it all —

A woman's voice, it seemed, nearby and yet somehow remote, fading now, then swelling again, wheezing like wind through a cracked window:

— I think I remember it all. . . —

And then it was gone. Perhaps it had come from the shore, perhaps from somewhere closer to the boat. Michael drew in his breath sharply, turning his head violently from side to side; but there was nothing to see except shadows among shadows. Now the cold was inside of him, in his chest. His limbs trembled, and he wanted to turn back to look to Laura and Oriens, but realized he was too terrified. He did not want to attract the voices to himself by moving. But still they sighed and hovered all around him.

— If only I could remember. . . —

This also was a woman's voice, but not the same one.

Michael started at the sound of a sob behind him, and then realized it had come from Laura. "It's horrible," she said again.

He continued staring ahead. The serenely, gorgeously sparkling waves beyond this miserable corridor of darkness seemed at last to be coming closer, alive and vivid under the open sky, and yet they somehow also seemed more tauntingly out of reach.

Then another voice emerged from the whispers, this one a man's:

— It was a very long time ago . . . how long I can't recall . . . —

And then another man's, more emotionless in tone:

— And I said to her, You must run, my love, you must flee —

And then, unbearably, shatteringly, the voice of a child, perhaps a young girl:

— Is that you, Mother? Is that . . . ? —

At this, Michael lowered himself slowly to his knees on the deck and bent his head under what was now an incessant eddying of murmurs and hisses and fragments of phrases, half heard or partly imagined or unmistakably clear. And somehow also, amid those fleeting ghostly moans, he heard Laura also occasionally moaning in pity or horror. He himself had never experienced a fear quite like this. It was every bit as intense as what he had felt when he was being drawn toward the spectral lights of the Shadow of the Deep, but somehow more deadeningly melancholy. This was terror without energy: the saturating dread of some sheer meaningless sadness he could not fathom, of the crushing banality of a darkness without end or a void without a bottom. It was almost as if the fear were something flowing into him from without, unnatural — bleakly magical — in its immensity and weight. He looked up and ahead again, past the lowering, stricken silhouettes of the trees, past the lusterless waters, toward the open river and its still excruciatingly distant incandescences.

"Are we moving at all?" Laura cried out.

"We are," Oriens replied, but even his voice had become grim and subdued.

— There were fires in the hills then . . . in the forest . . . and nowhere to hide . . . nowhere . . . —

— In those days, many died . . . many were never heard from again . . . —

— You must flee now, my dear one. I cannot be saved, but you must be. —

— My mother was there. Have you seen . . . ? —

And then one voice, an older woman's perhaps, somewhat louder and more strident than the others, piercing the haze of whispers:

— And they said to me, It is in the wind, in the heavens, in the stars. You cannot escape from them. —

But then that voice too melted back into the general clamor. At that moment, the boat swerved toward the island with particular force, and Michael heard Laura groan aloud once again as she and Oriens struggled to shift the tiller and steer back toward the middle of the passage.

— I am so lonely . . . —

That the voice of a boy, perhaps.

— How long has it been? How long will it be? How long yet? —

A girl? Two girls, perhaps, speaking almost in unison, so that their voices seemed to echo each other?

"It is not far to go," called out Oriens, surprisingly feebly.

The cold was in Michael's bones now, in his heart. He clenched his fists and drew his arms in tight against his body. He shook violently, once, twice. He closed his eyes and bowed his head again. He felt tears on his cheeks, he felt his teeth grinding together. He swayed back and forth, willing the boat forward.

— Do you know me? Do you know my name? I can't remember . . . —

— I told him to run, to leave me, but he wouldn't go . . . he refused . . . —

— Please tell her that I miss her so . . . I recall so much . . . —

— Please, I beg you, tell them to let us go. —

— I still dream of her too, and know she hasn't forgotten me . . . —

— I saw him in the smoke-filled sunlight, under the hill, in its shadow, lying in the grass . . . just lying still . . . —

— Please . . . —

— The air full of smoke, drifting in the sunlight . . . red and golden . . . —

— Please . . . —

And on and on. Now all the voices were audible, all the words clear and distinct. Terror upon terror. Sadness without end. Michael felt a scream welling up within him.

— If you know me . . . if you would help . . . —

— Lonely . . . so very lonely here . . . —

Then, as quickly as it had arisen, the storm of whispers ceased, and Michael felt the boat under him almost career forward as it immediately gained speed, and the air about him was suddenly growing warmer again. There was even a slight breeze blowing against his face, fresh with the scent of clean water. He swallowed his scream just as it reached his lips, opened his eyes, and breathed deeply. His body felt brutally cold, but he also felt a sudden almost pleasant tingling in his arms and legs, as if his blood had been stilled but was now flowing again. He did not move, though. He did not want to look back. He wanted never to see the lines of those trees again. After several moments, he heard the sound of Laura softly weeping, something that a week before would have seemed all but unimaginable to him. And he had been weeping too, he realized. Still he waited, as the cold within began to dissipate, and the warmth of the open air began to penetrate his flesh, and he began to breathe more evenly, and he was able to wipe the tears from his eyes and cheeks. But the horror still clung to him.

Only after they had journeyed on for several minutes could he feel his limbs recovering enough of their vitality to allow him to move. He rose from the deck stiffly and, still trembling, walked toward the rear of the vessel, looking down at his feet so that he would not catch so much as a glimpse of Ghostwood receding (much too slowly) into the distance behind them. When he reached the stern, he raised his eyes to Oriens, who returned his gaze with a solemn, almost indignant expression. Then he looked at Laura, who was bent forward, staring downward, shaking. He knelt beside the bench, placing his hands gently on her shoulders as much to comfort himself as to reassure her, and she raised her face to him, streaked with tears, with a look of pure grief in her eyes. They said nothing, but after a moment they rested their heads together and remained still.

After several moments more, Oriens spoke: "The maker of this world is unspeakably cruel."

Michael and Laura still said nothing.

Then, more bitterly, he added, "To know this world — truly know it — is to have found a corpse."

This time, Michael did not demur.

"I think," Oriens continued, "I should like to drown it in fire. I should like . . ." He paused, and then his voice became milder: "But, for now, we must pass by."

THEY CONTINUED DOWN THE RIVER FOR MANY HOURS more, saying little, and shortly before dawn they found the sheltered area the white bird had described, where the water slowed between two sandbanks near the southern shore, under the thick overhanging shelter of amber, purple, and ruby autumn leaves. They slept the better part of the day, ate less than usual, washed as best they could, slept some more. When the last of the day had glistened away into nothingness at the western fringe of the world, they unmoored the boat and—still exchanging only the barest and briefest remarks, and never once mentioning the ordeal of the night before—set out again on the wide, faceted, shining breast of the waters.

PART FIVE
Kenopolis

But we were fools. Already they had seen
Our foreignness. They gave us food to eat
Envenomed with oblivion. Soon the green
And surging swells had filled my mind, day's heat
Enveloped me, and I forgot the king
My father, and my home where dawn's light gleams,
And served their king instead. The precious thing
That drew me there, the pearl, was lost in dreams.

— from "The Hymn of the Pearl"

I

THE NIGHT'S TRAVEL HAD BROUGHT THEM OUT of the mountains by the time dawn arrived. The last of the high peaks had yielded a couple of hours earlier to the humbler elevations of the foothills, and the forests had yielded in turn to brush, thorns, and gorse and then to high grasses. And now, in the first clear light of day, the wide level stretches of the westernmost lowlands came into view, darkly green and softly yellow, untended sward here and shining fields of grain there, narrow canals glittering like sparse threads of silver in the immense gleaming fabric of the flats, a few small weirs just visible among the nearest of them, and everything quite open to the gradually brightening sky and to a horizon that seemed impossibly far away. Michael, after his several years sheltered in the close compass of green summits and deep woods, knew for the first time since they had set out in their boat how it felt to have absolutely nowhere to hide—no refuge, no path of escape—and he said so to Laura and Oriens. They did not reply, but from Laura's manner he could tell that she was feeling something similar; and Oriens, though his expression remained impassive, nodded in accord. But at least they were no longer alone on the river.

As Hyperion broke over the eastern edge of the world, with no mountains or trees to shield their eyes from its dazzling brilliance, they could see the black silhouettes of fishing vessels and merchant transports suspended in the scarlet abyss of sky and water ahead. And, well before the disc of the sun had entirely detached itself from the line of the land, their boat — its railing now draped with nets and hung with coils of fishing line — was in among the others, gliding calmly between trawling boats of various sizes and then, for more than two hours, alongside two large barges of raw lumber. No one paid them any obvious attention, though Michael constantly feared that someone sooner or later would realize that, unlike the other vessels on the river purporting to be out after fish, theirs was trailing neither nets nor lines in the water. Then again, why would anyone bother to notice, or to care? Surely no one apart from the authorities knew that there were fugitives to be found. The fishermen were deeply engaged in their own work, casting or hauling nets, dropping weighted lines for the rarer fish of the deeper waters, yelling back and forth, calling from one boat to another, steering into or away from the shoals, floating downstream or motoring upstream; and those manning the merchant barges clearly had no concern other than keeping to the broad middle current of the river in something like orderly succession, paying practically no heed to the smaller vessels at all. Still, if the police should pass, in either aerial barges or anemokinetic speedboats — and surely they would — the sight of two boys and a girl by themselves on a flatboat that was clearly neither trawling nor angling, in spite of all its theatrically distributed fishing gear, could hardly fail to excite their interest. "You'd better go under the awning," Michael said to Oriens. "Your eyes and hair stand out too much."

"Yes," said Laura, "that beautiful hair . . . that hair of yours stands out."

Without any change of expression, Oriens complied. A few moments later, Laura rose from her bench by the tiller, lifted its seat, and withdrew a flat gray fishing cap with a broad bill. "I thought so. Here, wear this." She tossed the cap to Oriens and he, thanking her with his customary courtliness, promptly put it on backwards. "Oh, no . . ." she said.

THROUGH MIDMORNING NO POLICE VEHICLES HAD appeared on the water or in the air overhead, but a little more than an hour before noon a great black aerial barge with blue trim came rushing from the west at full speed, its rotors positively roaring. Michael and Laura exchanged looks of something close to panic, but both succeeded in remaining still. The barge did not slow down as it approached, however, and was past them in a few moments, a hundred feet overhead and hurtling eastward. Quizzical voices arose to left and right; one fisherman shouted out to another on a different boat, "Must be an accident," at which the second shook his head and shouted back, "Probably contraband." Then everyone returned to work.

"Shouldn't someone be looking for us?" Laura asked. "Someone?"

"I think they are," said Michael. "But they seem confused about where they should be looking."

"Perhaps," said Oriens from under the shade of the awning and the low slant of his cap's bill, "because they have failed to find us on the river already, they do not expect to do so now. If they have searched only during the day, when we have been hidden from sight, and have not been willing to go out in the night for fear of the Shadows, perhaps they have assumed that we could not be traveling at night either. And perhaps they now have no notion where to look."

"It seems pretty foolish of them," said Laura.

"As I have said," replied Oriens. Then, after a moment, he added, "I did not know those vessels could move so swiftly."

"Oh," said Laura, "they can go very fast. At full speed, they can go from Kenopolis to Brightrill in about seven hours. But normal citizens can't use those sorts of aerial cars; only the authorities can. My father has flown them, though. He used to . . ." She paused for a moment. "I'm not sure what it was he did exactly, but he's the only person from around Brightrill who's ever been in one without being under arrest."

"How fast can vehicles travel on land?" Oriens asked.

"Oh, land vehicles are only drawn by horses," said Laura.

"It's not physically possible to make autokinetic vehicles that move at ground level," said Michael, "except for trains, of course. Phosphoric engines can't be made that small and still be powerful enough to move over surfaces with friction, because the vapors don't generate enough heat except under great pressure and in large quantity."

"I ask," said Oriens, "because I believe I can leave this world only from the place where I arrived. That is where my ship is anchored in the upper air, in the region of sublunary fire. So, when I find my sister, we shall have to return to your home forests by some means, and may have pursuers to elude."

"Oh," said Laura. And then, in a more emphatic voice: "Oh, I didn't realize. We'll have to go back by boat then, back up by way of the locks. I hadn't even thought of that."

For two minutes or so, Michael stared at the water, flashing and scintillating on all sides and far off ahead along the path of the river, tapering away toward the horizon in innumerable sparkling prisms and mirror shards, foaming in small crystal waves about the hull of the boat, occasionally affording a glimpse through a wavering ribbon of transparency into the upper depths where fish flickered past as bright bolts of iridescence. Finally, he said, "It seems to me they should've been more thorough in searching for us. It's strange they weren't."

"Oreiotopia is very large," said Laura. "My father always says whole armies can be swallowed up in the mountains. That's why the region has never been easy to control."

"They weren't searching all of Oreiotopia," said Michael. "Still, yes, I suppose you're right. But it seems as if there should be more patrols here at least."

"We're still a long way from the city," said Laura.

THREE HOURS FARTHER DOWNRIVER THERE WERE seven large common piers and several common slips in a long alcove on the northern side, at either end of which stood a tavern. Dozens of fishing boats were moored there, most of them already carrying impressive loads of fish in great open tubs or in their deep concave sterns, and fishermen were seated on benches and at tables all along the shore, eating from tin plates and drinking from pewter tankards, talking volubly, laughing, calling out for more beer to the girls bearing pitchers from table to table while deftly evading presumptuous hands. Michael was the first to see an empty slip flanked by two of the larger fishing craft, and Laura guided their boat into it. When they had moored, they used blankets and hooks from the storage chest to convert the deckhouse's awning into a tent, still attracting no obvious attention, ate from their provisions, spread out their bedding, and surrendered to their exhaustion amid the sounds of cheer and of boats gently knocking against their slips, and amid the mild warm breezes of the day and the odors of fresh water and freshly caught fish. If anyone had yet noticed the oddity of an ostensible fishing boat manned only by three children and carrying no catch, there was no sign of it. The raucous voices of the men scarcely intruded upon their sleep, though Michael was twice roused by his own troubling dreams (wolves and umbral figures in the forest again), and he found that, as the afternoon had worn on, most of the boats had returned to the water.

When he awoke for the third and final time, though, it was night and the slips were full again, and the fishermen were gathered at the tables and in the taverns in larger, louder groups, now with the additional noise of some rather disorganized singing. Oriens and Laura had already awoken and were eating dried fruit, coarse seed bread, nuts, and cheeses. Seeing Michael stir, Laura urged — commanded — him to eat as well, and a few minutes later they were discreetly putting out from their moorings and swinging back into the flow of the river. The large merchant craft were still out in number, in a long and widely spaced convoy, but only a few of the smaller vessels remained on the water. Laura eased the boat into a course parallel to a long barge laden with crates, stacked high and tightly bound with heavy ropes, but was careful to keep about thirty yards away, beyond the field of light cast by the lines of phosphoria strung along its railing. There were clouds overhead, and so even when the moons had risen the river remained dark. And, unlike the other boats, theirs had no lights of its own burning at its prow or stern. And so they traveled, inconspicuously borne on the easily gliding currents of the river, through the lowlands and down toward the city. Sometime after midnight, two speedboats, obviously police, went by in quick succession in the opposite direction, but did so on the far side of the barge, much faster than they would have done had they been on surveillance. Perhaps, Michael thought to himself, the truth of the matter was that there simply were not enough police properly to search so vast an expanse of land, sky, and river as they were trying to cover. That the authorities lacked foresight now seemed obvious; but perhaps they were also far less resourceful, far less numerous, than most people knew.

It was still in the early hours after midnight that the sulfurous glow of Kenopolis appeared on the horizon and then began slowly to swell upon the darkness before them. Gradually, the high, oblong, brazen towers, stippled with scattered lights, became visible against the dark gray sky, and then in time the glowering yellow of port lights and streetlamps and hovering aerial vehicles as well. As they neared the vast harbor, opening out on the southern side of the Phlegethon, the city loomed above them with such monstrous immensity, and its shoreline awaited them with so enormous an embrace, that it scarcely seemed real. Michael had been much smaller when he and his father and Paichnidia had left for Oreiotopia, and since then he had forgotten just how huge and jagged and soaring the Kenopolitan skyline was. He had also forgotten the noises of the city. Sounds now flooded in upon them from every quarter, especially as they steered into the harbor and toward the reflection of the cityscape spread out like gold foil upon the water's dark vitreous surface: machinery, the sudden waking roar of the barge's massive anemokineton, the churning of the water behind it, the drone of port authority aerial cars in the distance, as well as innumerably many other sounds, all intertwining in grandly elaborate discords.

The great mouth of the harbor was unguarded, as always, since it would have taken more than the entire police force to create a cordon capable of spanning it; but there would be customs agents and police at the docks and at all the open canals. Laura's father, however, had told her and Michael where the disused docks lay, and where along the poor end of the port's northeastern crescent the Red Clover canal was to be found, and how to recognize the old, empty Red Clover warehouses. So, not long after entering the harbor, their motor inaudible under the sound of the barge's, they detached themselves from the larger vessel's shadow; and as the convoy broke apart, each vessel heading for its own dock, Laura was able to steer furtively around and through the shadows of other slowly motoring barges, toward the unlit extremity of the old warehouse district, without much fear of being noticed.

It took them almost thirty minutes to cross the stretch of open water beyond the diverging larger vessels and to reach the sagging wharves of the northeast end, where not a single phosphorion was burning. Both moons had already set, and had it not been for the dim glow cast by the city lights beyond, this whole section of the harbor would have been more or less invisible under the clouded sky. As it was, it was only when they were within fifty yards of the wharves that Michael and Laura could definitely make out the large, faded clover — its shape, not its color — painted high up on the bare brick façade of an abandoned warehouse. The mouth of the canal, which was the standard twenty-five feet wide in order to allow traffic both ways, had at some time in the distant past been closed off with a heavy iron chain stretched between two large posts, about three feet above the current level of the water; but, also at some time in the distant past, the ring bolt on one post had been sawn through (maybe by smugglers, maybe by "our circle"), leaving the chain to hang from the other straight down into the water.

"Father says this is a dangerous part of the city," said Laura.

"It seems deserted," remarked Oriens.

"Not entirely," said Michael.

With the anemokineton on its lowest, quietest setting, Laura maneuvered the boat into the canal and began heading up the waterway, keeping to the right side. The canal walls were high, stony, ominously dark; at the present water level, they rose above the boat a good dozen feet and more; and once, when the prow of the boat brushed against the one on the right, a surprisingly loud hollow echo ran along them. An unpleasant mustiness emanated from every side, and a fetid and at times acrid pungency rose from the water. It was, on any view, little more than a grim, cavernous trench. But Michael found a certain comfort in its darkness; he preferred concealment to the sense of exposure that had oppressed him from the moment they had reached the foothills.

"The water here seems to have a kind of oil on its surface," said Oriens, peering over the railing. "And there are small creatures swimming in it."

"Rats," said Michael.

"Are they poisonous?"

"No," said Michael, "but the water is."

"Will it damage the boat?" Oriens asked.

"No," said Michael. "But it wouldn't be safe to drink."

"I was not tempted to do so," said Oriens.

"The lanes up in the city all have bridges over the canal," said Laura, "but I don't know how we'll know which one is Trifle Lane."

"Oh, that's easy," said Michael, feeling some satisfaction in usurping Laura's usual privilege of speaking with a native's special knowledge: "there's a sign under every bridge, on either side, and a paved landing for embarking and disembarking, and steps leading up to the street."

"Oh," said Laura.

There were no real bridges or lanes for a long way, however, only the occasional loading platform with a rusting steel stairway leading up to a decaying storehouse and to a narrow metal gantry spanning the canal. No voices descended from above, no lights shone in the darkness overhead; and the only sounds were the murmuring of the anemokineton and the sloshing of waves continuously folding away from the prow and dashing with a soft hiss against the stone walls. After a little more than a mile, however, the somber glow of the city's lights began to invade the canal, and the avenues' stone bridges began to appear, with their distinctively Kenopolitan rows of flame-shaped finials on the parapets, and the sounds of other human beings began to sift down from above. Yet, as the boat progressed, Michael began to realize that what he was hearing was not quite the mixed urban clamor he remembered from years before, but rather an altogether more unsettling combination of noises: curt, commanding shouts, twice a shrill whistle, heavy boots ringing on cobblestones, singly or in troublingly regular synchrony. Under the first of the bridges, the lettering on the large street sign bolted to the wall was impossible to make out, as was also the case under the second and third bridges, but they did not dare light a phosphorion. Laura's father, however, had told them that Trifle Lane was a great many blocks from the harbor, and by the fourth bridge the light had become just strong enough to make the sign — "Wise Dragon Lane" — barely legible. It was strong enough also, at least just as the boat passed under the bridge's arch, to illuminate two rather squalidly dressed men — one in old sailor's flannels, the other wrapped in a bizarrely large woolen coat better suited to the winter months — huddled together at the back of the paved platform on the left. Laura gasped on seeing them and Michael rose to one knee; but Oriens merely stared in unperturbed silence. Each man had long, lank hair and an unkempt beard; neither moved; both simply stared at the boat vacantly, not even bothering to follow it with their eyes as it went by; and one of them, in a hand that was weakly propped upon his knee, held a long clay pipe from which a sickly wisp of viscid smoke floated upward into the shadows of the barrel vaulting above. There was a faint sweet fragrance in the air, like that of nectar-heavy blossoms just beginning to decay. And then the boat was past the bridge and the normal odor of the befouled waters returned in all its purity.

"Were they ill?" asked Oriens.

"I think they were smoking the Dreaming," said Michael. "Oneirodakryon, that is — a kind of drug that comes from an eastern tree sap."

"A medicine?" asked Oriens.

"No," said Laura.

"Yes," said Michael, "in a sense."

"For what illness?" asked Oriens.

Michael lowered his eyes to the unctuous water. "Life," he said, "in this world."

"Oh, Michael," said Laura impatiently, "don't be so . . . what's the word? . . . so *morbid*."

"Sorry," said Michael after a moment. "I miss my father." What he had been thinking, however, was how foolish he had been to speak to Oriens of the beauty of this world only a few nights earlier, and that perhaps Ghostwood or this long dismal ditch was the true face of Kenogaia, however prettily veiled it often was: a narrow and menacing passage through corrupted waters, in silence and darkness, among broken souls.

"What does it do for them?" persisted Oriens.

"I don't really know," said Michael, "but I think it lets them see other worlds . . . dream other worlds . . . better than this one."

Oriens was silent for several moments, and then remarked, "Dreams like that, I suspect, are often memories that have been buried deep within one's souls."

Eight more bridges passed overhead, seven more dissolute figures went by, sprawling or limply reclining on landings on one side or other of the canal, and as the boat progressed the light gradually grew in intensity, and the noises from above grew louder and more frequent; but still the city did not sound like itself, and Michael became increasingly agitated at the cold cheerlessness of the sounds it did make, and at the way they made the clingingly dismal atmosphere of the canal seem even bleaker than it already was. He also began to wonder why he had neither seen nor heard any sign of aerial omnibuses, since his memories of the city were filled with them. The only vehicles he had noted by the time the boat reached the next bridge were police cars in flight, passing above crosswise at three different junctures, each time too quickly and at too great a height to be searching for anything in the deep trough of the canal. "Could we pause here?" he suddenly asked. "I want to look." The light from the street was for some reason vividly pink, the road sign — "Holy Convalescents Avenue" — was clearly visible, and there was no one on either platform.

"Why?" asked Laura, turning off the anemokineton even as she spoke.

"The sounds up there," said Michael, tying a rope to one of the platform's short, stout iron bollards, "there's something wrong with them. I just want to see what's going on, before we go farther in."

Laura began to whisper a protest, but Michael's curiosity had already carried him over the railing and onto the platform, and he quickly and quietly dashed over to the flight of concrete stairs curling upward toward street level. Just before reaching the top, he stopped, drew into the bridge's shadow, and peered out over the edge of the stairs into the avenue. The nearest lit phosphorion was an enormous sphere of frosted pink glass hanging above the opulent bronze and beveled glass doors of an establishment whose name, as inscribed in decorative red cursive on a large pink sign, was "The Pirate's Paradise." Beyond the door's panes, however, all was perfectly dark, and no sounds emanated from within. In fact, the entire street — its grand goldstone buildings and ornate frontages showed it to have been once an extremely prosperous district — was devoid of any traffic, either horse-drawn or pedestrian; and the only human presence was a distinctly disturbing one. Along the pavement on the same side of the street as the stairs where Michael crouched, standing at attention in a single line perhaps twenty yards away, were ten or so men in the jet-black and blue-piped trousers and tunics, long-billed hats, aeroballistic pistol holsters, black gloves, and high leather boots of police agents, each with a long baton dangling from his right hand; and pacing back and forth before them was another, rather squat police agent, this one with an officer's distinctive tricorn hat, its tall purple plume swaying high above his head, and a thin, pliant swagger-stick clutched in both fists behind his back. Michael would have descended the stairs again on the instant, but no sooner had he seen the police agents than the officer, reaching the far end of the line, wheeled around so that he was facing the bridge — in the process, revealing a particularly bulbous nose and a sharply receding chin — and Michael did not want to attract his notice by any sudden movement.

Not that, from the sound of things, the officer was likely to pay much attention to anything but his own words. "Now, men," he was calling out in a piercing but thin voice, "it's fifteen minutes till your shift goes on duty, and then five hours till the general curfew is lifted for the day. I know you've all heard it before, but I'm required by regulations once again to repeat your orders. I know we all find it dull, but these instructions come down from the office of the presiding minister, Lord Theoplast himself; so please save any questions until I'm finished, as sound etiquette dictates. So, then: The curfew remains total. Anyone found before the end of watch out of doors and not carrying a current permit duly validated by one of the eighty-two government agencies empowered to issue such permits is to be detained, manacled, stamped with luminous dye, and stored in the nearest temporary disposal pen, to be collected thence by the therapeutic detention wagon on its next patrol and taken to the local Ochlosyntactic Services facility for processing and preliminary remedial intimidation. That, at least, is the procedure for full adults or infants — ah, fully ambulatory infants, that is, needless to say. If, however, the violator of curfew should be a child between the apparent ages of eleven and sixteen, he or she is to be held at the place of capture and reinforcements are to be summoned immediately by a series of calm but vigorous and continuous insufflations of your emergency whistle — though without any display of panic, as that might embolden the children under charge. An order of special vigilance remains in effect for all such children, both male and female, alone or in number; and especially special vigilance is ordered for one boy in particular, of whom we have been able to obtain no photeinic image, either eisoptrographic, skiographic, or chromatographic — such, it seems, is his deviousness and perversity, his sly diffidence and furtive aversion of friendly eyes — but a lad believed to be possessed of extraordinary physical beauty and delicacy of address. He might even be described as offensively beautiful. Yet he is also known to be a dissident, and therefore almost certainly subversive of etiquette. Indeed, one of the infallible signs by which he is likely to be recognized is that he *has* no etiquette. If he is encountered, he is to be stopped; but on no account must you attempt to subject him to extraordinary restraint, physical violence, emotional coercion, or verbal abuse. You must in fact refrain from speaking to him any more than is strictly necessary, or from giving him any information for which he might ask, or from disclosing to him your name or the names of any of your relations, therapists, priests, or pets. You are not to consult him regarding your taxes, or the taxes of your relations, therapists, priests, or pets. Neither are you to seek his advice on matters of personal moment, romantic or otherwise, or to engage him in philosophical, metaphysical, or ethical colloquy. Above all, do not ask his opinion on questions of etiquette. In all such spheres, he poses a grave threat to your psychic and physical wellbeing, as also to that of your colleagues. He is, I warn you again, and as others have already learned to their surpassing sorrow, extremely dangerous, despite his apparently exquisite comeliness and sweetness of manner — though, as I say, a manner lacking in true, honest etiquette. He is also believed to be traveling in the company of at least two other children of the same approximate age and physical dimensions, one a boy, one a girl; we may assume that the latter might be slightly smaller than the former, and somewhat differently shaped, perhaps with distinctive hair or attire, but do not allow this to confuse you; it is an entirely normal phenomenon. And there may be some others as well, given the susceptibility of immature minds to examples of poor etiquette and to cognitive or psychological dysfunction. They too if discovered, are to be held in custody but left largely undamaged until reinforcements have arrived. Be vigilant, men. We must not let these fish slip through our nets. They are agents of social, spiritual, fiscal, and psychological disorder, terrorists whose aims are nothing less than the absolute annihilation of our whole way of life and of our etiquette. Am I understood?"

A bored murmur of inarticulate assent rippled along the line of men.

"Am I understood?" the officer repeated more loudly, now with a hint of the whip in his tone.

"Yes, sir," the agents answered, this time distinctly, though no more enthusiastically, and in only the roughest approximation of unison.

"Right, then," the officer continued, "are there any questions before we have our calisthenics drill?"

There was a momentary pause, a few heads uneasily turning and looking back and forth, and then the agent at the near end of the line — a fellow with great square jowls, a nose like a large snail's shell, and a bristling black mustache — raised a hand and called out, "Sir!"

"Agent Nimbleclam," responded the officer, striding down the line, "what do you need to know?"

"Lieutenant Thrashturtle, sir," said agent Nimbleclam in a hoarse and thick-tongued voice, lowering his hand, "I am frankly perplexed and obscurated. Are these children in fact fish, as you now say, rather than human children? Because I've been assuming that we were looking for human children, not fish, and if I've been mistaken all this time . . ."

"Ah, no," Lieutenant Thrashturtle interrupted, waving his swagger-stick lightly before agent Nimbleclam's nose, "any confusion on that score is entirely my fault." He stepped back and addressed the whole line of men. "How careless of me. I should guard my figures of speech. I was not speaking literally, but in what men of letters call a meta- . . . that is, a meta- . . . yes, a metaphorical, um, ah, tripe — or *trope* rather. That is to say, a pictorial image meant to illustrate an idea by similarity or, ah, analogy. Forgive me, as I know that most of you haven't received alpha-psychic schooling, and it was thoughtless of me to have spoken metaphorically . . . as though you were officer or priest material. The seditious bairns we seek are in fact human — human children with all their sparkling, effervescent charm and touching guilelessness and delightfully mischievous boisterousness, but also all their lamentable deviousness and perversity and frequent lapses of decent etiquette. You must not judge or despise them for that, of course, but you must arrest them. And in doing so, incidentally — I'd quite forgot to say this — you absolutely *must* address them according to the most precise rules of perlocutionary rhetoric, taking care to distinguish the voice jussive from the voice petitionary, the voice minatory from the voice hortatory, and so on. The direct imperative is preferable to the less compelling and more abstract injunctive gerundive and infinitely preferable to the invariably effete prescriptive subjunctive. *Oratio recta* only, moreover, and never *oratio obliqua*. This is vital." Lieutenant Thrashturtle paused for a moment, clearly for effect. When no one seemed to react, however, he continued. "As I was saying, in appearance this boy is quite enchantingly . . ." But here he had turned around to walk back toward the other end of the line again and Michael, seeing his opportunity, lowered his head and stole back down the stairs to the platform.

"What's going on?" Laura whispered as he climbed over the boat's railing.

"Police," said Michael, quickly loosing the rope from the moorings with one hand and pushing away from the bollard with the other: "they're all about. There's a city curfew."

"Oh, dear," said Laura, sounding momentarily like her father, as she switched on the anemokineton. "Oh, dear."

Three more bridges passed above them. At the second, there was another figure on the platform on the opposite side, this time a man drably dressed in old work flannels and lying on his back with outspread arms, apparently fast asleep if not dead, and with a clay pipe — its stem broken — lying beside him. At the third, the marching of several police agents' boots rang out directly overhead on the bridge; but apparently no one up there thought it worthwhile to look over the side into the canal, and by the time the boat cleared the bridge Michael looked back and saw no one there. Then there was a longer gap between the bridges, nearly twice the normal distance, and the canal was submerged in the enormous shadow of a huge, gray, undistinguished concrete tower rising high above on the right. Then came another, more tenuous bridge, with no finials running along its parapets — it was really little more than a slender steel catwalk with open railings — the sign beneath which read "Corvine Alley." Beyond that was another normal avenue bridge, where the light was fuller and clearer again, and there was no one on either platform; this, at last, was the bridge of Trifle Lane. With a deep sigh, Laura turned off the anemokineton and Michael tied the boat to two mooring bollards, fore and aft.

"What if someone steals it?" Laura suddenly whispered, as if the thought had not occurred to her until now.

"Well," said Michael, beginning to gather a few still unpacked items of clothing into his knapsack, "no one is likely to find it by night, what with this curfew, except maybe some Dreamers; and in the daylight, with all these police around, I think most people would be afraid to . . . But, well" — he stood up, knapsack in hand — "does it matter? We can't worry about it now. We have so much else to worry about. First, we have to get through the night without being caught."

II

THEY DECIDED TO SEEK SHELTER AT THE FRAVASHI house. A private residence, they reasoned, especially during a curfew, was surely more likely than a shop—even a shop with living quarters above it—to have someone in; and a single man was surely more likely than an entire family to be out. But the address Laura's parents had given them was, by Mr. Magian's account, two cross-streets away, and lay along a boulevard now patrolled by police agents. It was perhaps only ten minutes away at a normal pace, but just at the moment it seemed as if a vast trackless waste separated them from it. They hesitated near the top of the steps for some time, looking up and down the street as best they could, listening for the soles of boots ringing on cobblestones or for the low drone of aerial thrust rotors overhead; but, for all they could hear, this part of the city might have been entirely deserted. Even the windows of the homes were dark, all of them, which seemed quite ominous.

"Should we not go now?" asked Oriens after several minutes. "If we wait, is it not more likely that our enemies will find us?"

And so they went, crouching low as they hastened across the street to the pavement on the far side and then drawing in as close to the buildings as they could. These were old homes, however — large, sternly angular, granite townhouses four stories high — and at first they were obliged to proceed by repeatedly venturing far out from the shadows of the walls to circumvent the large flights of polished stone stairs rising from the pavement to the front doors. Still no one else was about, and they moved as quickly as they could without making any loud sounds.

When they reached the first intersection — with Ember Avenue, according to the sign midway up the corner lamppost — they pressed themselves against the end of the final building, just beneath a low ornamental cornice, and looked up and down both streets. Now, at last, they did see someone, far down Ember Avenue, at the end of the block: the figure of a police agent, strolling more than striding, swinging his baton back and forth in indolent arcs; but he was walking away from them, and after only a few moments he turned the corner of the next street and disappeared from view. Even so, the intersection was wide and fully lit by streetlamps, and it took them several seconds to gather the courage to make the dash across to the opposite side. When they reached pavement again, they discovered that the homes here were even larger and that the stairways rising to their doors were conveniently flanked on both their sides by smaller flights of steps leading down to the sunken landings of the service entrances.

Now it was possible to proceed more quickly, as they could stay for the most part out of sight under the shadows of the great front porches and below the level of the pavement, exposing themselves only for brief intervals as they ascended from one landing and slipped along to the next. And, again, there were no lights inside the homes, no sounds, no signs of anyone awake within. Each of the downstairs doors had panes of glass in its upper half, and generally one or more narrow windows on either side; but the servant hall or kitchen or whatever else it was that lay beyond the glass was in every case perfectly dark. Twice they paused, lingering in a sunken stairwell when they thought they might have heard someone above on the pavement; but both times they realized it was nothing and soon resumed the undulating course of their journey along the row.

"Does a curfew mean there can't be any lights on inside after hours?" Laura whispered at one point; but Michael merely shrugged his shoulders.

The next intersection — at a street called Via Indevia — was somewhat broader than the previous one, as if the scale of the city were shifting as they moved from the merely respectably prosperous district near the bridge toward the profligately prosperous district a few streets onward. Again they pressed close to the edge of the last house on the block for some time, as though clinging to a ledge-wall above a deep canyon, looking and listening intently for patrols; but no police agents were in sight in any direction and, again prompting one another with wordless glances, they fled across the open space as quickly as they could without raising a clamor from the stones, and then hastened over the pavement and down the service stairs of the first house on the opposite side.

"Four more to go, I think," said Laura.

As they began to move toward the stairs leading up to the pavement, however, a single shrill whistle sounded in the distance, somewhere behind them, echoing along the stone façades, and they became motionless.

"They've seen us," said Laura.

There was no sign of pursuit, however: no shouts, no clatter of boots, no beams from phosphoric torches sweeping across the stairwell's entrance. Instead, a single, clear, casual, quite cheerful voice called out from — it now seemed — just around the corner above, on this side of the intersection: "Hello, there! Is that you, Nimbleclam?"

And, from what seemed the corner opposite, on the other side of Trifle Lane, another voice — equally affable but somewhat lower and thicker — called back: "Yes. Is that you, Limpsnake?"

"Yes, yes," the first voice replied. "Our patrols seem to be overlapping."

"Wait there," called Nimbleclam. "I'll join you. It's getting boring all on my own." And then there was the sound of boots crossing the road at a leisurely pace. "Good to run into you," said Nimbleclam when he was obviously standing only yards beyond the top of the stairs.

"Indeed," said Limpsnake, from just as nearby. "This seems so pointless, really."

"Which way are you going?" asked Nimbleclam.

"Oh, I thought I'd head down to the bridge now, and then over to the other side. Nothing's happening here."

"Well, then, I'll come along," said Nimbleclam.

"Is that on your patrol route?" asked Limpsnake.

"Well, no, but who's to know? It doesn't make much difference, one way or t'other."

"No, I suppose not. I should be doing my nightly check of the quarantined house, but why bother? There's no one there, and I couldn't see anyone from the street if there were."

"By the way," said Nimbleclam, as if just recalling something very interesting, "these children we're to keep a special eye out for . . ."

"Yes?" said Limpsnake after several seconds of silence.

"Had you heard anything about them being . . . well, being *fish*?" asked Nimbleclam.

"Fish?" said Limpsnake. "No, no, I hadn't."

"Well, I hadn't either," said Nimbleclam, "but apparently it's been going about."

"Oh?" said Limpsnake, with a note of bewilderment in his voice.

"Well, anyway," said Nimbleclam, "on no account should we be looking for fish. These children may very well be fish, for all we know — word is they probably are — but they don't look like fish."

"Oh, yes?" said Limpsnake.

"Yes," said Nimbleclam. "There's no need to look for fish at all."

"That's good to know," said Limpsnake. "Thank-you for filling me in on that, mate. My, my. There could've been considerable confusion on that score. You'd think our briefings would cover these matters."

"Wouldn't you just?" said Nimbleclam. "That's officers for you: always worrying about punctuality and neatness and metaphorical tripes and proper etiquette and proper pronunciation and rhetorical modalities and whatnot, but never giving us the information we really need to do our jobs."

"True, all too true," said Limpsnake. "But who gets the blame when things go all topsy-turvy, ay? That's the question. Us. Well, all right, let's be going, then."

The sounds of their boots retreating across the street and down the far pavement and of their interweaving voices dwindled away.

Michael took a deep breath. "All right," he whispered, "four more houses, then."

And so they went, swiftly but carefully, down into the next three service stairwells and up and out again, pressing against walls and skirting the edges of the light from the streetlamps, Michael and Laura making scarcely any noise, and Oriens making none at all. But, just as they were crossing the last stretch of open pavement, they were brought up short by the quite horrible sight of a long, gently glistening puce cord strung across the entrance to the final service stairwell, fastened at one end to the iron handrail bolted into the stone wall and at the other to the flame-shaped finial that crowned the volute of the front stairway's thick marble newel post. And just below the finial there was a large, circular, yellow adhesive label affixed to the post itself, reaching halfway down to the curtail of the bottom step, on which was printed in bold black letters that stood out clearly in the lamplight, "Warning: Exorcism and Chemical Sanitation Site (dangerous organic, syn-thetic, and psychic contaminants)." Just below that, a second label — smaller, diamond-shaped, and bright red — read, "Warning: Criminal Investigation Site (gloves and decorum required)." Below that, a third label — larger again, shaped like a blue flower with many petals — bore words in the thin, fluent script of the Sacerdotal Authority: "Violation of this cordon constitutes profanation of a temporary sacred temenos. Transgressors will be arrested, subjected to a corrective confessional regimen, and in extreme cases remanded to the Bureau of Psychopompic Therapy (but denied sacra-mental disposition of their remains)." Another cord was strung across the bottom of the main staircase itself with a puce and silver quarantine seal dangling from two steel clips midway across. And Michael, lifting his eyes in stunned misery, saw that the large white oblong of some official notice was clumsily pasted over the heavy glass panels of the wide front door at the top of the stairs. "This was the house the police agent meant," he whispered. "Are you sure this is where the Fravashi family lives?"

Laura looked at him with a forlorn expression, withdrew a small slip of wrinkled paper from the pocket of her pants, unfolded it, and held it up before her eyes to read the address in the light of the streetlamp. "This is the house," she said, glancing up at the number on the large brass plate above the door.

Michael bit his lower lip in silence for a few seconds. "They've been taken," he said almost listlessly.

"Let us go down," said Oriens. "Surely we should not remain here."

"Yes," said Michael, stirring from his daze, "yes, we should."

Bending low to pass underneath the cord, each of them descended to the servants' landing. Here too a notice was pasted over the glass of the door, but it was illegible in the darkness. After a moment's hesitation, Michael took his phosphorion from his knapsack, lit it, and read the notice in a whisper: "This property sealed by order of the Office of Inquisition into Spiritual Maladies, and its occupants taken into protective therapeutic custody, pending counseling, catharsis, and absolution. Entry strictly prohibited, under penalty of indefinite incarceration and possible excommunication." He extinguished the light.

"Oh, the poor Fravashis," said Laura, very quietly. "Poor Persy. My parents will be . . ." She paused momentarily and then added, very quietly, "What now? The confectioner's?"

"Oh, no," said Michael in a weary voice, "not with this curfew. We'd get caught this time, I'm sure of it. I don't know how we made it this far. We have to stay out of sight."

"Would it be ill-mannered to enter this house?" asked Oriens. "As this is the home of friends, would we not be welcome here?"

"No one goes into quarantined houses," said Michael. "The penalties are very severe."

"I think we're past worrying about that," said Laura after a second. "Wherever they catch us, the penalty's likely to be the same. And that police agent said he isn't even going to bother to check the premises. I think even the police don't go into quarantined houses. Only priests and ministry officials."

"It would not be discourteous, though?" asked Oriens.

"Oh, no," said Laura. "Mr. and Mrs. Fravashi would insist."

"We'll have to break this glass," said Michael, "if we can . . ." But, as he laid his hand unthinkingly on the door's lever handle, it gave way and the door opened. "It's unlocked," he said. He looked at Laura with an eyebrow raised in suspicion.

If she could make out his expression, however, she ignored it. "I suppose no one bothered after the family was arrested," she said. "No one's going to break quarantine, after all."

"I . . . I suppose not," said Michael, though not with much certainty. He moved slowly forward into the darkness, relighting his phosphorion once he had advanced several yards. Laura and Oriens followed. They found themselves in a large pantry with black floorboards and with shelves along both walls, full of jars, boxes, and casks. At its far end, a pair of plain wooden double doors on swinging hinges admitted them into a large kitchen with a white tile floor. There were two great iron ovens there, each with a phosphoric vapor range on top, canopied by an apron of bright copper and a flue leading up into a broad black stove pipe, as well as four large sinks with taps; against the wall opposite them, between two other swinging doors, there was an immense steel refrigeration cabinet; in the middle of the floor stood two large work tables, over which a dimly glinting chaos of pans and pots and ladles and whisks and so on hung on racks suspended from the ceiling, along with dozens of large knives hanging with handles-downward from magnetic strips. Even by the light of a single phosphorion it was clear that everything was in immaculate order, and there was no fragrance of food or of rot in the air, or any crockery or service on the washboards, or any indication of recent use.

"Do they have servants?" asked Michael.

"I sure they must," said Laura. "But no one will be here now, under the quarantine."

"I know," said Michael. "It just doesn't look like they were all suddenly arrested and taken away."

"Maybe the police let the servants put everything in order before leaving."

The righthand door at the other end of the kitchen led to a flight of service stairs, somewhat steep and rather narrow, that went up to the first floor. Slowly, listening intently for the slightest noise, they ascended, still guided by the single light of Michael's phosphorion, and emerged at the top through a single door into a kind of anteroom with three long unadorned sideboards. From there, they passed through another, much more ornate swinging door, around a large ebony screen lavishly gilded and painted with figures from myth — dragons, gryphons, gigantic mountain fays, firebirds, sidereal gods — and into a spacious and rather grand dining room. A plush, elaborately patterned carpet lay underfoot, a coffered plaster ceiling spread overhead, and two splendid crystal chandeliers hovered over a long dining table of dark, polished wood, paled about by matching chairs.

"They're very wealthy, aren't they?" said Michael.

"I suppose so," said Laura. "They've certainly done well for themselves since leaving Oreiotopia." Then, after a moment, she remarked, "At least all the curtains are drawn." She pointed towards the blue satin drapes hanging down to the floor at the far end of the dining room. "Otherwise your light would be shining out into the street."

"Oh, yes," said Michael, lowering the phosphorion. "Sorry."

"In all the worlds I have visited in this cosmos," said Oriens, "some persons live in great comfort and security, but others in want and fear. It is a great evil."

"Our economics and social pathologies tutor," replied Laura in a quiet, absent tone, "Miss Osteodes — she says it's inevitable that economies have to work that way."

"It is a great evil," Oriens repeated simply. "Therefore it is not inevitable."

They moved on, out into the enormous front foyer, whose floor was also richly carpeted and whose ceiling must have been at least two stories high, though right now it was lost to view in a gulf of shadows. Opposite them stood the main entrance to the house. A large staircase led up to a long, open, balustraded landing overhead, and to the private rooms beyond. Off to their right, open double doors revealed a sitting room full of splendid furnishings and, visible through a smaller door at its rear, an adjacent drawing room, and to their left a broad passage led back to a sunroom, its linen curtains pulled across what were obviously glass paneled walls. They wandered about from one room to another, looking for nothing in particular, Michael becoming increasingly aware of how grim and sad the emptiness of the house seemed to him. He had, he realized, been desperate for the safety that the Fravashi family had seemed to promise, and for the comfort of finding allies here who might help him search for his father. Now he could hardly imagine what to hope for. And his father suddenly seemed infinitely far away. He knew now that just below the surface mist of his confusion lay a dark sea of pure fear, into which he might quickly sink if he allowed himself.

"Well," said Laura in a weary voice when they had returned to the foyer for a fourth time, "we should sleep, upstairs I suppose."

Michael was afraid that tears were beginning to form in his eyes, and so he kept his back turned to Laura and Oriens. "Yes," he said, without turning around, "that would be wise. For just a few hours, though. I think time is getting short."

The upstairs was as impeccably clean and neat as the downstairs had been. There was certainly no evidence of a sudden forced eviction or arrest. The beds in the capacious bedrooms seemed freshly made. Laura prevailed on Oriens — who was not conscious of any differences among the accommodations — to take the master bedroom, and then she quickly identified Persephone's room, two doors down the corridor, and claimed it for herself. Michael found Epiphanius's room soon thereafter, around a corner, nodding admiringly when he spied its large shelves of books — many of them with an appearance of great age and, therefore, of questionable legality — but he was too exhausted and preoccupied to investigate them as he normally would have done. He set the alarm needle of the hexagonal clock on the wall to just before six and released its three dangling chimes from their bracket. Then he undressed, found a washroom door farther along the corridor, found a fresh nightshirt folded under his pillow and donned it, and a few minutes later slipped in under the bed's covers. He noticed before extinguishing his phosphorion for the night, however, that the emerald green blazer, black trousers, and golden cravat of a school uniform were neatly hung upon a suit-stand near the wardrobe; and before falling asleep he had formed in his mind the first rough sketch of a plan.

"BUT WHY RISK BEING CAUGHT?" ASKED LAURA THE next morning with a hint of asperity in her voice. The three of them were sitting on the carpet of the sunroom in the pale early morning light, made paler by the thin white curtains. "You're just going to get yourself arrested. We can wait till dark."

"No, no, really," said Michael, "it's much safer during the day, when people are supposed to be out on the streets. And it makes perfect sense. And his clothes . . . the boy . . . what's his name again?"

"Phane," said Laura: "Epiphanius."

"Yes, well, his clothes fit me, and his school uniform is right there . . ."

"Do you even know if the schools are running now?" asked Laura impatiently. "Maybe the curfew has closed them. And . . . and how do you even know what school it is, or where it is?"

"It's the Temple academy here, the Ephebeia of the Clavorum Opificis Magni Aedes," said Michael. "The school escutcheon is right there on the blazer. It's the private boy's school of the largest Temple in this precinct — the Great Demiourgeion, they call it here — you know, the one with those gigantic relics — the two giant nails left behind when the Great Artisan finished building the lower heavens. The school's very, very prestigious. A lot of archpriests and government ministers went there. My father graduated from it. But it doesn't matter. I'm not going to classes. I just want to be able to walk outside without being noticed. As for whether schools are in session . . . I can wait to see. I'll look out first for other school uniforms. If they are, I don't think police agents would interfere with someone wearing a uniform from an alpha-pneumatic Temple academy."

"Can you be certain of that?" asked Oriens in a calm voice.

"No, he can't," said Laura crossly. "And," she said, turning to Michael, "why you?"

"Oriens can't go, obviously. His eyes and hair . . ."

"Why not me?" asked Laura.

"I have Phane's uniform right there," said Michael.

"Persy must go to school somewhere too," said Laura. "Does the Temple have a girl's school too?"

"A Koreia? I don't know. I think maybe . . ."

"Wherever she goes, I'm sure I can find her uniform. I can go."

Michael turned his eyes to the soft silver light pouring in through the curtained walls of glass. "Don't be ridiculous," he said softly.

"What does that mean?" Laura's voice was now nearly furious.

"I mean," said Michael quietly, "that you're the pilot of the boat . . . and the Fravashi family knows you, and if they're released and come back . . ."

"That's all nonsense," said Laura curtly.

"It was my idea," said Michael in a stubborn tone, "and I've already found the uniform . . . and . . ."

"And?" said Laura. "None of this . . ."

"And your parents already lost Rafe," Michael blurted out, a little more loudly than was necessary, "and you should wait here for them until we know whether we have another plan."

"Oh, Michael," said Laura after a moment, her voice sinking away, "please don't. It's not fair."

Several more moments passed in silence before Oriens asked, "Are you sure this Mr. Goëtus will be there?"

"If he's still free," said Michael, "I think so. A shopkeeper keeps his shop during the day. Listen, shall we eat something?"

But, as Michael began to rise, Oriens reached out and gently took him by the arm. "Michael Ambrosius," he said.

"Yes?" said Michael resuming his seat. "You can call me just Michael. We're friends."

"Forgive me," said Oriens, "I mean no offense. I wish to give you something, for your protection." And reaching around behind his neck, he raised his hands over the top of his head as though holding something between them, though nothing was visible at first; but, as he brought his hands away from his body, a thin golden cord shimmered into visibility and then, as it swung away from his chest, a small silver pouch with embroidered blue flowers appeared. Laura quietly gasped and Michael felt a cool shiver run down his spine.

"The jewels you brought with you," said Michael.

"Yes," said Oriens blandly. "They are very powerful, and I shall tell you as much as I can about what they can do. This cord cannot be broken, not even by the hand of a god, and so long as you wear this purse about your neck no one but you in all this world can touch it, much less take it from you or remove any of its gems. Nor can anyone take one of these gems from your hand unless you freely give it."

"I mustn't take them," said Michael. "They're for your protection. Your whole reason for being here . . . your journey . . . your sister . . ."

"And your father?" said Oriens. "Again, no one can take them from you. They are safe with you. And my hopes for finding my sister lie in your hands, so in protecting you they protect her and me. Even now, my guide is seeking out a way to reach her, and we shall await you here, so that we may all go together and win her back."

"I can't be certain . . ."

"You can, if you wish it. You must simply master your doubt. Then you will become invincible. Not even a god can change victory into defeat for one who has vanquished himself."

"No," said Michael, more pathetically, "I truly can't."

"I am sorry," said Oriens, now with a faint but kind smile, the otherworldly blue of his eyes seeming to shine even more brightly than usual, "but you fail to understand. You have said I am your friend, and I say you are mine. You are not free, then, to refuse my gift, or to fail to bring it back in order to protect us with it; and so you must return to us safely."

Michael lowered his eyes. "I won't take them."

"I command it," said Oriens, his voice still calm.

"Command?" whispered Laura, in a tone not of protest but of curiosity.

"Yes, command" — his back grew somewhat straighter, his gaze more penetrating — "I, your liege, Prince Oriens Anatolius of House Enteles, regent and heir to the Kingdom of Pleroma, son of the High and Hidden King and of the Queen Beyond the Veil, and brother to the Princess Aurora Orthrina, keeper of the vessels of light."

Michael smiled bleakly and raised his eyes to look directly at Oriens. "You're not my prince," he said. "I'm not from your world."

"Oh, but you are," Oriens replied, stretching out his arms and placing the cord over Michael's head and around his neck, so that both cord and purse vanished in an instant. "You think you know yourself, but your true self is hidden from you. As my guide would say, within you there are two birds seated upon a single bough, and one eats of the fruit of the tree and is sated by it, and so is content to stay where it is, but the other does not eat, and looks instead to the skies and remembers its true home, and longs to take wing. Heed the second bird's wisdom. Follow its desires. You have passed through many lives, worn many names, been made to forget again and again, wandered in this dark prison of Kenogaia, this sorcery, this maze of dreams" — he withdrew his hands and folded them together in his lap — "but the glory that sleeps within you is from above, is from my kingdom, and is mine to call upon, and mine to awaken. And, in truth" — here his smile, for all its kindness, took on a hint of regal haughtiness — "your father pledged himself, and therefore his entire house, to my cause long ago. You cannot break faith with him."

III

THE DAY WAS SLIGHTLY WARMER THAN WAS COM-
mon in mid-Autumn, but only pleasantly so. Michael saw now that
the distance between the Fravashi home and the bridge beneath
which they had moored their boat was not nearly so great as it had seemed
at night, or when traversed in a state of constant, quiet dread. Having left
the house by the service entrance and ascended to ground level as quickly
and diffidently as he could, he had discreetly insinuated himself into the
flow of foot traffic. This had proved fairly easy, since every one of the
pedestrians thronging the pavements seemed to be hastening along with
downcast gaze and in morose silence, or at most trading whispers with
companions whose eyes theirs did not meet. Michael too tried to keep his
eyes down, but could not help but look up now and again at the crowd.
Unlike those of the almost uniformly pallid inhabitants of Brightrill (Mr.
Philon excepted), these faces were as various in complexion as all the distinct
peoples of Kenogaia: black and white and brown and olivine and coppery
and tan. Nothing could lighten his mood, but he was at least reminded of
how rich the life of the city was, how it had all delighted him as a child,
and how much he had at first missed it on moving to Oreiotopia.

Not that he had time to dwell on such thoughts just now. From here,
the Via Indevia and Ember Avenue were both visible; and, at the far end
of the street's long corridor of immense town homes — their stones softly
gold, or pearl, or darkly bronze, or ruddy — the bridge was a just perceptible gleam of polished pastel stone in the morning light. Pressing his
chin against the smooth silk of his cravat, he continued moving forward,
matching the general pace. He was conscious that his heart was beating
rapidly and that he was grinding his jaws, and so he knew he must be
quite afraid; but somehow he felt (as he frequently had these past few
weeks) as if he were at a slight remove from himself, watching from a safer
vantage — or, perhaps, as if he were dreaming, half aware that he was not
awake, and half unaware. Then too there was the odd atmosphere of unre-
ality emanating from the city itself. Certain things immediately reminded

him of early childhood: the feel of pavement underfoot, the fragrance of stone, tar, coal smoke, and phosphoric vapor in the air; men attired in what was apparently the current style (jackets cut long, with glossy lapels and broad shoulders, bright cravats in solid colors, two-tone shoes); women arrayed in what also must be the prevailing fashions (tightly tapering knee-length skirts, shoes or boots with high stiletto heels, billowing sleeves, hair in florid masses of curls or swept into shining cowls, lips positively effulgent with crimson or scarlet or coral-pink lipstick); children in trim school blazers and either sharply creased trousers or stiffly pleated skirts and serge stockings. But other things were queerly absent: voices raised in mirth or anger or simple casual conversation, the cries of news-sheet vendors, children laughing, the happy chaos of people strolling or running or crossing one another's paths, or gathering in small groups in the middle of the pavement while others tried to get around them. It was obvious that no one felt it wise to linger or to diverge from his or her normal route. And there were no carts out, no hooves ringing on the cobbles, no sounds of steel-hooped wheels.

As he came to the Via Indevia, Michael briefly raised his eyes. A tall police agent was standing on the curb, idly tapping the palm of one hand with his baton, serenely staring toward the opposite side of Trifle Lane, and paying absolutely no attention to the pedestrians who were obliged to swing wide to get around him. Then, just as he was about to lower his gaze again, Michael noticed an emerald blazer and gold cravat like his own, on a blond schoolboy about his own age coming from the opposite direction and carrying a green satchel on a shoulder-strap; and both satchel and blazer were emblazoned with the escutcheon of the Clavorum Opificis Magni Aedes (a field gules, two crossed nails, a hammer, four stars of differing hues, and both moons). The boy did not look up as he passed by. It was only a moment later, as Michael was stepping down from the curb and crossing the road — past a crossing guard in her official bright orange tunic, silently and sternly waving her orange paddle — that he realized with a small twinge of terror what it probably signified that the other boy had been walking the other way. At once, the dreamlike feeling disappeared, his distance from himself collapsed into a stark immediacy, and he tried to swallow, but without success. Quickening his steps ever so slightly, he looked up again at the backs of the figures ahead, resolutely striding onward, as well as at the grim downturned faces swiftly passing by in the opposite direction. As he stepped up onto the curb again, he glanced obliquely at the opposite side of Trifle Lane, where at once he saw two other boys, about his own age, also wearing the Temple academy's uniform, also carrying satchels, also walking in the opposite direction. Then he noticed two dark-haired girls perhaps a year apart in age, wearing what was obviously the same blazer (though in a feminine cut, with wider lapels), greet the two boys with very slight nods of the head and then hurry past them in the same direction as Michael was taking. For a moment, as he lowered his gaze again and tried to suppress a grimace of dismay, it occurred to him that perhaps it should have been Laura making this trip after all.

Still, though, he continued forward, letting the flow of the crowd carry him along, trying to appear unworried. He came to the end of the pavement, crossed Ember Avenue, and had nearly reached the bridge, when he felt a hand fall gently but powerfully upon his right shoulder, and heard a somewhat gruff voice say, "Young sir, excuse me." And as the hand brought him to a halt and began to turn him about, the voice added, "Pardon me, but I need you to stop." Michael raised his eyes to the plump but imposingly weathered features of a very tall police agent, who smiled wryly and asked, "Are you going to school with the girls today, young sir? I might have tried it myself at your age, but you won't fool anyone."

"Ah, no," said Michael vaguely, clearing his throat. "No, I wasn't."

"Well, then," said the agent, releasing his shoulder but also looking him over with a quizzical expression, "I don't mean to seem rude, but you're going the wrong way."

"The wrong way?" Michael said, affecting a slightly distracted tone.

"You do belong to the COMA school, don't you . . . don't you, young sir?"

"I, well, I . . ."

The agent's brow furrowed.

"I'm sorry," said Michael, "I wasn't listening. What did you say?"

"You're supposed to be heading to the COMA academy, aren't you?" And the agent's eyes passed slowly over Michael's chest, from right shoulder to left hip, as if considering the absence of something that should have been there.

Then, however, Michael realized in a single instant both what the acronym meant and why the police agent kept addressing him as "young sir." Attempting to appear as calm and natural in his movements as possible, he straightened his posture, threw back his shoulders, thrust out his chest, and assumed what he hoped looked like the confident expression of a child of privilege addressing a social inferior. "Yes, of course," he said a little curtly,

"I'm at the Clavorum ephebia." Then, adding a hint of impatience to his voice: "Why are you stopping me?"

"Now, young sir," said the agent, at once stepping back slightly and assuming a more emollient smile, "I'm only asking because the academy is in the other direction, and under the current circumstances everyone's supposed to go directly about his or her business without any detours or . . . you know, playing about."

"Yes, well," said Michael, trying to sound haughty, but not too much so, "I've —" And then it occurred to him: "I've forgotten my books, you see."

"Oh, yes," said the agent raising a knowing index finger, "I did notice you didn't have your book bag about you, young sir. That explains it, then."

"And it has my music sheets," Michael needlessly added, thinking to justify himself a bit further, "and there's choir practice today. I'm a chorister, you see." He seemed to recall that this was an especially impressive credential for Temple scholars.

"Oh, yes?" said the agent with a sudden note of elation, his eyes widening happily and the crags of his lined face seeming to become somewhat softer. "I do love the boys' choir at the Temple. I go to Caeruledian evensong whenever I can. Confidentially, young sir, I was in choir myself in school."

"Oh," said Michael, tilting his head to one side, "were you at the COMA academy too, then?"

At once, the happy expression deserted the agent's face and he swallowed uneasily. "Well, no sir, naturally." He took another step backward. "But I went to a very good school . . . for my station, obviously. It was a secondary modern beta-psychic progressive school, with alpha-psychic rating in arts and music."

"Ah," said Michael, sniffing slightly and attempting to assume a generously condescending expression, "I'm sure it was quite fine."

"Yes, young sir," said the agent, now lowering his gaze to the pavement. "Good of you to say so. Well, then, you'd best be on your way, I suppose. I'm sorry to have stopped you."

"Very well," said Michael very dryly, and began walking away, feeling all at once a very real distaste for his own behavior and real pity for the agent's small but piercing humiliation, and yet also immense relief at having slipped past the danger.

From there it was only about two dozen yards to the bridge, where Michael had hoped he might be able to see whether the boat was still moored to the bollards below; but as he began to ascend the gently sloping arc of the span he realized that the parapet was solid throughout, with panels of pink marble set between the ornamental balusters, and too high to look over without stretching up on one's toes. This — when everyone else was moving so steadily, quietly, and sullenly forward — would have been to invite dangerous attention. And anyway, he thought to himself, it would matter only if he and the others succeeded in staying free (or alive) long enough to return to the boat. So he simply crossed the bridge and continued on.

THE SHOP WAS EASY ENOUGH TO FIND, JUST TWO blocks beyond the canal, on the same side of the street as the Fravashi house. A circular sign of glazed white hung above the door from a short brass pole, announcing in ornate black letters that this was "Glyka Goëtika: Confections and Sweets." There was, however, no indication of whether the shop was open or closed. Michael, glancing quickly from side to side to satisfy himself that no one passing by was looking up from the ground, tried the handle and found it unlocked. He entered quickly, sounding the small bell at the lintel, and closed the door as gently as he could. There was no one in the shop, but a sonorous male voice instantly and amiably emanated from the other side of the green curtain in the doorway behind the varnished counter: "Just a moment, if you please. I'll be out directly."

The shop was tastefully paneled and floored in a deeply polished red wood of some kind, lit by the mild yellow glow of small phosphoria set in sconces all along the walls, and filled with handsome display cases: narrow octagonal ice-cabinets capped by clear glass domes, under which cakes or tortes or other confections, with deep brown or golden crusts, or brightly colored icings or translucent glazes, were displayed on dark blue velvet like precious jewelry. Overhead, suspended from a white, molded-tin ceiling, a large fan with five leaf-shaped blades was turning so lethargically as scarcely to generate a draft. At once, Michael felt slightly more at ease. Something in the sober, delicate, traditional appointments of an old city shop was comforting to him, and summoned up some indefinable but happy feeling he recalled from early childhood, and he was quite content to stand there for a few moments allowing the sensation to soak in.

After a few moments, the head of a middle-aged man — a slightly receding hairline, thin curls of dark hair falling over the tops of his ears, short trim sideburns, an extremely neat mustache and goatee, a monocle mistily glowing at his left eye — appeared from behind the curtain. "Yes?" And then, at once, a look of consternation came over his face and he stepped out entirely into the room. "Now, you know you shouldn't be coming in here during school hours, don't you?" he asked, in a firm though very kind tone of voice. "Especially with martial law in effect. It's not sensible, lad."

Michael stared at him for a moment — taking in the exceedingly stylish cut of his long, forest-green jacket, the dark bronze of his narrow satin lapels and waistcoat, the bright red silk of his cravat, the frilly ivory cuffs of his shirt, his gracefully slender form — and then asked, too softly and perhaps a bit doubtfully, "Are you Mr. Goëtus?"

"Yes," said the man mildly, tilting his head back casually, an expression of curiosity appearing on his face. There was a definite elegance about this man, Michael immediately concluded. There was something distinctly elegant even in that small gesture.

"Mr. Symeon Goëtus?"

"Yes." Now the expression of curiosity deepened. "The very one. Why are you asking?"

Michael attempted to speak a little more loudly, with only minor success. "I'm Michael Ambrosius."

Mr. Goëtus said nothing.

"My father is Valentine . . . Prof. Valentine Ambrosius, and I'm . . ."

At once, Mr. Goëtus stood more erect, the monocle fell to his cravat on its black silk lanyard, and he interrupted Michael with a sudden, somewhat plosive, "Oh, good lord!" He hurried, though with considerable grace, from around the counter and past Michael, locked the door, hastily lowered a sign on a chain into the window from its casement, and pulled down two blue shades on rollers. Michael found himself admiring Mr. Goëtus's pinstriped copper and russet trousers and the shining ginger and white leather of his shoes. That strangely soothing feeling — that indistinct recollection from early childhood, just at the edge of his memories — was still making him oddly calm. And there was something about this man's manner, even in an obvious state of agitation, that reminded Michael of the existence of a certain kind of urbane bearing that one never encountered among Oreio-topians. "How in the world," said Mr. Goëtus apprehensively, turning to look Michael over again, "did you get here? The last we heard, your whole region was entirely cut off."

"By boat," said Michael simply.

"Boat?" An expression of both astonishment and incipient joy appeared on Mr. Goëtus's face. "What boat? From where?"

"From home," said Michael. "We came down the Phlegethon. Our own boat — we steered it ourselves."

"All the way from Oreiotopia?" Mr. Goëtus took a step toward Michael and gazed at him in frank amazement. "All the way? But, my God, that's extraordinary. How..." Then he paused, raising his hand with almost theatrical poise. "But wait. We, you say? We who? Is... is *he* with you?"

Michael hesitated to answer, though he was not certain why. Perhaps, he reflected, it was because the atmosphere of the shop was making him a little *too* comfortable. While he remembered all the better tradesmen of Kenopolis as being extremely courteous, and debonair to a fault, he could not recall any who exuded quite such practiced, even aristocratic suavity. "Do you mean my father?" he asked evasively.

At this, Mr. Goëtus's expression became vacant, and then grave. He lowered his hand and his voice became considerably less elated. "No, I don't mean your father. He was arrested weeks ago. I know that. I'm so sorry."

"Do you know where he is, then?" asked Michael, becoming more alert. "Have you heard anything?"

Mr. Goëtus shook his head. "I know he's been detained," he said, "and I have to think he's being kept somewhere over at the Central Ministry building. Everyone of importance tends to be interned there, at least at first. But no, I haven't heard anything certain."

"But he's alive?" asked Michael, now in a pleading tone.

"I don't know even that much," said Mr. Goëtus, his voice becoming gentler. "I assume he is — I feel sure he must be, actually — he's so important... and knows so much..." His voice shrank to a whisper.

"Then they're torturing him?" said Michael, now entirely returned to the present, and wholly miserable again.

Mr. Goëtus sighed and placed his hand lightly on Michael's shoulder. "They will certainly be using therapeutic methods of some kind. But" — he began to guide Michael toward the back of the shop, around the counter — "they aren't going to risk hurting him, I'm sure. He knows too much. They'll try to... persuade him, but not... not to damage him. Come, through here." He moved the curtain aside and ushered Michael into a fairly spacious office with white plastered walls and a large but simple desk covered with papers and account ledgers and pens and inkwells, a single phosphorion glowing at its center in a glass base. At the opposite end of the room was a pair of swinging doors. "No, I wasn't asking about Valentine," Mr. Goëtus continued. He led Michael to the old leather armchair in front of the desk, removed his own jacket and hung it from a peg on the wall — revealing in the process a pair of very old-fashioned puffed sleeves — and seated himself behind the desk on a swivel chair. "I mean is *he* here? You know" — he leaned forward and whispered conspiratorially — "the visitor?"

Again, Michael hesitated to answer. But Mr. Goëtus was staring at him with such earnestness, and with so deep a look of kind concern in his eyes, that Michael could not account to himself for his own reserve. "You know about him?"

"Of course. How could I not?" The confectioner leaned back again, placed his elbows on the arms of his chair, and brought the fingertips of his hands together almost as if he were about to pray. "I've been waiting for him practically my whole life."

Michael did not know what to say to this.

"Is he . . . does he really look like a child?"

"Well, yes, he is a . . ." Michael caught himself, but realized he had already divulged everything. "Yes, he came with me. And, yes, he's like me. I mean, he looks to be about my age."

"Where is he now?" asked Mr. Goëtus, an audible note of stress entering his voice. "Is it just the two of you?"

Michael yet again hesitated to answer and instead stared down at his own hands, limp in his lap. Where else was he to go, though, and whom else was he to trust? "No," he said. "My friend Laura came with us."

"Laura," Mr. Goëtus repeated to himself. "Whom do I know by that . . . ? You don't mean the pretty little Magian girl, do you?"

"She's not so little," Michael replied, a bit defensively, still looking down. "She's the same age as I am."

"Oh, yes," said Mr. Magian, nodding thoughtfully. "I suppose she would be by now."

"And she's not just pretty," added Michael. "She's a better sailor than I am. And she's braver too."

"And what of her parents? Have they been arrested also?"

Michael shrugged sadly. "We don't know. They were in hiding when we left, and Mr. Magian was injured and couldn't make the journey. So we had to leave them."

For some seconds, neither of them said anything. When Michael finally raised his eyes, he saw Mr. Goëtus cleaning his monocle with a handkerchief and staring pensively into the air above Michael's head. This continued for several seconds. At last, Mr. Goëtus placed the monocle back before his eye, thrust the handkerchief into his waistcoat pocket, and shook his head wonderingly. "I have no doubt she's as courageous as you say. She was quite a fierce little thing when I last saw her — too long ago for her to remember, of course. Just three or four, I believe. But, really, just the three of you, on your own, all the way down the Phlegethon. And they couldn't catch you. My, my." He lowered his eyes and gazed directly into Michael's. "It beggars the imagination. You're a remarkably brave little band, I have to say. If she's braver than you, then you must be a company of heroes. Good God, I'm quite sure I wouldn't have had the courage for that journey."

"We didn't have much choice," said Michael. "There was no safer way, and none as quick. They'd have caught us if we'd stayed, and my father's here."

"Even so," said Mr. Goëtus.

"And Oriens needs to . . ."

"Oriens?" Mr. Goëtus interjected.

"That's his name. The visitor, I mean. He's called Prince Oriens."

"Prince Oriens," Mr. Goëtus repeated, almost as if turning the name over in his mouth to see how it tasted. "How very remarkable. Please excuse my atrocious manners. I should offer you something to drink or to eat." He laughed tersely. "It's more than I can quite take in. I can tell you're a lad of some breeding, and . . . . But you said he needed something? Something here in Kenopolis?"

Michael looked down again. "I think he'd better tell you himself."

After another pause of several seconds, Mr. Goëtus said, "Where is he? Can I meet him?"

"We're staying nearby. We're hiding out in an empty house."

"The Fravashi home, I imagine. I hope."

Michael said nothing.

"Don't worry," Mr. Goëtus added after a moment. "It's probably better that you don't say. I know the Fravashis were arrested last week, and the house was searched and exorcised. It's quarantined at the moment, which might be the best sort of protection you'll find for now. Still, it's not ideal. The penalties for . . . well, that's the last thing you need to worry about. Still, sooner or later a psychic sanitation detachment will come to scour the place again, and perform secondary and tertiary exorcisms, and someone from the OSFS — the Office of Seizures, Forfeitures, and Spoliations, that is — will have to come to assess the property and furnishings and other possessions, in order to determine the family's ability to indemnify the state for the cost of their therapeutic incarceration, and for any penances or absolutions or corrections, or physical or spiritual adjustments, or psychopompic services and . . . and disposal of remains, if it comes to that."

"Where else can we go?" asked Michael, again meeting Mr. Goëtus's gaze.

"Here, I think," Mr. Goëtus replied. "I don't know where else for now. My own rooms are upstairs, but I also have a hidden apartment downstairs. There's a large storage cellar, you see, and a secret . . . well, the space isn't luxurious, but it's got cots, and a bath, and four separate quarters. I think it's safer than where you are, but . . ."

"But . . . ?" Michael prompted.

"Time, you see," said Mr. Goëtus. "Time's definitely against us. They've had your father for what, a month? And we've really no plan as to how to proceed, have we?"

Michael shook his head glumly.

"Right, yes." Mr. Goëtus looked away to the antique cloisonné clock on his wall. "It'll be a good seven hours till schools let out. I don't think you'd be wise to go out before then. What's that you're wearing? That's the COMA uniform isn't it? A pity. They're over on the other side of the bridge. But nothing's to be done about that. And we can't call over to the Fravashi home. The anemophone will be shut off there or, worse, one of the intelligence services will be listening in."

"Laura and Oriens aren't expecting me till then, anyway," said Michael. "And they wouldn't answer even if we rang."

"Of course not," said Mr. Goëtus. "You're all obviously too clever for that. Look, stay here, eat, rest, and then we have to get you back to your companions."

"It's . . . the police are out."

"Oh, I know." Mr. Goëtus began tapping his forefingers together meditatively. "I hope I won't disappoint you. I'm not necessarily the ideal tactician for a situation like this. I was raised in a family dedicated to the secret knowledge, true, and I've been prepared all my life for the eventuality . . . but, of course, to be prepared in the abstract isn't the same as to be expectant in the concrete, if you take my meaning. I never really thought I'd live to see this day." He placed his hands flat upon the desk and looked into Michael's eyes with a particularly apologetic expression. "I'm an artist, you see, in the culinary realm, and quite an accomplished one I like to think. That's my artist's atelier, so to speak, over there." With a charmingly drooping wave of his hand, he indicated the double doors. "I actually don't even do it for the money — my family was quite well off — but I'm very good at what

I do, and take pride in my craft. But espionage, intrigues, secret societies, seditions, subversions . . . I have no particular aptitude there. I'm working here entirely under the impulse of faith, I assure you, not out of some great confidence in my own proficiency. I don't want to give you any illusions." He sighed deeply and shook his head. "If I could pass the responsibility on to someone else, I would. Sadly, there've been too many arrests lately. We're few and scattered now. It's somewhat terrifying to me, I have to admit. But, I assure you, I'll get you back to your friends, and we'll get you all back here safely, come what may."

If nothing else, Mr. Goëtus's candor and air of composure gave Michael a bit more confidence than he had felt for some time. At least, he did not feel quite so utterly abandoned. "You don't seem very afraid to me," he remarked.

A slight, sly smile appeared on Mr. Goëtus's face. He tilted his head back and held his hands out before him with upturned palms, in a gesture of whimsical haplessness. "Well, whatever happens, one must preserve one's sense of style. In the end, it's often all we have. Balance, equipoise, a small, stubborn sense of personal dignity — there are times when that's what has to carry us through the dark places. Even so" — he spun his chair partially around, reached up to his jacket hanging on its peg, and extracted from one of its side pockets a plain but brightly burnished silver flask, larger than any other Michael had ever seen — "a little something to fortify the nerves never hurts." He turned back around as he unscrewed the cap. "A cordial of my own making. Not, I fear, for the young." He took two swallows, replaced the cap, and smiled again at Michael. "All will be well, I'm sure."

"May I ask, do you know how we'll get to them?"

"Yes, you may," said Mr. Goëtus with a touch of blithe playfulness, setting the flask aside. "We're in danger of making things too complicated. There are tradesmen's entrances in those large houses like the one you're . . . camping in, as it were . . . in the alleys around back."

"I hadn't noticed one," said Michael.

"Oh, but it's there. And you and I, I think, have an absolutely delicious torte to deliver this afternoon, one that I'll have ready by the time the schools discharge their imps. It will be something of a masterpiece, I predict."

IV

MR. GOËTUS SOON SAID THAT HE HAD TO open the shop again for fear of arousing suspicions. Before doing so, however, he led Michael through the kitchen— which was of only moderate size, with only a single large oven and a small work table of polished steel—and up a rather steep flight of steps to the small but tastefully appointed parlor of his apartment. There Michael rested in a comfortable upholstered armchair of antique design. A little later, Mr. Goëtus brought a plate of neatly cut sandwiches made from some sharp salty cheese and very freshly baked herb bread, along with a small dish of varied fruits and a pot of wonderfully aromatic tea. After eating, Michael drowsed through the early afternoon, dreaming at one point of his mother walking with him beside a mountain stream—in Oreiotopia, where in life she had never actually been with him—telling him that she was sorry to have been away so long, and that she had missed him terribly, but that she knew he would be well. He woke only when Mr. Goëtus roused him with a gentle shake of the shoulder and told him that it was time to go.

"How?" asked Michael, stretching his limbs, feeling far more peaceful than he had for many days.

"We've a delivery to make," said Mr. Goëtus, "to your uncle, the canon. You recall him, don't you? Very important fellow."

"BEFORE TWILIGHT," MR. GOËTUS TOLD MICHAEL AS they were crossing the bridge together, "I'll be out making my normal deliveries from my cart. Hold that a little more level, if you would."

Michael slightly adjusted the angle at which he was carrying the white, blue-beribboned box containing the torte. Another like it dangled on twine from Mr. Goëtus's hand.

"And?" Michael asked.

"So be ready, the three of you, near the back entrance. I'll come along the alleyway and ring twice, pause, then ring once again. Remember that.

Don't so much as peer out the window unless you hear two rings, a pause, then a third ring."

"Yes, I'll remember."

"And be there well before nightfall. With curfew, I have to finish my deliveries before dark, or we'll be detained and searched."

As in the morning, the pedestrian traffic flowed steadily, somberly, almost noiselessly, with no one stopping to greet acquaintances or to take in the view or gaze in at shop windows. It was nothing like Michael's childhood memories of Kenopolis. Once only an aerial omnibus passed overhead, and the bass drone of its rotors sounded outlandishly loud above the eerily quiet streets. The distance between shop and house seemed even shorter than it had in the morning, in part because Michael now had a full sense of where he was, but mostly because he did not have to walk it alone. He was beginning to think they would reach their destination without incident when, just as they came to the Via Indevia, a rather thin police agent with a young, pink face emerged from behind a lamppost and raised his hand. Michael attempted to remain calm, but Mr. Goëtus became at once affably animated. "Hello there, my good man," he said, with a loud heartiness that was almost shocking amid the nearly total silence. "How can we help you?"

"Out a bit early for deliveries," the agent said in a high voice, "aren't we?"

"Yes, indeed," replied Mr. Goëtus, as if the question had delighted him. "It's a special day, my good man. A high canon of the great Demiourgeion is celebrating his name day. Or, rather, it's being celebrated for him." Mr. Goëtus nodded in Michael's direction. "His nephew and I are taking a cake of my own confection for a little gathering at his house, a surprise for when he returns from afternoon benedictions. And, of course" — he raised the box he was carrying — "a few choice savories as well."

"Oh," said the agent, drawing himself up, "a canon?" He looked at Michael and touched his cap deferentially. "Good day, young sir."

Michael smiled courteously but not warmly and replied with just a slight nod of his head.

"Bit of an honor for you, sir," said the agent, turning his eyes back to Mr. Goëtus.

"Maybe so," answered Mr. Goëtus with a jovial smirk, "but upon whom else would they call for such an occasion, after all?" Michael could not help but admire the confectioner's effortless grandiosity.

"Yes, I imagine no one," said the agent. "But, forgive the inconvenience, for the transport of merchandise during the present circumstances I'm required to see your mercantile license, with a current certification."

"Oh, of course," said Mr. Goëtus, reaching into his breast pocket with his free hand, withdrawing a small teal card, and holding it up before the agent's eyes.

The latter stared at it for only a moment, and then, with an abrupt officiousness, practically snapped, "Good, sir, very very good." Then he stepped smartly backward and behind the lamppost again.

Mr. Goëtus smiled encouragingly at Michael and said, "Onward, my lad."

There was no great difficulty for Michael in getting back into the Fravashi house unobserved. Absolutely none of the pedestrians was looking up from the pavement, and the police agent was now far away and walking in the opposite direction. At the right moment, Mr. Goëtus placed his box atop Michael's and pretended to be searching for something in his jacket pockets, and Michael slipped behind him and down the stairs to the servants' entrance. In an instant, he was inside, had left the boxes in the kitchen, and was up the back stairs.

He found Oriens and Laura in the sunroom, seated on the floor against opposite walls, each wearing clothes they had evidently borrowed from the wardrobes upstairs: Oriens in black trousers and a loose gray pullover shirt, a soft, broad-beaked black wool cap in his lap; Laura in a plain but fetching gray dress with pearl-colored clasps down the bodice and a pair of simple black cloth shoes. At first they did not notice Michael's approach. Each was staring away, as if lost in thought, toward the milky haze of daylight pouring through the curtained walls of glass. But then Oriens turned his head, and then Laura, and as Michael reached the middle of the room the latter had risen, set aside a small red volume she had evidently been holding in her lap, run quickly across the carpet, and taken him in her always surprisingly powerful embrace. Oriens also rose and gracefully bowed his head in greeting.

"Oh, Michael," said Laura after a moment, detaching herself and stepping back, "I wasn't sure you'd make it back, you idiot. Why did you insist on going out there? As soon as you left, I knew it was foolish."

"Thanks for your confidence," said Michael, "but I did manage to make it back, and I found help." He straightened his jacket. "You know, you've hugged me more in the last week than in all the years . . ." Then, seeing that her eyes were rimmed in red, and perhaps a little swollen, he asked, "Were you crying? Were you really that worried?"

"No, it's not that." Then she scowled. "As if I would. Be sensible. I don't cry when I'm nervous. You might, but I don't."

"Are you well?" asked Oriens. "You have suffered no harm?"

"I'm perfectly fine," said Michael. And at once he realized how very happy he was to be with the two of them again. Something vaguely like hope was beginning to rise up in him. "Look," he said after a moment, "I have a great deal to tell you. We're not going to be safe if we stay here, but we do have friends in the city. One, at least. Oh, and I've brought some food."

"MICHAEL," SAID LAURA QUIETLY, HESITANTLY, PER-haps an hour before twilight, "the reason I was crying earlier . . ." She paused and lowered her eyes.

The three of them were seated on the floor of the sunroom again. They had descended to the kitchen to eat the sandwiches and much of the torte sent by Mr. Goëtus while Michael recounted the day's events, and then had prepared their knapsacks for the night's departure with more borrowed clothing and practical supplies (Michael changing into an ordinary shirt and trousers in the process), distributing the remains of the chrysastra blossoms they had brought with them (still moist and golden and fragrant) among their various pockets. Then, at last, they had returned here to await the first signs of evening. Oriens again was seated on the other side of the room, evidently deep in contemplation.

"Yes?" asked Michael after several seconds of silence.

Laura reached into a pocket of her dress and withdrew the small red book he had seen her holding earlier. "It's this," she said. "It's Persy's journal. I found it in her room, just under her pillows. The authorities don't seem to have searched here very thoroughly at all."

"Maybe it wouldn't interest them."

"Oh, it would," said Laura gravely. "It's full of the sort of things anyone would be in dreadful trouble for saying. I know I shouldn't be reading it, but I was just so desperate to know what had happened to them, and . . ." She shook her head, and a faint trembling of her chin and lower lip told Michael that she was struggling not to start crying again. "It's so horrible."

Michael breathed deeply, not really certain he wanted to hear any of the details, but could see that Laura needed to tell him. "Go on," he said after a moment.

"They were persecuted," said Laura, with indignant dejection. "For months.

Terrorized. The Office of Inquisition into Spiritual Maladies kept visiting, and interrogating the whole family, and kept threatening to take Phane and Persy into protective custody. Well, you know what the OISM is like."

"I've heard stories," said Michael.

"They started taking her father or mother away, sometimes for hours, but then sometimes for days at a time without any explanation. And when they came back they were always in a bad state. Once her father was gone for three days and returned weak and shaking, like he hadn't eaten all that time, and wouldn't say what happened, but just said he hadn't slept well since being taken away. And another time her mother came back with a badly injured hand in a bandage and with her hair all clumsily cut very short." Here Laura did have to pause to suppress her tears. "And then they took Phane for two days. Her parents were mad with worry. And when he came back he could hardly talk. And then it was Persy's turn. She was taken out of class at her koreia and three OISM counsellors took her in an aerial car to some institute for wayward children, and made her wear manacles on the way, and she had to put on an inmate's uniform and sleep on a hard cot, and she was there two days with all sorts of people asking her questions about her parents, and what sort of things they taught her, and how religious they were, and whether she'd ever heard them say anything impious or demented, and whether she thought they needed therapy or shrivening. They told her she might not be able to go home again, ever."

Michael, who had felt a tightness gathering in his chest as Laura spoke, finally interrupted, "Please, I don't think I want to hear any more."

But Laura could not stop yet. "There was some doctor there who told her that her parents had been abusing her because her diet lacked sufficient sedatives and sugar, and there was another that thought her hair should be shaved off for hygienic reasons . . ."

"Please," Michael repeated.

Laura shook her head. "She came back home then, at least. They left her hair alone. Of course, her parents were frantic and she was scared out of her wits. Sorry, I'm starting again." She sighed deeply. "Persy began keeping the journal about a year ago, but I think she already knew there was some danger on the way. Here" — Laura opened the volume to the first page and held it up in the slowly fading daylight — "this is how she begins: 'These are my secret pages. I am writing them in case I am no longer able to tell anyone what has happened to us.' And she doesn't write about normal things, friends or things she's bought or school." Laura lowered the book again. "It's all about her parents' beliefs, and about how they're waiting for the visitor from beyond the stars" — she glanced over at Oriens who still appeared to be lost in his own reflections — "and how he might . . . save them."

Michael said nothing, though he too now looked over at their companion. Was that what Oriens intended? He had never said as much. Was he here for anyone other than his sister, really? And, if he should find her, would he have any purpose then but to return with her to their kingdom beyond the stars, leaving everyone else behind? What did he intend for those who had waited for his arrival in hope, even when they did not know exactly what they were hoping for? Michael turned his eyes back to Laura, who was already gazing at him with an expression that — to his mind, at least — seemed silently to imply those same questions. He smiled a little feebly. "We must be kind to one another," he said, not entirely sure what he meant by it.

Laura, however, looked at him and nodded solemnly, as if she understood his meaning perfectly, then looked down at the book again. "Here," she said, turning the pages till she found what she was seeking, "listen to this. 'Father always says to remember that the Demiurge cannot see into our inward thoughts, no matter what the priests and teachers say. The light within us is beyond his reach. The palace of the spirit has inner chambers that he can never enter. As long as we dwell within that light, he cannot touch us.'"

"Dangerous words," Michael whispered.

"What's 'Demiurge' mean again?"

"You know," said Michael. "It's just from the word for 'Artisan' in the Noble Tongue. That's why temples are called Demiourgeia."

"Oh, right," said Laura with another shake of the head. "Stupid question."

"The ancient tongues weren't your favorite subject," said Michael.

"You mean I wasn't any good at them."

"That too. Does the diary tell you for certain what became of them?"

Laura nodded morosely. "About a week or so ago, the family received a notice that on the following day at noon they were to present themselves at their own front door to be taken into custody. There was a warrant for their arrest on charges of 'epistemic and psychic malfeasance.'"

"That's bad," said Michael grimly.

"There's a final entry from that night. Persy wrote a final . . . I don't know, a kind of prayer or confession that she says her father taught her. It's . . . oh, she has such pretty handwriting . . ." — Laura flipped to a place about three quarters through the volume, after which (Michael could see) the pages were blank —"Here it is: 'Remember, O my spirit, that the invisible world dwells within you, and that your true self dwells unseen within the souls and within the carnal frame that entomb it. But there is nothing hidden that will not become manifest. If you bring forth what is within you, it will be your salvation. Only that which you do not possess can destroy you. So fear nothing. Let the mind be subdued, like an unwavering lamp set in a windless place. This world is ablaze with splendor, like a royal chariot; it beguiles us with its grandeur. But the wise are detached from it. We have come from the light, and the place where the light came into being on its own is established in itself. That kingdom is within you. That light is what you are. So awaken, O my spirit, my priceless pearl deep in the ocean of oblivion; and, having awakened, overcome the world.'"

After several seconds, Michael stirred. For a brief moment, as Laura was reading, he had become almost unaware of himself; but now he came to himself again. "I've heard that before, I think. An old book . . . my father once read that to me, I think. Then he said not to repeat any of it. I'm sure that's what he read to me. Is that the last thing she writes?"

"Yes," said Laura, closing the volume and replacing it in her pocket. And, again, it was obvious that she was forcing herself not to cry. "I keep thinking of my parents," she whispered.

Michael said nothing else. He merely looked around the room and noted that it was beginning to grow dim.

"Should we go now?" Oriens suddenly asked, his clear voice breaking so suddenly through the portentous silence that had fallen on the room that Michael's whole body flinched and he drew in his breath sharply.

The light had become much milder in the past several minutes, and below the low casements of the glass walls had acquired a faintly violet tinge. "Yes, you're right," said Michael. "The evening is coming."

Oriens rose adroitly to his feet, while Michael and Laura got to theirs somewhat more laboriously. Before any of them had taken so much as a single step, however, Michael turned fully to Oriens and said, "May I ask you something?"

After a regal bow of the head, Oriens drew himself up straight. "Ask what you will, Michael Ambrosius."

"You say you are . . . my liege," Michael began. When Oriens simply continued to stare at him impassively, he cleared his throat and continued: "I accept this, even though I don't know anything of your world."

"It is your world too," said Oriens.

"I believe that also. And . . . and you've also called me your friend, and I am. So I ask this as a friend."

Still Oriens gazed at Michael, betraying no emotion; but, in the gradually deepening shadows, the brilliant sapphire of his eyes seemed to glow with an especially unearthly beauty.

"When you've found your sister, what will you do then?"

"Rouse her from her sleep," said Oriens mildly. "Take her back to her home."

"I mean," Michael continued, lowering his eyes, "what of us? What of this world and those here who've waited so long for you to come? Will you leave us behind? Will you leave this world as it is, in . . . in his hands?" He raised his eyes again.

Oriens smiled. "Do you think the kingdom from which I come is so careless of its own children? What the sorcerer stole from us is a treasure we will never freely relinquish. I have come for all the lost."

"How will that be?" asked Michael, his voice diminished to a ghostly rasp.

"I do not know," said Oriens, donning his cap and pulling its bill forward to overshadow his eyes. "No such world as this has ever existed before, and how difficult it will be to break the chains that hold you here I cannot foresee. Perhaps it will prove very hard. I do not know how long a labor it will require of me. But this I do know: the sorcerer made this world only by enchanting my sister in endless sleep, and the prison he has built exists only because she dreams of it, age upon age. What then do you think will happen when the dreamer awakes?"

AS MR. GOËTUS HAD SAID, THERE WAS A BACK entrance to the house, behind the kitchen and at the end of a large store-room with more shelving on either wall. Having found it, Michael, Laura, and Oriens had less than fifteen minutes to wait before they heard a horse-drawn wagon slowly approaching along the cobbles of the back alley and coming to a halt outside. Then came the signal—two pulls upon the bell-chain, then a pause, then a third ring—and Michael moved the small curtain aside from the door's single window pane to make certain that it was Mr. Goëtus waiting there. Behind the confectioner stood a horse-drawn wagon with a high canvas hood, harnessed to a sturdy bay mare. And beyond that stood the back wall and rear entrance of another stately town home. In quick succession, Laura, then Oriens, then Michael slipped out of the house, past four metal trash cans and a water-trough, over uneven cobbles with stray blades of grass protruding from between them, and up the retractable steps at the wagon's rear. Michael noted Mr. Goëtus attempting and failing to catch a proper glimpse of Oriens under his cap as he glided past. "Go forward, past the boxes" Mr. Goëtus told them as he folded up the steps and tied the rear flaps closed. It was dark within, and anything but spacious, but enough daylight still showed through the hood that they were able to find the clear area hidden behind towers of empty decorative cardboard boxes tied together with twine, and to settle themselves close together on the blankets spread out there — though these last proved small protection when, a moment later, the wagon lurched forward and began jolting its way along the remaining length of the alley. Soon, however, they felt themselves turning onto the smoother surface of the Via Indevia, and then onto that of Trifle Lane.

They must have been very near the bridge, Michael thought, when the wagon came to a halt and, a moment later, a man's courteously fatigued voice floated in from outside: "I'll need to see your mercantile license, if you please, sir." Michael felt Laura squeeze his hand anxiously.

"My pleasure, old man," Mr. Goëtus's considerably heartier voice replied.

And then, in a more clipped manner than at first, the other voice proclaimed, "Everything's in order, clearly. My sincere apologies, sir, I ought not to have stopped you."

"Nonsense," Mr. Goëtus's voice called out as the wagon started forward again. "Just doing your job, after all."

The sound of their wheels altered as the wagon began to rise up the arc of the bridge, becoming more richly resonant, and altered again at the end of the descent to the other side. Then the wagon turned, and then turned again a little later, and once more the cobbles of an alley sent uneven shocks through the boards and meager blankets on which the three companions were seated. Finally, they came to a halt. A moment later, Mr. Goëtus was unlacing the canvas flaps and urging them to move quickly: "My back door's open. Go in directly and up the steps. I'll meet you up there when I've stored my cart and unharnessed the horse and returned her to the stable. That's just a block away." They obeyed, Michael noticing that the air was now quite seasonably cool and glancing up briefly at the pearl-colored sky spread out above the brick walls and gables at the backs of the shops and glimmering with the ghosts of rainbows. The alley was already immersed in soft blue shadow.

What greeted them at the top of the back flight of stairs was a small dining room, attractively — even, perhaps, a little daintily — decorated with porcelain figures (a girl on a swing, a boy with a herder's crook, small pink pigs sleeping amid long grasses, and so on), and aquarelle paintings (flowered meadows, forested mountains, the sea at twilight, and so forth), and vases filled with long-stemmed flowers of various kinds. Heavy, wine-red curtains hid the room's single window, and in the center of the floor, on a carpet of evening blue patterned with fantastic white flowers, stood an antique oval dinner table and a matching set of chairs, all beautifully crafted from polished wood of a deep umber. Wearily and wordlessly, they laid their knapsacks together in a single heap in one corner of the room, and seated themselves around the table and waited.

After ten minutes, Laura spoke: "This seems pleasant," she said, though without any enthusiasm.

"Yes," said Michael absently.

"How long are we going to hide here?"

"I don't know."

Another fifteen minutes passed, and then they heard the door below open and close and the sound of a single person ascending the steps, and Mr. Goëtus entered the room. The twilight had so deepened in the room that at first he was obviously unable to see them. But he waved his hands over the two phosphoria ensconced on either side of the door, and the room was at once bathed in their glow, and he turned to look at his guests properly. "Oh, my . . ." he breathed on getting his first full sight Oriens, who was seated directly opposite him. He gazed for only a moment, turning his head to one side and then another; then he removed the monocle from his eye, slipped it into his breast pocket, removed a large silk handkerchief from his jacket, which he bent over to spread out on the floor, went down on one knee, and in a tone of abject awe said, "Your Majesty, it is my very great honor that you should grace me with your presence. All I have is at your service."

Michael expected Oriens to reply with his usual simplicity of manner. Instead, however, his face assumed a look of calm dignity, and with practiced formality he said, "We thank you for your hospitality, we gladly acknowledge your obeisance, and we rejoice in your fealty. You and your house have the friendship and blessing of House Enteles."

Mr. Goëtus visibly trembled, but did not raise his eyes. "Thank-you, my liege."

"Please stand," said Oriens.

Mr. Goëtus slowly returned to his feet, shook out and folded his handkerchief, restored it to his pocket, and only then raised his eyes to look at Oriens. His expression was one of rapt wonder, perhaps not unmixed with fear. "I have never seen such . . . beauty," he said, his voice now quite hoarse with emotion. "All my life, I've heard you would come. But I never imagined, not for a moment, that I would see you in this world."

"Please," said Oriens, "sit with us as our friend."

Michael was all at once aware of his own discomfort. For all of the mystery and strangeness and gracefulness of Oriens, Michael had never ceased to think of him as a boy his own age, quite remarkable in many ways, but still a boy. And he had never before seen an adult abase himself before a child like this, or a child speak to an adult with such an air of authority, and something in Michael rebelled at what felt like the impropriety of it all. But then, he also began to think, perhaps he himself had failed to address Oriens as he ought to have done. He looked across the table to Laura, who met his eyes with a dumbfounded expression that was probably much the same as his own.

Mr. Goëtus, by contrast, seemed quite pleased, and — removing his jacket and hanging it on a rack near the door — he sat down across the table from Oriens with a grateful and humble expression. "Thank-you, my liege."

Then Oriens said, "Please address me as a friend. Michael Ambrosius is disturbed by these rituals."

Michael was startled by the remark, but said nothing.

"Oh, I couldn't, my . . ." Mr. Goëtus began to say. "I mean, rather, that . . ." Again he fell silent.

"I am thankful for your courtesy," said Oriens. "The manners of my kingdom now seem to me like something from very long ago, and you recall my home to me by using them so gracefully. But we are all children of the same light. We are all free citizens of the same city, you no less than I. I crave friends in this place, not subjects. I have begun to think that this whole terrible world exists only because my kingdom has too long been governed by these formalities."

Mr. Goëtus merely stared at Oriens for several seconds, saying nothing, and slowly a look of serene happiness displaced the deferential timidity in his eyes. "What I really feel most, my . . . what I feel most is joy," he said at last. "We've waited for you for so long. These formalities, as you call them, are just tiny fragments of knowledge we've gathered over the centuries. Your arrival has long been foretold, promised, but why you would come, and from where, we can't even guess. We only know that we hope . . . hope for deliverance. So I long to understand. Can you tell me who you are? Can you say where you come from, and why you're here?"

"I can," said Oriens with a compassionate smile. "I believe I can also tell you the same about yourself."

V

S LIGHTLY LESS THAN AN HOUR LATER, AFTER
Oriens had finished relating his tale, an exceedingly quiet Mr. Goëtus
drew a shaking hand across his brow and began distractedly polish-
ing his monocle with his handkerchief. After two or three minutes of this,
he rose, retrieved his flask from his jacket on the coat-rack, and—with a
shy smile—drank rather deeply. Then, when he had replaced the flask, he
blandly remarked that he should bring dinner up for his guests. Oriens
thanked him and mentioned that he did not eat flesh. "Neither do I," said
Mr. Goëtus. When Michael and Laura offered to help, he directed them to
a small corner-cupboard in the shadows beyond the curtained window and
asked them to set out soup-dishes, plates, goblets, and utensils—though not
for him, as he had already eaten. The food had apparently been warming
the entire time, as Michael, Laura, and Oriens scarcely had time to lay the
table before a tureen of some cream bisque, redolent of herbs and roasted
nuts, a large platter of freshly baked breads and various cheeses, bowls of
berries and pears, a large block of butter, and pitchers of cold water and clear
bitter cider had been spread out before them. Mr. Goëtus excused himself to
tidy the kitchen below while the three friends ate. The meal was delicious,
and was soon devoured almost in its entirety to the accompaniment of
very little conversation, and seemed to put all of them in somewhat better
spirits. Michael began to feel free to forget his fear for a little while, and
even to luxuriate a little in a sense of safety.

"You three certainly know how to flatter the chef," Mr. Goëtus remarked
on entering the room again. "I was going to join you for a few moments
and ask you to tell me about your mighty journey. I suppose that can wait
till a later day, however."

"It was easier than I expected, really," said Michael.

"I don't think the authorities are quite as bright as they should be," added
Laura.

"No, perhaps not," said Mr. Goëtus, gathering up dishes, "but you mustn't
underestimate them even so. If nothing else, they have numbers on their

side. No," he added when Michael and Laura made as if to rise, "I can take care of these things. And I've a little dessert as yet to bring up."

"I don't know if I could," said Michael.

"Oh, but you must," Mr. Goëtus replied with cordial firmness. "I'm a confectioner, after all. I can't let you retire from my table without a taste of some of my better efforts. I'd be desolate." He carried away the tureen and soup-dishes on a prettily polished wooden serving tray, returned a moment later to carry away the remaining dishes, and then returned one time more. Now he bore a silver platter on one side of which was an assortment of small fruit tarts, on the other an artfully chaotic heap of what looked like exquisitely fragile and smoothly rippled amber glass in the shape of trees' leaves, and in the center a stack of small white plates with a pair of serving-tongs. "Tarts first," he said, serving two to each of them.

At the first bite, Michael was almost overwhelmed by the sheer richness of the flavor. It was sweet, but not excessively so, and the freshness and vividness of the fruits, nuts, honey, burnt butter, and exotic spices, perfectly balanced by the short crust and the custard base, were nearly intoxicating. "You *are* an artist," he said.

Mr. Goëtus laughed delightedly. "I do my best."

"That's the most delicious thing," said Laura. And then, having finished it: "What's in it?"

"Most of the ingredients are obvious to the tongue," said Mr. Goëtus with a knowing wink. "Those that aren't, however, are deep secrets of the craft, which I'm not at liberty to divulge."

Laura responded with a surprisingly giddy laugh. This in turn made Michael laugh.

Mr. Goëtus turned his eyes to Oriens and stared at him with an especially inquisitive and hopeful look on his face. "And you, my liege — I mean, Oriens — what do you think of my humble offering?"

Oriens was just swallowing the last of the tart with a meditative air. "It truly is a delicacy," he said. "In none of these worlds have I tasted any food quite so pleasant."

Mr. Goëtus seemed deeply moved by this. "I'm honored." Then he smiled again, and clapped his hands together. "There's one more for each of you. Please, they're small."

"It is very agreeable," Oriens remarked on finishing the second tart. "More so, it seems, with each bite."

Michael, who had been about to make a similar observation, nodded.

He was conscious that a welcome feeling of relaxation was settling upon him — of tranquility, even. There seemed no need to say anything.

"I think I'll sleep well tonight," said Laura, with a contented smile.

"I should hope so," said Mr. Goëtus. "Now, for the final flourish." He rose from his chair, took up the serving platter, and walked around the table to Oriens. "In my family, we've always observed an old custom of hospitality. The final viand of the night — or the final liqueur, as the case may be — is tasted by the guest who has traveled the greatest distance to be at the table. And I think we can say with some confidence"— he laughed dryly —"that you have traveled farther than anyone in history." He extended the platter toward Oriens. "This is a honey-brittle of my own decoction. The honey comes from the red seraph-bees of the southern mountains, and is flavored with a nectar distilled from fire-blossoms and morphinium berries and certain spices of the remote East. I consider it my finest achievement."

Oriens bowed his head graciously, took up one of the leaves, and held it up before his eyes. "It is very lovely to look at," he said, almost dreamily.

"It's still lovelier to eat," said Mr. Goëtus.

Oriens continued to smile in an absent way, absorbed it seemed in the exquisite translucency of the brittle. Then he took a small inquisitive bite from it. "It melts on the tongue," he observed, almost as if to himself.

"That's part of the artistry of it," said Mr. Goëtus.

Oriens took another, larger bite, and his smile widened.

Just then there came a sharp crack at the room's window, on the other side of the curtains, as if something had struck the glass from outside. Mr. Goëtus scowled and turned his head sharply. To Michael, this seemed somehow amusing, and he laughed again. Then the sound repeated itself twice.

Mr. Goëtus set the platter down and, in quite an irate voice, said, "What's that, for God's sake?" He strode to the window and yanked the curtains apart. There, in the light cast through the window by the room's phosphoria, something sparkling and white was visible just on the other side of the glass, and then Michael saw that it was the white bird that he knew so well, lunging forward and fiercely striking a single pane with its beak, three times, then three times more, its brilliant azure eyes flashing in and out of the light. Mr. Goëtus stepped back from the window. "What is it?" he said. "It's hideous."

"Oh, no," said Michael, though without any feeling of urgency, and laughing slightly again. "It's beautiful, and it's a friend of Oriens. His . . . what's the word...?" This too amused him. "His pneumatagogue. In the Noble Tongue, that would mean . . ."

"Well," said Mr. Goëtus impatiently, "whatever it is, no bird's going to break through that window. It's adamantine glass."

"Oh," said Laura casually, "like the windscreens on the police barges. My father used to . . . to . . . ." But her voice died gently away. Michael looked across the table at her, and she stared back at him with an expression of blissful serenity.

The bird struck the window again, four times, more sharply than before, but its beak left no mark on the pane. So it flapped its wings still more rapidly, drifted back until it was almost beyond the range of the light, and then rushed forward again with greater force, striking the glass so violently that it sounded as if a bough had snapped from a tree overhead, but still without any effect.

Slowly, it occurred to Michael that he ought not to feel so peaceful — he was sure that the bird's sudden appearance should disturb him deeply — but it was very difficult just at the moment to summon up a proper sense of anxiety. Then he realized that perhaps he should try at least to force himself to feel the panic that was floating just out of his mind's reach. "Something's wrong," he said. It was hard to make his mouth form the words, as if his jaw was too tired for the task.

Mr. Goëtus turned to Michael. "Something's wrong indeed." His expression had become cold.

Michael tried to rise, but realized that he could not. A warm languor was spreading through his limbs, and must have been doing so for some minutes, but until this moment he had not grasped that it had rendered him almost wholly immobile.

Mr. Goëtus stared at him for a few seconds longer, practically sneered, and then went to the corner cupboard, opened its lower doors, withdrew an antique aeroballistic pistol with a long, black metal barrel and a white bone handle, and returned to the window. "I detest vermin, pigeons as much as rats," he said. "Revolting things. Happily, I'm an excellent marksman." But, as he placed his hand on the small brass handle at the bottom of the sash, and before he could raise it, the bird turned in the air and was gone in a flare of prismatic white and gold. Mr. Goëtus waited several seconds, until he was apparently satisfied that the bird had fled. "Well," he said, "at least the larger quarry won't elude me." He laid the pistol on the window sill, returned from the window, and fixed his eyes on Oriens.

Michael followed his gaze, though it cost him considerable effort to turn his head even a few inches. Nothing that had just happened, it appeared, had registered at all on Oriens. He had evidently finished the first leaf of honey-brittle and was now holding up another before himself, staring at it in enthralled silence, the piercing sapphire of his eyes marvelously contrasting with the soft shimmer of the honey's amber.

"Please, have some more," Mr. Goëtus said, the silky refinement of his voice all at once seeming sinister in a way Michael had not noticed before now. Oriens, however, merely smiled at the confectioner and bit into the brittle.

Now Michael understood that what was stealing through him was not peace, but a deep, deadening stupor. And at once his superficial feeling of amusement vanished, and he knew that what he was truly feeling was misery. He could tell too from the blurring of his vision — though not from anything he could feel — that tears were welling up in his eyes. "Don't . . ." he weakly murmured, but could manage nothing more. He turned his eyes ever so arduously to Laura and saw that she too was shedding tears, and that she was no better able to wipe them from her cheeks.

"Oh, have another," said Mr. Goëtus. "They're as light and delicate as dreams. They don't fill you up any more than clouds would."

"Please don't . . ." Michael hissed.

"What you see here, Master Ambrosius," said Mr. Goëtus, not looking away from Oriens, "and you too, Miss Magian, sweet girl, is the essential advantage the trapper has over the hunter. The latter exhausts himself chasing after his prey, while the former need merely set his snares and wait. And what a long game it's been, for me and my family, waiting for this particular animal to fall into our nets. But the prize is mine now." He turned his eyes to Laura, then walked over to her and placed a gentle hand on her head. "You were such a hilarious little thing, last I saw you. And you" — he looked across the table to Michael — "I remember how happy Valentine was the day you were born. I even visited you in the maternity ward. And now . . . ah, this is a pity."

"Please let us . . ." Michael whispered, but again could not make himself say more.

"You poor silly children," Mr. Goëtus continued. "You really imagine no one guessed you'd come down the Phlegethon? Or that the Fravashi house wasn't constantly under surveillance? We could have found you along the river at any time, or arrested you when you got here. But clearly this creature you're traveling with is a very dangerous beast indeed. Caution was paramount. It was sobering enough that he was able to kill one of the Brethren, and one of their best stalkers at that, I'm told. But to wound one of the Great Ones, to the point that it still can't rise from the depths . . . ah, that's all but unimaginable. And then, just to drive the point home I expect, he even blasted a police barge out of the sky, and spirited its whole crew away, for God's sake."

"That wasn't . . . him . . ." Michael succeeded in rasping.

Mr. Goëtus was not listening. "No, it's clear he's a formidable thing. But"— he smiled more broadly still and raised his hands histrionically, as if inviting applause — "so, as it happens, am I." He looked again at Oriens. "Oh, go ahead, young man, that one too. It won't hurt you."

Michael turned his gaze ever so slightly again, and with even greater effort than before. Oriens was once more gazing admiringly at a leaf of the brittle — the last, it seemed, as the silver platter beside him was now empty. "It is so very delightful," he said. "It is like nothing I have tasted since . . . since . . ." He raised his eyes to Mr. Goëtus, with an expression of bemused uncertainty.

"Since departing your father's kingdom?" asked Mr. Goëtus.

"My . . . father's . . . ?" Oriens smiled. "I do not think I understand."

"No," said Mr. Goëtus, "I know. I know. You have no kingdom, do you?" With this he walked to the window again, took down a phosphorion from the wall, lit it with a brush of his fingertips, waved it three times back and forth in front of the glass, replaced it in its sconce, and returned. "But I knew that already. Just as I know what you really are. We aren't as benighted down here below the moons as you imagine. So let me tell you what I know about you. You're an aetherial daemon, aren't you, descended from the upper planetary spheres. An incubus. Yes? A spirit made from superlunary fire. You see, we know all about it. You're fooling no one. We've known for some time about the great rebellion going on in the higher heavens, and how the rebels have striven for some centuries now to overthrow the Great Artisan's celestial governments. And we've known for some time of the emissaries that have been sent into this world to sow discord, and that one of your kind was coming to wreak havoc here below, to initiate the final campaign against your God. We've kept that intelligence from the common believers, obviously, for their peace of mind. But it was foolish of you to think we weren't prepared for you. As terrible as your powers may be, you merciless little fiend, we've God on our side. And you were a fool to think you could possibly prevail against the Great Artisan's designs."

Oriens stared up at Mr. Goëtus with an almost radiant grin. "Since you offer, I will have one more," he said. "They are wonderful." And he bit into the last leaf of brittle.

"What I hadn't anticipated," Mr. Goëtus continued, his expression now becoming graver and his voice somewhat bitter, "was the sheer callousness of your deceits. You come into this, the best of all possible and compossible worlds, and do you rejoice in it, or praise its maker? No. Instead, you attempt to make it seem like a prison to those of us so fortunate as to inhabit it. And you do it with such cynically expert aplomb. That's the truly shocking and chilling thing. I mean, how cruel of you to devise so very pretty a fantasy, such a dewy, glistery, gleaming little fairytale, and how horrid of you to enchant, to mesmerize honest souls with a story that could never be true. That's the kind of dreaming that turns men into addicts. You see the wreckage of such dreams scattered under the bridges and all along the wharves and alleyways of this city. You didn't even scruple to corrupt these innocent children here. And now they'll have to be . . . " He paused, looking first at Laura and then at Michael with what seemed to be sincere sadness. "Well, they'll have to be purged and corrected, if they're not entirely beyond repair. If they are . . . ah, then, it's on your head. Not that I imagine for a moment that a monster like you has a conscience to wound."

Oriens had finished eating, and he laughed. "You are very entertaining," he said.

Michael wanted to call out to him, but now it was wholly impossible. He could not even part his lips.

Mr. Goëtus breathed deeply, as if containing his anger. Then he went down on one knee and took Oriens by the shoulders — albeit cautiously. "The time for dreams is at an end, though," he said, his tone all at once painfully solicitous. "Friends are coming for you, to take care of you."

"Friends?" said Oriens simply.

"Yes," said Mr. Goëtus. "You need never dream such things again."

"Thank-you," said Oriens.

And at that moment Michael heard the back door far below open, and several heavy footfalls ascending the stairs rapidly and loudly, and in an instant the door to the dining room opened and in stepped a very familiar figure — tall and slender but with broad shoulders, his face pale and narrow, his chin sharp, his nose prominent, his lips thin, his body clad in an opulently glossy black suit, a black silk cravat, and an impeccably blocked, elegantly creased, narrow-brimmed velvet hat — and Michael felt his heart begin to drum in his chest. Mr. Lucius looked about, took in the situation with a savage grin, at once somehow jovial and malevolent, and then raised a hand to beckon someone in from the landing. Two more of the Brethren entered, though not the two who had visited Michael's house the night of his father's arrest. These were younger; one was very thin and exceedingly tall, the other short and rather stout, and neither wore any discernible expression on his face. "Well now," said Mr. Lucius, "is everything in order, then?"

"Of course," said Mr. Goëtus with some annoyance. "The signal wasn't an accident. Did you bring the arch-therapist with you."

"She's just coming now," said Mr. Lucius, also in a somewhat acerbic tone. "I have to make sure everything's actually secure first, however. I wouldn't want some oversight on your part to put anyone at risk, now would I? And my responsibility . . ." His voice came to an abrupt halt. He was staring intently at Oriens, apparently seeing him fully for the first time. "Good gracious," he said after a moment, "you are most ridiculously beautiful, aren't you, my aetherial?"

Oriens gazed back at Mr. Lucius vacantly. "You are most beautiful too," he said.

Mr. Lucius flinched. One of his two assistants, however — the tall, thin one — said, in a murkily deep voice, "Yes, he is *very* beautiful."

Mr. Lucius sighed but did not turn about. "Don't talk to the daemon," he snapped. "Concentrate on the work at hand."

"Yes, Lord Lucius," the tall thin one replied. "I wouldn't normally talk to him, of course."

Mr. Lucius nodded. "Right, then."

"It's only," the tall thin one continued, "that what he said was very astute — if that's the right way to put it. Very incisive. Many of us have been wanting to say that very thing, and so when he said it . . ."

"Enough!" Mr. Lucius snarled. He turned his eyes to Laura and then to Michael. "Well, well, my succulents, so we meet again. Or, rather, I should say . . ."

"As it happens, my lord," the short stout one suddenly interrupted in a high, oddly wispy voice, "we've all felt that it was something very worth saying, but we've really never found the right occasion."

"Quiet!" Mr. Lucius roared, his eyes narrowing furiously. "Another word from either of you, and I swear I'll have you skinned." Silence fell over the room and Mr. Lucius turned to Michael, pointing an unnaturally long index finger at him. "Rather, you and I meet again, young Master Ambrosius, whereas" — he turned his eyes and finger to Laura — "you I just missed meeting last time. But now we can . . ."

"Does that mean both of us?" the tall thin one suddenly asked. "We should both be quiet, then?"

Mr. Lucius's eyes grew wide, the sinews of his jaw grew taut, and he turned to his subordinates. "Of course both of you. That's what 'either' means."

"I wasn't entirely clear on that," said the tall thin one. "If you think about it, it might just mean one or the other of us should be quiet at any given moment, but not necessarily both of us at once. *Either*, you see, one or the other."

"That was my thought, to be honest," said the short stout one. "It's a very subtly ambiguous locution, my lord, if you don't mind my saying."

For several wordless moments, Mr. Lucius stared at them, his hands clasped before him, his lips pressed together, his whole body rigid with restrained wrath. Then he lowered his head and sighed. "Just the two of you slip downstairs now," he said coolly, though perhaps a little lugubriously, "and see about the arch-therapist . . . the lady who came with us, that is . . . the extremely attractive one in the long white coat. All right?"

"Both of us?" asked the tall, thin one.

"Yes," said Mr. Lucius, visibly struggling to remain calm, "that's what 'the two of you' means. Both. Both at once. And she's to be brought upstairs . . . courteously. She's not an enemy . . . or a meal."

"I wasn't wholly clear on what the 'just' was meant to . . ." began the short stout one.

But something in Mr. Lucius's eyes must at last have made the proper impression on them, because they both came to attention, touched the brims of their hats submissively, and departed the room.

"I see that the Brethren are as incandescently brilliant as ever," said Mr. Goëtus after a second.

Mr. Lucius turned slowly about with a grim smile. "Some among our ranks are perhaps less than ideally clever. And yet their faith is beyond question. The Secretariat for Spiritual Sanity has been in the vanguard of the armies of righteousness for centuries, and the Lupine Brethren have been in the vanguard of the Secretariat all that time. Can your lot over at Global Security and Hygiene boast quite so illustrious and *unmarred* a tradition?"

Mr. Goëtus uttered a single sardonic laugh. "You have me there. We've lost a few to apostasy, I admit. And, I have to say, my family has only been obliged for four successive generations — five, counting mine — to live incognito among a sect of noisome heretics, to associate with them constantly, to risk the contempt of our fellow alpha-pneumatics, awaiting the day when we might at last discharge our sacred commission. You're right, that's nothing. What's that sort of continuous, unrewarded, unremitting fidelity as compared to the blind obedience and spontaneous loyalty of brutes. I mean" — Mr. Goëtus smiled impishly — "you don't mind me putting it that way, do you?"

"Not at all, my temerarious," Mr. Lucius replied. "Apart from a gift, there's nothing more delightful to receive than an insult. It provides one something to . . . chew over, so to speak."

"Still," said Mr. Goëtus, "I do wonder about the breeding of you fellows. I mean, I know yours is an ordained order, and that these fashionably austere habiliments of yours are a kind of clerical garb, but I still find it a mite rude that none of you ever thinks to take off his hat when he comes into my home."

Mr. Lucius sneered. "*Breeding* is precisely the issue there," he said. "We find it unpleasant to remove them. It feels unnatural."

Mr. Goëtus tilted his head to one side. "What? Why unnatural?"

"What do you imagine all this beautiful haberdashery is?" said Mr. Lucius, running his fingers delicately along his lapels and lightly flicking at the handkerchief protruding from his breast pocket. "What do you think becomes of our hides and gorgeous sleek fur when we're in this form?"

"You mean they're your . . . pelts?" said Mr. Goëtus. "You're born with them — or, rather, whelped with them? I had no idea."

"Evidently not."

"Well" — Mr. Goëtus seemed to be vaguely embarrassed — "my apologies, then."

Mr. Lucius nodded.

"Good God, you don't shed do you?" Mr. Goëtus suddenly asked in a tone of exaggerated distaste, looking about the room with a comic pretense of distress.

Mr. Lucius's eyes narrowed and his smile became especially vicious. "No, never fear. We don't shed anything — except, of course, the blood of those who're so rash as to provoke us."

Mr. Goëtus arched his eyebrows and uttered a sarcastic gasp.

"I amuse you?"

"You bore me."

"Why, then," said Mr. Lucius, the smile fading from his lips, "I shall have to contrive to make our next encounter more exciting for you, once this current business is done."

"And how do you propose to do that?" asked Mr. Goëtus with a sniff.

"By tearing out your throat with my own fangs," said Mr. Lucius calmly, "and then gorging myself on your heart and entrails."

Mr. Goëtus stiffened, the monocle dropped from his eye to hang from its lanyard, and his expression instantly changed from one of confident disdain to one of poorly concealed disquiet. "Well, I mean . . ." It was obvious — or so Michael thought — that the confectioner was only now beginning to consider at how great a disadvantage he was in regard to Mr. Lucius. Slowly, as casually as possible, he turned his eyes to the pistol lying on the window sill, as if calculating its precise distance away. After a few seconds, though, he lowered his head, obviously chasing away whatever impulse had momentarily possessed him, and swallowed audibly. "I think," he said, "we may have allowed our playful bantering . . . this genially adversarial persiflage of ours, as it were . . . to lose its levity."

"Nothing of the sort," Mr. Lucius replied with a dulcet lilt to his voice. "I find myself very entertained."

Just then, the sound of someone lightly ascending the top steps to the landing — clearly a woman wearing high heels — came through the door, followed only a moment later by the woman herself: extremely lovely, beautiful in fact, and surprisingly young, her long brown smoothly lustrous hair tied back, her cheeks tastefully rouged and lips painted almost ruby-red, wearing a pair of rimless spectacles and a rather short white lab-coat over her blue dress — plain but expertly cut to show off her very impressive figure — and clutching a clipboard.

"Ah," said Mr. Goëtus with a deep sigh, his posture becoming at once more relaxed, "there you are. You're the arch-therapist, I presume?" He restored his monocle to its proper place. "My Lord, if therapists in my day . . ." He stopped himself and glanced uncertainly at Mr. Lucius.

The young woman looked back and forth between the two men with an amiable but quizzical expression. "Is everything quite all right?" she asked in a voice that to Michael sounded almost maternal in its gentleness.

"Why, yes," said Mr. Lucius, turning to her with a warm leer, "now that you're here, my winsome, everything is splendid."

"Oh, Lucius," the woman replied, waving her free hand airily, "don't be such a charmer."

"It's in the blood," he replied, "and the bone." Then to Mr. Goëtus he said, "Allow me to introduce Dr. Erasmia Axiomorpha, the youngest therapist ever to receive full certification from both the Kenopolitan Academy and the Psychodynamic Theology Association, one of our foremost experts in arsenodeleastics, and the youngest woman ever to receive arch-therapeutic ordination — as well as, if I recall, the newest inductee into the Congregation for Rational Science."

"Ma'am," said Mr. Goëtus with a polite bow of the head. "I'm truly impressed and honored."

"Oh, pay Lucius no mind," Dr. Axiomorpha replied. "He's an old friend and he insists on making me sound more remarkable than I really . . ." She stopped speaking. Her gaze had also now fallen fully on Oriens. She raised her hand to her mouth, pressed her fingers against her lips as if to suppress a gasp, glanced at Mr. Lucius with wide eyes, and then looked at Oriens again. "Oh, my," she whispered. She dropped her gaze for several seconds, breathed deeply, and appeared to be composing herself; then she looked up again, but now with an expression of excruciating tenderness. "Oh, my darling, darling boy!" she gushed, almost singing the words. Handing her clipboard to Mr. Lucius, she nearly ran around the table and behind Laura to where Oriens sat. "You poor child!" She pulled another of the chairs so near that when she sat on it her knees must have been pressed against his leg, and she took his hands in hers and stared deeply, caringly, piteously into his eyes. "We've been searching for you absolutely everywhere. We nearly gave up hope."

"Have you?" asked Oriens with a look of fascinated delight.

"Yes, indeed," said Dr. Axiomorpha, and she seemed now to be struggling not to cry. "What do you remember, dear?"

Oriens looked confused at this question. "The meal I have just eaten," he said. "It was very pleasant."

"No, no," Dr. Axiomorpha replied with a wince of still deeper pity, "I mean can you remember why you're here? Do you know who you are, to begin with? Or where you come from? Or can you guess where you're going to go from here? Does any of this make sense to you, darling?"

Oriens continued to look confused for some seconds; but then the pleased expression returned to his face and he said, "You are very beautiful."

Dr. Axiomorpha smiled, but still with a look of pained sympathy in her eyes. "You're a bit young for that sort of talk, don't you think?" She gave his cheek an affectionate caress, and then a slight pinch. "Anyway, I see. I'm sorry to tell you this, but there was an accident. This was just a month ago. You and your parents were in your private aerial car when something went wrong with one of the rotors, and the car hit the top of a tree and came down in a field outside the city. You struck your head — you wandered away in a daze, as best we can tell. And we've been frantically searching for you ever since."

"My parents?" asked Oriens, his brow furrowing, his gaze momentarily floating away toward the ceiling.

Now Dr. Axiomorpha's expression became all at once somber, tragic, haunted; she sighed deeply and shook her head; she removed her spectacles, laid them on the table, and gently took Oriens's face in her hands, directing his eyes back toward hers. "Steel yourself, dear. I have some very bad news. Are you ready, darling?"

Oriens smiled.

"The emergency corps at the scene of the crash did all they could for your mother and father, but he died before they could get him to the hospital, and she died the next day, despite all the doctors' very best efforts."

"That is a sad story," remarked Oriens absently.

By now, a surge of desperation had succeeded in breaking through the last layer of Michael's opiate trance, followed by a still greater surge of rage. He wanted to scream, to rush at this woman, to choke her with his own hands, but still he could neither move nor speak.

"Would you like to cry, darling?" asked Dr. Axiomorpha.

"I do not think so," said Oriens.

"Not at all?"

"No."

"You brave, dear boy," she said, and leaned forward and kissed him adoringly on the cheek, leaving a vivid trace of lipstick behind. "I'd like to gather you in my arms and just hug you forever — and kiss you a thousand times more."

Oriens grinned almost ecstatically, and Michael was curiously conscious of a small twinge of envy somewhere amid the writhing impotence of his own anger.

"But, of course," she continued, her voice and expression becoming somehow even more earnest, "we first have to see to your wellbeing. So I'll tell you what we'll do. You come with me and we'll go visit a clinic where we can begin to help you recover your memories. You'd like that, wouldn't you? And don't be afraid. You'll sit right next to me all the way, and I'll be with you the entire time. It's a wonderful place, and I have so many friends there, and they'll all be your friends too. Believe me, they're experts at psychological and spiritual adjustment. First thing tomorrow morning, we'll take you to make confession and then it's off to psychometric analysis."

"Confession?"

"You know — of your sins and delusions and such. I'll be with you to help you along."

Again, Oriens furrowed his brow. "I do not think I remember anything to confess."

"Oh, don't fret your sweet head over that." Dr. Axiomorpha rose and, placing one hand under his near forearm and the other on his back, encouraged him to rise as well. "We'll tell you what your sins are, and how to feel appropriately guilty about them, and how to find comfort in the forgiveness we provide." She began to guide him around the table, drawing him close against her shapely hip, fondly stroking his shoulder and arm as she did so. "Oh, and we'll also see to your emotional problems and your psychic dysfunctions — your deep sense of alienation, for instance — and we'll talk you through them, and see you get all the proper medications." She shook her head at Mr. Lucius when he attempted to return her clipboard. "Before you know it, we'll have moved on to discussing your career. After all, your father was quite an important man of business." They passed through the door, but Michael could still hear her speaking for a few seconds as they began to descend the stairs: "He left you a controlling concern in the Pamphagos Group, which . . . well, there'll be time for that, my dear, when you come into . . ." And then her voice was no longer audible.

Michael had no defense against his despair, and no way of expressing it. He simply wanted the world to disappear.

"It seems a rather elaborate method for dealing with the creature," said Mr. Lucius, indifferently laying the clipboard on the table, "now that he's been rendered quiescent. Better to have done with him, it seems to me: kill the machine and fling his little light into the abyss. Surely the Land of Hel can hold him."

"You don't understand," said Mr. Goëtus, staring at the empty doorway. "What dwells in that creature is more than just some little light, like yours or mine. Do you still not grasp how dangerous he is?" He reached into his waistcoat pocket and withdrew a small glass phial half filled with some cloudy green fluid and stopped with a dropper set in cork. "Who else has ever defeated — ever crippled — one of the Great Ones? Are you really eager to provoke someone who can do that? The only things protecting us from all that horrendous power right now may very well be his fleshly body and all those sidereal and planetary souls wrapping it tightly in. No, no, dealing with him will take time. If we're precipitous, we invite cataclysm."

"I know nothing of that," said Mr. Lucius scoffingly. "I certainly don't believe in 'planetary souls,' whatever those are. We Lupines don't have the appetite you Venefici do for all that wild arcane nonsense. We don't pretend to know the natural philosophy of the upper heavens or their . . . fauna. But surely it doesn't matter. The Great Artisan wouldn't allow him . . . "

"Please," said Mr. Goëtus, "don't finish that sentence. Our God has fashioned us for his good ends, but he doesn't intervene to rescue us from the bad ends we might make for ourselves. At least, that's what we in the order of the Venefici believe, with all our wild arcane nonsense." He filled the dropper and removed it from the phial. "These two you can take now. This will make them sleep, for about five or six hours perhaps, but its somnifacient virtue will also purge their bodily humors of the paralytic and euphoric agents I fed them. So keep them restrained till you get to the sanatorium, just in case." He went first to Laura, applied the dropper briefly to her lips, removed it, and then looked at her with a frown of doting melancholy. "She's such a brave and pretty girl, isn't she?"

"She looks quite delectable," replied Mr. Lucius.

Mr. Goëtus stared coldly at Mr. Lucius for a moment, and then began to walk around the table to Michael. "Our instructions are clear," he said. "No harm is to come to either child. They've much to tell us about that creature. And, don't forget" — Michael very vaguely sensed the glass tip of the dropper through the numbness of his lips, and then tasted something on his tongue at once sickly sweet and bitterly astringent, like malted vinegar mixed with salt and heavy treacle and some especially sour herb — "it's always possible they can yet be saved."

Already, these words seemed to Michael to be coming from somewhere far away, echoing down a long stony corridor, and the room was rapidly fading into darkness. His mouth and throat felt as if they were full of ice. And soon he felt nothing.

PART SIX
The Archons

I kissed the scroll and broke the seal and read,
And soon the covenant that marked my heart
Began to stir — a shadow, nearly dead —
And then illusion's veils began to part.
My spirit, born to freedom, once more yearned
For others of my kind, and liberty.
Old memories revived, faintly discerned
Among the dreams that still imprisoned me.

— from "The Hymn of the Pearl"

I

MICHAEL WOKE SLOWLY, ALMOST DELIciously, aware at first only of a soothingly empty tingling in his limbs and of a slight sensation of being in motion, as though he were slowly swinging side to side in a hammock, and of a taste in his mouth like honey and burnt butter. On opening his eyes, however, he found himself staring up at a bare concrete ceiling with a single recessed phosphoric panel at its center, its light tinged faintly acid green by its glass. After many moments, he became conscious of the coarseness of the sheets and the hardness of the mattress of the bed in which he lay, and then of the thinness of the pillow beneath his head. He sat up and instantly felt a combination of mild vertigo and mild nausea rise up in him like a wave. He braced himself with his hands on the edges of the bed, took a deep breath of air that tasted damp and stale, and the feeling slowly subsided. Then, breathing deeply again, he discovered to his dismay that he had no clothes on beneath the sheet and thin gray blanket covering him. He looked around anxiously in every direction. The head of the low metal bedstead was set against the middle of a wall in a fairly spacious foursquare room, all of it, with the exception of the white tiled floor and its variegated stains, in unpainted concrete. There were no windows. A small white wooden table and single white wooden chair sat opposite the foot of the bed, a white wooden dressing screen in three hinged sections stood across the room to the bed's right with what appeared to be trousers and a pullover of gray flannel draped over it, and a white dressing gown of a distinctly clinical kind hung from a hook on the back of the room's dull green metal door, a few feet from the table. Now that the covers had fallen from his chest, he felt how cold the air around him was, and began to shiver.

Only then did the events in Mr. Goëtus's rooms come seeping, and then pouring, back into his memory. Involuntarily, he pressed his fists against his temples, closed his eyes fast, and bowed his head. He could hear his own small, suppressed moan of anguish before he was aware of it issuing from his lips. And then he realized that his whole body was shaking, not from the cold but from the violence of a sudden panic, and he could not make it stop. "Control yourself," he succeeded in whispering to himself after nearly a minute of continuous spasms. "You have to be calm." But his mind was filled with despair, with the terror that he would never see his father or Laura again, or Oriens . . . "You have to be still." But he could not, and after several minutes, weakened by his own inability to draw another deep breath, he fell back against his pillow, striking the top of his head glancingly against one of the steel bars of the bedhead. There he lay inert for what seemed a very long time, struggling to breathe more steadily, forcing himself to become gradually calmer (if no less miserable), pressing his hands desperately against his bare chest . . . pressing. . . .

He slowly realized, however, that his chest was not *entirely* bare after all. Looking down at his hands, he saw that they appeared to be lying quite flat against his breastbone, and yet he also clearly felt the slender cord and soft fabric of the purse of jewels that Oriens had given him. For several moments, he lay very still, holding the invisible object close to himself; and his anxiety began to diminish. His breath gradually became even, his body's shudders slowly ceased. He briefly considered attempting to extract one of the jewels from the purse, just to gaze at it, remembering the sense of peace that that otherworldly light had given him on earlier occasions. But then he decided that it was not worth the risk of exposing his secret now. Someone might be watching. He turned his eyes in their sockets in every direction. He alone could touch the purse, he remembered Oriens telling him, and he alone could remove it. And perhaps, he began to reflect as the minutes continued to pass, this was an advantage for which his captors could not possibly be prepared — if only he could find the right moment to exploit it.

His next thought, when at last it took distinct shape, was for clothes. Why it had taken so long for this to occur to him, he could not say, but attributed it to the lingering effects of his drugged meal. He looked from the gown on the door to the shirt and trousers on the dressing screen and decided on the latter. He pulled the covers away from his feet and began to swing his legs over the side of the bed, but then instantly heard a small shrill bell ringing, out of sight below the foot of the mattress, and felt the tiny pull of the string tied around his right ankle; and he had only just untied it when the door to the room swung open with a startlingly loud protest from its steel hinges. He pulled his legs back into the bed. A tall, thin, but apparently quite solid woman, with a pale, lined, plain face entered, clad in the distinctive habit of a nurse of the Sisters of Rational Pity: a long white frock reaching all the way down to her ankles, tied at her waist with a cincture of braided black rope, a black cowl over her hair and shoulders, and black canvas shoes with flat soles. A steel key — no doubt the one with which she had just admitted herself — hung from her right wrist on a short white woolen cord. Michael gathered the covers up against his chest. For a moment, the nurse gazed at him with an expression that seemed somehow to combine curiosity with profound boredom. "Can you stand, boy?" she asked in a cold clear voice that had a slightly metallic timbre.

"I think so," said Michael.

She frowned momentarily and then closed the door behind her. "The proper answer," she said, "would be 'I think so, *ma'am*.'" Then she stared sternly at Michael for several seconds from icily gray eyes.

"Oh," said Michael, finally understanding what she was waiting for. "Yes, *ma'am*, I think so."

The nurse sighed. "Someone your age shouldn't need to learn manners. Apparently your parents were somewhat derelict in your upbringing." She reached into a pocket of her frock and removed a small pad of paper, which she began to read. "Michael, is it?" she asked as if the answer was really of no interest to her.

"Yes . . . yes, ma'am."

"Well, Michael," she said, looking up at him again, "this sanatorium is a remedial penitentiary for maladjusted children, and a place where discipline and order and hygiene are maintained inflexibly at all times. You can be excused for an infraction of the rules, but only until you've been told what they are. At that point, you're expected to have mastered them. The slightest failure to comply thereafter will be punished. Do you understand?"

"Yes, ma'am," he said quietly.

"And one rule you've already learned," she continued in a fatigued monotone. "When addressing an adult, you must always say 'sir' or 'ma'am,' without fail. Or, alternatively, you may address an adult by his or her proper title. For instance, you can address me also as 'Nurse' or 'Sister' or by my full name, Sr. Theomenia. As long as you're respectful. Understood?"

"Yes, ma'am," Michael replied, trying to conceal the resentment her tone was already inspiring in him. Then, as calmly as he could, he added, "Can you tell me where my friends are . . . ma'am?"

"Another rule is that children do not ask questions here." She shook her head in obvious disapproval. "It's not your place and it's extremely impudent.

If you absolutely must ask something, in an emergency, you must first ask permission to ask. Is that clear?"

"I think so, ma'am, yes."

"And another rule is that, when an adult enters the room, you are immediately to stand at attention until instructed to do otherwise. So" — she gestured for him to rise with her hand — "up you get."

"But . . ." Michael clutched the covers of the bed. "But I haven't any clothes on."

Sr. Theomenia frowned more fiercely and stared at him impatiently.

"Ma'am," Michael added.

Her irate expression dissolved back into a look of tired indifference and she shook her head again. Replacing the pad of paper in her pocket, she said, "Your modesty is charming, of course, but quite out of place. What with medical exams and hygienic inspections and lab tests and therapies and corporal punishments and such, no one's going to put up with girly bashfulness on any child's part. Personal dignity is a social privilege that even normal children enjoy only partially, and that delinquent children forfeit entirely. This isn't a holiday camp, boy."

Michael said nothing, but neither did he move.

"Child," Sr. Theomenia continued, a slight note of anger entering her voice, "I'm the one who undressed and decontaminated you before you were put to bed. You've nothing left to hide. Now obey me."

Again, though, Michael did not move, except gently to touch the unseen cord around his neck with a single fingertip. "No, ma'am," he said, without any inflection.

For a moment the nurse merely glowered at him. Then she sighed resignedly, took the gown from its hook, tossed it onto the bed, and turned her back to Michael. "Quickly," she said. Michael had scarcely pulled the ridiculously flimsy garment around himself and tied it closed by the six sets of short strings sewn down the front before she turned about again. "Now get up this instant," she snapped at him, in a voice that clearly signified the end of her patience.

Michael pulled the covers away and stood, almost losing his balance as he did so. The gown reached halfway down his shins, but was no protection against the chill in the room.

"Stand up straighter," said Sr. Theomenia curtly, "heels close together, hands flat at your hips, shoulders back, chin up, eyes forward."

Michael did his best to comply.

"'Yes, *ma'am*,'" Sr. Theomenia prompted, her tone growing even sharper.

"Yes, ma'am," said Michael. "Yes, Sister."

"One yes is sufficient." She drew closer, fixed a grim, infuriated, and yet somehow still deeply bored gaze upon him. "Now, listen to me very carefully. I won't be this indulgent again. Neither will anyone else. I've been unusually tolerant because you're new, and you're probably still a bit sedated, and because I'm not sure yet why you're classified as a special and delicate case. But henceforth you will most certainly obey all the adults here without the slightest hesitation, or suffer the severest consequences. Believe me, you don't want to discover sooner than you need to how we deal with contumacious children. This facility has several trained paedoko-lastic specialists on call at all hours, licensed in corporal, psychological, and psychopharmacological correction, and under normal circumstances you'd already be on the way to one of them for your defiance. Never again play the insidious brat with me, and never say no to me when I give you a command. Do you understand me?"

Michael nodded, genuinely beginning to feel uneasy and exposed. "Yes, ma'am." Then he added, in a more subdued voice than he intended, "I understand, Sister." The gown felt as light as gossamer now, and the floor beneath his feet as though it were slick with frost. He could not help notic-ing, moreover, how menacingly sinewy the nurse's hands and wrists looked, and what broad shoulders she had for a woman.

"The rules here are simple enough," she continued, "as are the prohibitions. Punishments will be imposed, severely and without fail, for disobedience, sloth, petulance, disrespect, psychopathy, furtive leering, theft, dishonesty, temerity, fingernail-chewing, impiety, devious darting or rolling of the eyes, vehement expostulations, disconsolate sighs, murder, slovenliness, sarcasm, and idiosyncratic opinions."

"*Murder?*" Michael said with a slight gasp, almost a dry laugh. "I mean: murder, ma'am?"

At this, Sr. Theomenia's expression became indignant (if in a weary way). "Do you mean to tell me you think murder shouldn't be penalized? What a very perverse child you must be. No wonder you've been sequestered."

"No, ma'am," said Michael hastily. "I meant only that I was sur-prised . . . well, I didn't think that that's something that needed to be. . . . Sorry, ma'am."

Sr. Theomenia stared at him for several silent seconds with what looked like candid distaste. Then she breathed deeply once again and returned to her original station near the door. "It's breakfast time. You'll be eating in your room for now, as you're not allowed to enter the general population yet . . . for some reason. On the other side of that screen is the entryway to your bath-chamber and general facilities. Towels and mats are hanging in the airing cupboard. A lever over the tub automatically fills it. You'll have seven minutes for your bath before it automatically drains again. Be thorough with the brush and soap you'll find there, not neglecting your hair. Dry yourself completely, hang your towel and the mat neatly back in the cupboard. There are a brush and powder by the vanity for your teeth. Leave the sink immaculate. There's a comb for your hair as well. Change into the clothes on the screen. You'll find canvas shoes there. Hang your gown up neatly again. You'll have three minutes to make your bed, and I mean very tidily. Your breakfast will be on the table here. You'll have twelve minutes to eat. After that . . . well, after that, I'm not sure. Normally, on your first day, you'd make confession, be processed, go to chapel, and then appear at midday assembly to make a public profession of your crimes to the other children. Then classification as either a convalescent or a criminal and assignment of a schedule of classes and therapies. Then you'd be left for about an hour with the currently dominant group of boy inmates, to establish your place in the social hierarchy, then sent over to the infirmary to treat any injuries. Then dinner, assignment of a cot in the boys' dormitory, bedtime prayers, and lights out. But apparently your case obliges us to wait for special instructions. You're not to come into contact with anyone for longer than a few minutes, it seems, not even the regular priest here. You really must have done something very . . . depraved." Her face once more assumed the same, oddly mixed expression of boredom and curiosity with which she had first regarded him. "Well, go then," she suddenly said, clapping her hands loudly, "unless you want me to drag you in myself and scour you raw."

"Yes, Sister," said Michael briskly, turning and hastening toward the screen, but also discreetly touching his hand to the invisible purse as he did so.

AFTER BATHING IN THE UNPLEASANTLY TEPID AND shallow water—infused, apparently, with some kind of acetic disinfectant—and after cleaning his teeth with the bitterly antiseptic powder, he donned the gray uniform, including the shoes that almost immediately began to chafe at the backs of his ankles. The trousers had an elastic waistband, and trousers and shirt alike had the consistency of a worn dust-rag. None of it was substantial enough to keep him warm. Sr. Theomenia was gone, and he cautiously checked to make sure she had locked the door behind her. He made the bed as neatly as he could and then sat down at the table before the bowl of cold porridge and the large glass of warm water awaiting him there. The porridge was flavorless, congealed, barely edible. Soon, however, the door opened and an orderly—a short, middle-aged man with fleecy white hair and an abnormally ruddy complexion, dressed in white clinical frock and trousers—entered. Michael stood to attention, but the man seemed not to notice; he merely gathered up the half-empty bowl and the spoon and left again.

Then practically nothing happened for a long time. With the exception of the same orderly bringing his lunch roughly four hours later — a bowl of flavorless brown soup sparsely populated with unidentifiable vegetables, a dry slice of coarse white bread, and another glass of water — and then returning to collect the remains twelve minutes after that, no one entered the room again till evening came. Michael was left to sit at his table, or to pace the room rubbing his hands together, or to slip into the bed a few times in search of warmth only to leap up again to smooth out the bedclothes at every fancied creak or whisper from the other side of the door. At least once every hour he approached the door and placed an ear against its cold metal, but not once did he hear so much as a footfall on the other side. And, as the day unfolded, his mood continually fluctuated, at times becoming mere restlessness, at times reverting to the panic that had seized him on first awaking, at times resolving again into an uncertain calm (especially when he thought of the purse of jewels), at times turning into prolonged periods of numbing despair irregularly punctuated by small inexplicable thrills of irrational hope, and at times becoming sheer rage.

What, however, it never quite became even for an instant, much to his surprise, was simple, unqualified fear. Even the spells of panic felt more like fits of extreme impatience for something to happen — an anxious sense of time already lost — than like true terror. He found this so strange, in fact, that two or three times he attempted to make himself afraid, just as a kind of exercise, by willfully recalling how dire his situation was. But it was no use. The most he could manage was a briefly sustained state of angry insecurity. No doubt, he thought, this was partly on account of the reassurance the purse of jewels provided him. But, as the afternoon wore on, he realized that it was also on account of all his adventures of the last several weeks. At some point, he had been carried over some emotional frontier that now lay irrevocably behind him. And before evening arrived he knew that they would never be able to make him as afraid as they thought they could — which, after all, was surely the point of all of this. The dreary cell, the inadequate garments, the revolting food, the nurse's condescensions and insults, the threats of punishment, the imperious commands issued to him as though he were a small, wicked, stupid child — all of it was meant to terrify him and render him submissive. But all it had accomplished really was to give him time to think, and he had so much more to think about than they could possibly have guessed.

Well before the orderly brought him his dinner — an insipid gray hash of some kind of macerated animal protein and some kind of grain, again accompanied by lukewarm water — he had resolved that he would act as compliantly as possible, and appear to surrender his will to theirs in every particular, but only until he could decide how and when to employ the weapon Oriens had given him. And then, he told himself, he would . . . he would do something quite . . . well, something.

An hour after dinner, Sr. Theomenia returned with a nightshirt folded over one arm, scowled at him menacingly for several minutes while he stood at attention, clearly inspecting him for the slightest deviation from the approved posture. Finally she placed the nightshirt over the dressing screen. "Go take your evening bath and clean your teeth again," she droned harshly, "change into that, leave the shoes where you found them, and give me your clothes."

"Yes, Sister," said Michael, and did as he was told, even somewhat exaggerating his haste to comply and trying to affect something of a timorous demeanor.

Then, as he stood once again shivering in his light nightshirt, Sr. Theomenia tersely commanded him to put his heels closer together and said, "Tomorrow is an important day for you. You'll be meeting our director, who will be the one to decide what comes next for you and for that girl who came here with you . . ."

Michael felt his heart suddenly begin to beat a little faster at the mention of Laura, and it was only with considerable effort that he prevented himself from reacting.

". . . and you had better be on your very best behavior . . ."

"Yes, Sister," Michael immediately interjected, as if excessively eager to please.

"Hush," hissed Sr. Theomenia angrily. "Reply only when I finish speaking. You'll also attend chapel, and perhaps make your public profession of sins. You are to make no attempt to communicate with the other inmate children, however. Do you understand?"

"Yes, Sister."

"As for private confession, that will apparently have to wait for another day. I'm sure you want to be shriven as soon as possible — at least, I'm quite sure that in your case it's a burning need — but apparently there are some delicate issues where you're concerned. Understood?"

"Yes, Sister."

"Very well. Time for prayers." She pointed to the floor beside the bed. "On your knees, then."

Michael hesitated, but so briefly that he was certain she had not noticed. He knelt on the hard cold floor, rested his elbows on the edge of his bed, and placed his hands together before him. He had never said evening prayers at home, or prayers of any kind outside school or temple. Apart from weekly attendance at temple, in fact, which was legally mandatory in any event, his father had never encouraged the slightest trace of religion in him. But he knew all the prayers he had been required to memorize in catechism class. So, when Sr. Theomenia told him to say the "O Great Artisan, molder of my flesh and soul," he recited it fluently, in as sonorously devout a voice as he could contrive. He did the same with each of the next four prayers she named, by the last of which his knees were aching abominably. Finally, she required him to repeat after her as she recited the sanatorium's special prayer in small digestible fragments: "King and Maker of all . . . heal us of our defects and diseases . . . liberate us from our oddities and harmful curiosities . . . keep us from prying and crying . . . teach us thy truth . . . help us to be obedient and decent . . . worthy and wise . . . pious and pecunious . . . functional and virtuous . . . normal and nice . . . and shape us by thy mighty hand . . . into vessels answerable . . . to all thy good purposes."

"Right, then," said Sr. Theomenia officiously, "into bed, flat on your back."

Michael rose stiffly but with as much decorously submissive haste as he could manage and got under the covers.

"Good," she said softly, perhaps slightly grudgingly. She bent forward and drew the covers up to his throat. Then she reached into one of her pockets and withdrew a small shiny metal box with a hinged lid, from which she extracted a chalky green lozenge of some kind, the size of a small coin. "You've been prescribed only a basic soporific and hedonic. Once your pharmaceutical schedule is drawn up, that will change. But for now this will at least make you sleep. Head right back against the pillow, mouth open." She extended the lozenge toward him. "Right now," she said with emphatic curtness, "wide, with your tongue out."

Michael wanted to resist, or to pause at least, but knew he should not defy her now, after having made such an effort to impress her with his docility. He opened his mouth.

"Wider, child."

He opened his mouth quite wide and extended his tongue, thinking perhaps that he could store the medicine in his cheek and only pretend to swallow it, and then dispose of it in the sink later. But as soon as she laid it on his tongue it began to melt, rapidly filling his mouth with a nauseous fruity sweetness mingled with some other, more acrid and artificial flavor.

"Goodness, child," Sr. Theomenia said, placing her fingers under his jaw and closing his mouth with a small slap, "you act as if you've never been sedated at bedtime before. Now lie perfectly still while it takes effect."

A pleasant insensibility was already stealing through Michael's body, starting from his tongue and quickly spreading through his limbs.

"There's a glass of water on the table if you wake," he heard Sr. Theomenia saying, "though that's unlikely."

Then he heard the door to the room groan open again, far away, then bang shut, at an even greater distance. The sickly green glow of the phosphorion in the ceiling sank down to little more than a dim briny sheen. "Oh," Michael breathed contentedly. He was floating now. He was happy — in an empty way. Gentle sea currents were carrying him away from shore and downward into dark green depths, where there were fabulous coral reefs and exotic fish. A strange, dreamy sense of security had settled over him, along with a feeling of gently undulating warmth all about and within him. And soon, once more, he was aware of nothing.

II

WHEN HE WOKE THE NEXT MORNING—AT least, he assumed it to be morning, since the ceiling phosphorion was glowing at full intensity again—Michael discovered that clothes had again been hung over the dressing screen while he slept, and these he could see were somewhat more substantial and formal than those of the day before. They were the same drab gray, but the trousers were of a fabric sufficiently heavy to have retained the creases ironed into them, and came equipped with actual belt loops and a gray canvas belt, while the shirt had buttons and a collar. There were even some proper undergarments and a pair of gray stockings. He rose quickly and went about bathing and dressing before Sr. Theomenia arrived, in the hope of forestalling a reprise of the former day's litanies of rebukes, threats, and injunctions. He had just made the bed and folded his nightshirt into what he assumed would be an acceptable oblong when the door emitted its loud complaint and he turned about and came to attention, expecting to meet Sr. Theomenia's frigid sneer. Instead, another nurse entered. She was wearing the same style of habit, but was fully a foot shorter than her predecessor and four or so feet wider in girth, with a much rounder, pinker, and younger face. Her expression, moreover, was one of vibrant, almost radiant cheer. "Oh, there you are, sweetie!" she effused in a voice so high that it sounded almost like a series of loud squeaks. "Already up and dressed, like a proper little gentleman." She closed the door behind her and then, quite astonishingly to Michael, wrapped him for several seconds in a strong, warm, rather gelatinous embrace. He tried to maintain his posture, keeping his hands at his sides, although he found it difficult to balance himself. When she released him, he came back to full attention and she giggled at the sight. "Delightful," she said. "So"—clapping her hands together before her—"did you have a nice cozy sleep last night?"

"Yes, ma'am," Michael replied, hearing in his own voice the slight disorientation he was feeling but had wanted to conceal.

"Ma'am, ma'am, ma'am," the nurse echoed with a comical frown, waving her hands in the air. "You make me feel like a venerable old crone. My name's Sr. Galera, and that's what you can call me. Or just 'Sister.' I like that best, I think, because we're all family here really." And she winked a brown, limpidly bovine eye at him. "And aren't you a handsome child?"

Michael attempted a pleased smile, not at all sure he had made it look sincere.

Sr. Galera said nothing for a few seconds, then arched her brows and looked at him expectantly. "I said, aren't you a handsome child, then?" Her voice had momentarily descended to a more typically human pitch.

"Oh," said Michael, realizing what was expected. "Yes, ma'am. I mean, yes, Sister. Or, rather, thank-you, Sister."

She laughed shrilly and clapped her hands together again. "Precious," she snorted, her voice once more piercing. "Just like that lovely little girl who came in with you, that wonderful Laura. Such a lamb."

Michael caught his breath. "May I ask, Sister . . . ?"

"Yes, sweetheart?"

"Is she well, Sister?"

"Oh, you're worried about your friend." A playfully sentimental frown appeared on her face. "That's just what I'd expect. You've obviously got a good heart, down there under all the silly mischievousness and depravity. I can tell. And don't you worry, she couldn't be in finer fettle."

Michael swallowed. "Thank-you, Sister."

"She's like you," Sr. Galera continued, "as good as gold when the tarnish is scraped away. Mind you, she's a spirited one. She's quite a snarly, scratchy little pet when she hasn't had her nap and milk and medicine, isn't she?" Again, she mutely awaited an answer with a cocked eye.

"Oh, yes, Sister," said Michael after a moment, "she's strong-willed . . . but very kind . . . and terribly brave."

"Well, of course she is, and we got along beautifully. I mean, there was a little difficulty at first, with her frame of mind so to speak, but she was an absolute delight once we got all that sorted out. Rambunctious, I think. That's what I'd call her. But now we're as close as can be, and she's a sweetly purring pet."

This was beginning to sound ominously implausible to Michael, but all he said was "Yes, Sister."

"That's only to be expected," she added with a gentle sigh. "I know the two of you are here because you've had some very hard times spiritually, and some truly, truly deep psychologically traumatic experiences. So it's natural for her to be a little contrary and wild. Once we get her on a good healthy pharmaceutical rotation, she'll get over that in a blink."

Michael wanted to say nothing to this, but again her expression told him he was expected to reply. "Yes, Sister," he murmured.

"Well, now," said Sr. Galera, walking over to the bed and collecting the nightshirt, "you've saved us a good deal of time by being up and dressed . . . and washed, I presume?"

"Yes, Sister."

"Good child." She came around to face him again. "You won't be breakfasting in your room today. Not with the other children either. But I've arranged for you and your little friend to eat with one another before you go to see the director together. You'll like that, won't you?"

"Oh, yes, Sister," said Michael, not needing to feign earnestness. "Thank-you."

"You two can catch up a bit."

"Yes, Sister. Thank-you very much."

Sr. Galera smiled with what seemed to be genuine fondness and then patted his cheek with a soft, plump, clammily moist hand. "Such a polite one. As I say, a little gentleman. Aren't you getting a bit tired, standing so straight like that?"

"Yes, Sister," said Michael, somewhat taken aback.

"I would think so," she said. "Well, I believe we can go now. It won't do any harm if we're a moment or two early."

THERE WERE NO WINDOWS IN THE CORRIDOR EITHER, and the walls were of the same unadorned concrete as those in his room, though the floor tiles were a dull blue, and the phosphorion panels overhead emitted a hazily purple glow that imbued everything with an especially desolate drabness. Dark green doors ran along either side of the hallway at intervals of about ten feet. Every surface seemed to emanate despondency. Michael had expected to see a guard or two stationed somewhere on the floor, or at least an orderly or two, but there were none. Sr. Galera kept pace about three feet behind him most of the way, humming merrily to herself, the rasping echoes of their footfalls blending a low sepulchral note into her aimless tune. At the end of the corridor, about forty yards from Michael's room, there was a hydraulic elevator. Sr. Galera unlocked its sliding door with the key at her wrist, guided Michael into the car ahead of her, directly under its overhead phosphorion, latched the door behind them again, and turned the car's dial several spaces. Just as the gushing water in the great resonant steel shaft below their feet had begun gradually to lift them upward, she remarked, "I expect you were hoping to see Sr. Theomenia again. I hope you're not disappointed."

"Oh, no, Sister," said Michael, "not at all."

"She was so sorry to miss you this morning. She took such a liking to you, but she's with the director just now, making her report on your activities from yesterday. I have to make my report after her, on your little friend, and her little bit of mischief last night, and then the two of you will meet him. He's a wonderful man. You'll adore him."

The elevator came to a halt, and the gauge by the door indicated that they had ascended to a level four stories up from the ground floor, which itself had apparently been two stories up from the floor where Michael's room was situated. Sr. Galera slid the door open and led him into a wider and considerably more presentable corridor, with clean, dark blue carpeting underfoot, walls and a ceiling painted a hideously cheerful yellow, and rows of real phosphoria, lambent with their normal golden glow, in respectable brass sconces. There were six or so doors of polished wood with small oblong windows of frosted glass in their upper panels, and at the end of the corridor Michael could see another corridor, running at a right angle. There was, as well, a hint of chemical perfume in the air, with a vaguely floral fragrance that was almost not unpleasant. Again, no guards or orderlies were anywhere to be seen.

"This way, sweetness," Sr. Galera chirped, leading him to the second door on the right and unlocking it with her key. "You've a little friend waiting to see you."

The room was surprisingly spacious but scarcely furnished at all. Directly to his right, perhaps ten feet from the door, was an unremarkable desk in the plainest utilitarian style and a simple swivel chair. Opposite the door, across a space of as much as six yards, was a table for two flanked by simple wooden chairs and set with a variety of dishes, utensils, and pitchers, as well as two covered steel platters. The floor was carpeted in the same manner as the hallway, the walls and ceiling painted a yellowing white. Again, there were no windows. None of the room's details, however, made any immediate impression on Michael, because Laura was there as well, standing at attention beside the table in a simple dress made from the same gray fabric as Michael's clothing, bound at the waist with a similar canvas belt, its skirt reaching her shins; she was wearing gray stockings and canvas shoes, and her hair was tied back tautly, with only a single curl free at either temple. Even across the room, her eyes met his, and he could see that she was struggling to contain her emotions. He felt the same struggle in himself, and it was nearly intolerable. But they both remained immobile for several seconds. Then, with a laugh that was almost a shriek, Sr. Galera threw her hands in the air and exclaimed, "Oh, goodness, you silly little piggies, don't be so formal! Go," she said, pushing Michael gently forward by the shoulders, "give your friend a proper hug."

Michael glanced back at the nurse hesitantly, but only for a moment. Then he strode quickly across the room and he and Laura embraced. He felt himself trembling, and felt her trembling too, and knew that he was perilously close to tears. "I didn't know what had become of you," he whispered weakly.

Behind him, he heard Sr. Galera clap her hands together delightedly and sigh with contentment. "That's much better." Then, after a few seconds, she added, "But that's enough now. Time to eat."

Michael and Laura detached themselves from one another and turned to face the nurse, though Michael realized after a second that he had not yet let go of Laura's hand. Sr. Galera approached, gesturing for them to sit, and they did so.

"This is normally just a detention area for children waiting to see the director, usually for disciplinary reasons. That's why there aren't any other seats. The children have to stand at attention till summoned. Good for the back, I hear, but a bit tiring I would think. But, confidentially, I haven't finished writing down my report for the director . . . you know, on how things went yesterday when you were getting settled in." She looked at Laura with a comically sulking expression. "I'll have to note down all the little difficulties we had last night, of course, but I think we're past that." She briefly laid a hand on Laura's head, to which Laura responded with a perfectly blank stare. "So I thought," Sister Galera continued, "that while I'm at the desk over there putting my report together, and since I have to keep an eye on both of you, that you two could have a nice little breakfast together, and a bit of a conversation. It's not really normally allowed, but we needn't mention it to anyone. So I had these things brought in."

"Thank-you, Sister," said Michael after a moment's pause.

"Yes, thank-you, Sister," said Laura in a voice barely above a mutter.

Sr. Galera sighed again. "After all, you may never have another chance

231

to talk to one another." She smiled affectionately at each of them and then retreated to the desk. The swivel chair creaked loudly as she sat upon it.

This last remark had all at once made Michael feel a kind of cold emptiness in his chest. He turned his eyes to Laura, but she was gazing down at the table listlessly. For a few moments, neither of them moved, but then he removed the cover from one of the platters and discovered two bowls of porridge. Unlike the previous day's breakfast, it was hot, and was topped with copious berries and toasted nuts and was accompanied by small pitchers of cream and honey. And, on uncovering the other platter, he found two oval dishes, each containing two poached eggs and a generous slice of extremely aromatic toasted bread, with a small dish of real butter on the side. "Look," he said softly, "have some of this. I don't know about you, but I'm ravenous."

Laura raised her eyes and attempted a smile, but achieved only a look of sardonic resignation. She let Michael place the food before her, however, and pour cream over her porridge, and fill her glass with the melon-infused water from one of the pitchers. He was even about to butter her toast for her when she took the knife from his hand. "I can do that," she said quietly.

Michael was, in fact, quite hungry, and this was the only appetizing food he had seen since the night of their capture, and so he began to eat with some enthusiasm. But when he saw that Laura was merely stirring her porridge over and over again distractedly, he paused to whisper: "You must eat. You've got to stay strong. We've got to be ready."

She looked at him inquiringly, and then wearily, and then began eating, steadily but with an air of indifference.

Michael began eating at a somewhat more deliberate pace, so as not to finish too soon before she did. "Honestly," he said after two or three minutes had passed, "I know things look horrible, but please don't give up yet."

Laura closed her eyes for a second and then gently shook her head. "I'm tired, Michael," she said.

A few more moments passed in silence. Michael finished the last of his eggs and toast and continued working away at his porridge, but now at a pace as dilatory as Laura's. "What happened?" he asked at last. "Why does the nurse keep talking about difficulties yesterday, or whatever it is she . . . ?"

Laura stared directly into his eyes, with just enough exasperation on her face to reassure Michael that she was still herself. But then she only looked down again, almost meekly. "Nothing," she murmured and took a small lethargic bite from her toast.

Somewhere in Michael, some deep anger was stirring. To see Laura so subdued and seemingly defeated — something unimaginable to him until now — somehow offended him more profoundly than anything he himself had endured. "If they've hurt you," he said, his whisper becoming fierce, "I swear I'll kill them."

At this Laura closed her eyes and drew a deep, melancholy breath. "Please don't, Michael," she said, the fatigue in her voice now tinged with impatience. "It doesn't make me feel any better if you don't talk like yourself."

"I mean it," he said.

"No you don't," she said, opening her eyes again and looking at him in a way that made it clear she found him touchingly absurd. "At least, you shouldn't. It makes everything more awful."

"Did they hurt you?" he asked more insistently.

Laura shrugged. "It wasn't much worse than what happens when you get sent to the praeceptor's office at school."

Michael hesitated for a moment to reply. "I, ah, don't really know what that's like. I never got sent to the praeceptor."

Now a slight spark of amusement appeared in Laura's eyes. Then she positively smirked. "Of course you didn't. I don't know what I was thinking."

Michael felt slightly relieved at this. At least, she sounded somewhat more like herself. "But they didn't hurt you . . . much?" he asked again.

Laura scowled. "Well, it didn't exactly tickle," she snapped, clearly finding the topic somewhat embarrassing. "It still doesn't. But they told me it would be worse in future if I don't behave as they want me to. Mostly it was . . ." She shook her head angrily.

"What?"

"It was humiliating," she said. "That's all. I think that's the real point . . . of everything here. To make us feel like we haven't any . . . you know, any dignity."

Michael glanced across the room at Sr. Galera, who was energetically scribbling away on a pad of paper with an orange-plumed pen, humming to herself aimlessly and cheerfully, her head bobbling up and down. He looked back at Laura. "Your nurse seems fairly nice, at least," he said. "At least, compared to mine."

Laura cast a baleful glance across the room. "She isn't. Not at all."

Sr. Galera happened to raise her head just at that moment, saw Michael and Laura looking her way, smiled almost rapturously, and blew them a kiss. Then, with a fond giggle, she returned to her writing.

233

"The one they assigned to me," said Michael, "spent the whole day ordering me about and calling me a — oh, I don't know — a little degenerate and a beast, and threatening to have me punished. It was all a bit vague, but I thought she was going to have me thrashed, or psychoanalyzed, or drugged, or all three."

"Well Sr. Galera didn't threaten anything," said Laura. "She just had it done. She sent me to someone called Miss Loveslug in their punishments ward here when I wouldn't say prayers, and then again when I refused to take my sedative."

"Twice?" said Michael, incensed, his voice rising in volume.

Laura glanced again at Sr. Galera, then raised her finger to her lips. "Quiet," she said. "Yes, twice. And when I still wouldn't swallow the pill she had two orderlies hold me so she could give me an injection instead. But she was very . . . *sweet* about it all. She kept calling me 'pet' and 'dearie' and laughing at me like I was a silly little baby, just being awkward, and she kept pinching my cheeks and stroking my hair."

Michael lowered his eyes. He did not know if he was furious or merely depressed. Perhaps he was both at once. It was an odd feeling, whatever it was. He ate the last of his porridge, saying nothing, and emptied his glass. He no longer noticed the flavor of anything. "Listen," he finally said, "we have to make them think they've beaten . . . think they've defeated us. You've got to do what they say, without any defiance."

He looked up again to see Laura staring back at him almost pityingly.

"Please." He added, somewhat pathetically.

"I can't," she said, nearly inaudibly.

"Please. Master your pride for just a little while."

"It's not pride."

"Your natural . . . strength of character, then."

"Why, Michael?" Laura said in a tone of utter fatigue. "What's the point of letting them have the satisfaction? We've lost already. They have us, and they have Oriens."

Michael looked once again toward Sr. Galera, still bent over her report. Then he turned back to Laura, dramatically widening his eyes and arching his eyebrows with what he intended as a conspiratorial expression, and tapped his chest meaningfully three times with his forefinger.

Laura looked at him with knitted brows, scowled, and shook her head uncomprehendingly.

Michael pressed his lips together resolutely, tried to stare at her with an even more penetratingly secretive look on his face, and tapped his chest again.

Laura stared at him for an instant as if he were mad, then rolled her eyes, sarcastically mirrored his expression back at him in an exaggerated form, and threw her hands open in annoyance. "What?" she whispered irascibly. "What are you trying to tell me? Is that your way of saying I'm in your heart, or something idiotic like that?"

At this, Michael felt himself relaxing. Being mocked by Laura was so familiar a sensation that it instantly comforted him. He smiled discreetly. "No, you . . . you little dunce," he replied, taking a certain delight in the word. "I'm telling you" — and here he lowered his voice almost to silence — "that I still have the jewels that Oriens gave me . . . here, around my neck."

For several moments, Laura's expression was wholly inscrutable. Then, ever so slightly, her eyes widened in earnest, she glanced cautiously toward the nurse, and then bent her head forward across the table. "They didn't find them on you?"

"They can't. Don't you remember? Only I can remove the purse . . . or hold one of the stones."

Laura's eyes fell away from his. For a few seconds, she was clearly lost in thought. When she met his gaze again, she asked, "Do you know how to use them? Or what they can do?"

Michael bit his lower lip. "Well, I know what Oriens told us when he made me take them. And we've seen how powerful they are. And, I think . . . I think they more or less know what to do for themselves . . . if you ask them."

Laura looked at him with hooded eyes. "That's not very precise."

"Look, we've seen Oriens use them. He gave them to me for a reason. And it's something we have that they don't know about."

Again, Laura's gaze drifted away from his and toward nothing in particular. Obviously, she was allowing herself to consider the possibilities that had suddenly opened before her.

"I mean," Michael continued, "we just have to wait for the right moment. So we have to make them think they've conquered any resistance on our . . ." But he had to pause, because a sudden fierce shock of pain in his left shin had converted his words into a sharp wheeze. "What, what . . . ?" he coughed out involuntarily, doing all he could to contain a shout of angry surprise. "What are you doing, you . . . ?" He clenched his teeth and pressed his lips together as hard as he could.

"Everything all right over there?" Sr. Galera called cheerily across the room.

"Wonderful, Sister," Laura promptly replied.

Michael managed a forced smile, hardly distinguishable from a grimace, and nodded. "Oh, yes, Sister," he coughed again. "Delicious."

"Splendid, splendid," Sr. Galera replied. "Almost done over here. You two finish up now."

"Yes, Sister," Laura called back charmingly.

"Are you insane?" Michael hissed through his teeth. "Why did you kick me?"

"You called me a dunce," said Laura blandly. "A *little* dunce, in fact. That 'little' sounded especially condescending, if you ask me."

"You . . . call me all sorts . . ." He closed his eyes to wait for a second cresting wave of pain to subside. "You can't go kicking me whenever you like just because you're a girl and think you can get away with it."

"Oh, I think I can," Laura replied, narrowing her eyes. "And you can't do anything about it. People would think you were such a coward if you went around kicking girls."

"It's absurdly unfair," he quietly moaned.

"I know. That's what makes it so lovely. Anyway, the soles on these shoes are just rubber. Don't whimper. I doubt I even broke the skin. Don't start crying or anything."

"I'm not going to . . ." Michael opened his eyes again and saw the first unforced smile Laura had shown him since he had entered the room. Then he felt his own expression soften, and he smiled back at her in surrender. "It's an abuse of an unearned social advantage — as my father would say. Even if you didn't draw blood."

Laura's smile lingered a few seconds longer, and even briefly widened; but then her expression became more sober and she laid a hand on Michael's wrist. "Do you really think you can use them?" There was a note of genuine hopefulness in her voice.

"I do," he said. "I have to. We can't just give in now. There's too much to lose."

Laura nodded and withdrew her hand. Pensively, she ate the last of her toast. Then, a slight perplexity clouding her expression, she said, "Can I ask you something?"

"Yes, of course."

"You heard what the confectioner said to Oriens? You know, about him being . . ." Her voice died away.

"An aetherial daemon, you mean?" Michael nodded. "I heard it."

"Have you considered whether . . . it might be true?"

Michael shook his head, but also averted his gaze from hers. "No," he said. "It can't be. We've seen enough to know better."

"I don't believe it either," said Laura. "I just mean . . . well, we really don't know anything about him except what he told us."

"It doesn't even matter," said Michael. "Even if I thought it was true, I'd still be on his side. Even if he's some kind of . . . heavenly dissident"— he turned his eyes to Laura's once again —"I'd want to join his rebellion against this world's God. But I know he's not that. I know that everything he told us was true. I know he doesn't lie. I can just tell. And then . . ."

Laura waited a few seconds, head turned at an inquisitive slant. "And then . . . ?" she repeated.

"I know the story he told us is true because . . . I feel like I already knew it. As if I could almost remember it. I knew the first time I heard it."

Laura nodded slowly. "Right," she said, "yes. I know what you mean. I felt the same way. It's like I already knew it was all true, and I'd heard it before, even though I hadn't. But . . . but I don't think the confectioner was lying . . . not lying for our benefit or anything. I think he really believed what he was saying."

"So do I," said Michael. "I think that's what he has to believe. It's what they all believe. Or most of them."

"Maybe, then," Laura added diffidently, "they might all be underestimating his power."

"I hope so," said Michael. "If the authorities really recognized him for what he is, I don't think they'd dare . . ."

Just then, however, the door to the room swung open and a tall, spare, lanky orderly with hair cropped close to his skull and a sullen frown on his gaunt face entered and, without a word, slouched toward the table. Michael and Laura both stood to attention as he approached, but he took no notice of them. He merely began gathering the dishes and utensils and platters together; and, when he had carried them away and — as was audible from just beyond the door — placed them upon some kind of metal conveyance, he returned for the glasses and pitchers. Cradling these in one arm, he closed the door behind him.

"Right," said Sr. Galera, rising from her chair, slipping her report into a purple folder. "That's the signal that the director is ready for us." On seeing Michael and Laura standing at attention, she snuffled whimsically. "Why are you both being so stiff and formal now? You didn't get up for *him*, did you?" she said, waving her hand in the direction of the departed orderly.

Michael and Laura exchanged glances.

"Yes, Sister," said Laura.

"I was told to stand at attention whenever any adult enters the room, Sister," said Michael.

Now Sr. Galera's laugh really was a shriek, scarcely distinguishable from a cry of terror or grief. She doubled over in mirth for several seconds, quivering like a custard in torment, and when she stood up straight again tears were glistening on her plump, flushed cheeks. "Oh, my goodness," she cried, trying to catch her breath and practically staggering as she came around the desk, gesturing for Michael and Laura to approach. "You stand up, yes, but only for *proper* adults. Not for *them*. Never for *them*." She had to bite her hand to contain the next surge of laughter. When at last she stopped shaking, she wiped the tears from the corners of her eyes. "The orderlies here are all congenital convicts. You know, gamma-somatics. Inmates who were ultimately designated as natural criminals . . . innate deviants. Assigned as permanent menials. That's what often becomes of incorrigibly refractory children, you know. Well, the ones that can be salvaged at all. The rest . . . well, we can't mend every broken cup they send us. You must have heard something about institutionalized incurables, surely." She shook her head in delirious astonishment as she opened the door and ushered them both into the corridor. "They're not even allowed to speak, for goodness' sake. You might as well salute the furniture. What in the world do they teach you out there in the wilds of Oreiotopia? Oh, my goodness! You little darling dears, you!" And again her shrill, merry laugh rang out, until it seemed to fill the corridor with its happy echoes.

III

THE ELEVATOR CARRIED THEM TO A FLOOR another three stories up. Here, the presentable gave way to the lavish. The upper halves of the wide corridor's walls were a shiny eggshell white, while the lower halves were elaborately wainscoted with panels of a dark wood so richly hued that dim pools of purple and crimson seemed indistinctly visible in its depths. Frosted windows in the long barrel-vault of the ceiling allowed the morning light to stream down at regular intervals like fans of sparkling mist. The hardwood floors shone with thick varnish. Brass sconces in the shapes of bare, slender female arms held glowing, cut-crystal phosphoria almost lovingly in their upturned hands. The air had an unnaturally dry chill of the sort produced by a mechanical climatistikon, something Michael had not felt since he and his father had moved to the cooler elevations of Oreiotopia. Instead of doors, rows of paintings in vivid colors stretched along the length of the hallway on either side: stirringly emblematic portraits of laborers, fishermen, farmers, lawyers, priests, and men of business, or of mothers, nurses, teachers, librarians, operatic sopranos, and barmaids, all resolutely or elatedly engaged in his or her trade, the men muscular and broad-shouldered, with handsome and prognathous features, the women statuesque and voluptuous, with enticingly radiant smiles or pouting berry-red lips, and each figure ingeniously depicted in a manner somehow both exuberantly carnal and starkly machinelike. At the far end of the corridor, opposite the elevator, the wall was emblazoned with the silhouette of an anvil encircled by a large gearwheel and ringed by an inscription in florid lettering: Incus Decoris et Modestiae, Fabrica Pietatis et Castimoniae.

"That's the school crest," Sr. Galera twittered as she guided Michael and Laura toward it. "Isn't it lovely? Not that anyone knows what it means."

"'An anvil of decorousness and modesty, a workshop of piety and . . . moral purity,'" said Michael, ". . . Sister."

"I'm sure that's as good a guess as any," said Sr. Galera, winking at him.

The corridor terminated in a wide rectangular atrium with large polished wooden doors at either end. "This way," Sr. Galera added, turning right and bouncing along before them with wobbling buoyancy.

No sooner had she knocked on the door than it opened wide to reveal the austerely angular figure of Sr. Theomenia, and at once Michael felt a small sea-swell of depression break over him. The older nurse said nothing, but merely stood aside and brusquely gestured for the three of them to enter. The director's office was impressively opulent: superb wooden paneling on every side and wooden coffering overhead, a handwoven carpet patterned with intricate images of vines and fruits and flowers, green, red, yellow, and violet against a rich midnight blue, chairs of lacquered rufous wood and polished ruby leather, an immense desk of scrolled and fluted ebony drenched in the morning brilliance pouring down from two more skylights, and beyond the desk three enormous windows with large panes framed in airily delicate brass. And there, seated at the heart of all that sumptuousness and leaning forward in his chair behind the great desk, was a figure that looked like nothing so much as a dapper but exceedingly despondent frog.

The very shape of his head seemed as if it had been altered by a powerful vertical vice, resulting in a symmetrical ovoid with a horizontal polar axis. His complexion was not so much sallow as lightly green. His mouth was unnaturally wide, with thick, tautly stretched lips the color and texture of earthworms. What ears he had were small and circular and somewhat recessed. His nose was broad and rather flat, as if it had been spread on his face unevenly by a butter knife, and had what looked more like nares than full nostrils. The sparse, slick tendrils of his hair were of some murkily nondescript hue and clung unguinously to his scalp. The dense convex lenses of his wire-rimmed spectacles made it seem as if his greenish-gray eyes were peering out at the world from the bottom of a shallow pond, through a thin layer of algae. If he had a jawline, it was not immediately evident where he kept it. His hunched, narrow, rounded shoulders, moreover, amplified the amphibian quality of his appearance. He was, however, dressed in the height of fashion: a high collar and pearl-colored cravat, a waistcoat of forest-green velvet, and a formal coat of lighter, lettuce-green damask with lapels of cream-white satin with pink borders.

"Director," said Sr. Galera as she handed him her report, which he received rather listlessly and without words.

Another purple folder with another sheaf of papers already lay open on the desk, and he placed Sr. Galera's next to it, opened it as well, and began reading. Occasionally his eyes passed back and forth between the two reports. Now and then, he glanced up at Michael and Laura, twice lingering on the latter with what looked like a glare of displeasure. Two or three times he sighed, in a reedy and gurgling way.

All the while, Michael's eyes were fixed on the room's windows, which afforded a view of the very center of Kenopolis. He really had forgotten how overpowering a sight the city's skyline could be: the immense skyscrapers of granite and bronze, steel and glass, marble and silver; slender pillars, massive obelisks, vaunting towers; cusped, roofed, pinnacled, terraced; sinuously embellished or sleekly minimalist; cornices, dentils, chevrons, volutes, modillions; cupolas, spires, arches, turrets. It all burned and glistered fiercely and ecstatically in the morning sunlight, except where it was submerged in the frozen cascades of its own gigantic purple shadows. Beyond all of it lay the shining, glassy, rippled surface of the great bay under a vast cloudless blue, the water and sky converging at the far horizon in a thin band of silvery haze. And in the very center of the city, rising higher than any other structure and spreading its annexes like great white wings stood the Central Ministry of the World Dominion with its titanic dome of blue and gold. Birds wheeled about it continuously like sparks gyrating around a fire. When he had been a child, Michael had been struck with awe every time he had looked at it, scarcely able to believe that anything so prodigiously huge and gorgeous could ever have been built by human hands. Just now, though, as he stood there in silence, its sheer immensity and magnificence seemed sinister — even atrocious. It was as if it were a kind of enormous monster perched upon the body of its prey.

"Well, then" — the voice of the director, which had the quality of a highly pitched croak, recalled him from his thoughts — "we seem to have a mystery here." He closed the folders and set them to one side, then raised his eyes to Michael and Laura. "You may sit, boy," he said, indicating one of the leather-upholstered chairs.

"Thank-you, sir," said Michael, seating himself.

The director looked at Laura with cold, reptilian impassiveness. "As for you, girl, I'm not at all pleased by what I read here." He jabbed a forefinger at the reports. Michael noticed that the pads of his fingertips were round and notably broader than the emaciated digits to which they were attached. "Not pleased in the least. You're not the first fractious child who needed to be disciplined on first arriving here, but I'd been given to believe that yours is a reasonably reputable family. Reading this, I might almost think you were the daughter of chimneysweeps. Two visits to the mastigatrix and an injection under restraint on your first night is hardly what I'd have expected from a well-bred young lady, even one who's traveled some distance down the road of vice. And it's certainly more than I'm prepared to tolerate." He leaned even further forward and Michael had the oddest feeling that a long tongue might at any moment dart out from between his lips. "What do you have to say for yourself, then?"

Laura stared steadily into the director's spectacles. Michael could see from the working of her jaw that she was struggling not to speak the words spontaneously rising up in her. Then, after a second, she dropped her head as if ashamed and said, "I'm very sorry, sir. I behaved horribly."

Michael drew in his breath very quietly in relief.

The director's expression did not change, but after a few seconds he leaned back again and, in a somewhat mollified tone, said, "Well, that's something, at least. Understand, girl, that you were treated with extreme delicacy. In future, you can expect no such leniency. This is a penal reformatory, which is to say a hospital for very sick souls. It is a place where radical surgeries and drastic cauteries are called for, not syrupy tonics in small doses. Do you understand? We don't have the luxury of letting nature take its course. Do you know why the disciplinary sciences are called 'kolastics,' girl?"

Laura raised her eyes uncertainly. "No, sir."

"Because in the Noble Tongue the word for corrective punishment is *kolasis*, which originally meant 'pruning' or 'docking,' as you would the trees in an orchard or the vegetation in a garden. Now, we know what happens when a garden is left to become unruly, don't we?"

After a few seconds, Laura apparently realized that she was expected to answer. "I'm not sure, sir."

"Weeds," said the director gravely, "and shrubberies swollen out of all proportion, and topiary reverting to a shapeless shambles, and excessive numbers of flowers in gross and undignified profusion, and vines and ivies all wantonly out of control. In short, decadence is what happens. Chaos. Corruption. Do you take my meaning, girl?"

"I think so, sir."

"And so we must prune every errant twig and leaf ruthlessly." He nodded in evident satisfaction at his own eloquence. "The alternative is a garden so overgrown that it can't be restored except with scythes and herbicides — or, worse, can't be restored at all and has to be put to the torch. An absolute horticultural catastrophe is what you get. The same is true of deviant children.

As they say, better ten strokes of the cane today than ten-thousand pricks of the hypodermic in days to come. Welts vanish in time, but the lessons they impart are indelible. So, understand, mercy is not an option here. For your own good, any repetition of last night's behavior will be met with the full force of our punitive license."

Now Michael was becoming indignant. It was one thing for them to try to terrify and humiliate him, but it was unpardonable for anyone to talk this way to Laura. And of course, he thought, there was the very real danger that she would not stand for it.

All she said, however, was "Yes, sir, I understand."

"Good," said the director with a nod. "You should emulate your young friend here. I see from his nurse's report that his behavior has been utterly impeccable from first to last."

Michael could not help but turn his head to glance back as Sr. Theomenia in surprise. "Eyes forward, child," she commanded with a snap of her fingers.

"You may sit too," said the director to Laura, "if you can." When she had done so, he leaned back fully and thrust his thumbs into his waistcoat pockets. "How often did your parents chastise you when you were growing up?" he suddenly asked, his eyes shooting back and forth between the two of them.

"You mean actual physical chastisement, sir?" asked Michael after a moment.

"Yes, of course."

"Never at all, sir," said Michael.

"Mine neither, sir," said Laura.

The director lowered his eyes for several seconds and slowly, lugubriously shook his head. "Tragic," he muttered. "It explains a great deal, though." He looked up again. "It may be prudent to put one or both of you on an accelerated castigation schedule for a while. Sometimes preventive punishment is the best medication. You may be the more obviously recalcitrant," he said to Laura, "but you"— he looked somberly at Michael —"according to the dossier I have from the Office of Children's Safety and Sanity, you're a bookish child, which almost always portends a certain degree of morbidity in physiological and sociodynamic development, especially in males. You may be the more sorely in need of regular proleptic correction."

Michael said nothing.

"But," the director continued, "there's not much we can decide on today, since we've been given special instructions for you two — instructions that baffle me, to be honest — telling us to wait before making any arrangements. As yet, also, you're prohibited from talking to the other children, even to make public attestations of your crimes. You're not even to be sent to the confessional yet. I don't understand that at all, since I would assume your spiritual wellbeing is a matter of prime importance. This institute was established by the Incudian Brethren — Order of the Anvil, that is — and our chaplain here, Fr. Wraithwight, is an Incudian priest with years of experience dealing with psychologically and morally damaged minors. He's a judicious and thorough confessor, one who doesn't flinch in the penitential prescriptions he sends us. And yet we can't avail ourselves of his wisdom, and we can't even give you any of the proper medications to ease the emotional transition into your new life here. So . . ." He threw his large froggy hands open in perplexity. "So it goes. Anyway" — he laid his hands flat on the desk — "here we are, then. So, let's at least be properly introduced. I'm Dr. Porphyrius Glabrus Glumgum, the director of this institution. My academic and professional specializations are in psychotraumatic therapies, counter-delinquency theory, and psychopharmacology. I tell you this solely to make it clear to you that you're in the hands of well-trained professionals. It's not an overture to a deeper companionship. We won't be interacting henceforth, as a rule. You're unlikely to visit me at all, unless you have to be brought here for reasons of extraordinary miscreancy. If that should happen, you will rue renewing our acquaintance, I assure you. But my hope is that the healthy regimen of this institution — the plain, bracing diet, the robustly interventionist pharmaceutical schedule, the strict hygiene, the scientifically rigorous methods of corporal and psychological punishment, the year-round schooling, the psycho-reconstructive techniques, the absence of desserts, and so forth — will ultimately heal you and make it possible to release you into the world again, under the care of your new families."

Michael grew tense at this, clutching the arms of his chair, but managed to say nothing. Out of the corner of his eye, he could see Laura stir abruptly, begin to lean forward, but then sit back again.

"That's rather a lot to hope for, I know," continued Dr. Glumgum, "but I'm an optimist. Ultimately you'll be segregated into the separate boys' and girls' sections here. At that point, you won't ever be seeing each other again, except in chapel, but your medications will make it so that that doesn't cause you the least distress. For now, you'll each continue in solitary confinement until we have further instructions. Is that clear?"

Michael despised this man with every cell in his body. "Yes, sir," he said. "Yes, sir," said Laura.

Dr. Glumgum stared meditatively at both of them for several moments, drumming his fingers on the desktop. As he did so, Michael noticed, the round pads of his fingertips seemed ever so slightly to catch hold of the surface of the polished wood and to pull free again only with a weakly adhesive reluctance.

"Morning chapel starts shortly, director," Sr. Theomenia suddenly interjected.

"I know, Sister." Dr. Glumgum wrinkled his brow (what little there was of it), sat back with his elbows on the arms of his chair, and brought his hands together on his abdomen, interlacing his fingers in a repulsively prehensile way. "Perhaps I shouldn't bring this up, but I can't forbear. Whatever this great mystery is that dictates we treat you two so gingerly, I know it involves another child, apparently one from a very important family. I know that it's a delicate situation, or a volatile one, and that there are issues of considerable social import here — even, it's been hinted, issues of state."

Sr. Galera gasped. "My goodness me!" she squeaked.

"It's not clear to me whether you two fell under his influence, or he fell under yours, but I know that it's quite a scandalous tale potentially. Apparently, there were all sorts of wild misdeeds involved, things that could . . . I don't know, bring the mighty low . . . or at least lead to difficult questions being asked in public assemblies. I suppose that's the reason for all the secrecy." His gaze hardened. The bruise-colored tip of his tongue momentarily emerged from between his lips. "Any light that you feel you can shed on this, you two? For your own good, perhaps?"

Michael and Laura exchanged glances of feigned incomprehension.

"No, sir," said Michael.

"No, sir," Laura concurred.

Dr. Glumgum pursed his thick lips disappointedly, scowled at both of them, and then raised his eyes to look over their heads. "So, Sisters," he said, his voice all at once sounding strained, "it seems I'm to be kept in the dark. Apparently my eight years governing this facility, my six higher degrees, my two awards for contributions to pharmaceutical and psycho-coercive rehabilitation, my immaculate record of service and achievement, my uncontested reputation for discretion and sobriety . . ." — his lips shuddered, his cheeks and strange small ears flushed a sickly livid purple, and he clenched his jaws as if attempting to hold back tears — ". . . yes, well, all of that, it seems, is of no consequence. The ministry has determined that I'll be responsible for these wretched little defectives, but that I don't deserve to know what that responsibility entails." He heaved a deep, prolonged sigh that trailed away into a soft whistle. Then, slowly, the look of exasperation departed from his features and was replaced by his original expression of dejected indifference. "Well, so . . . anything else we need to discuss here?"

"Hair, director," said Sr. Galera gaily. "They both need their hair cut hygienically, the girl especially. I'm glad to take her over to the tonsorial ward after lunch and have her shorn."

Again Michael grew tense. And again, with all the power of his will, he repressed the anger welling up in him. When he looked at Laura, though, he saw that she was struggling even more violently not to react. She was staring down into her own lap, and for a moment her jaw and lips quivered.

"It's not the least trouble," added Sr. Galera.

"Alas," said Dr. Glumgum with a petulant frown, "we're prohibited even from that. We are, as yet, to make no changes in their physical appearances. God alone knows why."

"Why, that's silly," said Sr. Galera.

"Even so," said Dr. Glumgum. "Anyway, you'd best get them to chapel. Remember, no fraternizing with the other inmates."

"Quite," said Sr. Theomenia.

ON THE WAY TO THE ELEVATOR, THE TWO NURSES CON-versed quietly with one another, drawing far enough ahead of their charges that Michael felt safe in whispering to Laura, "It'll be all right. I know you almost lost your temper. Just a little longer."

"Actually," said Laura, "I was about to cry. I'm not quite as brave as you think. I like my hair."

Michael stared ahead malevolently at Sr. Galera. "So do I," he said. "I always have. Even that time when I pulled it so hard that you started crying."

"We were seven years old," said Laura.

"It's . . . it's glorious," he added earnestly.

"Oh, hush, you fool," she replied, though not very severely.

ON THE GROUND FLOOR, AT THE END OF A DRAB HALL-way with walls painted an institutional gray and a floor tiled in black, behind plain double doors of crudely varnished pine, was the chapel. Its interior had no windows. The altar was large and hideous, having been fashioned in the efficientist-mechanist-brutalist style that had been in vogue some decades ago. Hanging on the wall behind it was the room's only other ornamentation: a large, clumsy image of an anvil and hammer, made of wood and painted a metallic black. The plain wooden pews were already full of children, perhaps a hundred of them, sitting in rigid silence, an aisle separating the boys from the girls—though on entering from the back Michael could not at first tell which were which, since all of them had their hair cropped in the same savagely short and carelessly uneven manner. It did not matter, in any event, as he and Laura were not seated among them but were instead taken to a separate pew set off to one side, the two nurses stationing themselves at either end.

After several minutes, a small bell chimed and everyone stood. Fr. Wraithwight entered in the vestments prescribed by the liturgical calendar: a strident scarlet and yellow cassock, a sky-blue girdle, a mauve chasuble with orange embroideries, a massive wig with bright pink ringlets, and a chaplet of silver foil decked with purple crystals. He was extremely tall but also seemed impossibly old and frail — not so much thin as spectral. He began the service without even glancing toward his congregation. His voice was little more than a susurrous wheezing sound that seemed like it might at any moment dissolve into a death-rattle. Rather than stand before or process around the altar in the course of the liturgy, he seemed instead to hover or waver or gently swirl about it, like an eddy of fog in a weak breeze. And yet he conducted the worship from beginning to end without pausing for so much as a second, a full hour and a half of litanies, responsory verses, readings, and a long droning sermon so dull that Michael forgot everything about it even as it entered his ears — except, that is, for the oddly frequent recurrence of the words "industriousness" and "sanitation."

Michael and Laura, under the vigilant eyes of the two nurses, joined in the service dutifully, reciting and responding and pretending to pay attention. There were hymns as well, sung without instrumental accompaniment in the wailing off-key voices of deeply bored children. The last of these, the recessional, was the best-known and most tedious piece in the whole hymnal, the famous setting (entirely in half-notes) by Alampes Phlyaretes of Ludibrius's poem "In all his works, the Artisan doth prove." It went on and on, for seventeen slow, monotonous, excruciating stanzas, and by the end almost every voice in the room had grown feeble and hoarse:

None saw him to his hidden smithy hie
To beat the burning ore to shining steel,
And forge the great machine of earth and sky
In ev'ry gleaming piston, spring, and wheel.
And yet we know it was his hand whose might
First kindled great Hyperion's deathless flame —
Set days ablaze, cast splendors on the night —
And so we magnify his holy name.

When at last the liturgy was done, Fr. Wraithwight, still not sparing a glance toward the pews, wafted away again on a gust of solemn silence, like a ground-mist dissipating in the dawn, and the children were led out in mute columns by a contingent of about a dozen nurses. Only then did Sr. Theomenia and Sr. Galera conduct Michael and Laura back to the elevator. It stopped one story below ground-level where, apparently, Laura's room was located. She and Michael were permitted at Sr. Galera's urging to embrace one another briefly, but not to linger over their farewells. Then the elevator took Michael and Sr. Theomenia down to Michael's floor.

Michael's lunch was the same as it had been on the previous day, and once more he spent the afternoon alone. Then another barely comestible meal, evening ablutions, prayers, and bed. As Sr. Theomenia was extracting the evening's sedative from its case, Michael requested to ask her a question.

"What is it, child?" she said impatiently.

"Why did you tell the director that my behavior was . . . impeccable, I think he said . . . ma'am?"

"Head right back, mouth wide open," she said, and placed the lozenge on his tongue. "Don't ask foolish questions. They annoy me, and if I'm annoyed don't think I won't have recourse to harsh measures."

He did not really believe her now, he realized, but before he could reflect on the strangeness of this fact he had lost interest in it. She was disappearing through the door and he was already sinking into deep, untroubled sleep.

IV

AND THEN, ALL AT ONCE, SHE WAS THERE AGAIN, staring down at him and saying something. For a few moments he felt as though he were dreaming. Then he became gradually aware that she was shaking him by the shoulders, not violently but nonetheless urgently. And now he could make out her words. She was calling him by his first name and telling him to rise, in a voice that was more anxious than commanding.

"What...?" he mumbled. "I don't . . . know . . ."

"You have to get up now," she was saying.

"I . . . I'm trying . . ."

Now she was pulling him upward by his shoulders. "Quickly," she whispered, almost as if she feared being overheard. "Something's happening. Someone's here."

"You called me Michael . . ."

"Oh, child, *up*."

He managed to turn the covers aside and to stand, though totteringly. The phosphorion overhead was glowing at full strength and, after a moment, the chill of the room reached him through his thin nightshirt and the bare soles of his feet. He began to grow more alert, grasped it must be morning, and did his best to bring himself to attention.

"There's no time for that now," Sr. Theomenia said. She cupped her hand under his jaw, took his face in a powerful grip, and forced him to look directly into her eyes. "Someone has come to see you — someone extremely important. Extremely powerful, in fact. You're to have breakfast with him . . . and with . . . well, someone else very important too. We have to get you ready. He's someone who may very well decide your fate. Do you understand?"

Slowly Michael nodded. "Yes, ma'am," he said.

"Get washed and dressed, and don't delay. I need you wide awake before we go. Quickly now." She turned him around and pushed him, though oddly gently, in the direction of the dressing screen.

In his daze, he practically careened forward, but on reaching the screen's other side he paused momentarily, staring stupidly. Rather than the gray uniform he expected to see, a formal suit hung upon a proper dressing stand: a dark blue jacket with sleek black lapels, a red waistcoat, a red cravat, black pressed trousers, a linen shirt with lace cuffs, all of it of obviously very fine materials and expertly cut. On the floor there was a pair of gleaming two-tone leather shoes in jet and white.

"If you don't get moving," Sr. Theomenia growled, "I swear I'll . . ."

It took him all of fifteen minutes to wash and dress, as well as to recover his wits fully. As he was tying the laces of his shoes, Sr. Theomenia paced back and forth near the door in obvious agitation, wringing her hands. Now her nervousness was beginning to communicate itself to him. "Sister," he said, standing up, "I'm ready, I think."

"Remember," she said, summoning him with her hand and straightening his cravat, "you must comport yourself perfectly. You must address him not as 'sir' but as 'my lord.'"

"Address whom, ma'am?" asked Michael, pulling his sleeves' cuffs out from the jacket's sleeves.

"Be absolutely respectful at all times," she continued, taking a small steel comb from her pocket and running it several times through his hair. "He has the power to help you . . . in fact, to do anything for you he wants, if he's so disposed. Don't waste the opportunity."

Michael did not know quite how to react to this. "I promise, Sister," he said after a moment.

"Good," she said, curtly and quietly. Then, passing her eyes over him, she added, "It fits exactly. We measured you precisely when you were brought in, of course, but how they did this so quickly . . ." Her face assumed a sterner expression again. "Come along, then. We mustn't be late."

Everything was happening so quickly that Michael could not quite tell if he was apprehensive, merely curious, or slightly hopeful, but decided not to try to discover which. He hastened after Sr. Theomenia, who was taking long hurried strides, and boarded the elevator with her. They got off on the director's floor again. In the atrium at the end of the corridor, Sr. Galera, Dr. Glumgum, and Laura were already assembled.

Not that Michael was entirely sure that it *was* Laura until he was a few yards from her. She, like him, was in formal wear — in her case, a dress of deep blue, its top elegantly fastened at the left shoulder by a gold brooch bejeweled with what looked like amethysts, its sleeves long and puffed out at the wrists, and its gracefully flared skirt extending to just below the knees. She was also wearing exceedingly stylish boots of dark blue leather with raised heels. He thought for a moment that perhaps a hint of rouge had been applied to her lips and cheeks, but then concluded that her dress was merely setting off her natural coloring to striking effect. What was most startling was her hair, which was fully down around her shoulders, brushed and gleaming and arranged in lovely waves. Michael had never seen her looking so enchanting, even on special occasions. But for the sullen glower of distaste on her face, the effect would have been flawless.

"Don't we just look precious," she said mordantly. "Like dressed-up dolls."

"None of that, you wretched girl," spat Sr. Galera. Michael looked at the younger nurse and saw that every trace of yesterday's invincible effusiveness was now absent from her face. Her expression was not merely anxious, but terrified: eyes wide, cheeks pallid, lips parted and twitching in helpless panic. "I swear, if you say or do anything to make me look bad, there'll be King Hel to pay."

"Oh, for goodness' sake, Galera," said Sr. Theomenia, "if you frighten her before she goes in, she's sure to make some slip. Girl" — she said, turning Laura around by the shoulders to face her — "you'll be fine so long as you remember that you're speaking to men who merit the most punctilious kind of respect."

"Yes, Sister," said Laura, with only a hint of surliness in her voice.

"You look very nice," Michael ventured hesitantly.

"So do you. Shut up."

"Remember to curtsy when you go in," added Sr. Theomenia.

This clearly left Laura at a loss for words.

"And you must bow," said Sr. Theomenia to Michael: "right arm across your midriff, left folded smartly behind your back."

"All right, ma'am," said Michael uncertainly.

"Yes," croaked Dr. Glumgum feebly, somehow drawing this single syllable out into a protracted tremolo.

Michael now took in the director fully for the first time. Rather than merely dapper, his attire today was absurdly resplendent. His coat and trousers were of a lusciously rich crimson satin, garlanded with intricately sinuous flocking, and his waistcoat and cravat were of a bright golden silk, and the two tones of his shoes were crimson and gold as well. Michael could not help but notice also, even making allowance for his hunched posture, what a very short man he was, and how precipitately his somewhat bowed legs tapered down from already narrow hips to almost impossibly slender calves and ankles; and yet his feet were positively enormous and (to judge from the peculiar design of his shoes) rather widely splayed.

"I don't know how to curtsy," said Laura.

"Oh, show her, Sr. Galera," quavered Dr. Glumgum.

"Like this, you stupid girl!" cried Sr. Galera shrilly, lifting the hem of her frock a couple inches and frantically bouncing up and down three times in rapid succession. Then she staggered against the wall from the spell of vertigo she had apparently induced in herself.

"Yes," said Dr. Glumgum, "like that . . . I suppose. Maybe a bit less violent and . . . awkward and . . . utterly graceless. Look" — his eyes began darting back and forth fiercely between Michael and Laura — "I believe we came to understand one another yesterday. I believe we even became friends, or at least initiated the process of friendship. And I daresay I wouldn't be presuming too much in thinking that, even in your brief tenure here, you've come to appreciate something of the spirit of the place . . . the benevolent purpose that animates it, guides it . . . its moral lodestar, so to speak . . . and even perhaps to take some reasonable pride in your own small contribution to its mission. So I think we share a real solicitude for this establishment's reputation. That's fair to say, isn't it?"

Neither Michael nor Laura replied.

"It's only . . ." He began wringing his hands and his thick lips began to vibrate like taut, plucked strings. "It's only that I need you to understand that . . . a great deal is at stake. We've never . . . and, well, how you behave . . ." There was a pleading tone in his voice, which evidently he himself now heard and disliked. "See here," he suddenly proclaimed with a strident whine somehow simultaneously pompous and injured, "no one has ever had cause to think me recreant to my duty. No one! And it would be quite unjust if either of you were to give that impression now, when men of such eminence have condescended to visit us. Oh, oh, oh" — he spun about three times, as if looking for an escape — "it's happening again, I just know it."

Now Michael was completely mystified. His eyes and Laura's briefly met, and it was obvious that she was no better able to make sense of the situation than he was.

"You see," Dr. Glumgum continued, his gyrations coming to a halt, his voice descending to a more restrained register, "this is the first time . . . ever. Our guests — well, our principal guest, to begin with — well, you know who the presiding minister of the World Dominion is, of course . . . the Chief Archon of the Great and Esteemed Council."

"Yes . . . sir," said Michael, beginning to feel genuinely unsettled.

Laura nodded apprehensively. "Yes," she said after several seconds, forgetting the "sir."

Dr. Glumgum turned his filmily bespectacled eyes up toward the ceiling in an attitude of anguish, and the slight bulge of flesh between his pendulous lower lip and his wizened throat that served as a kind of chin quivered from the vehemence of his emotions. "Yes," he said, forcing the word out in a strained peep, "Lord Cosmas Theoplast himself is here."

Michael caught his breath. Behind him, he heard Sr. Galera squeaking fretfully.

"The most powerful man in the whole world is . . . in my office even now. This very moment. And," added the director, lowering his eyes to Michael and Laura again, "he's brought the minister for Psychotherapeutic Affairs with him. The very man, actually, who . . . ." He wagged his head from side to side a few times in apparent discomfort. "The same very eminent gentleman who actually appointed me to this position, after he very graciously, ah . . . removed me from the faculty of the Kenopolitan Academy . . . which was a promotion, in fact, in case you're unaware. That's something easily misunderstood . . . ." He stood in silence for a moment, staring aimlessly at the floor, exhaling in a slow sustained stream through pursed lips so that they made a soft fluttering sound.

"I believe it's time," Sr. Theomenia said after nearly a dozen seconds of this.

Dr. Glumgum turned his eyes to her abruptly, with the harried look of someone who might suddenly run away. Then he swallowed, breathed deeply, and said, "Yes, of course, Sister. I'll just go and . . . ." He lifted a trembling hand in the direction of his office. "So, yes, I'll just . . . yes . . . ." He turned, shuffled toward the door, and tentatively knocked four times with one of his oddly protuberant knuckles.

The office door swung open and the light of morning, pouring through the large windows opposite, spilled around the edges of the imposing figure of an extremely tall, massively muscular, strikingly handsome, very darkly complected man wearing the deep green and golden-piped uniform of an officer in the World Dominion Security Detail. Dr. Glumgum took two timorous steps backward, looking up into the impassive gaze of this titan, and struggled for several seconds to force words out of his mouth. "I have six higher degrees," he said at last, in something like a brittle chirrup. When this elicited no reaction, however, he cleared his throat, attempted to stand more erect, and said, "The young patients whom his excellency the lord presiding minister wishes to see are here."

The security officer stared down witheringly at the director for what seemed an unnecessarily long time and then casually glanced back over his shoulder, saying only, "My lord?" His voice was intimidatingly deep.

From inside the office, a voice not quite as deep and far more melodious replied, "Admit them, of course. We're eager to meet them."

With a disdainful smirk, the officer stepped aside.

"Come, come," called Dr. Glumgum to Michael and Laura, waving them on urgently. "Thank-you, Sisters."

Both nurses briefly lowered their heads and then hastened away, the younger one quickly outpacing the older.

In the office were two men standing together before the central window pane, looking out over the city with their backs to the room, apparently engaged in conversation.

"My lord," said Dr. Glumgum with a quiet cough.

The two men continued to exchange words for another ten seconds or so before turning about. One of them, the taller and (presumably) older, was handsome, fair-skinned, with eyes of a blue so striking as to be visible from across the room. He was not especially old to judge by his face — no wrinkles to speak of, except a few at the corners of his eyes — but he was crowned with thick, flowing white locks and had a neatly trimmed white beard and mustache. His attire, with the exceptions of a silver pin in his cravat and a slender silver chain extending from a pocket of his waistcoat to one of its buttonholes, was also white, obviously of the rarest fabrics and superbly tailored. He was, moreover, instantly recognizable. Michael had seen his image — in painted or photeinic portraits — countless times before, in school, in the library, in the postal office, at civic festivals. The other man was slender, black, younger perhaps, slightly smaller, also bearded and mustachioed, with daubs of gray at the temples, and was wearing an equally luxurious but more restrained ensemble of charcoal, dark silver, and black, with a cravat of twilight blue.

For a long moment, no one said or did anything. Then Michael, remembering Sr. Theomenia's instructions, stiffly bowed. Laura, even more stiffly, made her best attempt at a dignified curtsy.

At this, the man in white smiled, shook his head slightly, and walked across the office to them. "Well, that was something of a disaster, wasn't it?"

he said in a mellifluous baritone. He came to a halt only a few feet from them, looking over the both of them with a cool appraising eye. "I feel I now know what it would be like to watch two fish attempting to dance. Really, I'd just as lief we dispensed altogether with ceremony, formality, deference . . . nervousness, ideally. Those are all enemies of candor, and I want to talk candidly to the two of you. You understand me?"

"Yes, Lord Theoplast," said Michael after a few seconds' hesitation.

"You know me, then," said the man in white. "Well, I won't pretend to be so humble as to have imagined you wouldn't. Laura, is it?" He reached out a hand and, when she raised hers in return, he took hold of it gently. "A lovely young woman, I see."

"Thank-you, my lord," said Laura in a hoarse near-whisper.

"There it is," said Lord Theoplast, releasing her hand and wagging a finger at her. "That's the sort of deference I mean, and the sort of nervousness I'd rather not see. An intrepid and lovely young lady like you should have all the confidence in the world. And, honestly, I'm not someone you need to be afraid of." Then he took Michael's hand, enveloping it warmly in both of his own. "And you're Michael, of course."

"Yes, my lord," said Michael, also barely above a whisper.

"I met your father Valentine at the Great Academy long before you were born. A very impressive man."

Michael stared into the almost porcelain blue of the older man's eyes, and opened his mouth to speak. A sudden pang of deep longing and sadness at the mention of his father had, however, robbed him of words.

But Lord Theoplast seemed to have heard him anyway. "Yes, I do know where Valentine is now. And, yes also, he's in good health and, I hope, good spirits. The two of you should sit down." He indicated the two chairs directly before the desk. "I should as well," he added, walking around behind the desk to the director's chair.

"Yes, my lord," said Michael, conscious that he was finding it difficult to breathe evenly.

". . . my lord," Laura echoed faintly.

When they had seated themselves, Michael summoned up what courage he could and asked, "May I see him?"

"In time, I should think. We have to clear away a few questions first. I've only just recently involved myself in this matter." Lord Theoplast sat and stared at them, waiting silently until both of them dared to meet his eyes with theirs. "Gaius," he suddenly called over his shoulder, "won't you honor us with your presence? This," he told Michael and Laura, "is Prof. Gaius Tortus, one of the most brilliant men you'll ever meet, and a true friend to young persons like yourselves."

"That's far too generous," said Prof. Tortus, in a voice every bit as refined as Lord Theoplast's, though neither so deep nor so plangent. He left his place by the window and seated himself in a chair to one side of the desk, facing Michael and Laura.

"I've brought him along," said Lord Theoplast, "because I rely on his expertise at times like this. You see, I'm somewhat inept with the young, never having been a family man myself. And you two, to make the matter more complicated, are at that very interesting age, aren't you? That fragile, volatile age. You're not still children, of course, but neither yet are you fully adults. You're in that liminal place — that penumbral in-between region — emotionally, intellectually. The night of childish innocence has passed, the full daylight of adult experience and responsibility hasn't yet dawned. You can think, can reason, can fend for yourselves, but you still have so much to learn — emotionally, practically. I imagine you're even feeling the earliest inchoate stirrings of romantic longing in your souls and bodies." A look of kindly melancholy and perhaps a trace of pity came into his eyes. "You're still pure . . . still unformed."

At that moment, a thin vaporous croak floated across the room. "Um, my lord, shall I just . . . ah, take a seat over here then . . . by the door?"

"Oh, Glumgrub," said Lord Theoplast, "you're still here. Good. Do you think you could see to some tea for us?"

"I can ring for it directly," replied the director. "I've already ordered it prepared. And it's Glumgum, my lord."

"Yes, Glumgum. How silly of me," said Lord Theoplast. "But I'd rather you fetched it yourself."

For a moment, Dr. Glumgum said nothing. He looked around the room, as if in incomprehension. "Myself? You mean, you want *me* to bring tea up from the kitchen . . . my lord?"

"Yes, that's the idea," said Lord Theoplast with an affable smile.

"We, ah . . . we have orderlies who . . ."

"Yes, but you're here already."

Again, Dr. Glumgum was silent for several seconds. Then, his voice resonant with tears heroically held back, he asked, "For both of you, my lord?"

"For the four of us," replied Lord Theoplast. "I daresay none of us has breakfasted yet."

"You wish me to . . . to serve tea to the children?"

"Yes, your best black tea, with plenty of milk. I imagine they're famished. Oh, and bring along some bread and butter and jam, if you would — the best you have. A selection of cheeses also. And I suppose you have your own supply of pastries and fruits laid in, yes? Director's reserve, so to speak?"

"I do, my lord," replied Dr. Glumgum, his voice growing almost inaudibly frail.

"Excellent," said Lord Theoplast heartily. "We'll have plenty of those as well."

"Ah, yes . . . of course. . . ." Dr. Glumgum oozed morosely toward the door, but then paused and turned back. "Shall I bring a fifth cup, my lord?"

"No, no. My security man is on duty."

"I meant a cup for myself, my lord."

Lord Theoplast grinned. "That would be delightful, of course, under normal circumstances. But we won't have need of you here today. The matters we have to discuss are rather confidential."

Doctor Glumgum's lips and jowls began to tremble. "I have six higher degrees, my lord," he said.

"Then fetching our tea and breakfast should be well within your abilities," said Lord Theoplast. In an instant, his expression of good humor had been replaced by one of baleful coldness.

"Yes, of course, my lord," Dr. Glumgum rasped, bowing low and backing out of the room.

With a small nod, Lord Theoplast dismissed his security officer as well. When the door had closed, Prof. Tortus remarked, "It still amazes me how very like a frog that man looks."

Lord Theoplast was already smiling again. "It's not all that surprising," he said casually, turning his gaze upward to the ceiling with a distracted air. "I believe he *was* a frog in his last life, and simply failed to make the transition from that incarnation to this with complete success. I expect he'll be a frog again next time too. He seems to have got himself caught in a kind of vicious loop."

The room became silent. Michael and Laura exchanged looks of distinct unease. After a few seconds, Prof. Tortus cleared his throat and laughed. "I fear they think you're serious," he said.

This roused Lord Theoplast from his thoughts. He turned his gaze back to Michael and Laura. "I jest, of course," he said after a few seconds. "It's only because you two come from Oreiotopia. That's something all those

257

old heretical sects from your region — the Escapists and the Purists and whatnot — are said to have taught, isn't it? The transmigration of souls?" He looked back and forth at the two of them. "Surely they taught you that in school."

"No, my lord, not really," said Laura.

"I don't think it's legal to teach those things, my lord," said Michael.

"Really?" Lord Theoplast reflected on this for a moment. "No, I suppose it isn't. I made that law myself, in fact. How forgetful one grows as the ages roll along. Well, then — a wholly unsuccessful witticism."

"I laughed," said Prof. Tortus. "Inwardly, at any rate."

Lord Theoplast cocked an ironical eyebrow at his companion. Then his expression became more serious. "Listen, my young friends, I could spend the better part of the next hour trying to put you at your ease. Really, though, I'd count it a kindness on your part if you'd relieve me of the necessity and simply take it on faith that I intend you no harm. But I also intend to speak frankly to you, and expect you to do the same to me. I think you know why we're here. No, don't say anything."

Michael closed his mouth.

"This is a rather dismal facility, as you know by now. And you haven't seen the worst of it. It's not impossible, moreover, that you'll end up here, or at a place equally bad, or worse even, and even that would be allowed only after some rather drastic alterations had been made in your . . . personalities."

Michael felt a chill spreading through him. The sheer phlegmatic calm of his manner made Lord Theoplast's words seem all the more terrible.

"It's hard *not* to be frightened when you say that, my lord," Laura remarked in a cautious tone.

"I know," Lord Theoplast replied. "And it would be a great waste to reduce two redoubtable young souls like you to . . . something more ordinary. Frankly, that may not even be an option. Things might have gone too far already. And the more radical forms of pharmacology and encephalic surgery are not exact sciences. In the end, it might be determined that the risk of exposing others — other children, tutors, confessors, reformatory staff . . . anyone, really — to you and your story is far too grave. Then . . . well, the most extreme measures would have to be considered. Even the most final measures of all. But that's not what I want. And, happily, what I want is usually what's most important."

Again the room was silent for several seconds. And again it was Laura who finally spoke: "What is it you *do* want, my lord?"

"There's the question of greatest moment," Lord Theoplast said. "Clever girl. What I want is for you to show me that you know the difference between reality and fantasy. And then, if I'm satisfied in that regard, I want your help."

"You, my lord? Our help?" said Michael.

"With what?" asked Laura.

"Ah, at last," said Lord Theoplast with a touch of genuine delight in his voice, "no 'my lord' that time. Good girl. As I said, ceremony is the enemy of candor. So, then, since you ask, my dear, I want your help" — he pointed directly at Laura and then at Michael — "and yours too, with rescuing your young friend — the one you know as Prince Oriens, I believe — from his delusions."

Laura gazed at Lord Theoplast, saying nothing. Her expression was perfectly inscrutable, but Michael knew she was near to losing her temper.

"You see," interjected Prof. Tortus, "we have a very deep concern for that lad's wellbeing. And, at present, though he seems to be in recovery, there are signs that he'll need the assistance of friends he trusts in order to surmount the psychological obstacles his unconscious mind has placed in his way on the road to sanity."

Laura's eyes narrowed. Michael, as inconspicuously as he could, reached over and touched her wrist. "Don't," he whispered.

At this, Prof. Tortus frowned. "Please don't be upset, young lady. I know you're not likely to believe what I'm going to tell you, but give me a chance before you close your mind. I really do care only for the health, sanity, and piety of all of you. We understand that you fell into league with a young boy who was lost and confused and who told you astounding stories, and did so with such earnestness that he was able to convince you of their truth. And this wasn't his fault, I hasten to add, because I assure you he believed everything he said."

Now it was Michael who could not hold his tongue. "We saw many things too," he said, not knowing why he felt compelled to say it. "It's not just what he told us."

A look of pure compassion emanated from Prof. Tortus's mellow brown eyes. "I know. I know. But what you saw you didn't really *see*, if you take my meaning. Have you ever heard of something called psychotic transference? No? Well, it's quite a well-attested and copiously documented psychopathological phenomenon. I did much of my doctoral research on it, in fact. It's a curious syndrome. A person in the grip of a powerful psychosis, especially if he's particularly charismatic and has a peculiarly compelling personality, can, so to speak, *contaminate* other minds with his own delusions and hallucinations and paranoias. The effect is so profound that those whom he affects not only believe in the things he claims to see, but actually come to believe that they have seen them also. I know it sounds incredible, but your friend was so sincerely certain that his visions were realities that he was able to communicate them to you, and even to revise your memories of your own experiences in the process. As it happens, you're both at an age when one is particularly susceptible to such influences. As Lord Theoplast said, it's that in-between age when everything becomes confusing, and everything seems both plausible and implausible. You're caught in a no-man's land between the credulity of babes and the disenchantment of adults. It makes your minds malleable. What you think you saw was, I assure you, only a phantom spectacle conjured up in your conscious minds by your unconscious minds' willing surrender to your young friend's fantasies. Essentially, he induced psychotic episodes in both of you, and thereby drew you into his own dark imaginative universe."

"How can you know that?" asked Michael quietly.

"Because it's all quite nonsensical," answered Prof. Tortus with a laugh. "Try to think rationally about this. We know from our agent, Symeon Goëtus, precisely what tale he told you. Extraordinary. Lovely, even, if you're drawn to that kind of fabulous twaddle. But how could it be real? Think. A fairy kingdom far beyond the reaches of the Kenocosm? A magical ship sailing the heavenly aethers? A stolen princess, a child-prince on an endless quest? Don't you see that it's all the stuff of fiction and psychological disorder? Can't you see what a pastiche of old fairytales and folklore and vulgar story-telling it is?"

"You're lying," Laura said, softly but clearly.

"Now, now, girl," said Lord Theoplast sternly but gently. "You're talking to a good man, and one who doesn't lie. You will speak to him respectfully."

"It's a blasphemous tale, as well," said Prof. Tortus. "It makes the Great Artisan out to be . . . I can hardly say it . . . evil. So be very careful what you say, young lady. Blasphemy is a very serious crime."

All at once, Michael realized that he felt oddly free to say whatever he liked just now. These men — the two most powerful men, no doubt, that he would ever encounter — felt it worth their while to try to persuade him and Laura to believe something obviously incredible. Why? Lord Theoplast could destroy the two of them with the slightest twitch of his finger if he chose. Surely he would not be bothering with this at all if he did not have some very real use for them. "The things we saw," said Michael, "how can we doubt them?"

"Let me stop you there," said Prof. Tortus. "You're making the classic error of assuming that you should trust your own direct experiences. But, in fact, isolated experiences are just subjective impressions, and subjective impressions are purely phenomenal — that is to say, they just take in surfaces and appearances, mere *phenomena*, which as you no doubt know, Master Ambrosius, with your grasp of the classical tongues, means 'appearances.' And such phenomena can include the *appearances* of things that aren't really there. I, on the other hand, am speaking out of a deep reservoir of abstract expertise. It's simply a statistical fact that extraordinary experiences of the sort you believe you've had are, well, *extraordinary*, which is to say outside the statistical mean, which is to say mathematically impossible. All but invariably, they're attributable to delusion. Otherwise, they're attributable to a misperception, of the sort an optical illusion might induce."

"But . . ." Michael began.

"Yes, yes, I know what you'll say. Statistics are abstract generalities distilled from an indiscriminate accumulation of isolated atoms of data, and so don't correspond to any particular actual states of affairs, while specific experiences are particular and immediate and so more trustworthy."

"I wasn't . . ." Michael began.

Prof. Tortus, however, took no notice. "But you're wrong. Wrong, wrong, wrong, in principle and in fact. It's the statistical that's real, precisely because it has been purged of every distracting and misleading element of lived experience and sensation and feeling and thought. I tell you, lad, sensibility is the enemy of sense. Sensuous intuitions, poetic inspirations, mystical intimations — it's all nonsense. The hard factual core of reality is statistical through and through. By contrast, personal affective experience is just an evanescent and numerically nugatory embodiment of one possible point or vector within the distribution of the statistical field of probabilities, and therefore not real or true in itself at all. Something's true or real, you see, only to the degree that it's accounted for by the probability curve. The more atypical the experience you think you've had, the more it's ruled out by the regularity of the statistical mean. Your imagined memories of your adventures with this unfortunate boy, for example, are so outlandish that they'd simply be excluded from a proper statistical calculus as anomalies, well in excess of any standard deviation from the median probability, and thus much too extreme to fit within any rational pattern of distributed likelihoods."

"But . . ."

"Hence, it's precisely because you're basing your beliefs on direct, unrefined, unreduced experience that you can be sure that those beliefs aren't to be credited. And it's precisely because I'm relying on statistics unpolluted by the particularities of direct knowledge that you can take what I'm telling you as scientifically established."

Not until a dozen seconds had passed could Michael think of anything to say. Even then, the best he could manage was a feeble, disoriented "What?"

Prof. Tortus smiled indulgently and briefly closed his eyes. Then, in a more deliberate manner, he said, "It's confusing, I know. But you must believe me and not your own memories here, because I'm an expert in these matters. Moreover, you're a child — or, at least, not yet quite an adult. You haven't even yet achieved full development in your frontal cortical lobes. By contrast, I'm an adult, and I'm a priest and a psychologist and an economist. Mind you, I'm not discounting practical knowledge, within its own proper, strictly limited sphere of utility. I deal with the most boringly concrete realities every day, the laws of finance and supply and demand and material production. But I also deal with the derangements of the mind and the sicknesses of the soul that can imprison us in hopelessness and delusion. So you must believe me simply because I know whereof I speak, while you are as yet too young to know even what it is you don't know. More to the point . . ." — here he breathed deeply and gazed more intently into Michael's eyes — ". . . for you it's an absolute imperative that you learn to doubt what you saw, because only in that way can you hope ever to be free again, or to have a future all your own, or . . . to see your parents again."

At this, both Michael and Laura became rigidly upright in their chairs.

"The parents of each of you, that is," added Prof. Tortus. "You should know, Miss Magian, that your father and mother were rescued only a few nights ago, and taken into medical custody."

"Rescued?" said Laura softly, a subtle ferocity entering her voice. "From what?"

"From the ruins of some Oreiotopian village called . . . what was it . . . Wildwater?"

"Wildwind?" asked Michael.

"That's it, the very one," replied Prof. Tortus.

"Ruins?' said Laura. "What do you mean?"

"We don't have a report on that yet," said Prof. Tortus. "We just know that all the inhabitants seems to have fled, since the place was quite empty, and that a significant number of houses had been knocked down by what we assume was a freak storm. Your parents were spotted by one of our aerial patrols. They were disembarking from a small skiff moored there. It's a good thing they *were* seen. Your father had an injured leg that was in danger of turning septic. Now they're both in care and thriving. But, like you, they have to be treated judiciously. This child who had such a deleterious effect on you seems to have worked some of the same sort of fascination in them, amazingly enough."

Laura lowered her eyes. Her shoulders became slack. She clasped her hands together in her lap. "Please don't hurt them," she said.

"As I've assured you," said Lord Theoplast, "that's not our intention. Look at me, young lady."

Slowly, Laura lifted her head.

"You too, young man."

But Michael was already staring at him.

"My desire is for you each to be reunited with those you love. My desire is also that the unfortunate lad who set all these events in motion should recover his memories and his sanity, and should be helped to cope rationally with the terrible tragedy that's befallen him, and should ultimately take his proper, very exalted place in society. But for any of that to happen, I'll require your complete cooperation. I should like to have your perfect trust as well, but I'm willing to allow that to evolve over time. I'm not, however, willing — or, rather, not able — to wait for your consent. The matter is placed before you now. Agree to be of assistance to us, or I must regrettably abandon you to a fate that I don't care even to think about. And that means also abandoning your parents to a fate as bad or worse. I'm sorry, but I'm charged with the welfare of an entire world, one that has no natural resistance to the kind of psychotic epidemic that the wild blasphemies and fantasies you've absorbed might set loose upon it."

Michael could not speak. Neither, evidently, could Laura.

"Listen to me," said Prof. Tortus. "As a priest, I'm obliged to assure you that there *are* spiritual realities, if we must use that terminology. But there's no eternal spiritual kingdom beyond this universe. The souls within you are exquisitely intricate and beautiful patterns of psychical and magnetic energy, cogitative ghosts directly fashioned and concocted within the machine of your body by the Great Artisan himself, destined by his grace to be transferred to subtle bodies after death and, if you're righteous in his eyes, preserved in Hyperion's Bower rather than in the Land of Hel. They're the most delightful and superb and ingenious machines of all, not fragments or sparks of some naturally eternal reality that have become lost here below. Our life — all life — is just an effect of the cunning arrangement of things that are essentially dead — matter, magnetism, random motions, what have you. Isn't that marvelous enough in itself? Think of it. The Great Artisan has the power to make what's essentially dead into an operative mechanical order whose functions are what we call life. Glorious. As a psychologist, moreover, I'm obliged to tell you that these ideas to whose sway you've succumbed are nothing more than desperate wish-fulfilment, illusions, idle fantasies for those who want to shirk off life's labors . . . opiate dreams suited to those who squander their souls on narcotics and inebriants and myths and fairytales. And, as an economist, I'm obliged to tell you that, were such illusions to become a pandemic, they'd bring about a cataclysmic economic contraction. They'd destroy all healthy ambition and appetite. It's only because men are driven by rational self-interest to acquire all they possibly can that the great machine of wealth-creation can function. These dreams that have so beguiled you — they're a poison. They drain the will of ambition, of acquisitive energy. All we want — all we could possibly hope — is to give you — all of you — the antidote."

At that moment, there came a knock upon the door.

Lord Theoplast continued to stare somewhat gravely at Michael and Laura for a few seconds longer, idly tapping a forefinger on the desk. Then his expression softened. "Open," he called out.

The muted thunder of the security officer's voice rolled across the room: "The small froglike man has returned with your tea, my lord."

"Excellent. Send him in."

Michael turned his head to see Dr. Glumgum enter, bearing a silver tray — clearly too large for anyone so diminutive — loaded with a large, floridly ornate porcelain tea pot, cups and saucers, spoons, milk and sugar, bread rolls and butter and jams, bowls of berries, wedges of white and yellow cheeses, and a tastefully designed three-tiered serving platter filled practically to overflowing with small cakes and pastries and savory tarts.

"Very good, indeed," said Lord Theoplast, rubbing his hands together. "Right here on the desk would be ideal. Pull your chairs up, you two."

Dr. Glumgum brought the tray unsteadily over, all of the porcelain tinkling loudly as he did so, and set it down with a small exhausted grunt.

"Oh, this looks delightful," said Lord Theoplast.

"I'm gratified, my lord," gasped Dr. Glumgum. "If you've no further need of me, I'll . . ."

"Pour out for us, won't you," said Lord Theoplast.

"I'm . . . to serve the tea, my lord? Serve . . . the children?"

"I'm sure they'll take milk. I know Prof. Tortus and I will."

Dr. Glumgum looked around the room with a desolate, haunted expression. "Gladly, my lord," he murmured. He laid out the saucers and cups, poured the tea and milk, asked if anyone wanted sugar — Laura meekly raised a finger to indicate a single teaspoon — poured four cups, and finally lowered his eyes in what to Michael seemed an attitude of abject defeat. "May I leave you to your victuals now, my lord?"

"This tea is splendid," said Lord Theoplast. "Rich and aromatic and with just the right snap on the tongue. Perfectly brewed."

At this, Dr. Glumgum raised his head, now with a faint look of hope on his face. "Thank-you, my lord. Thank-you very much indeed. I do flatter myself that I know my teas."

"Clearly you do."

"I bring the water to a full rolling boil every time."

"Capital," said Lord Theoplast, taking a second sip. "I knew you were the man I could trust to do the thing right."

Dr. Glumgum began visibly to quiver all over. "Oh, thank-you, my lord," he gushed. A look of sincere and humble gratitude spread over his features. "I can't tell you what it means to hear you say so. A man of such discernment, after all — it means the world to me."

"You honor me in saying so," replied Lord Theoplast. "I certainly hope you made some for yourself."

"It's brewing down in the kitchen even now, my lord."

"Well, I won't keep you then."

"Thank-you, my lord." Dr. Glumgum was almost weeping with joy as he turned to leave.

"Oh, and Glumgum," said Lord Theoplast just as the director had reached the door, "remember, we all have our parts to play, even the most pusillanimous among us. I rely on you greatly, and you've not disappointed me."

Now Dr. Glumgum's tears could not be restrained. "Thank-you, my lord," he said, removing a handkerchief from his jacket pocket, raising his spectacles from the broad low slope of his nose, and dabbing at his eyes. "This is a very great day for me." Then, obviously galvanized by emotions he could not fully express, he executed a spectacularly obsequious bow — one thin leg extended, one arm high aloft, the handkerchief briefly unfurling from his bulbous fingertips like a festive pennant — then turned and, with a surprisingly lively gait, practically hopped away.

For a moment, the security officer remained where he was by the door, staring intently toward Lord Theoplast, his hand resting on his holster. Michael turned to look in the same direction.

"Just out of curiosity," asked Lord Theoplast, "did either of you tell the stories of your adventures, or the stories your young friend told you, to anyone here?"

"No, my lord," said Michael.

Laura shook her head. "No."

"Are you sure? As I understand it, you've had only limited contacts. Just two of the resident nurses, one staff disciplinarian, some orderlies, and our good director there. Are you quite certain you divulged nothing at all to any of them?"

"Quite certain, my lord," said Michael.

"Not anyone," said Laura.

For a few seconds, Lord Theoplast seemed to be reflecting on this. Then he cast a meaningful look toward the officer, accompanied by a small, almost imperceptible shake of his head. Michael glanced back in time to see the officer tilt his brow forward ever so slightly, as if acknowledging an instruction, take his hand from his holster, and then withdraw, quietly pulling the door closed behind him. A chill crept down Michael's spine and flickered over the surface of his skin.

"That's a relief," remarked Prof. Tortus. "Personnel redactions are always such an administrative nightmare."

"Listen, my young friends," said Lord Theoplast, rising from his chair, "things have become a bit grimmer than I wanted. I didn't come here to issue an ultimatum. I assure you, I'm prepared to whisk you away today into the waiting arms of your friends and families, if I can do so in good conscience. But I can't be cavalier. I've the wellbeing of a whole world to consider. I'll need an answer from you soon, but I think some food will help you decide wisely. My colleague and I will take our tea over there by the windows. We have to confer for a few minutes. But I'll be very disappointed — nay, very vexed — if, by the time I return, a considerable quantity of this food hasn't disappeared." And with that he and Prof. Tortus took their cups and saucers and retreated to the back of the room again.

After a few seconds, Laura whispered, "We don't have any choice, do we?"

"No," Michael whispered back. "No. But we do have these." He lightly touched the purse through his shirt and cravat. Then he reached for a plate.

V

ICHAEL, LAURA, LORD THEOPLAST, PROF. Tortus, and the huge security officer emerged from the elevator at its highest terminal, which turned out to be the building's rooftop. There, across an expanse of metalled concrete, a large private aerial car awaited them, its flawless black finish adorned with fluid coils and curls of silver trim. A uniformed chauffeur and another security officer stood by its open doors. The city rose around them, gigantic and splendid, a fantastic panorama of looming massifs and deep canyons and shining peaks. The wind was strong and cuttingly cold up here, disarranging Laura's hair and causing it to whip at her eyes so that she had to gather her locks and hold them behind her neck; but, when Lord Theoplast invited her to approach the car with a courtly sweep of his hand, she clearly did not want to do so. "I've never been in one," she called out over the breeze, staring uneasily at the overwhelming skyline.

"Never?" he called back. "Not even an omnibus?"

She shook her head. But, with Michael's hands on her shoulders and his voice in her ear telling her that it was actually extremely safe, she finally shuffled forward and slipped into the back of the car, under its hard canopy of blue adamantine crystal. Michael sat beside her on the plush red leather seat, and Lord Theoplast joined them, sitting opposite on the facing seat. The security officers and Prof. Tortus took seats a few rows further forward, on the other side of a closed glass partition. The rotary lift motors began to pulse and thrum, the car rose on its columns of air as smoothly as a feather rising on a gentle gust of wind, and Laura drew back from the windows and gripped the sleeve of Michael's jacket. "I don't like heights," she remarked rather loudly.

Michael, on the other hand, after a brief glance at the almost featureless concrete building from which they were departing, was carried back in memory to other flights over Kenopolis, never in conditions of such luxury of course, but always with a sense of exhilaration at the dazzling magnitude of the spectacle.

268

"And you the daughter of a former pilot," said Lord Theoplast. "Well, my apologies, but it won't be long, I promise."

"Where are we going?" Laura asked.

"There." He pointed toward the great dome of the Central Ministry.

Michael had suspected as much, but it still seemed incredible.

"First, though," said Lord Theoplast, "I have to tell the two of you something — just you two. I don't want you repeating this even to my friend Gaius. Do you understand?"

They both nodded.

"You're bright children . . . bright young adults, rather. I'm not going to condescend to you. I know that nothing Gaius told you convinced you. I doubt that anything could. And do you know why?"

Neither of them answered.

"I'll tell you. It's because it's ridiculous. He believes it, and there's some truth to what he says. There is indeed such a thing as contagious dementia. A deeply deluded person can communicate his delusions to others — but only up to a point. And I think the two of you have had a number of experiences situated well past that point."

Again, Michael and Laura said nothing, but now they looked at one another uncertainly.

"Don't fret," said Lord Theoplast. "We can be frank here. Gaius trusts his own expertise, as well he should. He's a psycho-epidemiologist of very high achievement, and one of the best encephalotomists ever to earn a degree from the Program in Psychic Surgeries. There's no therapeutic distinction higher. But I think it was your father, Michael, who said that expertise is often just self-deception certified by others."

"I don't recall that," said Michael hesitantly.

"Valentine Ambrosius was something of a provocateur in academic circles, with an ill-disguised taste for daring ideas, well before you were born. I remembered another of his epigrams today, actually, when Gaius was talking about dangerous myths. It was something like, let's see — 'Myth is the true, if symbolic, memory of the immemorial; history is the false, if factual, memory of the unforgettable.' Maybe it was phrased a bit more ingeniously."

Michael had in fact heard his father say something like this on occasion.

"Clever, but in that case wrong," added Lord Theoplast. "It was that sort of brilliant contrariness and fondness for the irrational that finally got him in trouble. And that ended up harming your mother, to be honest. Her tribulations were the result in large part of his recklessness — his strange theories about cosmology, history, ancient stories . . . his strange doubts regarding the science of the instantaneous subtle air currents exploited by anemophones, for instance . . . his inability to curb his appetite for controversy, even when it made things dangerous for the both of them. She let her own research be corrupted by his obsessions, and her sanity to be compromised by his fantasies."

"I don't believe that," said Michael, softly but firmly.

"No, I know you don't. It doesn't matter, really. What's important now is that you and your father — and you too my young, pretty Miss Magian, and your parents — all of you, that is — can move forward to a peaceful life together — in some green and remote place once again, unmolested by the authorities, fully provided for — but only if, today and hereafter, the two of you do what I'm about to ask." His face betrayed no emotion, but this only made his words seem more ominous. "I'm not a cruel man, but neither am I sentimental. I long ago reconciled myself to the hard decisions it's incumbent on me to make whenever the security of the Dominion or the welfare of its subjects is at risk. I accept now that, in doing what must be done even when I find it unsavory, I relieve others of that burden. So understand, I can't permit myself the pleasure of granting small mercies." He stroked his beard thoughtfully, his eyes shifting back and forth between them. "I know from the reports I've read that our man Goëtus injudiciously allowed the two of you to overhear certain remarks regarding a rebellion in the upper heavens — one that's been raging for ages — and regarding also the true identity of our celestial visitor. Under normal circumstances, that indiscretion on his part would have spelled your doom. The terror, the confusion that that knowledge would ignite among the faithful could lead to a social and religious conflagration of unimaginable proportions. It would burn for centuries. I simply couldn't allow the news to get out. But in this case, happily, it's for the best that you know the truth. If you can come to accept it, it will disabuse you of the fantasies that this daemon sowed in your minds, and make it easier for you to see that your happiness — yours and your parents' happiness, that is — is all that should concern you now."

"Why," Laura said in a quiet, cautious voice, "should we believe you rather than him?"

Lord Theoplast smiled sadly. "Rational self-interest, perhaps. Loyalty to those you love. And, if you think about it, it's obvious which of the two stories is more plausible. Still, that can wait. In a sense, it also doesn't matter. In the end, the rebellion will fail, because the Great Artisan is omnipotent. There is no other God beside him. He allows his creatures free will, true, even the daemons on high who've turned against his benevolence and who resent his love for his Kenogaian children — and that, incidentally, *is* the cause of their rebellion: their anger at his great partiality toward human-ity — but at the last he won't allow his creation to be destroyed. They'll be judged one day, and the Land of Hel will receive them. Even if you can't yet believe that your friend is what I say he is, however, you should at least bow to the inevitable. He has lost, whatever his purpose here. We're trying to help him, believe it or not. No one's beyond salvation as far as we know. But, even if we can't, he can do us no harm now."

This, Michael thought, was clearly a lie. It was a plain contradiction: Lord Theoplast had only just said that he would not hesitate to do what he thought necessary; surely he would have destroyed Oriens immedi-ately — not to mention Laura and himself — if he had thought it could be done without risk. Here too Mr. Goëtus had certainly revealed too much. It seemed clear that the authorities feared what would happen if the spirit within Oriens were released from its souls and fleshly body. All Michael said, however, was: "What do you want us to do?"

"Clever lad," said Lord Theoplast turning his eyes to the dome of the Central Ministry building, rapidly taking up ever more of the view ahead. "You're learning from Laura. I want you, in short, to corroborate the story we've told your daemon friend. We want to integrate him into a new life in this world, make a friend of him, even an ally. We want to convince him that this is his true home. And we even want to put him in a position of considerable social advantage, because we know that he has great talents that could, with help, be restored to the side of righteousness. The Great Artisan, no doubt, has uses for him yet. We've told him that his true name is Theophilus Hypermachos, and that his parents were recently killed . . . well, as I recall, you heard that arch-therapist woman tell him . . . what's her name . . . ?"

"Axiomorpha," muttered Michael.

"Indeed. What a good memory you have. Well, that's the story. But it's a tale that comes with a great many benefits. We believe that, now that he's assumed a Kenogaian body, he will age like any normal male. When he achieves his seeming majority, he will inherit control of the Pamphagos Group, which you know, I hope, is probably the largest corporate entity in the world. He'll live a life of ease and prosperity, surrounded by the finest things, given the best education, dining on the rarest delicacies, drinking the rarest wines. He'll have homes, great sailing and flying yachts, private carriages on trains. Soon, perhaps, there'll be beautiful girls and then, in time, engrossingly beautiful women. He already shows encouraging signs of delight in feminine beauty. He's clearly charmed by his therapist's . . . charisma, let's say. In time, he'll be assigned an ideal wife, perhaps have children, live to a grand old age, fall asleep at last in the embosoming arms of his maker, and be borne away to the paradise of Hyperion's Bower. Really, if you still think of him as a friend, you should want all that for him."

"So why would you need us at all?" Michael asked.

"Ah. Because *he* does, it seems. We've kept his food liberally dosed with the most effective psycho-metabolic distillates known to natural philosophy. We've employed the best pharmaceutical and psychological methods at our disposal. And, for the most part, we've succeeded at rendering him receptive to his new life. The mad fables he told you — his fairy kingdom, his captive sister, his millennial voyage through the planetary spheres — all that's receded now into a kind of dream for him . . . stories recalled from the nursery. If we can erase every last trace of his old life from his memory as quickly as possible — and that's the urgency of the matter, because speed is necessary, we believe — we may prevent him from reverting to his former state. There's only one problem. While his mind is willing to relinquish its otherworldly fantasies, it seems resolutely unwilling to relinquish its memories of you two. He doesn't recall exactly who you are or what adventures you've had together. But he does remember . . . I don't know, his affection for you. I suppose celestial daemons are as emotionally susceptible as the rest of us. He remembers parting from you the night we captured him. He remembers the boy who was his friend. He remembers the fierce pretty girl with the lovely ruddy hair, for whom perhaps he felt a slightly different kind of affection. Perhaps an incipient romantic tenderness. Who knows?"

Michael saw Laura lower her eyes and fold her hands in her lap.

"And he clings fast to those memories, as a kind of indistinct obsession, a dissonance lingering in the otherwise untroubled harmony of the new story we've taught him about himself. And, so long as he does cling to them, they keep a door open in his mind that can only lead back to what he used to be. And, should that happen, we'll have to give up on him and . . . well, you can imagine."

Michael struggled to conceal the anger rising in him. "What must we do, then?" he asked quietly.

"Be his friends, of course," said Lord Theoplast with a slight, inscrutable smile, "just as you've been all along. But be his *old* friends, as it were, who grew up with him, who've always known him as Theophilus — Theo, you call him — and who worried about him horribly after the terrible accident, and who even helped find him and bring him back to Kenopolis. You'll visit him today briefly to renew *that* friendship, and you'll visit him with regularity in days to come, and you'll follow our promptings and you'll learn the lines we teach you, and you'll fill his mind with new memories, until you've wholly submerged your real friendship with him in this fictional friendship, and all the psychic currents in his head can flow back together into a single untroubled stream. Right now, the two of you haunt him. You're a mystery he can't penetrate, an ache he can't soothe. So you must change yourselves from ghosts into ordinary, very solid, very old childhood companions for him. You must bring him peace of mind. And you'll do it" — and now the faint smile vanished, and a frigid hardness came into Lord Theoplast's eyes — "because you know that his life, and yours, and that of your parents all hang suspended on the single thin thread of your ability to convince him. Do you both understand me?"

The immense dome now filled the sky, and Michael could see details that he had never before been close enough to make out. He now saw that its shimmering, beautiful surface — deep, richly varying liquid blues of morning and crystal blues of evening, circlets of interlinked diamond patterns in darkly beautiful gold, tenuous vertical bands of lighter gold thinly bordered with a green like forest shadows — was a mosaic, composed from innumerable enameled tesserae. The turret at its apex was a pavilion of crystal, marble, and gold whose broad roof of blue tiles swept steeply downward from its lofty pinnacle and dramatically upward at its eaves, with small green copper rainspouts in the shapes of half-opened flowers at regular intervals all around it. And the marble colonnade at the base of the dome, where it rested atop the main body of the enormous white marble ministry building, formed a peristyle encircling a broad loggia that ran around the entire structure. It was toward this that the car was now descending.

"Do you understand?" Lord Theoplast repeated, more emphatically.

"Yes, my lord," whispered Laura, still staring down at her hands.

"We understand," said Michael.

ONCE THE CAR HAD PASSED BETWEEN TWO OF THE great columns and come to rest on a low steel platform within the loggia—whose marble walls and floors were brightly illustrated with mosaic images of gardens and forests and oceans—Lord Theoplast, Prof. Tortus, and the large security officer conducted Michael and Laura through a hammered copper door and down a long, otherwise deserted, spaciously echoing corridor of porphyry and rose marble, inlaid with wavily striated agate—a corridor hundreds of yards long, all eerily lit by softly glowing, widely interspersed phosphoria—until at last they came to a semicircular chamber of black polished marble, immense and shadowy, containing three large elevator doors, one of copper, one of bronze, and one (set between the other two) of gold.

"We're under the very center of the dome," remarked Lord Theoplast, "and from here we'll go up to its very summit. I keep my private apartments there, at the top of the world so to speak. But at present I've ceded them to your young friend. It seemed at once the most secure and the most spectacular place to keep him." With this, he took hold of the silver chain he wore on his waistcoat and withdrew a small key in an antique design, but fashioned from crystal or perhaps (if such a thing was possible) diamond. It glittered like a minute prism between his fingertips. There was a keyhole next to each elevator, and it was the door to the far left (the copper one) that he now unlocked and slid open by its heavy handle. "The main building below us is home to no fewer than four-hundred and seventy-two government agencies," he added, leading the way into the elevator's car, "but the dome is occupied only by the battalions of my security detail and representatives of those various sacred orders that concern themselves exclusively with the spiritual security of the Dominion."

Even the interior of the car was luxurious. Even the wheel of its dial—which Lord Theoplast turned to the highest setting—was wrought silver dusted with flakes of diamond. The water rose from the deep cisterns below into the great resonant metallic shaft and carried them up and up, for so long that Michael began to wonder how even the great dome's summit could be so high. But finally they reached the top and stepped out into a large foyer, again of marble, this time white, dazzlingly illuminated by the sunlight descending through the glass ceiling. Directly across from them stood a single enormous door of polished bronze into which was molded—from lintel to threshold, from jamb to jamb—the massy image of a face identical to Lord Theoplast's, with eyes wide open and terrifying in the accusing intensity of their huge gaze. The same face stared out even more implacably from a large oil painting hanging on the wall to the door's left, this time attached to a figure clad in an exorbitant purple and silver military tunic from many centuries past, its left breast ablaze with a constellation of honorific gewgaws — medals, ribbons, badges, and one especially splendid medallion in a solar design. Below the picture frame was a large brass banderole bearing a legend of two lines in dimly reddened mezzotint:

> Alti sunt montes Oreiotopiae, sed quanquam
> altiores montes cadaverum inimicorum eius.

"Welcome to my humble eyrie," said Lord Theoplast. Then, noting Michael's and Laura's stares of wonderment, he added, "Lest you think me an insane egoist, let me assure you that neither of those portraits is of me. Both depict one of my forebears, Field Marshall Kronos Theoplast, the hero of the campaign against the Purist heretics."

"He looks exactly like you," said Michael.

"That," said Lord Theoplast, gently guiding Michael and Laura forward with a hand on each of their backs, "is what I believe is called an 'atavism': when, that is, someone's features or qualities uncannily recapitulate those of his ancestors. It all has to do with the longevity of the generative germ-plasm, I imagine. But, I assure you, I've never dressed quite that sumptuously. I know you're good with the classical tongues. Can you translate?"

"Yes," said Michael: "'High are the mountains of Oreiotopia, yet higher still the mountains of his enemies' corpses.'"

"Indeed," replied Lord Theoplast in a mordant tone. "Those were the days, what." He heaved a deep reflective sigh. "A sentiment from a more savage age, when the martial virtues were more prized than the humane. A barbarian's bombast. The boast of a butcher. I keep it there, where my eyes will fall on it every day, to remind myself of why I continue to discharge my responsibilities — to remind me that the values and stabilities and harmonies of our enlightened age are frail, friable things, and that if I don't strive to preserve them against every threat, no matter how minor, the world could very easily descend into wars and schisms and slaughters once again. It's a reminder to me of a possible future self I have no desire to become — a self I must never let myself become as a result of foolish laxity in the present."

"I'm still not persuaded that it's healthy to fixate on such things," observed Prof. Tortus.

275

It occurred to Michael that the regularity with which Lord Theoplast kept hinting that he and Laura might unfortunately have to be killed was beginning to make the threat seem not so much terrifying as tedious.

The security officer pulled the bell-handle and a moment later the door swung open to reveal the shorter and stouter of the two Lupine Brethren who had attended Mr. Lucius three nights earlier. Immediately, a look of stark horror overspread his broad face, he emitted a high yelp of alarm, and then he dropped to his knees, quaking and whimpering miserably. "Oh, good gracious, my lord, we weren't expecting you!"

"What in God's name are you talking about?" cried Prof. Tortus angrily, kicking the poor creature in the ribs with some force. "We told you we'd be coming back little more than an hour ago. Get up and let us in at once."

Clutching the lapels of his jacket wretchedly, eyes downcast, the man rose to his feet again. "If it please your majesty," he whined.

Lord Theoplast groaned softly. "I've granted my usual staff a leave of absence for the duration of your friend's visit," he said to Michael and Laura.

"It's only that I was unprepared to see your divine preponderance back so early, and I . . ."

"Yes, yes, yes," said Lord Theoplast mildly, waving the man back from the door and attempting to usher Michael and Laura in ahead of himself. "I understand completely. Inform your master of our arrival."

"You see, my lord, if I'd known it was you . . ."

"Quite."

"Well, I'd have been properly composed, and in the most admirably dignified state . . ."

"Yes, I see. Go tell your master we're here."

"I'd even have brought a tray of biscuits . . ."

"Now!" shouted Prof. Tortus.

With a small affrighted yap, the fellow turned and scampered away.

Lord Theoplast stood and watched him go, as if momentarily absorbed in some depressing reflection or other. "Wait out here," he told the security officer. Then, affecting a kindly smile, he swept an open hand before Michael and Laura, inviting them to enter.

VI

THEY WERE STANDING IN A GREAT CIRCULAR room, almost entirely surrounded by solid walls of glass and gracefully spare, diamond-patterned reticulations of what Michael suspected was platinum, far too fine to have any but a decorative purpose. The only visible load-bearing supports were perhaps a dozen slender, silver-plated poles spaced at regular intervals around the room's circumference. Opposite the door through which they had just entered was another, very similar door, also set in a span of marble wall.

The room was drenched in the light from the east, though the air was cool and dry, obviously issuing from unseen climatistic vents and evenly distributed by the five large, slowly turning fans equidistantly spaced overhead. Deep carpets of midnight blue — adorned with images of stars and moons, gardens and lakes — were spread here and there on a floor of rose and white marble tessellations. All the furnishings were from the East: luxurious couches and divans, deep enveloping chairs, small side-tables of complexly filigreed gold, exquisitely painted vases, and gold, silver, and ormolu lamps in the shapes of trees with phosphoric globes of cut crystal hanging from their boughs like ripened fruits. And at the very center of the room, twisting up through a circular aperture in the sky-blue glaze of the ceiling, was a bronze spiral staircase with railings shaped like winding and flowering vines. But, as extravagant and exotic as everything in the room was, it was what lay outside, beyond the encompassing glass walls, that truly overwhelmed Michael's senses. The enormous gleaming dome sloped away in every direction like a vast, engulfing sea-swell, rising out of a city that stretched away on every side like an ocean of fluctuating hues, opalescent waves, shadowy emerald depths, with small moving motes of color just visible in its lowest fathoms, in the avenues and along the pavements. Above it all, countless birds wreathed the air in undulating ribbons of gauzy gray, hazy magenta, and translucent blue.

"I keep my quarters overhead," said Lord Theoplast. "This room I call my panoptikon. When I stand here, I fancy I can see almost everything in the world."

"It must all seem like a dream from this height," said Michael.

Before Lord Theoplast could reply, however, several figures in the garb of the Lupine Brethren began descending the circular staircase, their heavy footfalls ringing dully on the metal steps. In all, seven came down, including all four of those Michael had seen on earlier occasions in Mr. Lucius's entourage — the one with a crooked nose, the one with a scar, the tall thin one, the short stout one — and the last of the seven was Mr. Lucius himself. "Well, well, my primped and purfled," he said on reaching the bottom, with creamy suavity but a caustic grin, "how very, very patrician we look this morning. Quite the little princelings of creation."

"Not now, Lucius," said Lord Theoplast impatiently. "You can see everything's secure. Bring him down."

Mr. Lucius bowed from the waist, arms outstretched and hands elegantly limp, then stood up straight and called up the stairs, "Bring him down, my delightful."

Even before her face had become visible, her astonishing figure — wrapped in an extremely tight-fitting, sleeveless, knee-length dress of fiery red — announced that it was Dr. Axiomorpha whom Mr. Lucius had addressed. Her hair was down now, cascading around her throat and over her bare shoulders and to either side of her plunging décolletage. She no longer wore spectacles, and she had donned a single strand of pearls and two teardrop pearl earrings. And directly behind her, lightly holding her hand, came Oriens. Only the high heels of her shoes made any sound on the stairs; his tread was as noiseless as ever. Like Michael and Laura, he was grandly attired, in his case in a suit of solid white very similar to Lord Theoplast's, though with a delicate sheen of lavender seemingly just below the surface of his moiré cravat, waistcoat, and lapels. His hair had been expertly trimmed and arranged in shining wavelets. And he wore spectacles whose deep blue lenses hid the brilliant sapphire of his eyes.

"My gracious lord," said Dr. Axiomorpha solemnly, performing as plausible a curtsy as her unyielding dress would permit.

Oriens, however, on seeing Michael and Laura, smiled broadly, released Dr. Axiomorpha's hand, and quickly crossed the room to them. "Oh, I knew it," he said in an elated voice. "I knew you were real. At first, they thought I was imagining you both, but I was certain they would find you if they only searched." He placed a hand on each of their shoulders. "I could not stop thinking about you."

Laura parted her lips, but before she could say anything Dr. Axiomorpha interjected, "*Theophilus* was adamant that we must find you. We knew only that *Theophilus* had suffered a trauma, and I'm afraid we were a bit slow at sorting out the real memories from the hallucinatory ones. And, of course, we didn't know anything about his childhood friends."

Laura closed her mouth.

"I have to ask you to forgive me," Oriens continued, withdrawing his hands. "I cannot recall your names. I know your faces, I remember that we have been friends. But your names . . . are lost to me."

"Michael."

"I'm Laura."

"Yes, Laura. That is right. I especially remember your beautiful red hair . . . how pretty you are. And . . ." — he looked at Michael, removing his tinted spectacles as he did so — "and I feel certain I remember that you . . . helped me when I needed help . . . Michael."

"Yes," said Dr. Axiomorpha, swiftly coming up to him from behind and taking hold of his arms, "of course, you silly dear, friends help one another all the time. But don't start confusing things again."

By this point, the six Lupine Brethren in Mr. Lucius's detail had taken up separate stations near the walls of glass, three on either side of the room, and another figure was descending the stairs. It was Mr. Goëtus. There was nothing of the dandy about him now. He was dressed in a plain suit of somber black that looked as if it might be a kind of clerical habit. Even the glint of his monocle seemed somehow more subdued. On reaching the floor, he performed a theatrically stately bow in the direction of Lord Theoplast and said, "My good and gracious lord."

Michael looked at Laura and saw that she was staring at the confectioner with an expression of pure hatred.

Oriens, however, appeared not to notice. "I do confuse things, I know. I know that after my accident I suffered many delusions and made up many stories. I am sorry if I have trouble recalling our friendship properly. But I do remember . . . I remember . . . that we *are* friends."

At this, Laura turned her gaze from the confectioner and toward the brilliant blue of Oriens's eyes. Her expression of anger yielded to one of pained tenderness. "Oh, yes, we are. Very good friends. We've missed you so very much."

"I am sorry if I caused you any grief."

"You've nothing to apologize for," said Laura, her voice beginning to break.

"Nothing at all," added Michael quickly. "We're simply glad to see you again . . . and to see you so well."

"I have been treated with great kindness by all my friends here," said Oriens, looking about the room and then back at Michael. "But I still felt the absence of the two of you. I felt a loneliness that I knew was not simply my imagination."

"Again," said Dr. Axiomorpha liltingly, "we were so very, very concerned for his wellbeing that we'd scarcely any time to disentangle the true memories from the false. But now we've found you two, and everything's going to be so much better." She looked at Michael pointedly, and then even more pointedly at Laura. "Isn't it?"

"Of course," said Michael blandly.

"Yes," said Laura, more blandly still.

Lord Theoplast had seated himself on a divan upholstered in what looked like white samite, bright with a delicate webbing of golden embroidery, his arms spread out along its back, his ankles elegantly crossed, his expression stern but placid. The effect was rather like a tableau of one of the sky-deities of myth seated upon his celestial throne in one of his more languorous godlike poses. "Our young friend has suffered a good deal," he said, "but I know that the two of you can help him recover."

From the corner of his eye, Michael saw Mr. Goëtus grimace and lower his head.

"Yes," added Prof. Tortus, who was standing a few yards to one side of Lord Theoplast and who Michael could see had also noticed the confectioner's reaction, "most definitely. We're all quite sure of that."

"Here, darling," said Dr. Axiomorpha, gently taking the blue spectacles from Oriens's fingers and placing them on his face again, "remember your eyes still need protecting."

"They do not seem injured," replied Oriens.

"We must do as the physicians say, dear."

Oriens continued to look back and forth, now at Laura, now at Michael. "I wish I could make it all come clear in my mind," he said wistfully. "I have such strong feelings when I see you, but everything is mixed up with dreams — mountains, forests, giants . . . drifting among stars . . . a land that . . . that . . . ."

"Yes, well," Prof. Tortus interrupted, "if you try to disentangle your memories from your delusions, you're as likely as not only to render them all the more inextricable from one another. Stop trying to remember the past.

Fix your mind on the present moment, and trust your friends to tell you what's real and what isn't."

"That's right, dear," said Dr. Axiomorpha soothingly. "They can tell you about their memories of you instead — picnics and outings, games played when you were all very small, and so forth. Not today, of course. You still need your rest till you're fully recovered. But perhaps in days to come." She looked at Michael and Laura. "I know you've just arrived, but you'll need to bid Theo goodbye in a little bit, as he's still recovering from his shock. But we'll all be back together soon . . . when we've all had some time to talk."

Again, Michael saw an expression of distaste contract Mr. Goëtus's features as he continued to stand apart, well beyond the stairs.

"Surely not right away," said Prof. Tortus, a hint of consternation in his voice. "They've just become reacquainted. It's a very perilous moment we've arrived at . . . a good moment for establishing certain things, before confusions can begin to reassert themselves."

"But it all seems so real at times," said Oriens, still gazing back and forth at his two friends. "I see you . . . there."

"It's my considered opinion," said Dr. Axiomorpha to Prof. Tortus, the sweetness of her tone beginning to sound somewhat strained and her smile beginning to lose some of its rapturous warmth, "that now's not quite the time. Our young friend mustn't become agitated. It's good that he's seen his friends — good that he's confirmed their reality in his mind — but there are things to discuss before we can simply leap into the therapy you've decided on."

"And it's my considered opinion," replied Prof. Tortus, drawing himself up haughtily, "that your opinion should defer to mine. You're very talented, but also very young and inexperienced. We need to . . . imprint some firm impressions in the . . . in the deeper strata of the *mens nesciens*, if you take my meaning."

Dr. Axiomorpha released Oriens and stepped away from him, toward Prof. Tortus. "I appreciate your credentials," she said, "and your authority. But my rate of success in rehabilitating young male patients is, I believe, notable." She attempted to reinvigorate her fading smile, but with rather tepid results.

"If you would, doctor," said Prof. Tortus, glancing at Oriens and then taking hold of Dr. Axiomorpha's arm to lead her a few steps away. He and she began to exchange animated whispers, punctuated by what sounded like several keen hisses of discord. Michael turned his eyes first to Lord Theoplast, who seemed to be lost in thought and staring off absently at the city outside, and then to Mr. Lucius, who stood on the far side of the room staring fixedly at Dr. Axiomorpha and Prof. Tortus.

"You," Oriens said to Laura, "I see you steering a boat on a river . . . in the moons' light. And I see you clinging to the roots of a tree in a great . . . a great storm, I suppose. Does that make any sense to you? Could that be one of those outings we have talked about?"

"What else do you recall?" asked Michael quietly, realizing that no one else was listening to the three of them just now.

Oriens stared at Michael for several moments, tilting his head one way and then the other. "A wolf," he said. "It is absurd, I know, but I seem to remember that you and I were once chased by a wolf . . . in the darkness . . . through a forest."

Michael merely gazed back at Oriens.

"Some of my memories . . . my fancied memories, I mean, seem even more ridiculous than that."

"They're not ridiculous," said Laura, casting an anxious glance about the room.

"If I were to tell them to you," said Oriens, "you would laugh."

"No," said Laura, "we wouldn't."

"Not at all," said Michael. "You'd be surprised what we'd think believable."

Oriens shook his head. "I think some things are too incredible for anyone to believe. I find it hard to imagine how things so ridiculous can seem so real at times. I would be ashamed to recount them."

"Do you remember how we met?" asked Michael.

"No," said Oriens. "It was when we were very small, was it not?"

"Do you . . ." said Laura tentatively, quickly glancing around the room again, "do you remember . . . searching for someone?"

Michael looked at her, his breath catching in his chest, but at once realized he had no desire to interfere. He had never really expected her to comply with Lord Theoplast's commands, anyway, no matter what the threat.

For his part, Oriens seemed to be considering the question seriously. "I have been looking for you," he said after several moments.

"Someone else?" said Laura, her voice becoming quieter but also more urgent. "Someone you care about . . . other than us?"

Again, Oriens seemed to lose himself in his reflections. "Yes," he said after several moments more, "I do. Someone *very* important to me. But I cannot recall . . ." He shook his head sadly.

"Oh . . . *Oriens*," Laura breathed in a desperate whisper.

Oriens stared at her, his lips parted.

"Think," she added. "Try to remember."

"You called me . . ." His voice died away.

Now, however, Mr. Goëtus had taken notice of them and was approaching. "What are you three young persons talking about?" he asked with unconvincing amiability.

"Outings," said Laura.

"In boats," said Michael.

Dr. Axiomorpha and Prof. Tortus ceased their sibilant quarrel and turned to listen.

Oriens looked back toward them. "Do I have a sister?" he suddenly asked.

At this, Mr. Goëtus merely frowned in incomprehension while Dr. Axiomorpha and Prof. Tortus exchanged confused glances. But Lord Theoplast instantly turned his head about and rose to his feet. "Why do you ask that?" he said harshly. "Did they tell you that you had?"

"No," replied Oriens guilelessly, looking again at Michael and Laura. "No one told me. I just seem to remember."

"Well, you haven't one," said Lord Theoplast crossly, advancing a few steps. "Doctor, tell him."

"Oh," replied Dr. Axiomorpha, plainly taken somewhat aback. "No, of course not, darling boy. We'd have told you right away if you had a sister."

"Of course," added Prof. Tortus.

Mr. Goëtus, however, walked a few paces yet farther away, his hands clasped behind his back, his head lowered.

"Tell him," said Dr. Axiomorpha, looking first at Michael and then at Laura. "You, girl, go on."

Laura hesitated for a few seconds and then said to Oriens, "You'd know if you had."

Oriens stared at her for some seconds, and then at Michael. "Do I have a sister, Michael . . . Michael Ambrosius?"

A loud groan of displeasure issued from Mr. Goëtus's lips. "I knew this wasn't a wise course of action."

"Oh, good," said Dr. Axiomorpha in a nervous voice. "You see, you've remembered your friend's full name." She looked at Michael. "Tell him, you . . . silly lad, you." She was obviously attempting a radiant smile, but was unable to produce more than a few seductive flickers.

Michael said nothing, however. He merely feigned a look of helpless bewilderment.

"Gaius," said Lord Theoplast with a slightly rising inflection in his voice, "I'm beginning to have my doubts regarding your recommendations."

"I assure you, my lord," said Prof. Tortus, "this is the very moment when we must intervene. If we don't start imprinting the proper . . . the true memories now, when his disorientation is at its most pronounced and his ideative apparatus at its most ductile, he'll begin to regress. His psychic shadow will reassert itself more forcibly and become more invincible. With every relapse there comes a correspondingly deeper induration of the delusive construct. All of this merely proves my point. Lad," he said, turning to Oriens, "I know it's all horridly confusing still. But it's also all quite explicable according to the best and most current psychological science. Your mind is filling in gaps in your memory the same way it fills in the blind-spots in your field of vision — you've heard of that, I imagine — by supplying visual data that aren't real but that seem to complete the total image. There's a syndrome — you know what I mean when I say that, yes? — a syndrome called 'mnemonic anamestosis,' which is the retrospective fabrication of false memories to compensate for true memories that you've lost. And the more precious the things you've forgotten, the more exaggerated the inventions necessary to fill in the evacuated spaces. You've been robbed of certain memories you especially cherish, principally of your parents, and so you've created an alternative construct of comparable symbolic power to supply the lack — a kind of fabulous psychic synecdoche for the erased memory of your real family. This sister-construct your unconscious mind has contrived for you is just a convenient placeholder for a much larger collection of memories. But you mustn't cling to the fantasy, or you'll never recover the reality. You mustn't let the false memory usurp the place of the true ones, lest it become a permanent obstacle to your full convalescence. Are you following me?"

"No," replied Oriens.

Dr. Axiomorpha sighed deeply. "Please let me take care of this," she said, seizing hold of Oriens almost frantically and drawing him away toward a particularly plush couch. "He needs therapy, not theory."

"It all seems real to me," Oriens remarked as he was being borne off.

"I swear, my lord," said Prof. Tortus, turning again to Lord Theoplast, "we're definitely not acting too rashly. If anything, we risk waiting till it's too late."

Lord Theoplast peered briefly over Prof. Tortus's shoulder. "And yet that very charming arch-therapist you've brought in seems to think a more cautious approach preferable. It was you, after all, who recommended her."

"And I was right to do so. She's the most gifted ephebics specialist I've ever certified. I mean, you can see for yourself that her qualifications for the deleastic therapy of a . . . *puer adolescens* are, well, obvious."

"Exorbitantly obvious," agreed Lord Theoplast dryly.

"Even so, she's also still only learning the art of psychometric engineering. You yourself can see, I'm sure, that the boy is at an especially unstable and impressionable juncture. Why else would he suddenly come up with this nonsense about a sister?"

Lord Theoplast stared at Prof. Tortus for a moment, then looked past him directly at Michael and Laura. "It's not quite that simple," he said. "There are details as yet unknown to you."

All at once, Michael was conscious of the starched collar of his shirt pressing uncomfortably against the base of his jaw.

"I foresee a considerable therapeutic success coming out of this," said Prof. Tortus, "if we apply ourselves now."

"Foresee?" said Lord Theoplast with a trace of acid in his voice. "I want assurances, not auguries."

"The question is whether the boy's been correctly prepared for today's treatment."

Lord Theoplast briefly pursed his lips. "Erasmia, is it?" he asked, turning toward the therapist.

"Yes, my lord," replied Dr. Axiomorpha anxiously, beginning to rise.

"Stay where you are," he said, more domineeringly than graciously. "What's your assessment of our current situation, Erasmia?"

"Well . . . I . . ." she began as she resumed her seat, but then fell silent, looking around uncertainly, first at Prof. Tortus, then at Mr. Goëtus, and finally at Mr. Lucius (on whom her gaze briefly lingered, almost imploringly). "It's very difficult to say precisely," she said, turning again to Lord Theoplast.

"Come, now, my dear," replied Lord Theoplast, his voice growing icier, "compose your thoughts. Don't behave as if you thought your entire career and social position and even perhaps your life depended on your answer."

Dr. Axiomorpha stared at him with wide eyes for several excruciating seconds. "No, my lord," she barely managed to murmur.

"You're even lovelier when you're afraid," said Lord Theoplast, with an odd, cruel gallantry in his voice, "if that's possible. It adds an additional, very attractive rosiness to your cheeks . . . a beguiling shiver to those rose-petal lips of yours. It accentuates your . . . vulnerability, which is very appealing."

Once again, Michael felt an unpleasant chill pass through him. His gaze drifted toward Mr. Lucius, who was now standing quite erect and watching Dr. Axiomorpha, his lips anxiously parted. And then he happened also to notice Mr. Goëtus discreetly taking a quick swallow from the large flask he kept with him.

All at once, Lord Theoplast's tone became more severe. "Come along, young woman. What's your recommendation? Nothing catastrophic is going to happen to you — unless you try my patience."

Michael could see that Dr. Axiomorpha's hands were shaking as she twisted them around one another in her lap. "I believe . . ." she began, so weakly and hoarsely that the words were scarcely discernible. She paused, swallowed, and began again more loudly. "I believe that we're pursuing the best course of therapy possible, in principle. I believe also, however, that we needn't be afraid of taking a more deliberate approach."

"I'm sorry," interrupted Prof. Tortus, "but I simply can't concur with my junior colleague's recommendation. With all due respect, delusional ideations are notoriously at their most virulent precisely when they've first been challenged. They're resilient by nature, and react with a force proportionate to the assault upon them. If given time, they regather their strength and become more resistant to . . ." — he glanced uneasily at Oriens and his voice sank to a conspiratorial whisper —". . . *aedificatio memoriae coercitiva*. Now's the time when the foundation absolutely must be laid."

"Oh, my God!" Mr. Goëtus suddenly exclaimed, striding toward Dr. Axiomorpha. "You're both making a terrible . . ."

But before he could finish his sentence he was forced to take two violent steps back again, as Mr. Lucius had suddenly and nimbly blocked his path, glaring savagely. "Have a care, my unpalatable. She's not some scullery maid to be scolded by a foppish candy-maker."

"Now I've had quite enough of you!" protested Mr. Goëtus, failing to conceal the quaking in his voice. "I'm not used to being ordered about by a . . . by a cur in a cravat."

"It's all right, Lucius," said Dr. Axiomorpha.

"It's intolerable," Mr. Goëtus corrected.

"It grieves me to hear you say so," replied Mr. Lucius. "Especially since you and I still have a dinner date to keep."

"It's absurd too," Mr. Goëtus continued, taking another step back, still shaking. "You, I mean, and your . . . juvenile infatuation. A lycanthrope pathetically enamored of a real human girl. Ideas above your species, if you ask me."

"A . . . *what?*" asked Dr. Axiomorpha vaguely, obviously diverted from other thoughts.

Before Mr. Goëtus could repeat himself, however, Mr. Lucius — a deep, positively inhuman snarl rising from his chest and throat — took two quick menacing strides forward, and the confectioner practically danced backward in his haste to keep his distance, the monocle falling from his eye as he did so.

"Enough!" said Lord Theoplast crossly. "Both of you — Lucius, Symeon — please come over here and join me and Gaius. You too, young woman . . . Erasmia, I mean. Right now." When all three had obeyed, silently and sullenly, exchanging apprehensive or threatening glances, Lord Theoplast detached himself from their circle and approached Oriens, hesitantly placing a hand on his shoulder. "Will you excuse us, Theo? We must confer on a few matters. Do you mind waiting a few moments?"

"No, not at all," replied Oriens. "May I talk with my friends?"

"Perhaps in a moment. That's what we need to decide."

When Lord Theoplast and the rest of his party had gone apart, all the way to the opposite side of the room, Laura smiled affectionately at Oriens, who was still sitting by himself on his couch, and then took hold of one of Michael's sleeves and drew him aside, almost up against the wall of glass, several yards from the closest of the Brethren. "They don't seem to know what they're doing at all," she whispered. "I think this is all falling apart."

"I agree," said Michael.

"If it does, they may change their minds about bringing us back here. This may be the last time we'll see Oriens."

"I know."

Laura glanced across the room uneasily, briefly pressed her forehead against Michael's shoulder, and then looked directly into his eyes. "They're not going to give us our parents back, are they?"

Michael shook his head somberly. "I don't think so. Not really. Even if they did, it wouldn't be for long. I don't think they'll ever let any of us go free again. I don't even know if they'll keep us alive longer than they absolutely have to."

Laura nodded gravely. "They won't. I'm not even sure they're going to have any use for us after today, if this . . ." She cast another glance at the far side of the room. "It's all so disorganized."

"They don't know what to do," said Michael. "They're afraid of Oriens. Even Lord Theoplast is. Otherwise things wouldn't be this chaotic. You

287

heard what the confectioner said when they caught him. They don't know whether they dare try to kill him or . . . imprison him . . . or whether they can really convince him he's this Theophilus they want him to be."

For a few moments neither of them said anything, but merely looked at Oriens, still sitting all alone, patiently and innocently waiting to be told what to do next. "We have to rescue him now," said Laura.

"Yes," said Michael. "But then he'll have to rescue us."

"Well," she said after a moment, assuming a slightly more spirited tone and straightening her back, "it's up to you, then." She placed her hand on his chest, roughly in the vicinity of the purse of gems. "Now or never."

Michael looked down at her hand, pressed his own against it, and nodded. "Yes," he said weakly, "I suppose so." He felt himself trembling and took a deep breath.

Laura suddenly rose up on her toes and kissed him on the cheek.

Surprised, he raised his eyes to her again. "What's that?"

She frowned. "What do you mean 'What's that?' It was a kiss. It was a friendly kiss, you idiot."

He stared at her.

"It's meant to give you courage," she added with a hint of vexation in her voice. "I'm your friend, you see. I'm also pretty, apparently. Everyone keeps saying so, at least. It's nice to be kissed by a pretty girl who's your friend when you're going to do something daring. At least, I assume it is." For a long moment, Michael feared she might kick him, but instead of a scowl she looked at him with a melancholy smile. "I'm right here beside you," she said in the tenderest tone he had ever heard her use.

"Yes, I know," he finally managed to say. In fact, he realized, just now she looked not merely pretty but truly beautiful, with her shining red hair unbound and set off against the deep blue of her dress and her dark green eyes staring at him with an expression at once resolute and startlingly gentle. "I'm sorry," he said. "I don't mean to be so stupid. I'm just trying to think what to do. And to work up the courage. You're much braver than I am, you know. And, yes, of course, thank-you." He quickly, clumsily kissed her on the cheek in return. "You *are* my friend — my dearest friend. And, yes, that was very nice. The kiss, I mean — being kissed by you. Very nice. I'm very glad you're here." He struggled to produce a confident smile. "Your hair is lovely," he suddenly added. His heart was beating rapidly. "And your dress . . ."

"Calm down," she said, her voice extremely kind. "You're babbling. You're as brave as anyone I know. Remember, Oriens said no one can take the gems from you. And you said the gems *know* what to do."

"I think they do. I hope they do."

"I'm frightened too," she said, resting her hand on his chest again. "But it has to be now. Please, Michael, we can't wait."

"I know." Michael looked through the glass at the city beyond. It was a hypnotic sight, with its soaring heights and plummeting depths and flowing colors. The ceaseless rise and fall of the circling flocks of birds was especially entrancing. He gazed at the long, streaming pennons they formed against the sky, trying to take in something of their grand, lazy tranquility. Then, slowly, discreetly, he reached under his cravat with his right hand, undid a button of his shirt, and slipped two of his fingers into the mouth of the purse. It loosened at his touch, as if of its own accord. Even more carefully, he felt for the gems with his fingertips. There were perhaps four in all now. As his fingertips brushed them he instantly sensed a strange, delightful vibration passing through his hand and along his arm, at once a kind of warmth and a kind of pulse of vitality. It was a wonderfully comforting sensation. Delicately, he caught one of them — smooth and small, somehow seeming to take hold of him even as he took hold of it — between his fingers and began to lift it out of the purse, still uncertain what he would do when he had extracted it entirely.

At just that moment, however, far off against the sky, he caught sight of a sudden, tiny, diamond-bright flash of light amid the flocks of birds, and then of whatever he had seen flashing several more times as it broke from the formation, veered off in a wide arc, and began unmistakably hurtling across the huge space toward where he was standing. Again and again, it caught the sun and glittered and sparkled with all the rainbow's colors, each time considerably nearer, moving with astonishing speed. A thrill of exultation and hope suddenly surged through him. He held his breath for a second, turned his widening eyes to Laura, impetuously kissed her cheek again — this time more competently — and then removed his hand from his shirt, closing it around the gem as he did so. A magnificent warmth flooded through his whole body. His heart ceased pounding in his chest. A feeling of incipient bliss was welling up in him, but he was far too excited to allow himself even a moment to relish it. "Oriens!" he suddenly shouted, taking three long strides into the room and stretching his closed hand out before him. At once, the five figures on the far side of the room broke apart and turned to him. Lord Theoplast, a look of amazement and rage on his face, pushed Prof. Tortus and Dr. Axiomorpha to either side roughly in his haste to get past them. The Brethren, all beginning to growl, started to move away from the windows and toward Michael. But he only called out even more loudly, "Prince Oriens Anatolius of House Enteles — look!" And he opened his hand.

The serene, pure, strangely mild radiance that poured from the gem pervaded and even overwhelmed the daylight in the room. Everyone became still. Even Lord Theoplast halted in his stride, an expression of utter perplexity — and perhaps fear — on his face. Nothing was audible for several moments, aside from a single gasp obviously uttered by Dr. Axiomorpha, curiously happy in tone, followed by a single meek canine whine from one of the Brethren. The unearthly glow filled the entire space. Michael felt almost as if he were himself gently falling forward into it, though he was perfectly still. He could have stood staring into that mysterious clarity forever, it seemed to him. Even so, he turned after several seconds to look back at Laura; she too was still, caught up for the moment in a calm rapture. Turning back to the room, he saw that Oriens had risen from the couch and was now removing his spectacles and dropping them onto the carpet.

"Look," Michael said again, his voice clear and untroubled. "It's the light of your true home."

Oriens took two steps forward. The vacant expression had departed from his eyes. "My home . . ." he said, gazing into the light, lifting one hand and reaching out toward it.

"Remember who you truly are," said Michael. Another light was now flashing and flickering at the periphery of his vision. He looked to see the white bird beating its wings, hovering just beyond the glass, the iridescence of its plumage especially vivid in the gem's light. "Remember," he repeated, looking again at Oriens. "Please."

Suddenly, a bellow of sheer wrath erupted from across the room, and Michael saw Lord Theoplast, who had apparently broken free of the gem's spell, rush toward him. "Give me that!" he screamed on taking hold of Michael's wrist. Twice he tried to seize the gem from Michael's hand but came away both times with nothing, and the light continued to blaze softly from Michael's open palm. He violently twisted Michael's wrist in his clearly very powerful grip; but the warmth from the gem seemed to give Michael the strength to resist.

"Oh, no," said Laura, almost fondly, stepping forward and placing a hand on Lord Theoplast's arm. "Please don't do that."

Lord Theoplast glared at her in rage, yelled, "Get off me, you horrid brat!" and struck her face so viciously with his free hand that she was thrown to the floor. "And you," he shouted at Michael, "let go of it!" He struck Michael's face as well, a tremendous blow across the mouth and jaw.

For a moment, Michael felt his legs giving way beneath him. But then it was as if the streams of the gem's warmth had simply caught him and raised him up again. He could taste the salty flavor of blood in his mouth, but the throbs of pain seemed distant and oddly irrelevant. He looked down toward Laura; she was sitting with her legs drawn up under her, holding a hand to a dark welt on her cheek, but with a strangely unconcerned expression on her face. Then he raised his eyes and saw that the door to the room was wide open. The security officer had evidently heard Lord Theoplast's outcries and had entered from the foyer with his pistol drawn; but the light from the gem had rendered him immobile, so that he now stood with his hands hanging idly at his sides, the pistol on the carpet at his feet. Finally, momentarily glancing at Laura again, Michael looked once more at Lord Theoplast, who was still impotently trying to grab hold of the stone, and all at once an enormous anger rose up in him — though, oddly, without lessening the deep calm flooding his body and mind. Staring directly at Lord Theoplast's face, repulsively distorted by fury and desperation, he spoke to the gem in a calmly scornful tone that he had never before heard himself use: "Drive this thing away from me."

Immediately, two dazzling bolts of white fire sprang from the gem. Lord Theoplast screamed as they struck his eyes, both of which began at once to shine in their sockets like blazing blue coals. He released Michael's wrist, pressed both his hands to his face, and went reeling rapidly away, continuing to issue agonized screams until he fell to the floor several yards distant and began writhing on the carpet, moaning loudly through clenched teeth.

Still the others in the room remained motionless. They seemed not even to notice his suffering. They simply continued to stare at the light of the gem, each of their faces wearing an expression of imperturbable contentment.

Then Oriens took three more steps forward. "Michael Ambrosius," he said, "that light — it is beautiful."

"Yes," said Michael. He looked again to the window and the fluttering bird. "It was you who brought it with you into this world. Remember?"

"I am trying," said Oriens.

Michael began to wonder how long one of these gems could continue to burn so brightly. He recalled Oriens telling him that they were extremely transitory things in this world. "I think we need help," he remarked. And then, again addressing the gem, he said, "Let it in."

The gem at once leapt from the palm of his hand in a brilliant streak and struck the window precisely where the bird was hovering; silently, it seemed to melt into a rainbow glow, which a second later expanded to wrap itself quickly all the way around the room's circumference. A moment later, the glass walls broke apart, not shattering so much as dissolving into thousands and thousands of fragments that simply spilled outward onto the surface of the dome and poured away into the air in ringing torrents. A strong, chill wind from the east entered the room through the empty, now quivering network of platinum, and with it came the white bird. It immediately rose into the blue ceiling's vault, began circling overhead, and called out in its bell-like voice — though now far more loudly than usual — "*Awaken!*"

It was like a thunderclap directly overhead, but it was like a great blast of wind, forcing everyone in the room except Oriens downward. Without the gem to bear him up, Michael sank to the floor, as if all the strength had instantly been drained from his limbs; and he saw the Brethren and the security officer and the therapists and the confectioner all falling to their knees as well, and then bending their faces down to the floor. Lord Theoplast had ceased moving or making any sound at all. Two of the Brethren had assumed the forms of wolves, brawny and bristling, but having done so they only groveled more cringingly and began emitting wails of distress. Michael was by Laura's side now, and each reached out to draw the other closer, so that they were leaning against one another, each supporting the other's head and shoulders. The wind was catching Laura's hair and dashing it gently against Michael's face, which helped somewhat to revive him. Oriens, however, remained standing quite erect the whole time.

"*Awaken!*" the bird cried out again, so loudly that it seemed its voice might bring the upper floor down on their heads.

"I am awake," said Oriens clearly. "You need not shout." And he stretched his arm out toward the bird, which instantly ceased its circling and alighted gracefully on his wrist. He briefly contemplated the beautiful creature, brought it near to his face, and said, "Hello, my very old friend."

Michael could see that the expression of stupor had wholly vanished from Oriens's face and had been replaced by a look of calm assurance. And in that moment — seeing Oriens standing above him, clad in immaculate white, the shining bird perched on his outstretched hand, his unearthly beauty and his shining sapphire eyes and his wind-stirred golden hair all set off against the blue of the ceiling — Michael could not help but feel a shudder of awe. But only for a moment. Soon the precariousness of their situation reasserted itself in his mind. "We have to go," he called out.

Oriens opened his mouth to reply but, before he could, the bird had leapt from his hand to his shoulder and whispered something into his ear. He nodded and the bird took wing. It soared over to Lord Theoplast's dormant form and, with surprising efficiency and power, snatched the silver chain from his waistcoat with its talons, tearing the pocket open in doing so. Then it returned, the glittering crystal key dangling in the air, dropping it into Oriens's open hand before settling again on his wrist. Then Oriens looked down toward his friends. "Michael Ambrosius . . ." he began. "Michael," he corrected himself, "Laura, can you rise?"

They attempted to do so, each trying to assist the other, but even together they could not get to their feet. After a few seconds, Oriens sent the bird aloft, slipped the key and silver chain into his own waistcoat pocket, and reached down to them, offering each of them a hand. With his help, they stood. Michael's legs were still unsteady, but already the feeling of weakness was passing. He looked at Laura, and she looked back with an encouraging if rather feeble smile.

"My sister is here," said Oriens.

"What?" said Michael, forcing the word out of his throat. "Where?"

"Beneath us, far below where we are now standing. But with this"— he withdrew the key from his pocket again —"we can reach her." He cast a glance around the room at the prostrate and quaking figures littering the broad floor. "We must go now, before our adversaries regain their strength."

Michael, Laura, and Oriens began to move toward the open door, but had scarcely taken three steps when a roar of fury forced them to halt and look back. Lord Theoplast, incredibly, was conscious and moving again, half upright and struggling to regain his feet, but then falling again to his knees. His eyes were closed at first, but after a second failed attempt to rise he opened them, and quite to Michael's astonishment they appeared to be unharmed. "Stay where you are," he said. "I'll have you torn limb from limb if you defy me." He looked about the room at his stricken servants. "Get up. All of you!" he yelled. "Seize them!"

But none of them was able to obey. Most of them stirred, but only weakly. Mr. Goëtus groaned at the effort. Dr. Axiomorpha gasped quietly. The security officer clenched his fists and pressed them uselessly against the carpet beneath him. Mr. Lucius was able at least to raise his eyes and glare broodingly across the room, but no more than that. Various of the Brethren made small helpless noises. The two who had assumed wolves' forms raised their tremulous haunches slightly, laboring to spring from their low crouches, but neither was able to do more than slink a few inches forward.

"Come back!" Lord Theoplast cried again, turning back to Oriens. A strong gust of wind caught his hair so that it momentarily streamed and guttered about his head like white flames. And then, evidently for the first time, he noticed what Oriens was holding in his hand. Frantically, he looked down to his own waistcoat, clutching at the torn pocket, and then tried even more strenuously to rise to his feet, only to fall forward on his knees again. "Thief!" he screamed, in a strangled voice. "You have no right! You have no *right!*"

"Come," said Oriens to his companions calmly, directing them past the security officer. The bird flew out into the foyer ahead of them.

"If you value your lives," yelled out Lord Theoplast "catch those children!" As Oriens closed the door, it was as if the voice were now issuing from the enormous, darkly shining, ferociously indignant visage glowering at them out of its dense bronze: "Bring them back! Every last one of you, on your feet!"

A moment later, Oriens had unlocked and opened the elevator. Another moment and they were inside its car, descending upon the pillar of water sinking away beneath them and echoing hollowly in the great metal shaft — down and down and down.

PART SEVEN
Kenoma

But then the spell was broken, and I woke.
I now recalled the Pearl, recalled my king.
Like thunder on the sea, the letter spoke
An incantation, and produced a ring
Of red sardonyx for my hand. I sailed
A skiff to where the serpent lay, and soon,
Bewitched by ring and spell, its power failed;
It closed its eyes and sank into a swoon.

I seized the Pearl, cast off the rags I wore,
And hastened to the radiant East, entranced
By joy. The letter came to me once more,
But now seemed like a lantern, whose light danced
Before me, urging me to journey on,
Through that hard, barren country, onward till
Dark Sarbak's citadel and Babylon
Were far behind, and I came to a hill.

— from "The Hymn of the Pearl"

I

ORIENS WAS STARING AT MICHAEL AND LAURA enigmatically. The beautiful white bird, perched on his shoulder, also had its gaze fixed on them. Sapphire eyes, eyes of azure. For a time, no one said anything. Then, after more than a minute, Laura spoke: "We didn't know whether we'd ever see you again."

"I did not even know I had lost you," replied Oriens, "except as something like a dream I could not quite remember."

There was silence for several seconds more. This time, Michael broke it: "I thought Lord Theoplast had been blinded . . . or killed."

"I do not believe the jewels from my father's treasure-house ever work more harm than is necessary," Oriens replied pensively. "Even so, I was surprised at how quickly he recovered. It makes me wonder. . . ."

But he was prevented from completing his thought by the sudden deep tolling of a great bell, outside and beyond the elevator but loud enough to penetrate its walls.

"That must be the alarm," said Michael. "Everyone will be after us."

"Below us," said Oriens, "there is another of these moving rooms."

"Elevators," said Laura.

"Yes," said Oriens. "It will take us all the way down to the place where my sister sleeps."

"Are you sure?" asked Michael.

Oriens briefly turned his head toward the bird. "My pneumatagogue has never failed me. He has watched and listened, and he can sense things that others cannot. He has found the way."

The alarm — slow, continuous, deep — continued. The sound of water below their feet ceased and the elevator came to a halt. When Oriens slid the door open, the bell became almost deafening. Even so, once they stepped out into the large, dimly lit atrium of polished black marble, they were still able to hear — in the intervals between the booming knells and blending with their reverberations — distant shouts and ringing boots echoing down the corridor from the great loggia. Michael even thought he could see men approaching from far away, though only as a tumultuous mass of seething shadow just beyond the long corridor's hushed glow of porphyry, rose marble, and agate.

"Quickly," called Oriens over the din, moving swiftly to the gold elevator door and inserting the key into its lock. "This is the way down." He slid the door open, this time with more effort than the other had required of him, and Michael and Laura dashed in before him. Just as he was closing it again, the blunt, hollow report of a distant aeroballistic pistol was audible, immediately followed by the extremely loud clash of a bullet against the door. Then the bell was again somewhat muted, and again the sound of deep waters rose up from the metal shaft below their feet and they were descending. After a few minutes, the alarm had altogether faded. And still the car sank down, minute after minute, for much longer than the journey from the top of the dome had taken.

"Are we going to go right through the world?" Laura asked at one point.

"I do not believe so," said Oriens, as if seriously pondering the possibility. "But I believe we are moving toward its heart."

For a time, Michael felt somewhat dizzy. He even briefly, as he had been prone to do in recent weeks, felt as if he were observing himself from a short distance away, as though all of this were happening to someone else. He looked at Laura, but she was still staring at Oriens, her expression impossible to read. He again noticed the welt on her cheek, breathed deeply, and tried to gather his wits. Then, loosening his cravat, removing the small silver stud from his collar, and unfastening the first two buttons of his shirt, he raised the invisible cord from around his neck and over his head. At once, a slim glimmer of gold became visible between his hands, and then the pouch with its silvery sheen and embroideries of blue flowers slipped out from his open shirt. "These are yours," he said.

Oriens considered the purse for a second. "I am content that you should keep them," he said.

Michael shook his head. "They've done enough for me. You may need them to find your sister, I think. And . . . and I don't think there're many left."

After a few seconds more, Oriens smiled and politely bowed his head. Michael draped the cord over his neck and released it, and cord and pouch alike disappeared from view even before Oriens had loosened his own cravat and collar and slipped them under his shirt. "I thank you, Michael Ambrosius," he said in a particularly courtly tone.

"They're yours, after all," said Michael.

"Only because you are generous enough to make them mine," said Oriens. "They belonged to you from the moment I gave them to you, and it is an act of great kindness for you to return them now."

Michael could think of no reply. And, at any rate, the elevator was at last coming to a rest, and the sound of water beneath their feet was growing still. "Are we there?" he asked, dropping the collar stud to the floor with a tiny clatter.

Oriens looked at Michael, then at Laura, dropped his collar stud to the floor as well, and smiled once more — though now with a hint of uncertainty in his eyes.

"She is near," the bird said suddenly, its vibrant voice causing both Michael and Laura to start slightly. "But there are dangers yet ahead. Prepare yourselves."

Michael found this distinctly unencouraging, but — briefly exchanging apprehensive looks with Laura — he reached for the handle of the elevator door before anyone else could. "Ready?" he asked. No one bothered to reply. With a deep breath, he pulled the handle, sliding the heavy door slowly but steadily open with scarcely any sound apart from a small, faintly resonant plaint of metal against metal. Outside there was light, but so pale and diffuse that it seemed only to make the surrounding darkness beyond it visible. The bird took flight as Oriens stepped forward, followed by Michael and Laura. They found themselves in an immense and empty room, a perfect cube to all appearances, perhaps sixty yards long, wide, and high. Its walls, floor, and ceiling were all of the same polished, midnight blue marble, through which ran thin twisting veins of a glowing white mineral.

"That's raw phosphoric crystal," said Michael, his voice seeming much louder in the stillness than he had expected.

At the far end of the room was a large, steeply arched aperture, perhaps nine feet high and wide enough to admit four grown men walking abreast. It was wholly framed in a broad band of dark crenelated gold, molded with the supple figures of two enormous, heavily scaled serpents, their necks entwined at the keystone, their faces turned in opposite directions, their fanged jaws opened wide. Beyond the aperture there was only more obscurity and more of the same ghostly light.

"It's so . . . cold . . . the light, I mean," whispered Laura, the room gently hissing with the echoes of her words. "It's as if . . . it feels like no one ever . . . comes here . . . ever could . . ."

The bird had twice circled the room overhead and was now spiraling downward again.

"We are in the deep places here," said Oriens. "I believe we are near our destination." He looked about him, though there was nothing to see. "I think we must be near Kenoma . . . the Emptiness, where my sister is held captive."

Michael only half digested these words. He was thinking of Laura's remark and of how apt it seemed to him. The room was physically cold, with a deep chill, but that was not what she meant. There was a feeling to this room, something that seemed to pervade the air, the depressing atmosphere of a place that no one ever visited, or ever should visit. And it was more than that too — something more desolate. It was almost as if pure absence had been given tangible shape and dimensions. The dim light torpidly emanating from the veins of crystal, the silence that the echoes of their voices seemed to make only all the more enveloping, the unadorned emptiness of the space — all of it seemed as if it had been forgotten long ago, or was perhaps everything that had ever been forgotten. And Michael could not drive the feeling from his mind. It was as though, just behind the dark blue of the walls, another, deeper darkness could be glimpsed, a night without stars or moons, fading away toward nothingness. A night from before the beginning of the world, before the first flicker of cosmic light. Nowhere at all. He was not sure he had the will to continue on. There seemed no purpose in doing so. In fact, he was sure he did not want to proceed any farther.

"Come," the bird called out, and its voice resounded from every direction. "We cannot tarry here."

Oriens nodded and said, "There is some enfeebling enchantment in this place, I can feel it. Something oppressive, heavy. It will rob us of our resolve if we do not move quickly."

"Enchantment?" murmured Michael, as if stirring out of a dream. "You mean actual . . . magic of some kind? A magic spell? Is there such a thing in this world?"

"Of course," said Oriens without looking at him. "How could there not be?" And he turned to cross the room.

Michael had to force himself to move, and Laura seemed to be walking with a lethargy like his own, but both followed Oriens without speaking, their luxuriously shod footsteps echoing around them in a chorus of stony sighs. And the white bird flew back and forth before them, repeatedly soaring ahead, returning, soaring off again, as if trying to urge them into taking flight as well.

They entered another, far larger chamber. It was a vast circular space, also all of marble — this time a smoky amber in color — and also veined with glowing crystal. Six slender, cylindrical columns, fashioned from the same marble, rose up to a much higher ceiling — so high in fact that only the thin webs of mineral luminescence running through the rock were clearly visible from below. Another arched aperture with the same gold molding stood before them; but there were identical apertures here as well, two to the left and two to the right. The bird circled the entire space, the glitter of his wings somewhat dulled in its gloom, before leading them straight ahead toward the room directly opposite. And, as he followed after Oriens, Michael felt his sense of hopelessness growing more onerous, and the cold soaking deeper into his flesh and bones. He breathed into his cupped hands. Still the sibilant echoes of their footfalls accompanied them like spectral whispers.

There followed a succession of such chambers, all equally immense, empty, and cold, each of polished marble veined with phosphoric crystal, differing only in hue: dark malachite green, tawny gold, deep wine-red, pale sky-blue, twilight purple, black, cinnabar flecked with pink, sea-gray, sea-green. In each chamber, there were numerous openings leading away toward hidden places, but the bird continued to guide them forward, always toward the opening lying straight ahead. Michael felt himself growing wearier as they progressed, and even somehow indifferent to what awaited them, but was certain that this was the result of the enchantment of which Oriens had spoken. Somewhere within himself he knew he must actually be quite desperate to reach their journey's end, whatever it might turn out to be, if only in the meager hope of finding his father. So he continued on, every now and again looking at Laura and seeing that her expression was tired and a touch despondent. Sometimes she looked back at him. Twice they attempted to smile encouragingly at one another, to rather dolorous effect. Then, at last, the party came to a chamber that differed considerably from the others.

Here too the walls, floor, columns, and high ceiling were of a single color, and here too the phosphoric crystal shed its soft glow over everything. But the stony surfaces were more roughly hewn, and had none of the gleaming smoothness of the previous rooms. Everything was lusterless granite, the color of the ocean on a moonless night. And, instead of silence, the room was filled with the sound of water, gently running and quietly splashing. This time there was only one other aperture, again directly ahead and surrounded by the familiar gold molding, and through this a corridor was visible, a pearl-colored light coldly smoldering at its far end. Two small springs of water, one on either side of the aperture, flowed in weak streams from slim, unadorned silver spouts in the rock, filling two rudimentary fountain basins with irregular edges carved directly into the granite, perhaps three feet above the ground, and then overflowing to disappear through what must have been drains in the floor. The white bird hovered briefly over the fountain to the right and dipped its beak in the water; then it turned about and alighted on Oriens's shoulder. "You may drink, if you thirst" it said. "The water is pure."

Michael realized that his lips, tongue, and throat were in fact quite parched, and he gladly went to the fountain where the bird had drunk, and Laura went with him. In the room's dimness, the crystalline light sparkled delicately on the splashing water. He gestured for Laura to drink first and she, with a grateful smile, thrust her hand into the fountain, drew in her breath sharply at its chill, and then drank deeply, filling her cupped palm four times. "It's delicious," she finally said, stepping back. Michael dipped his hand in and found the water nearly as cold as ice. He too drank deeply, until his thirst was wholly quenched, five handfuls in all, delighting in the water's purity. Somehow the chill of the water within him made the chill of the air around him less unpleasant, and he felt all at once more alert. Oriens was drinking from the other fountain, somewhat less greedily, while the bird, perched on a slightly elevated and so dry portion of the basin's edge, was repeatedly dipping its beak directly into the stream from the spout. When all of them were sufficiently refreshed, they gathered before the mouth of the passage.

"How long have we been walking?" asked Michael after a moment.

"Thirty minutes, perhaps," answered Oriens.

"Twenty-three," the bird corrected, gracefully circling above their heads, "and sixteen seconds. Eighteen now."

"Is that all?" asked Michael.

"It feels so much longer," said Laura, wrapping her arms tightly about herself.

"This place has weighed upon us as we have walked," said Oriens. "As I said, there is some subtle magic here. But I believe we are near our goal. And, unless I am mistaken, the water of these springs dispels the enchantment."

"Yes," the bird said simply, its clear voice like the peal of a small bell.

And, in fact, Michael no longer felt weary and indifferent. Now he was eager to proceed.

They all turned their eyes to the corridor before them. No veins of crystal glowed from its walls and so its length was hard to judge; it was illuminated only by the mild white light coming from its far end; but it appeared to be bare granite all the way along, with rough walls and a rather low, crudely barreled vault.

"If you are ready, then . . ." Oriens began.

At that moment a faint, distinctly lupine howl broke out somewhere far off, emanating from the entranceway at their backs but obviously coming from somewhere well beyond the adjoining room. Two more howls followed, just as distant, but with a slightly different timbres, clearly coming from a different direction.

"The Brethren are following," Michael whispered.

"We must be swift," said Oriens.

They began to run. The floors of the corridor were as roughly hewn as its walls, and in the poor light Michael and Laura more than once stumbled, Laura at one point falling to her knees with a gasp of irritation but rising and continuing forward before Michael could help her to her feet. Oriens seemed to glide along, never losing his balance, while the bird — at times no more than a vanishingly small flicker of iridescence in the darkness before them — led them onward in his pendular hence-and-hither way. The corridor, it turned out, was no more than fifty yards in length, and as they approached the light it became stronger and more inviting. At its very end, the corridor was positively awash in a soft splendor pouring in from beyond. Still, Michael was wholly unprepared for what met his eyes when they stepped into the open.

The same granite as before, but now fully lit and even in places flashing with small fragments of quartz or moonstone, rose up to a ceiling perhaps a hundred feet above, and spread away a hundred feet or more on either side toward towering walls; directly opposite, however, a good hundred yards away, was a wall just as high and wide, but consisting entirely in phosphoric crystal, fully aglow and casting a cold brilliance over everything like a coating of frost. Michael drew in his breath sharply and paused for a moment in amazement. He had never imagined that such a thing was even possible: so dazzling and yet so placid, so immense and yet of such uniform purity that, apart from a few cloudier streaks of white, it looked as if it might almost have been composed entirely of light. Oriens and Laura also came to a halt. They had no choice, as between them and the crystal wall the floor was split by an enormous jagged fissure, perhaps sixty yards across and running from one end of the room to the other, with no way around. Where they now stood was a broad ledge perhaps twenty yards wide; on the other side was another of roughly the same width; and it was obvious that the fissure itself opened over a chasm. All that connected the two separated sides of the room was a narrow bridge of what looked like sullenly dark, polished bronze, three feet wide at most, fixed to either ledge by short, stout posts driven into the rock, and with extremely thin handrails whose widely spaced spindles were almost dainty in their slimness. Laura heaved a wretched sigh. The bird soared out before them, for a moment rising upward before the shining crystal wall, practically disappearing in its glow, visible only as a small spark of prismatic brilliance amid a sea of gentler incandescences; then it swung back out over the fissure and, drawing in its wings, plunged straight downward. After ten seconds or so, Michael cautiously approached the edge, placing a hand on the railing of the bridge and gazing down. There was nothing to see below the far extent of the wall's ambience except impenetrable darkness. Then he realized that the sight was rather terrifying and he backed away again.

As he did so, the bird streaked shimmeringly up again from the shadows and alighted on the bridge's railing. "I could not reach the bottom," it announced simply.

"Is my sister beyond that wall?" asked Oriens.

"She is," answered the bird. "I can sense her now, very near. I can hear her singing in her dreams. We are separated from her by only a few last veils — but they are veils of adamant. There is a door in the wall at the bridge's end."

"I see nothing," said Oriens, staring intently across the distance.

"It is there even so," the bird replied. "I believe the key you carry will open it."

"I . . . I don't like heights very much," Laura remarked in a wavering voice.

"We must cross over," said Oriens blandly.

"Heights, you see," Laura added: "they frighten me. They always have."

Oriens looked at her kindly. "It is frightening," he agreed. "Would you like to take my hand as we cross?"

Laura took a step toward the bridge, stared into the fissure, and then drew back again. "I think I'll be holding onto the railing," she said. "What there is of it. But . . . but thank-you. If . . . but if there's some other way. . . ."

The high, plaintive wail of a wolf came drifting down the corridor at their back.

"You grew up in the mountains," said Michael.

Laura frowned at him coolly. "Mountains are large. I didn't grow up on the edge of a cliff." Then her expression became merely anxious again. "Don't be so absurd," she added mildly.

Several howls and a few barks came echoing along the corridor, nearer than before.

"They have found us," said Oriens without any trace of fear in his voice. "They have reached the chamber that we just left. We will cross over now." Then to Laura: "Please lead us to the other side."

Laura's eyes widened. "I can't . . . no . . ."

"I am afraid you may hesitate and be caught if you go last," he added, reaching out, taking her hand, and gently but insistently leading her toward the bridge, keeping his eyes fixed on hers the whole time so that she could not look at the chasm. He placed her hand on the railing. "I cannot bring myself to go any further unless I know that you will cross over first, and I know you will not hesitate if our fates are in your care."

"It's not fair," she whispered resignedly.

"Don't look down," said Michael.

"It's not even flat," she added, pointing at the bridge with her chin. And, in fact, the surface of the span was slightly convex all the way along and very smooth, as if designed to make footing needlessly treacherous.

"Then you must be deliberate in your tread," said Oriens, his tone still perfectly calm.

"I know," Laura murmured. "I'm just . . ."

At this moment, a chorus of excited howls made it obvious that a large company of the Brethren were amassing at the far end of the corridor. Michael felt a pang of terror shoot through his whole body. "Please," he said desperately.

With one last "Oh," as much of exasperation as of fear, Laura took hold of the handrails to either side and strode resolutely forward. The heels of her new boots rang out dully on the bronze, and her gait was somewhat uneven; but she continued onward at a surprisingly brisk pace. Even from behind, Michael could see that she was keeping her head tilted slightly upward, staring into the gulf of light before her rather than down into the abyss below.

"Now you," said Oriens, a note of urgency entering his voice.

Michael did not hesitate. Like Laura, he kept his eyes turned upward to the wall of crystallized light, gripped the slender rails, and strode forward.

At once, both of his feet slipped to his right, one thrusting itself between two spindles and over the lip of the bridge, and he momentarily felt as if he was going to slide right through the railing. His heart began pounding ferociously. But he regained his balance and, taking a deep breath, continued forward as quickly as he could, placing one foot directly in front of the other, striving not to allow the new, unscored soles of these cumbersome shoes to slip down the convex surface a second time. He could only assume that Oriens — whose tread was never audible — was behind him. The air above the chasm was icier than that in the chambers behind them, and seemed to be rising up in slow continuous gusts, bringing a damp and acrid mineral fragrance with it. By the time he was half the distance across, Laura had just gained the opposite ledge and was leaping away from the bridge toward the shining wall. And suddenly he had a sense of being horribly alone. He felt as though he were enveloped by the emptiness, almost adrift in it; and, for no good reason, he turned and looked over the side of the bridge into the darkness below. It was vast and deep and terrible, and seemed to fall away forever and ever into depths beyond depths; below the broad band of rough granite illuminated by the wall's light, the shadow was as dark as ink and as huge as the sky at night. All at once, this slender span of metal beneath his feet — though it was perfectly solid and immobile — seemed to him like little more than a fragile, swaying thread of gossamer, certain to break beneath the weight of his next step, or to melt away on the air. Reacting rather than thinking, he quickly cast his gaze directly upward instead. But this was no better. In the huge, high granite vault of the ceiling the light from the crystal wall became sickly and grim, and the sight of it spread out so thinly and so far overhead made him dizzy. He looked down at his feet, but could not make them move.

"You must continue on," the voice of Oriens quietly told him, only a few inches from his ear. "They are here."

Now Michael could hear the clamor of the Brethren's growls and barks and elated whines as they poured out of the corridor onto the ledge behind. He raised his eyes, his limbs still not obeying him, and saw Laura staring at him from the bridge's end with an expression of genuine terror on her face.

"Come on, Michael," she called out to him. "Come on, you idiot!"

That last word calmed him, or roused him from his stupor, or both. He found he could move again and began striding shakily toward her. It was as if she were drawing him to herself with her gaze, and he gratefully surrendered his will to hers. He kept moving, steadily but deliberately, trying to defeat his ghastly sense of vertigo, reassuring himself that the bridge was not really swinging from side to side despite his body's attempts to convince him that it was; his heart pounded in his chest, his mouth was dry, his breathing was shallow and rapid; but then, endless seconds later, he too had reached the end of the bridge. Laura took hold of his arm, pulling him forward, and he stumbled toward her on weak and trembling legs. "I see what you mean about heights," he said very quietly.

No one had time to notice the comment. Laura was continuing to pull him away from the bridge and Oriens, directly behind him, was pressing him forward with a hand on his shoulder. The bird darted in front of him but then swiftly wheeled about in a graceful arc only inches from the wall and hurtled back across the chasm again. Michael turned and saw that more than a dozen enormous, bristling, slavering black wolves had already ranged themselves along the far ledge, and still more were rapidly issuing from the corridor's mouth. So great was the rush, in fact, that one of those near the front of the company — clearly distracted by the sight of the bird — did not realize that his fellows had pushed him to the very brink of the fissure, and when he rose up on his hind legs, snarling savagely, attempting to catch the bird in his teeth as it rushed by over his head, he succeeded only at hurling himself over the edge. He yelped in terror, and the yelp instantly became a human cry of angry frustration as his wolf's body all at once became a man's, clad in the familiar black habiliments of the Brethren. He was near enough to the bridge to catch hold of the railing by one of its thin bronze spindles, but the violent momentum of his body immediately tore him away again and he fell, and as he dropped out of view, twisting and flinging his limbs in every direction, he cried, "What a bother!" Michael, watching the thrashing figure swallowed up in the sea of shadow below, found the sheer absurdity of the remark somehow piercing, despite his own fear. A twinge of pity made him lower his eyes and bite his lip.

"It's like glass," said Laura.

Michael looked over his shoulder to see that she and Oriens had their hands pressed against the shining wall, searching for a door's edge or a keyhole. But then the sound of the wolves howling and snarling suddenly increased in volume and ferocity, and he turned again to see that the bird was soaring back and forth above them, just out of their reach, working them into ever greater frenzies as they leapt impotently upward, snapping at the air and falling over one another, and even occasionally biting one another in anger. Then one of them cried out quite distinctly, in the same sort of horrible, bestial, bellowing roar of a voice Michael had heard only once before: "Stop at once, you monster!" Then another, with a slightly more mournful canine wail: "You perfidy! You inedible thing, you!" And then yet another, in a harsh, congested growl: "Try that with me, you dismal pigeon!" And then several were crying out at once, with only stray phrases audible amid the din: "You vexation!" "Vermin!" "I'll grind you up proper!" "Vicious, vicious . . . !" "Such turpitude!" "Irksome morsel!" "I don't care for you at all!" ". . . murder . . . !"

"I have found it," Oriens suddenly called out.

Michael turned to see Oriens pressing one finger against the wall, a little more than three feet from the ground, and reaching into his waistcoat with his other hand. Laura signaled frantically with both hands for Michael to join them. But Michael looked back to the other side of the chasm. The bird was now darting toward him and the Brethren, still howling at it in rage — "Devious brute!" "Piniony pestilence!" "Vindictive rabbit!" "Impolite daemon!" "It's not a rabbit!" "Cruel fairy!" "Wicked Eyes!" "It looks like a rabbit!" — were surging toward the bridge.

"Now!" Laura's voice rang out just as the bird passed by, about a foot over Michael's head.

He turned. There was indeed a door, an oblong of only average size, standing open into the darkness beyond it, with Oriens and Laura stationed to either side urgently gesturing for him to come. He did not hesitate any longer. As he ran to the opening, he heard the pads and nails of the Brethren's paws begin to pound and drum and clatter and scrape on the bridge.

"Quick, quick!" yelled Laura, grabbing him by a lapel as he reached her, pulling him along while she half tripped through the doorway, the bird streaking in just past his right ear. And then Oriens was through as well and, just as the Brethren were reaching the near end of the bridge, he pushed the door shut and thrust the key into its hole again. At once, the commotion was silenced. For a moment, neither Michael nor Laura nor Oriens turned around. All three continued staring into the wall's light. Then, exchanging a variety of uncertain glances, they all turned about at the same time. Several seconds elapsed before any of them said anything. Michael was the first to speak. All he said, however, in a hint of a rumor of a whisper, was "Oh my . . ." — because, as had so often been the case over the past several days, he could not think of any words adequate to what he now saw.

II

"WHERE ARE WE?" LAURA ADDED A FEW moments later, and her voice, quiet as it was, rebounded with a cold, stony clarity.

"We are near the limit of everything, I think," Oriens replied, his words chasing hers across the echoing space before them.

And an immense space it was — perhaps a thousand feet or more across and no less high. Even the great wall of light behind them could do no more than cast a tenuous network of scintillations over its surfaces. To Michael, it summoned up memories of certain nocturnal scenes he had taken in from his father's watchtower in the mountains, when Aurea had sunk beneath the horizon and only Argentea's crescent was still shining in the sky, and everything — valleys, treetops, distant peaks, the rooftiles of his house — was immersed in a cool, glistening, silvery brightness. But in this place there was none of the inviting enchantment of that chilly beauty; there was only a glacial, brutal bleakness. The chamber was more or less circular, essentially a vast rotunda, hewn like the previous room out of darkest granite. Here, though, the walls were polished smooth again and everywhere ornamented with scrollwork and elaborate pilasters and bas-reliefs of sylvan scenes, populated — as far as Michael could make out — by fays and dragons and fabulous birds. Slender, cylindrical pillars, perhaps a dozen arranged in a circle, rose magnificently from ornate bases up to the ceiling and then appeared to branch out symmetrically into the webs of ribbing and fretwork that filled its huge vault. On the far side of the rotunda, opposite the crystal wall, there was a large portico: its roof was a massive, richly decorated entablature resting atop the lushly foliated capitals of eight thick, fluted columns; its frieze was festooned with floral medallions and leafy garlands; and its jutting cornice was crowned by a huge pediment in the shape of a single broad triangular gable. The whole structure was fashioned from deep blue marble with white mottling. A small battalion could easily have marched ten abreast through its colonnade. And yet none of this was what was most astonishing about this place.

It was not until Michael, Laura, and Oriens had advanced well out into the great chamber — cautiously, without speaking, the bird soaring and circling and glittering overhead, the sepulchral reverberations of Michael's and Laura's footfalls lapping and overlapping in every direction — that they saw clearly what they had been able to glimpse only partially, as it had been obscured by two pillars, from their position by the crystal wall. And, when they reached the center of the rotunda, they could not help but pause for several moments, staring up at it in silence. Set on a wide dais, at the top of five broad steps, roughly twenty feet from the wall and reaching maybe seventy feet in height, was a colossal statue, with everything carved from cream-white marble, though somewhat discolored and worn down by time. The image was of a god seated upon a magnificent throne. It looked like it was meant to depict King Hyperion, judging by the figure's splendid robes, his flowing locks, the luxuriant ringlets of his beard, his scepter capped with an image of the blazing sun, his royal orb adorned with elaborate astrological devices, his diadem of stars. Of course, thought Michael, it could be some other planetary god of old. He had seen all of them at one time or another portrayed in a form similar to this. None that he had ever seen before, however, had borne, as this one did, the visage of Lord Theoplast.

"I don't understand," said Laura. "It looks too old . . ."

The bird gracefully swung down from the ceiling and glided about the figure in three wide rings, a tiny flare of shifting colors beside its plain, pallid immensity. There was something unreal, even preposterous in the scale of the thing, and something especially absurd in the grandiosity of those familiar features looming over them like a vast mountain crag. Having seen Lord Theoplast in the attire of a modern man, it was impossible not to find all of it somewhat ludicrous — the antique robe, the elegant laxity of the hand bearing the scepter, the sinewy forearm from which a loose long sleeve had fallen away, the single sandaled foot protruding from beneath folds of broidered selvage, the regal loftiness of the chapleted brow, the pompously impersonal and august mien . . . all of it. The artistry — or, at any rate, the craftsmanship — was superb, at least as far as could be discerned in this twinkling gloom; but even this only seemed to heighten the absurdity. In a different setting, it would probably have struck Michael as wholly laughable. But, just now, he was far too conscious of his own confusion, and of the unpleasant premonition spreading through his mind and over the surface of his skin, to be properly amused.

"Is that another case of . . . what was it?" Laura continued.

"Atavism," Michael replied, but with a distinctly doubtful note. He realized that his breathing had quickened.

Oriens, who had now turned his back to the statue and was staring in the opposite direction, shook his head. "No," he said, "I think there is another explanation."

"What?" asked Michael.

But Oriens, still looking away, did not reply. Michael and Laura turned to see what had captured his attention, and once again joined him in silent amazement. After several moments, as if by unspoken agreement, they all three began moving forward together, coming to a halt about ten feet from a large circular pool of water, itself perhaps fifteen feet in diameter, set between two of the room's pillars and rimmed about by a low, rounded lip of smooth, almost translucent alabaster, as white as milk and rising no more than a few inches above the floor. The water was so perfectly still and captured the pale radiance of the crystal wall with such purity that it seemed to be itself nothing but light. On the far side of the pool, another twenty feet or so away, a large portion of the wall was flat rather than rounded, like the wall of crystal through which they had come, though not nearly as high. It rose probably no more than forty-five feet from the ground, and was of the same dark blue marble with white mottling as the distant portico, running perhaps sixty feet from end to end. At its center was a gate set in a broad lancet arch, half the height of the wall, the doors of which were entirely fashioned from what appeared to be seamless, uniformly blue, and gently sparkling sapphire; two ponderous rings of dark gold hung from the doors, and there were two oval doorplates with keyholes and four heavy hinges with long tapering braces, also all of gold; the arch's frame was gold as well, wrought in the shapes of two slender, leafless trees with intertwining branches. It was very much like the gate Michael had seen in his dream on the night that Oriens had first descended from the sky. But more astonishing still was what lay above it.

Stretched out on a long cornice, from one end of the wall to the other, was another colossal statue, this one the recumbent figure of a girl, on her back and asleep, carved entirely from the same sapphire as the doors. She was clad in a grandly beribboned and embroidered gown and wore small, elegant slippers with dainty bows; her hands were folded upon her breast; her eyes were closed; a garland of gracefully small flowers rested upon her head; her hair spilled down over the cornice in smoothly lustrous tresses with loose curls; her profile was exquisitely lovely. All of it, moreover, was rendered with extraordinary subtlety and delicacy of detail. And then — rising above this massive figure, reaching all the way up into the vault of the ceiling, and seeming to melt away among the ribbing there — was what looked like a curtain of perfect darkness, or a wall of solid shadow.

Michael tried to speak, but a combination of confusion and foreboding had momentarily rendered him unable to do so. Everything here seemed too gigantic to be real and yet too unimaginable to be an illusion. He closed his eyes for several moments and strove to regain his composure. Then, looking up at the immense figure once more, he again attempted to speak, this time producing a hoarse whisper: "What is this place? It looks like a . . . like a . . . gigantic tomb." The echoes of his voice rattled desolately around them. "What's that darkness above her?"

There was no answer. But after several seconds Laura's voice, quiet but full of anguished pity, broke from the silence: "Oh, Oriens. . . ."

Michael turned to look. Oriens was standing between him and Laura, quite motionless, simply gazing at the figure on top of the wall. His expression was one of candid sorrow, and tears glistened on his cheeks. Laura had placed one hand on his shoulder, and with the other was gently brushing one of the tears away. Michael could say nothing now. He realized that, if he had attempted before this moment to imagine Oriens as weeping, or for that matter as overcome by any emotion at all, he would have been unable to do so. And all at once, quite uncannily, he thought he could actually see how old — how ancient, in fact — Oriens truly was. There was no change in his friend's appearance, but even in the ghostly light of this place there was a grief visible in the unearthly blue of those eyes that seemed as if it could have been stored up only over many long ages.

"Oriens," said Laura again, withdrawing her hands, "please don't be sad. We're here with you."

After a moment, Oriens lowered his gaze and raised a hand to his face, as if only just discovering his own tears.

"Here," said Laura, taking the handkerchief out of his jacket's breast pocket and handing it to him.

"I know you are with me," he said, looking down absently at the handkerchief. "Forgive me. That is the image of my sister."

"I know," said Laura.

"It has been such a very long time since . . . Oh, I see what this does." He raised the handkerchief to his face and began dabbing at his eyes and cheeks.

"She sleeps within," said the bird as it alighted on the near side of the pool's rim, its face turned toward the gate, "beyond those doors."

"Just beyond?" asked Oriens.

"I cannot tell," replied the bird. "We are at the border of the Emptiness. Distances are different there. But she is very near. She dreams within."

"Is she all alone," asked Oriens.

"Yes and no," replied the bird blankly. "There are other presences within . . . disembodied . . . scarcely aware. They are certainly unaware of her."

"Disembodied?" whispered Michael. "You mean dead?"

The bird dipped its beak into the pool, sending a few thin glassy ripples spreading across its luminous surface. Then, lifting its head, it said, "Neither dead nor living. They are in the twilight land between one life and another . . . wandering and dreaming and forgetting . . . eating from the fruit that grows there and drinking from the streams that flow there, which bring oblivion. Some have been there for many years, even centuries. They remain as long as it takes for them to shed what they have been . . . and until they are called back to become something else . . . to die again into the flesh."

"Die?" said Laura, scarcely audibly.

"Birth, death — as you will," said the bird. "Each is the other. The carnal body is a tomb for the spirit. What is truly alive can never truly die, but the living can be born ever anew in a body of death, a prison of perishable flesh, never remembering."

"Never remembering . . . ?" Michael prompted after a moment.

"Never remembering their former lives," said the bird.

"Never remembering," said Oriens, "that they are gods." But then he raised a hand, plainly to prevent any further questions. Breathing deeply, he folded the handkerchief, replaced it in his pocket, lifted his eyes to the sapphire doors, and began to speak, softly at first and with an evident effort to contain his emotions: "Aurora . . . sister . . . little sister, can you hear me?" Then, taking a still deeper breath, he called out loudly, so that his words echoed strikingly throughout the rotunda: "Aurora, it is I, your brother . . . Oriens! Can you wake? Can you come to me?" He took two steps forward. "Wake! Come forth! Come to me, if you can!"

"She cannot," said the bird.

Oriens appeared to take no notice, though now his voice became somewhat less peremptory. "Arise from your sleep, my darling. Please hear me. Hear my voice. Wake. Aurora, come forth."

The bird momentarily spread its wings, as if considering an attempt to fly over the wall and through the great curtain of darkness, but drew them in again almost immediately. "No," it said, "there is only one way. She hears you, but to her it is only a voice in a dream, a voice among countless others. Her sleep is deep. Many centuries have passed for her and nothing has roused her. To free her, you must go in and find her."

"Go in . . . where?" asked Michael.

"Into the Prison of Souls," the bird replied. "This is where the Princess Aurora Orthrina is held captive, lost in a sleep of ages, and she cannot free herself."

"The Prison of Souls," said Laura with a quaver in her voice. "That's what the Land of Hel is sometimes called."

"Yes," remarked Oriens simply.

A small moan escaped Laura's lips and she took three slow steps backward.

Michael once again felt his skin tingling, much more palpably this time. Like Laura, he began to move farther from the gate. Quite against his will, his mind was momentarily invaded by vague but horrid images of human figures writhing and screaming in agony, a landscape of roiling smoke and lashing flame, a crimson sky full of falling ash and flakes of fire and dark fays borne on the sable wings of butterflies, wielding their flaming swords and scourges, with the huge shadowy form of King Hel in his crown of iron spikes towering over it all. For a moment, all the hideous terrors that his catechism teachers in school had tried to sear into his imagination from earliest childhood seemed about to overwhelm him.

"Do not be afraid!" Oriens suddenly commanded, looking back at them, now over one shoulder, now over the other. "Come back at once."

Michael was startled by the calm but unreserved authority in his friend's voice. And he could tell from the glances that he and Laura quickly exchanged that she was too. And perhaps that surprise was enough to free both of them momentarily from the worst of their fears. With only the slightest hesitation, they both obeyed.

"You must not allow the lies you have been told to weaken you. We are too close now to falter. Do you understand me?"

"Yes," said Laura, almost meekly.

"Yes," said Michael. Briefly, he was tempted to change this to: "Yes, sire." Just then the phrase might have felt perfectly natural to him, and even oddly comforting. He looked again at Laura, expecting perhaps a smirk of disdain, but she was far too absorbed in staring at the sapphire doors.

After a moment, Oriens spoke again, his voice returning to a less commanding register. "Speak to me as a friend, Michael Ambrosius — Michael.

314

It is friendship I require from both of you right now. There is no reason to fear this place. It is only one more prison, at the heart of a world that is nothing but prisons within prisons. Everything here is captivity. The whole Kenocosm is already your house of durance — its every sphere, its every world, this globe at its center, all the powers that reign over it, the seven souls that enshroud the light within you, the flesh that seals you in, the cycles of forgetting in which you are bound, the always turning wheel of birth and death and rebirth without end. This is simply the first — the beginning — the earliest and most central of its prison cells, and so the last we must penetrate. Held fast within is the captive for whose sake all the rest of you are imprisoned. If she can be set free. . . ." He fell silent. After a moment he smiled wistfully, first at Michael, then at Laura. "We are so near, after all," he said, removing the small, prismatic crystal key by its chain from his waistcoat pocket. "I imagine this unlocks these gates as well."

"There is another with her," the bird suddenly remarked, a slight inflection of surprise in its bell-like voice.

"Who?" asked Oriens with a frown of uncertainty. "A sentinel?"

"No," replied the bird. "No." It cocked its head to one side, as though listening intently for some distant sound, and remained in this attitude for nearly half a minute while no one spoke. Then, straightening itself and flapping its wings twice in apparent agitation, it announced, "It is the one called Ambrosius. The father, the one called Valentine."

Laura seemed to react before Michael did, emitting a sudden harsh choking sound and a prolonged "No" — half speech, half inarticulate moan — that died away miserably.

Michael was momentarily paralyzed. An extraordinary weakness all at once descended on him, especially intense in his legs, and a deep chill filled his chest and radiated into his arms and throat. And even when, after a few seconds, he was able to move and respond, he merely took a few feeble steps forward and sank down onto his knees next to the bird, murmuring, "No, no, no," in so subdued a voice that he sounded as if he were mildly correcting a small child's charmingly harmless error. He dropped his head and covered his face with his hands, certain that he was about to be engulfed by grief, but still too shocked to surrender to it. "They've killed my father," he said. "They've killed him."

"No," the bird instantly replied, turning about on the pool's rim so gracefully that it hardly seemed to shift its feet. "He is not dead. He is not one of the disembodied souls who roam there."

It was a moment before Michael could quite make sense of these words. He was shaking violently, struggling to control his thoughts. But after a few moments he took his hands from his face and gazed into the bird's small, brilliant eyes. "What do you mean?"

"Ambrosius is still alive," said the bird. "He still wears the flesh of this world — though it is growing frail."

Michael could not think. The shaking in his body refused to subside. His breathing was rapid, his mind slow.

"How is this possible?" asked Oriens.

"Nothing dies in that place," said the bird. "Nothing truly lives either. It is a dark dream of a place. But there is no reason why an embodied man should not be imprisoned there."

"But how could he have entered?" Oriens persisted.

"That I do not know," the bird replied, and turned again to face the gate. Then it added, "He will go mad in time if he stays there. If he drinks from the water of that place or tastes of its fruit, he will begin to forget everything, and to wander in a nightmare."

Michael, still unable to master the trembling in his limbs, was able at least to look up at Oriens and say, "We have to find him."

"Yes," Oriens replied, "of course we must."

"How did he . . . ?" Laura began.

But her question was curtailed by a deep voice suddenly ringing out from the direction of the great portico and then almost immediately drowning in the swells of its own echoes: "You there, you three, stop what you're doing at once! Get your hands up!"

No one complied with the actual command, but the sudden noise of it jolted Michael awkwardly to his feet. There, from far across the room, the tall security officer who had earlier accompanied Lord Theoplast was advancing toward them with his arm outstretched, aiming his pistol at them. For so imposing a figure, however, he seemed to be moving extremely tentatively, and even at this distance Michael could detect a certain tremulousness in the hand holding the pistol. "Show me your hands!" he shouted.

Oriens stepped forward, and as he did so the bird fluttered onto his shoulder. He did not raise his hands, but he did hold them out before him, empty palms upward. "I am holding no weapon," he said calmly.

The officer halted. "And your accomplice there?" He gestured vaguely in Michael's direction. "I don't see his hands."

Michael, still shaking, thrust his hands out before him, palms forward.

"The girl?"

Laura did the same.

The officer stared at them for five seconds or so, but then slowly looked away and all around, and the shivering of his hand became more violent. "Where . . . where is this?" he said, obviously more to himself than to them. Michael could see the astonishment on his face as he took in his surroundings: the vast space, the immense height of the ceiling; the shimmering pool, the marble wall, the sapphire doors; the giant figure of the sleeping girl and the huge veil of darkness stretching above it; the great wall of shining crystal; finally, the white marble colossus. His gaze lingered on this last for an especially long time; and, when his eyes suddenly widened and his mouth fell open, Michael knew that he had recognized its face. "What on . . . ?" he breathed, but the question died away in its own reverberations. He turned his eyes again to the three companions. "Where are we?"

"The heart of your world," Oriens replied simply.

The officer stared at them for several moments with a stricken expression. "I don't . . ." he began. Just then, however, the sound of voices and footfalls and even a few snarls and snorts — quiet at first, but soon rising to quite a racket — began to emerge from the portico. He ceased speaking and glanced back behind him.

Oriens quickly whispered, "Keep watch from above," and at once the bird sprang from his shoulder and shot upward.

One by one, the six Brethren who had been present in Lord Theoplast's "panoptikon" emerged from the shadows, first three in human shape, then two still in the forms of wolves, then another in human form. Then came Mr. Lucius, his sallow features an especially sickly hue in the pallid light. And all of them, Mr. Lucius included, cast their eyes about them in wonder and dread. The wolves cowered and began to slink about the foremost of the columns supporting the entablature; the men hesitantly wandered back and forth near the entrance peering up from lowered heads, as if expecting someone or something to hit them; even Mr. Lucius seemed unable not to stare now in one direction, now in another, in the dazed manner of someone not quite able to believe — much less interpret — what he was seeing. One of the wolves whined lugubriously. One of the Brethren in human form (the one with the crooked nose) suddenly remarked, surprisingly vociferously, "This is all very terribly unsettling, if you ask me."

Mr. Lucius, sneering and dropping his head in an attitude of angry exhaustion, snapped, "Silence!" Then he called out, "They're here, my lord."

The Brethren became still, either decorously erect with heads slightly bowed or crouching with quivering hindquarters thrust in the air and snouts deferentially lowered. After a moment, Lord Theoplast stepped out from the shadows of the portico and, almost casually, began to approach the three companions. Across the huge, wanly illuminated space, clad in all his sumptuous glimmering white, he looked like a ghost suddenly wavering into visible form. When he had come half the distance, he paused beside his security officer and turned about. "Come along, then, all of you. There's no going back now."

Slowly, three more figures emerged from the portico's darkness: Prof. Tortus first, closely followed by Dr. Axiomorpha, and then, hanging somewhat farther back, Mr. Goëtus. All three moved with a timorous hesitancy, looking about the room with the same expressions of amazement that everyone else except Lord Theoplast had worn on entering; and, one after the other, their eyes passed over everything and came at last to rest on the face of the immense figure of the enthroned god.

"Don't linger," said Lord Theoplast crossly.

They tore their gazes from the statue and made their way to Lord Theoplast's side with obviously anxious alacrity. All three were more disheveled than they had been when Michael had last seen them — disordered cravats, tousled hair, three missing buttons on Prof. Tortus's waistcoat, Mr. Goëtus's monocle hanging on its lanyard with a visible web of cracks in its lens, the skirt of Dr. Axiomorpha's dress torn open more than a foot along one seam — and all three were clearly terrified. Mr. Lucius stationed himself behind them, a few paces away.

"I don't . . . don't . . ." Prof. Tortus rasped, but then simply cast his eyes about the room again.

"My lord," said Mr. Goëtus in a reedy voice, "Where are we? What does it . . . ?"

But Lord Theoplast raised an imperious hand and said, "Quiet. I'll attend to you three presently." He turned to the security officer. "I think you can put that away," he said, placing a finger on the pistol's barrel and guiding it downward. "We mustn't risk an accident."

The officer met Lord Theoplast's gaze with an expression of bewilderment and awe, as if seeing something terrible there that he had never before noticed. "Very well, my lord," he answered, slipping the pistol into its holster.

"If you would just retreat for now . . ." Lord Theoplast waved a hand in the direction from which he had just come.

"My lord," the officer replied, touching the bill of his cap but not altering his expression. Then he withdrew with some haste to a position near the portico.

Lord Theoplast turned his gaze on Oriens, Michael, and Laura and held it there for several seconds, considering each of them in order, saying nothing and betraying no emotion. Then he sighed, looked down pensively at the torn pocket of his waistcoat, and finally raised his head to stare directly at Oriens. "Impressive," he remarked impassively. "I would never have imagined you could have found your way here, or that you would have known to steal my key. I expect that that all has something to do with that feathered familiar of yours. Where is it?" He glanced about the room for a few seconds and then turned his eyes upward. "Ah, yes," he said after a moment or two, "there it is, the little . . . *famulus*."

Michael looked up and soon saw the bird in the vault of the ceiling, a tiny shining spark turning in slow circles.

"And you, young Master Ambrosius . . ."

Michael looked down again, into the empty blue of Lord Theoplast's eyes. "What?" he asked curtly.

"Oh, it's straightforward insolence now, is it? All I was going to say is that you're more resourceful than I was prepared for. After all your possessions had been confiscated over there at Glumgrub's reformatory, I would never have suspected that you had any weapons concealed about your person, and certainly none so potent. That was all quite a revelation. Some sort of magic in it, I suppose. Well, well. I don't know whether you three meticulously planned all of this out in advance or simply stumbled into it by chance, but you've all acquitted yourselves splendidly." He looked at each of them in turn again. "You're a formidable little band . . . certainly far braver than I anticipated. Yet even so, as you see, I remain unscathed, and you remain outnumbered — by roughly the entire population of the universe."

"You have witnessed only a portion of the power at our disposal," said Oriens.

Lord Theoplast smiled indulgently. "No doubt. But I assure you that you've seen almost nothing of the real power I command. And you won't catch me unawares again." He glanced at the confectioner and the two therapists, and then at Mr. Lucius. "Unfortunately," he said looking at Oriens again, "that little display the lot of you treated us to up there revealed considerably more than is quite convenient. Especially for my, ah, let's say my *retainers*. I'm afraid, through no fault of their own, they've been compromised, and now I must decide whether to take them — some of them, at least — deeper into my confidence, or whether instead to . . . well, to wipe the slate clean, so to speak." He turned to Prof. Tortus. "I should regret that especially in your case, Gaius."

Prof. Tortus's eyes widened; his jaw shivered; he swallowed deeply. "My lord, we've been friends for years."

"Precisely my point," replied Lord Theoplast.

"I've never failed in my loyalty to you."

"Not in loyalty, no," Lord Theoplast agreed. "But, in the role of advisor, as the events of this morning so grandly illustrate . . . ." He waved his hand lazily in the direction of Oriens.

"Please, my lord," Dr. Axiomorpha suddenly interjected in a despairing tone, "we're devoted to you and to the Dominion. And we've seen nothing we . . . ."

"Silence, girl!" yelled Lord Theoplast with sudden severity. "You I scarcely know at all, and your destruction wouldn't cost me a moment's remorse."

She instantly dropped her eyes, bowed her head while the echoes of these words finished raining down on her, and then took two tottering steps backward. Mr. Lucius, with genuine fear in his eyes, stepped forward and placed a hand gently on her shoulder, but at this she gave a sudden start, pulled away, and moved a few inches closer to Prof. Tortus instead. Mr. Lucius dropped his hand to his side, his expression all at once more disconsolate than frightened, and turned to walk a few paces off.

As he had earlier, more than once, Michael felt an impulse of icy revulsion at the sheer insouciance of Lord Theoplast's cruelty.

"Why must you threaten them?" asked Oriens.

"Oh, well, that's your doing, really," replied Lord Theoplast with an acid suavity, turning to Oriens again. "I like to keep my secrets, you see. In fact, the continued order of this world depends on me doing so. And this place is one of those secrets. That's why it's locked away. Oh, I have more than one key, by the way, and that" — he pointed over his shoulder at the portico — "is the front entrance. You came by way of the tradesman's door, so to speak . . . the postern gate . . . not that anyone but me ever uses either." He frowned. "Another secret I jealously guard is the one you gave us a glimpse of when you exposed us to that wretched light that momentarily overpowered us. Really, you may have left me without discretion in this matter altogether. But there it is, I suppose. It wouldn't be the first periodic purge I've been obliged to execute. No one, not even God, always gets his way."

"My lord," said Mr. Goëtus in a shocked voice, "please, I humbly beg you, don't blaspheme."

Lord Theoplast looked the confectioner and, after a moment, an expression of mild amusement appeared in his features. "I assure you," he said, "that's one thing I'm quite incapable of doing. But your piety does you credit. I'll try to keep that in mind when deciding whether to have you executed." He turned back to Oriens. "The Great Artisan is glorified in his servants, but not necessarily well served by those who glorify him. Things fell apart quite rapidly up there in my apartments, didn't they? An absolute disaster. Even I quite lost my composure for a moment. If nothing else, a price must be paid for the dismally poor counsel I was given."

"Not given by me, though, my lord," said Mr. Goëtus in a pleading voice.

"It was you who listened to that counsel," said Oriens, "and you who chose to heed it."

"Yes," conceded Lord Theoplast after a moment, "very true. I confess, the novelty of the present circumstances rendered me uncertain as to my course of action, and susceptible to foolish suggestions. Happily, I'm immune to the consequences of my own poor choices. Serving no one, I need bear no one's wrath."

"We all serve the Great Artisan," said Mr. Goëtus, his thin voice now shaking nearly to pieces.

At this, Lord Theoplast closed his eyes and allowed himself an almost jovial smile. "Do we? Do we all *serve*?" He raised his right arm and pointed toward the immense white statue, though he kept his eyes shut. "There's the Great Artisan. At least, as sculpted by a very fine artist whose name has long since been forgotten. That's the single oldest image of your God found anywhere in this world." He lowered his arm and opened his eyes, still facing Oriens. "And whose visage does it bear?"

Mr. Goëtus's looked back and forth between the statue and Lord Theoplast several times before venturing any reply. "My Lord, I know of your family's illustrious history — all those generations of great men, all those viceroys of the Great Artisan here in Kenogaia. And of course there could have been no better model for any artist to use in depicting the face of the unseen God than one of your ancestors. But still, we must all serve his justice in the end. I make my appeal to the Great Artisan himself, and beg you to consider all that I and my forebears have endured in faithful service to. . . ."

"Yes, yes," Lord Theoplast interrupted, plainly becoming bored. "I assure you, your appeal is heard. Have faith. But know also that there are things you can't understand, and deliberations in which you can have no voice. It's rather more complicated. . . . In any event, enough of this for now."

Mr. Goëtus lowered his head and said nothing else.

"It is strange to me," said Oriens, "that anyone at all would submit to the God you speak of."

Lord Theoplast stared at Oriens again. "What else can one do? Can a bottle reproach the glassblower? Can a clay bowl rebel against the one who molded it? But in my case I suspect you understand very well."

"I believe I may," Oriens replied.

"Understand what?" Laura asked.

"Lucius," called out Lord Theoplast without turning, "I think the elevator bringing our other guests will have arrived by now. Be a good fellow and go collect them, won't you?"

"Yes, my lord," Mr. Lucius replied in an indifferent monotone, listlessly striding off across the great space and into the shadows of the entranceway.

Lord Theoplast's eyes were still fixed upon Oriens. "May I come closer without causing you alarm?" he asked.

Oriens slipped his hand into the open collar of his shirt and a moment later withdrew it again as a closed fist.

"Ah," said Lord Theoplast, "that's where you keep your little secret, is it?"

"Draw near if you must," said Oriens, "but know that I will not allow you to harm my friends."

"Of that I have no doubt," said Lord Theoplast. He looked at Mr. Goëtus, Prof. Tortus, and Dr. Axiomorpha. "Consider yourselves under arrest for the moment," he told them. "Go wait with my security man." And, as they wordlessly obeyed, he turned back to Oriens and began again to approach.

III

"**Y**OU NEEDN'T MENACE ME," SAID LORD THE-oplast, coming to a halt five feet or so from Oriens. "I want to avoid any further unpleasantness. But surely you must grasp that yours is a hopeless position. You're wholly surrounded, there's no way out, what you want you can't have, and if you force the issue you may be able to resist me for a time, but in the end you'll fail, and in the meantime there'll certainly be casualties." He cast a brief but meaningful look at Michael and Laura. "And don't be so foolish as to think that that little trinket concealed in your hand is enough to defeat me. Concealed here"— he raised his right hand before him, also closed in a fist—"is the power to create and to destroy on a scale you can't imagine. The instruments and agencies available to me far surpass the little arsenal of tricks you brought with you into this world. You've entered my realm now. Everything here serves me. And those who oppose me ultimately lose everything—home, liberty, life . . . the lives of those they love . . . ."

"Like my father," said Michael with a note of pure hatred in his voice.

"Indeed," replied Lord Theoplast, lowering his hand. "And if you ever hope to see him again, you'll. . . ."

"You threw him in there," Michael nearly shouted, pointing at the sapphire doors.

"My, my," replied Lord Theoplast with a look of almost delighted surprise on his face, "once again, the quality of the intelligence you've gathered astonishes me. How could anyone"— he momentarily glanced up at the ceiling again — "have known that? But, yes, it's quite true. I brought him here myself, just the two of us, the morning after you three were captured. It required no physical force. I merely told him that you were in our power, and told him what I would have done to you if he failed to comply with my instructions. I let him drink from this pool — just a taste, mind you — to sustain him for a short time, just to prolong his despair a bit, and then merely opened the gates and . . . ushered him in. He went without so much as a snivel of complaint."

"But why?" asked Michael in an agonized voice.

"Why, to torment him, of course. None of our customary methods had elicited any useful information, and I had grown weary of his intransigence. It's my belief that there's no greater psychic torture than to wander the Emptiness while still bound to the flesh, with its vulnerabilities and needs, growing weaker and thirstier and more hopeless and more mad."

"But you already had us," Laura protested. "You didn't need to hurt him."

"Well, yes, that's true enough. At that point I could've had him disassembled, I grant you, and it would have been satisfying to do so. But it seemed prudent to keep him largely intact for now, just in case it should prove useful to dangle him in front of you in the flesh, as an inducement to cooperation. I can't foresee every contingency."

"But why do you have to *continue* hurting him?" said Michael, taking a step forward with both fists clenched before him. "Why not just keep him prisoner?"

"Oh, to break him. After all, who knows what more he might yet be able to tell us about our young visitor here?"

"But you didn't have to . . ." Michael whispered.

"And because it pleases me to do so!" Lord Theoplast suddenly yelled in rage, the echoes of his voice all at once rolling like thunder around them. "Because he defied me! Because he provoked my wrath!" His lips were pulled back from his teeth, almost as if he were a wild animal about to attack. "Do you think we're playing games, boy? Do you think my patience is inexhaustible? And it wasn't the first time, either. Valentine was an insufferable nuisance to me even before he was ever born. Life after life, he incessantly continues to. . . ." But then, just as suddenly, he stopped speaking. A few moments later, the echoes subsided as well.

While Lord Theoplast had been speaking, Michael had been lowering his shoulders, as if about to leap. But now Laura was in the way, facing him and pressing her hands against his chest. "No," she said, "don't you dare."

"What do you mean, 'life after life?'" asked Michael, still leaning forward.

"No!" Laura repeated, striking him sharply on the chest with an open palm. "You'll have to hurt me to get past me."

Michael looked at her, at her earnest green eyes and flushed cheeks and disordered hair, and slowly relented. "I would never," he said quietly.

"Well, that's touching," remarked Lord Theoplast a moment later, his voice calm again. Then he breathed deeply and idly straightened the cuffs of his jacket. "Excuse my vehemence. I really shouldn't yield to anger. It's undignified. And, to be fair, Valentine wasn't entirely useless to me. He played his part. Once we took his woman away and expelled him from the faculty at the Academy, and he retreated — predictably — to the land of heresies, and of those horrid blue and white trees that grow like . . . like inextirpable weeds in those endless mountains, we knew we needed only to keep watch from a distance. We knew he would never stop . . . he would lead us to you." He stared at Oriens.

"Yet you failed to capture me," Oriens replied. "And even when you had me in your power you could not hold me."

"Please," whispered Michael to Laura, trying to move her gently aside.

"No," she whispered back, pushing against him again. "I'll kick you."

"Well, we have you now," said Lord Theoplast.

"Forgive me," replied Oriens, "but that is not certain."

"It really is, you know. Where do you imagine you can go?"

"There." Oriens pointed toward the sapphire doors.

"Well," said Lord Theoplast with a slight laugh, "I suppose I could accommodate you, if you really wish me to. It's rare that the fly volunteers to become more deeply enmeshed in the spider's web, I have to say. But, if that's your fancy . . ."

"But I intend to come out again, and not alone. As you know."

"You wouldn't find it an easy feat."

"Perhaps not," said Oriens. "And you will not open the way for me in any event. You know I can wake her."

Lord Theoplast's eyes narrowed; his mirthless smile became a malevolent scowl. "Don't challenge me . . . Oriens Anatolius of House Enteles, Prince and Regent of the City of Pleroma, son of the High and Hidden King and of the Queen Beyond the Veil. Don't risk a battle you can't win. As I've said, you've tasted only the tiniest morsel of my power. Here I rule, and there is no one equal to me."

Oriens met Lord Theoplast's gaze with an enigmatic smile of his own and an almost imperceptible bow of his head. "We thank you that you no longer pretend not to know us."

At that moment, the voice of Mr. Lucius rang out — "They're here, my lord!" — and he emerged from the portico's shadows accompanied by two rather haggard figures, moving at a laboriously shambling pace: a fairly tall man, bald and bespectacled, limping on his right leg and supporting himself with a simple crutch under his right arm, and a rather small, very slender woman, with dark gray hair tied back. Both were dressed in the shapeless gray flannels of the incarcerated or institutionalized, he in a pullover and trousers, she in an unbelted shift reaching halfway down her shins, and both in gray laceless canvas shoes. Each of them was looking all around in obvious wonder and fear. It took Michael only a moment to recognize Mr. and Mrs. Magian, though the former had lost some weight and the latter seemed even more angular than in the past. It took him only another moment to catch Laura firmly by both arms from behind as she loudly cried out, "Mother! Father!" and tried to spring past him toward them.

"Laura!" Mrs. Magian cried out, stretching out her free hand.

But Mr. Lucius quickly thrust himself into the Magians' path, wagging an admonitory finger. "That's far enough, my masticables," he said.

"Oh, let me go!" Laura yelled at Michael, struggling to pull free; but he would not release her. "Let go of me, you idiot! Oh . . . ."

"No," Michael said in a stern whisper. "No." Then, after a few seconds: "You can fight me all you want, but I'm not letting you go." And then, when she still failed to yield: "I *am* actually stronger than you, you know."

"Oh," Laura moaned again in frustration. "Let me . . . just let me . . . ." But gradually she ceased fighting. "Please, Michael," she said in a more beseeching voice, "it's not fair. Let go."

"No," he said again, attempting a tone sufficiently peremptory to convince her of his resolve. "Stand still."

"Don't tell me what to do," she said weakly.

He momentarily allowed his grip to become gentler. "I wouldn't dare," he said.

"This is altogether precious," said Lord Theoplast suddenly, wearily rolling his eyes. "Watching you three constantly leaping to one another's defense is positively debilitating — especially since it's entirely pointless. Lucius!" He gestured sharply for the Magians to approach. "Send them over, for pity's sake, before we're all swallowed up in noble sentiment."

Mr. Lucius bowed his head and stood aside, and the Magians at once rushed — at least, as best they could with Mr. Magian hobbling alongside his wife — across the intervening space. Only when they were a few yards away did Michael at last release Laura, and she ran to them. The three of them embraced, Mr. Magian dropping his crutch with a ringing clatter and nearly losing his balance in his haste to take Laura into his arms; all three wept and exchanged incoherent noises of fraught longing and frantic tenderness; Mrs. Magian kept kissing Laura's head as if desperately drawing nourishment from doing so. Then, after about a minute, Mrs. Magian looked at Michael and summoned him too with an arm outstretched over Laura's shoulder and an almost impatient wave of her hand. With a glance at Lord Theoplast — who was watching in obvious boredom — he strode swiftly into the general embrace, closing his eyes as Mrs. Magian's hand ran through his hair and then drew him in. He felt Mr. Magian's hand fall firmly on his shoulder and felt Laura, somewhat caught between him and her parents, quaking with emotion. After nearly a minute more the four of them slowly began to loosen their holds on one another and to separate, though only by a few feet, and without entirely detaching their hands from one another.

"Where are we?" Mrs. Magian gasped. "How are you here? And what . . ." — she looked up and down at Laura and then at Michael — ". . . just what in the world are you two wearing?" She ran the fingertips of one hand along the sleeve of Laura's dress. "And what . . . ?" She ran a single fingertip, more lightly, along the welt on Laura's cheek.

"My goodness," said Mr. Magian in a frail voice, coughing as he did so. "You too?" He was, Michael saw, staring at Oriens now.

"Yes," Oriens replied.

Mrs. Magian also looked at Oriens, and with the same expression of anxious bewilderment. Then she turned her apprehensive gaze toward Lord Theoplast and a moment later emitted a short, tiny, aspirated shriek of alarm. Mr. Magian quickly turned his head and, also after only a moment, exclaimed, "Oh my goodness! Dear me!"

Lord Theoplast adopted a courtly leer. "Yes, I'm who you think I am. I'm also, however, somewhat fatigued. It's been a taxing day already, and it's scarcely half spent. You can all share your stories later, if circumstances allow. But for now I'll thank all of you to remain silent. As for you, my . . . *young* prince," he said, facing Oriens again, "my young *ancient* prince, rather: the matter is very much in your hands. How much suffering are you willing to visit on your friends in pursuit of an impossible prize? How much pain are you willing to bring into their lives? How much pain did you bring with you into this world?"

Oriens said nothing. For several moments, though, his attention seemed to float, from Lord Theoplast to Michael and the Magians to the sapphire doors and back to Lord Theoplast again. At last he remarked, "I love my sister. I cannot leave her here."

"And yet you must and will," replied Lord Theoplast calmly. "I swear by that power that made and preserves all the worlds, if you do not consent to lay aside your weapons and surrender yourself to me, I will scatter your friends each to a terrible and lonely end, and none of them will ever see any of the others again. Don't provoke me further. I have it in my power to reunite this family here or to shatter it forever. I have it in my power to retrieve young Master Ambrosius's father from the land of shadows or to banish him there for time everlasting. The only real power you have — ultimately, at least, once your tricks have been wholly depleted — is to determine which among those choices I make."

Oriens contemplated his friends. His face was emotionless, apart perhaps from a faint trace of remorse. For many moments he said nothing. Then he stared directly into Michael's eyes. "What would you have me do?" he asked.

Michael stared back, briefly glancing at the detached frown on Lord Theoplast's face, but otherwise fixing his eyes on Oriens. He could feel the intense disquiet of the Magians next to him. He was aware of his own fierce longing to see his father again, as well as his almost equally fierce loathing of Lord Theoplast, and of how the two impulses contended with one another in him. He was aware also that anything he might say could bring unimaginable consequences. But, curiously enough, he felt no indecision, but only cold, grim certainty. "Everything he says is a lie," Michael answered. "Nothing he promises can be trusted. I don't think he'll allow any of us to live long once he has you."

With a terse, humorless laugh, Lord Theoplast said, "If you think me such an ogre, boy, it makes precious little sense to provoke me further. You seem to forget, again, that you've already lost this game. Why, then, do you think I'm giving you the opportunity to comply at all, if not to spare everyone here more grief?"

"Perhaps," said Oriens, "you are not so confident of having us under your sway as you pretend."

Lord Theoplast's expression hardened, his eyes became emptier. For a moment, it was obvious that he had withdrawn into private thoughts. Then, with a slight sardonic tilt of his head and arching of his eyebrows, he said, "Very well, as you wish." Without turning around, he called out, "Lucius, would you and your men and the prisoners please move as far back as you can?"

"My lord?" Mr. Lucius replied in an uncertain voice. "Back?"

"That's right," replied Lord Theoplast, still not bothering to turn about. "All of you, lupines and anthropines alike. You'll want to be at something of a distance. But don't leave. No one is dismissed."

After a second or two of hesitation, Lucius, the Brethren, the security officer, the confectioner, and the two therapists all began to stir, and then — as if all of them had simultaneously grasped that something dreadful was about to occur — they began moving with considerable speed.

Lord Theoplast walked to the edge of the pool. "You know," he said after several moments of staring into its radiance, "we're at the threshold of ages long past in this place. This wellspring" — he pointed at the pool — "was here before the foundations of this world were ever laid." He dropped his hand to his side. "Or so legend tells us. The last living waters before the end of all things. The frontier of the void. Back then, there was only a shining mere in a dim wilderness, at the border of the Emptiness. It came to be called Lake Hyaline by those few spirits who knew of it — the spring of crystal waters — though there was little need to call it anything. When this world was made, some of those waters were captured here in this enchanted pool, like wine in a chalice, but sweeter and more . . . incorruptible."

Michael looked at Laura. She was staring at the pool, wearing an expression of incomprehension.

"And when this citadel was built," Lord Theoplast continued, "this spring became both the first and the last outpost of the infant cosmos, a final marker before the entrance to an inviolable mystery — the mystery from which this world and all the worlds on high were born. At least, again, so ancient legend tells us. Legend so ancient, in fact, as to have been forgotten by everyone but me. It also tells us that here, deep down in these seemingly peaceful waters, a dragon was imprisoned, and that he sleeps there, and will continue to do so till the end of time unless wakened by those who would seek to plunder the treasure concealed behind those doors, or to desecrate the fane they protect. And then . . . well, we know what legends are." He raised his eyes to the giant figure supine atop the blue marble wall. "This place is called the Temple of the Dreaming Wisdom. At least, that's what I call it. No one else has any name for it at all. It's my private chapel — a privilege only ever enjoyed in any age by this world's governor. I come here when I need to retreat from my labors up above. The imagery is rather touching, don't you think? Even rather tender? The Great Artisan seated upon his celestial throne, keeping watch in the great night of the world over the sleep of his beloved daughter, making sure that nothing disturbs her, seeing to it. . . ."

"She is not his daughter," Oriens interrupted calmly.

Lord Theoplast turned around and looked at Oriens with a dejected smile. "As I say, we know what legends are. But, learn this, Prince of House Enteles: some legends are true not because they record what was, but because someone had the strength to *impose* them upon the past — and has the strength also to make them true in the present." He left the side of the pool and approached to within an arm's length of Oriens, then paused for several long moments, as if attempting one last, definitive assessment of his adversary. "I'm very tired, you know," he finally remarked. "You can scarcely imagine how tired. And I'm near the point of not caring anymore." He attempted a grin, but it quickly waned. "You look quite dashing in that suit, by the way. My private tailor cut it, you know. Quite a famous designer, in fact. Cornelius Pavo. Do you like it?"

Oriens said nothing.

"Well," Lord Theoplast continued, "I think it quite fine. It almost makes me wonder — seeing you there — whether perhaps, in more fortunate circumstances, I might have made you my son."

"I am not your son," Oriens replied.

"Oh, that I know," said Lord Theoplast. "I know it all too well. More's the pity." He breathed deeply, pursed his lips bitterly, turned, and walked slowly away, back in the direction of the portico. When, however, he had traversed half the distance he all at once wheeled about so that he was again facing the pool and the sapphire doors. Now his expression was solemn, almost priestly. He lifted his hands high over his head, almost in an attitude of liturgical invocation, and cried aloud, "O *draco vetus, qui inter umbras latibuli tui quiescis: Orire! Laede! Occide!*" At this, everyone else in the great rotunda became perfectly motionless, and remained so as the echoes resounded on all sides. Even when the echoes had faded, no one moved and nothing happened for many moments. Then, his hands still upraised, Lord Theoplast cried out even more loudly, "O *perditor antique, serpens huius voraginis sempiternalis, audi me! Occide! Interfice inimicos meos! Veni!*" Again the echoes died away in the glacial silence. Again all was still for many seconds. And again he cried out, "*Ex abysso — ex barathro — veni!*"

And this time, well before the echoes had dissipated, he was answered. An enormous, deafening, and yet almost inaudibly deep noise — something like the tolling of a huge bell, something like an atrocious bellow of rage, something like thunder — seemed to well up from below the ground and actually to throb through the granite floor and walls and pillars of the room. Then a sudden, terrifying vibration shook everything, as if the very earth had moved. At this, all the frozen postures in the room immediately thawed into motion. Only Lord Theoplast stayed where he was, simply dropping his arms to his sides. The Brethren began dashing about in complete disarray, though in a generally disordered way they were moving toward the shelter of the portico. Even Mr. Lucius turned and began to run, as did the security officer and his three prisoners. There were shouts of confusion and yelps of terror and a great torrent of discordant, reverberating noises. Dr. Axiomorpha cried out shrilly when the heel of one of her shoes snapped off and she fell to the floor; but Prof. Tortus, who was just behind her, caught hold of her and more or less dragged her along till she regained her feet, kicking off both shoes as she did so. Michael, Oriens, and the Magians were briefly uncertain which way to flee, starting in various directions at once, but Oriens pointed toward the great enthroned colossus on the other side of the room, calling out, "This way, behind there!" With Laura and Mrs. Magian leading the way and Oriens and Michael supporting Mr. Magian on either side, they ran and staggered across the space, and were just nearing the stairs of the marble dais when the deep, nameless noise surged up all about them again, louder this time, and once again the whole room shook. Michael turned to look around. He saw one of the wolves, under a descending haze of silvery dust, bounding away into the darkness of the portico with a howl of terror. He also saw the rest of Lord Theoplast's party rushing in the same direction; but Lord Theoplast himself, still motionless and staring ahead, shouted, "If you leave, your lives are forfeit!" They all came to a halt, and then turned to look at him; but they all also continued to drift, now on their heels, toward the entranceway.

Then Michael felt himself being pulled backward by the collar and heard Laura yelling at him, "Get down, you fool!" For a moment, he found himself sprawling alongside her on the broad white marble steps, but then they both leapt up again and hurried around the edge of the dais to where Oriens and Mr. and Mrs. Magian were waiting. There they all turned, all five of them peering out over the stairs at the other figures in the room.

"Guard the entrance," Lord Theoplast called out with a brief glance at his security officer. "No one is to leave." Then he turned his eyes back to the pool. Michael saw the officer hesitate, stare incredulously, then slowly move to the mouth of the portico, withdrawing his pistol from its holster. Once there, however, he let his arm hang limply at his side, as if the weapon were only a pointless formality.

Then a shrill "Oh!" from Laura caused Michael to turn his head, first toward her and then in the direction she was looking. A second later he saw what she saw, and tried as best he could to control the paroxysms of fear that began to shake him.

IV

OMETHING WAS RISING FROM THE POOL—SLOWLY,
massively, relentlessly—or, rather, not so much something as the
absence of something, somehow made concrete. It was perfectly,
abysmally black, without any features at all. As it emerged from the
shining surface of the pool, moreover, it appeared to displace none of
the water around it; and, the more it took shape, the more shapeless it
seemed, because—like the immense veil of shadow stretching up above the
wall behind it—it seemed to be composed of pure darkness. For several
moments, Michael was certain that it must be the huge and malformed
head of one of the Shadows of the Deep. But then, as it continued to ascend
from the pool, he became just as certain that it was larger than that—a
head, yes, but on an even more titanic scale and even more monstrous in
form. As it at last detached itself entirely from the surface, and he could
see it fully silhouetted against the dully gleaming sapphire and blue marble
behind it, he realized that its shape was not like a man's head, but something more like the blunted rhombus of a reptile's, with a severe ridge
jutting upward at its crown and with sharp frills extending from what
could only be its jowls. And, as it still continued to rise, it was followed
by a long, thick, serpentine neck, bristling with spines. When the head was
fully twenty feet or more above the pool's surface, with still only its neck
visible as support, it turned to one side, seeming to look directly at Lord
Theoplast, and in so doing revealed the ridge on its crown to be the topmost of an extensive row of barbed serrations. Curving its neck backward
but tilting its face forward, it parted its long jaws and bared enormous
fangs, like a snake about to strike. But it merely held that position for a
prolonged moment, then all at once stretched its neck straight again and
surged upward, so that the bulk of its body now began rapidly emerging
from the water. It seemed too large for the pool's dimensions, almost as
if it were issuing out like a great swelling column of smoke and only
then assuming fully solid form. At the base of the neck were what at first
appeared to be immense shoulders on a torso like a gargantuan obelisk,

but which then turned out to be the joints of great wings, like the wings of a bat; and these unfurled themselves all at once into two great, irregular tents of total darkness, almost entirely obscuring the marble wall behind them. And still none of the creature's movements, no matter how huge or violent, made any sound at all.

The rotunda, however, was full of jarring noises and their clamoring echoes: the high piercing cry of the remaining wolf; the alarmed shouts of the other Brethren; a shrill, horrified shriek from Dr. Axiomorpha as the wings were spreading out; an equally shrill and quavering cry of "Please, my lord!" from Mr. Goëtus; Mr. Lucius yelling, "Keep your stations!" at his subordinates; Lord Theoplast roaring, "Stay where you are!"

By now, Michael felt as if he had been plunged into an icy pond; the violent shudders continually passing through his body almost caused his legs to give way under him. He was vaguely aware of Laura gripping his arm so forcefully that he could feel her fingernails through the sleeve of his jacket. Mrs. Magian, at their backs, had her arms protectively around both of them and was pressing them to herself. But Oriens, whom Michael could see only from behind, was actually standing a few feet nearer the front stairs of the dais than he had been a moment before, and his posture was so still that — from behind, at least — he appeared to be wholly unperturbed by what he was seeing.

And then the dragon — or dragon's shadow, or dragon-shaped rent in the fabric of reality — emerged fully from the water, still not disturbing its surface, raising its four huge legs over the lip of the pool in quick order, striding three steps forward, lifting its enormously long tail high in the air and waving the three spikes at its tip back and forth above its head. The creature was simply too large for Michael's senses to take in all at once. His impressions were more like a collage of disjointed fragments, none of them seeming properly to coalesce into a single coherent image: a brief glimpse of forelimbs, difficult to discern against the backdrop of the wings, another glimpse of curved talons as the two huge hindfeet came out of the pool, another of the looming vastness of the wings, still another of the dreadful winding of the serrated neck, and all of these things emerging from and dissolving back into featureless gloom as the creature heaved its body upward and forward. And now it was no longer silent. Each of its footfalls was a deep, fulminant shock, passing through the stone in palpable waves. And when it opened its jaws again, stretching its neck up so high that the outline of its head disappeared against the curtain of darkness behind it, it gave vent to a shattering roar — of anger, perhaps, or of despair, or simply of brute bewilderment — that seemed at once to reach registers both lower and higher than the ear could quite absorb, as well as every register in between. The din persisted for what seemed an excruciatingly long time, and even after it exhausted itself with a sound like a gale dying away in a pine forest its echoes thundered around the room for several seconds and seemed to crash into one another overhead in the ceiling's vault. It was the same cry Michael had heard the Shadow of the Deep uttering that night in the forest in Oreiotopia, but magnified in range and amplified by the stone walls. It was not only terrifying, he realized as he leaned back into Mrs. Magian's embrace, and as she drew both him and Laura closer to her; it was unutterably, devastatingly sad — with, it seemed somehow obvious, an ancient sadness. And out of its fading echoes there again arose those other, smaller, more numerous noises: the voices of Lord Theoplast's party crying out, howling, begging to be allowed to flee. But, as Michael briefly looked away to the portico, he saw the security officer weakly but insistently waving his pistol at the others and refusing to allow them to approach.

Then the dragon lowered its head again and turned entirely toward Lord Theoplast. With three mighty, hammering strides it crossed the distance, its vacillatingly nebulous form set off indistinctly against the dimly glistening pillars and walls. It came to a halt perhaps ten yards from him and stood up on its hind legs, its wings unfolded and aloft like two giant pavilions, its spiked tail swaying in the air behind it. The contrast between its black immensity and the now minuscule white figure of Lord Theoplast briefly struck Michael as dreamlike in its disproportion. He was quickly shocked back into the immediacy of the moment, however, when the dragon cried out again in an even more desolate voice. It was as if all the wrath and lamentation in the world were pouring out of it all at once; and again the echoes rolled over and through everything for a horribly long time. When at last they faded, Michael could hear a few last, faint, miserable protests emanating from across the room: one low, long, plangent canine whine, the sound of Dr. Axiomorpha freely weeping, a sustained timorous groan almost certainly coming from Mr. Goëtus, a feeble "My lord . . ." from Prof. Tortus. But Lord Theoplast took no notice. He merely stared upward into the towering, overspreading darkness, and even at this distance Michael could see him smile; then, slowly, calmly, he lifted a hand and pointed toward the enthroned colossus. At once the dragon twisted its neck about and turned its head, and then swiftly brought its whole body around, settling upon all four of its feet again with another thunderous crash, and its wings momentarily seemed to Michael like a starless night tumbling down upon the world.

"Oh no, no, no," said Laura, gripping Michael's arm even more frantically.

At this point, Mr. Magian had hobbled to his daughter's side, and he took her and his wife into his broad embrace, and then Michael too as best he could, and seemed to be trying desperately to drag all of them away behind the great statue. The only effect, though, was that all four of them began to stumble over one another's feet, and Michael's weakened legs again nearly gave way. "Oh my goodness," said Mr. Magian in frustration.

Oriens, however, had still not retreated. In fact, he had evidently taken yet another step or two forward, as he was now standing beside the marble dais's lowest step, entirely exposed. Laura called out to him, but her voice was immediately drowned out by another terrific, devastated roar from the dragon and by the loud percussion of its footfalls as it strode slowly forward.

Then, however, quite a different sound did succeed in breaking through the pounding echoes: the piercing but still somehow bell-like cry of the white bird — rather as if an eagle's cry had been transformed into music — as it dived straight down from the vault of the ceiling in a streak of sparkling brilliance, directly at the creature's head. To Michael, it looked like a shooting star descending toward a mountain ridge. The giant figure came to a halt and quickly looked upward, and then just as quickly dropped its head in a defensive crouch as the bird swept past and upward and around again. Rather than darting at the dragon a second time, however, the bird assumed a station in midair, hovering perhaps twenty feet away from the huge jaws, flapping its wings with such deft precision that its position hardly wavered. Slowly, even cautiously, the dragon lifted its head, as if genuinely wary of the small, flickering, iridescent thing confronting it, and for several seconds rocked gently from side to side. Then the bird spoke: "Ancient One, I know you." It was like a lovely chime ringing out in the vastness of the rotunda, momentarily conjuring everything into stillness. "I know you. I know whence you have come. This is not your true home."

Still the dragon did not move forward.

"Who has made a prisoner of you, invincible king of the realm of sleep?"

Now the dragon drew its head back somewhat, but made no other movement.

"Who has enchanted you?" the bird continued. "Who has bound you and your children in these terrible forms? Lord of the Forest of Dreams, who has made a phantom of you?"

The dragon remained still.

"Who has robbed you of your beauty? Who has despoiled you of your ancient glory, and of your mystery?"

At this, the dragon drew its head back slightly further, and its wings began to sink down at its sides.

But then Lord Theoplast's voice burst out, almost choked with anger: "*Draco, audi me!*" His face, Michael saw, was again quite hideous with rage. "*Pare deo tuo! Obsecunda! Occide!*"

The great shadowy head turned toward the voice.

"*Creatura mea es! Laede!*"

The dragon hesitated for many moments, as though confused. It returned its gaze momentarily to the bird, with a kind of curious or dazed graduality, and then back to Lord Theoplast. And then all at once its whole body shuddered. A violent spasm seemed to run down the length of its neck and it swung its head around to the bird again with a savage suddenness, roaring out once more. The bird instantly began to drift backward, but the dragon was already raising its wings and had, before the bird could flee, brought them together ferociously in the air above its head. The effect was like a great blast of wind, but attended by some greater force as well, because it struck the bird powerfully enough to send it spinning away, beating its wings wildly but unable to prevent itself from striking the scepter in the hand of the white marble colossus with a dreadfully sharp sound. It dropped limply to the floor before the dais and Michael was certain it must be dead. One of its wings was thrust upward at an awkward angle, the other was no less awkwardly folded under its body. "No," Michael breathed, wincing at the pang of hopelessness in his chest. But then, quite incredibly, the bird began to move. It stirred its disordered pinions, rolled its body over, rose onto its delicate legs, primly ruffled its feathers, and wagged its head, as though it were merely shaking off droplets of water.

Michael had no time to be astonished. When he returned his gaze to the dragon he saw that — just as had happened with the Shadow of the Deep — a spectral glow was beginning to well up from deep within the darkness of its chest, and to take shape as a spiral of light, gray and ghastly white. He allowed himself to stare at it too long. Before he had had time to think what he was doing, he became aware that the same fascination and thoughtless stupor that had drawn him toward the Great One that night in the forest was beginning to take him over now. With an almost painful exertion of his will, he forced himself to close his eyes and to cry out, "Don't look at it! Don't look!" But, even as the words were leaving his mouth, he felt Mr. Magian releasing him, almost languorously, and Mrs. Magian lightly withdrawing her arms, and he knew that both of them had already succumbed. He opened his eyes to look at Laura and saw that hers were tightly shut. She was holding his arm in both hands while he, without being conscious of it, had gripped one of her wrists. "Your mother and father," he shouted as loudly as he could, "you've got to stop them."

"Oh," Laura cried, as if he had thrown water in her face, and immediately she let go of him, practically flung herself against her father's substantial but unsteady form, and pushed him so hard that he staggered backward into her mother.

Another shattering roar erupted from the monster. Michael glanced up, shielding his eyes with a hand on his brow as if that might protect him from becoming enthralled, and saw that the dragon had come to a halt in the very middle of the rotunda, its huge head and upraised tail swaying back and forth in contrary directions like counterbalances, its wings fully outspread to either side. The wheel of hoary light had grown to fill the entire space of its huge upper torso, sluggishly, grotesquely spinning, and now a sound of wind was rising from every quarter, hissing among the stone columns, and the wind was also full of voices, groaning, whispering, weeping, and the swirling light seemed also to be dim clouds drifting above a cold, barren waste, somewhere deeper within the darkness — just as had all happened before. And, as he had then, Michael felt an almost dreamy desire to reach out toward the light, to touch it, to go to it; and, again with all the resolve he could summon up, he closed his eyes, crying out, "No, I won't!" Then he realized that, while looking at the dragon, he had also seen Oriens, still standing by the lowest step of the dais. He half parted his eyelids and squinted at his friend, who seemed from behind clearly to be staring directly at the Shadow dragon, but who showed no sign of moving toward it. Michael tried to call to him, but there was no strength left in his voice. He also found, as he feared he would, that the rushing sound gathering around him was now becoming an actual and increasingly forceful wind, pulling at him, drawing his elegant jacket and trousers taut against his back and legs, and he felt the soles of his shoes beginning to slide forward on the stone of the floor.

Desperately he reached out toward the dais, but there was nothing to take hold of on its smooth marble surfaces. And he heard Laura's voice, rising to a frenzied pitch: "I can't hold them! I can't stand up! Help me!" He spun about as best he could and lunged toward her. She was still attempting to restrain both her parents, but the constantly strengthening wind was aiding them as they pressed forward, obviously oblivious to her, and was dragging her along as well, causing her long skirt to flutter and snap and her hair to whip and stream out behind her. Then her feet flew out from beneath her and she fell, and Michael tried to catch her, and he fell too. The wind was a storm now, wailing and thrashing at them, and with a sense of vacant terror Michael felt himself beginning to rise from the floor. He clawed in panic at the granite beneath him, but again there was nothing to grip. "Oh, Michael," Laura practically screamed, and Michael called out her name in a pathetic croak. His body was already rising free of the ground, with only his palms and the toes of his shoes still touching the stone, and the wind was stealing his breath away and forcing him to keep his eyes tightly closed, and he felt himself slipping along the polished granite floor, and he knew that in a moment the wind would be too strong for anyone to resist and would carry them all into that horrid light and horrid darkness, and a chill of final resignation spread through his limbs. "I'm sorry," he muttered quite meaninglessly, at everyone and no one.

But then, in an instant, the wind ceased. Michael dropped to the floor with an involuntary groan, and heard Laura utter a similar noise. It took him a moment to regain his breath and to turn over, and only then did he dare to open his eyes. Everything — absolutely everything in this enormous space, right up to the high vault of the ceiling and all the way to the most distant reaches of the rotunda — was bathed in a strange, serene, otherworldly light, full of warmth and entrancingly lovely colors. At once, the terror departed from Michael's body and mind. He sat up. Oriens was now standing farther out in the open with both arms high above his head. Evidently he had at some point extracted a second jewel from his pouch, as now one was shining out of each of his upraised hands. The jewels remained fixed where they were, not falling from his palms, though they were opened outward toward the monster. And two feet or so above his head the bird was hovering in place once more, the shimmer of its iridescent feathers and the flashing of its bright wings made even more beautiful by that unearthly splendor. Everything had grown quiet. Michael glanced briefly toward the portico and saw that everyone on that side of the room had ceased moving and was staring at Oriens. Even Lord Theoplast seemed momentarily stupefied — his arms hanging at his sides, his eyes gazing absently, his lips slightly parted. The dragon too was now perfectly immobile; the ghostly light had vanished from its chest. Slowly, Michael rose and then assisted Laura to her feet, though he kept his eyes on Oriens the whole time. The familiar feeling of perfect peace was washing over him, the warmth of the light was soaking into him, and he wanted to take in as much as he could.

"Ancient One," the bird called out in a voice less urgent and more melodious than before: "Look. See and remember."

"Look," Oriens said, loudly but calmly. "Remember. Know yourself."

The giant figure seemed frozen in fascination. If its eyes had been visible, Michael was certain he would have seen them intently fixed on the two burning gems.

"Remember," Oriens continued. "Recall who you are, and where you have come from, and where you must go again to be free of this world."

"Remember," said the bird.

"I know you too, now," Oriens said. "At first, I had not recognized you, as my wise companion had. I have never seen you in any shape, but I know this form is not yours. Remember who you truly are. Remember the Forest of Dreams. Remember the voices of your children. Recall the songs they sang before the sorcerer came."

"Remember," said the bird.

Now the dragon did move, but somewhat drowsily. It folded in its wings, and lowered its tail, and straightened its neck so that once again the outline of its head disappeared against the great veil of shadow behind it.

"You know this light as well," Oriens said, his voice becoming almost soothing. "It is the light of our world, yours and mine. It is the light of the home of all who are imprisoned here. Look at it. Remember."

"Remember," said the bird.

And all at once a sound like a soft but deep sigh issued from the monstrous figure. There was no hint of ferocity in it, though there was still an unmistakable sadness.

"You are too mighty for me to conquer," said Oriens. "But I do not need to fight you. We are not your enemies. It is not we who brought you here."

"Remember," said the bird.

"I have walked many times in the shade of your realm," said Oriens, "embraced by your hidden presence, under your care, dreaming the dreams you gave me. We are friends of old. Until now, I did not know you were here."

Just at this moment, however, Michael noticed something small and bright moving off to the side, and looked to see Lord Theoplast shaking his head and raising his hands to his temples, clearly struggling to throw off the spell holding him in place.

"Remember," said the bird.

Lord Theoplast looked away from the shining gems and upward at the dragon.

"Waken," said Oriens.

"Remember," said the bird.

Now Oriens raised his voice: "O, *rex magne, tu qui regnavit olim in silva umbrosa somniorum* . . ."

But then Lord Theoplast positively shrieked in fury: "*Draco tenebrarum, audi me* . . . !" That, however, was as much as he was able to say. At the sound of his voice, the dragon stirred from its trance, but this time turned about suddenly on Lord Theoplast, strode toward him, unfurled and shook its wings threateningly, and roared in rage. "No! Wait!" Lord Theoplast cried out, an anxious warble suddenly invading his voice, his eyes widening in obvious astonishment and fear. "No, don't! Wait!" He raised his hands before him absurdly, as if to fend off a blow, and began stumbling backward. The dragon took another stride forward. "Stop!" cried Lord Theoplast in a surprising high and undignified tone. But the monster took another step forward, and now Lord Theoplast turned and ran, past Mr. Lucius, who wheeled around and followed him.

Everything happened very quickly then. Michael could only watch. And so deep was the serenity that the light of the gems had infused in him that he could not even feel any real horror at what he saw. The remaining wolf succeeded in dashing away through the entranceway, but no one else did. The monster's thunderous footfalls ceased, but the storm wind had already risen up again, this time instantly at full force, and the ghostly light was again burning in its breast. Lord Theoplast and Mr. Lucius had thrown their arms around one of the portico's foremost columns and were clinging to it; Mr. Goëtus had done the same on the portico's opposite side. The four Brethren in human form, however — the one with a crooked nose, the one with a scar, the tall thin one, the short stout one — were immediately caught up into the air, mouths open wide but with their cries drowned out in the wind, writhing and flinging their limbs about impotently, until they simply disappeared into the seething light and impenetrable darkness. A moment later, they were followed by the security officer, who was just emptying his pistol into the dragon when he was lifted from his feet. Then Prof. Tortus, pushing Dr. Axiomorpha before him toward the confectioner, was torn away from her and off his feet, flipping rapidly backwards through the air several times like a rag doll flung by an angry child, until he too was plunged into the darkness and spiraling light. Dr. Axiomorpha succeeded in grabbing hold of Mr. Goëtus's sleeve with one hand while reaching for his lapel with the other; but he instantly yanked his arm free and pushed her backward brutally with an upraised foot, and with a scream that was just audible through the tumult of the wind she too was carried away, tumbling into the gale, arms and legs thrashing, and then was gone. Across the distance, Michael watched Mr. Lucius open his mouth to cry out; he even fancied he could faintly hear a howl of anguish; and a twinge of pity momentarily managed to penetrate his unnatural calm.

The wind stormed on for another minute or so, some of its draft reaching Michael where he stood. But then it simply died away, as if the monster's rage had been exhausted, and the turning wheel of spectral light simply shrank to a wisp of sickly white and flickered out. For a moment, the dragon stood silently, its wings outspread again over its head, waving its tail from side to side almost lethargically, as if pondering what to do next. Seizing the opportunity, Lord Theoplast released the pillar and fled into the darkness of the entranceway. Mr. Lucius, however, did not. With an absolutely savage cry, at once human and bestial, he rushed toward the confectioner — who had fallen and was just rising again — and leapt lithely through the air. As he did so, he was no longer a man, but rather a huge and brawny wolf, one with a thicker, glossier, darker coat than Michael had seen on any of the other of the Brethren. At the last moment, Mr. Goëtus saw the beast coming and was able to utter a single terrified "No!" But then the wolf closed its jaws upon his throat, pulled him viciously away from the pillar, back into the room, and dragged him several yards across the floor twisting and kicking and flailing ineffectually with his fists. The wolf held him fast and continued to shake him back and forth until he grew limp, and only then ripped its jaws away. With one or two last pitiful convulsions, Mr. Goëtus's body became perfectly still. The wolf raised its head, opened its lips, and bayed loudly in a tone that to Michael sounded like a combination of hatred, triumph, and utter misery. Then, pausing briefly to lower its head in what seemed clearly an attitude of grief, it turned and bolted away into the darkness of the portico.

At that same moment, the dragon cried out one last time, no less terribly than before but maybe more forlornly. Then it crossed the remaining distance separating it from the entranceway with a few strides, each shaking the room, reared up on its hind legs, and brought its whole body down with devastating force upon the portico. The single large gable of the pediment cracked in two, followed by the cornice, then by the medallioned frieze, and then by the architrave; finally, the eight fluted columns shattered and the whole structure came crashing down, sending up a great dark cloud of dust. The sound was like an avalanche in a mountain pass, and it did not subside for many seconds. For many long moments thereafter, the great shadowy form lay still, stretched out upon the ruins as if all its strength were spent. At last, though, it gradually lifted itself up from the debris of the now obviously sealed entranceway. For a few moments longer, it remained there, appearing to survey the destruction it had wreaked. Then it turned around and, without sparing a glance in any other direction, returned to the pool, its listless tread echoing much less tremendously than before, sounding now more like distant thunderclaps in an adjoining valley, while its wings dragged across the floor with a noise reminiscent of a flowing river. Then it dipped its head into the pool and a moment later — although, again, it appeared to be much too large to accomplish the feat — slipped its entire body soundlessly into the water, seeming as before not to stir the surface, and vanished entirely.

In that same moment, the lovely, limpid glow of the two gems faded from the air, and only the bleak light from the crystal wall remained. For a time, there was silence.

V

"IT SEEMS TO ME," SAID MICHAEL TO ORIENS, "THAT your enemies don't have any real idea what to do about you."

The two of them were seated — along with Laura and her parents — on the steps of the great marble dais.

"No," Oriens agreed, "it does not seem that they do."

"And yet they've had . . . centuries, I suppose, to prepare."

"It is their own fear that defeats them," said Oriens. "Not knowing what to do, they act impulsively, and so erratically." He rose from the stairs and stared across the rotunda toward the pool and gate. "But they will not cease trying. And I have only one of the gems from my father's vaults left. I must go into Kenoma now."

Michael also rose. "I have to go with you. I have to find my father."

"Yes, of course," Oriens replied. Then he looked about until he found the bird, casually perched on the large toe of the white marble colossus. "Will you lead me yet a little farther, my old friend?"

The bird said nothing but stretched its wings and took flight, soaring across the great chamber and alighting again on the near lip of the pool. Laura and her mother rose and helped Mr. Magian to his feet and the whole party crossed the room as well.

"What about us?" asked Laura somewhat hesitantly after they had come to a halt. "I'll go in with you, if you need me to." Her tone was anything but enthusiastic.

Michael was about to reply, but Oriens spoke first: "I would prefer you to stay with your father and mother. If we fail to return soon, you must show them the way out."

"The wolves have gone," remarked the bird.

"How can I?" asked Laura.

Oriens removed the key from his waistcoat pocket and allowed it to turn and flash for a few seconds on its chain. "Once these doors are unlocked," he said to the bird, "will I have further need of this?"

"This is the last portal to be unlocked," the bird replied, "the last veil to be parted."

"Then," said Oriens, turning to Laura, "I shall leave the key with you so that you can go back the way we came."

"I don't think I can," she replied weakly.

"I am sorry that I have brought you all to this place," said Oriens. "It was never my desire to endanger anyone but myself."

"Not without you and . . . and not without Michael," Laura added, as if she had not heard him.

Michael found it impossible to suppress a dour laugh. "You just offered to go into the Land of Hel with us," he said. "Please, Laura, don't pretend you're too afraid."

"I'm not," she answered. "And how long are we supposed to wait? You don't know what you'll find. We won't know what's happening to you."

"It is not really the Land of Hel to which we are going," said Oriens. "That is all a lie. A cruel legend devised by malicious minds. Do not fear." Then he turned to the bird. "Will you leave me if I ask? Will you come back here and warn them to flee if I cannot return?"

The bird dipped its head with a courtly solemnity. "I will."

For another minute or two, Laura protested her unwillingness to abandon her friends, her willingness to go with them, her doubts as to her own courage. But at last her mother took her by the shoulders and said, "Darling, we need you." So she lowered her head, obviously fighting back tears, and said, "If you don't come back, Michael, I won't forgive you."

"Yes you will," said Michael. "But you won't need to."

"These waters will refresh you for the journey," said the bird. "They will strengthen your bodies and your resolve. Drink deep before going in. All of you should drink. The waters here both refresh and nourish."

"But the . . . the dragon?" asked Laura.

"The dragon sleeps again," it replied, "many fathoms down. He will not harm us. You should wash your wound as well," it added, looking toward Mr. Magian. "These are healing springs."

"Oh, my goodness," said Mr. Magian. "That's good to know. Well, yes, I . . ."

"They will soothe your cheek as well," said the bird, abruptly turning to Laura. "And your father," it added, turning to Michael, "he too should drink."

"How?" asked Michael. "From what? We haven't. . . ." But then he paused and raised a finger significantly. He dashed across the room as swiftly as his awkward shoes allowed, slowing to a hesitant pace only as he drew

344

near the body of Mr. Goëtus. Fortunately, the upper half of the corpse was thickly shrouded in dark blue dust and rubble from the collapsed portico, so he was not obliged to see either its face or its torn open throat. Hastily, he knelt down and, after a moment's search, withdrew the large silver flask from the hip pocket of Mr. Goëtus's jacket, then returned to his friends, pouring out the liquor — which had a remarkably strong and unpleasantly saccharine fragrance — as he ran. "This should do nicely," he said, kneeling down again beside the pool, but then paused. He had expected, on leaning over the water's edge, to see himself and the dim gulf of the ceiling above mirrored in its surface. Instead, no less than when it was viewed from an oblique angle, all that it reflected was a mild white brilliancy, as though the pool really were filled to the brim with liquid light. Michael dipped his hand into the cool water only to see it wholly disappear beneath the surface. And yet, when he removed it again, the water in his cupped palm was perfectly transparent. "It is magic," he whispered. He tasted the water and found it delightfully pure — sweet, even. He briefly submerged the flask in the pool, withdrew it, shook it a few times, and emptied it onto the floor, then lowered it in again and filled it.

When all had drunk deeply, Michael discovered that he was not only refreshed, but thoroughly invigorated. All his fatigue had vanished, as had all those aches in his body of which, until they were gone, he had been only half aware. When he saw Oriens rise from the edge of the pool, he positively sprang to his feet, and followed along to the sapphire doors. Mr. Magian, with the assistance of his wife and daughter, seated himself on the floor, resting his back against a nearby column; but even he seemed remarkably lively in his movements. The bird was circling swiftly overhead, seemingly enjoying the revived power in its wings. Just as Oriens was about to insert the key into one of the keyholes, Laura called out: "Wait, wait!" She ran to them, threw one of her extraordinarily tight hugs around Michael, held him for several seconds, then went to Oriens and, somewhat more tentatively, did the same to him; then, looking away so as to hide her face from them, she simply told Michael, "I meant what I said," and returned to her parents.

The key turned easily in each keyhole, releasing a bolt each time with a loud metallic report. Then Oriens held out the dangling key to one side, and the bird swept down and took it from him, dropping it in the lap of Laura's skirt as she sat by her father. She closed her hand on it without raising her eyes.

"Are you prepared?" Oriens asked.

"Yes," said Michael, though without much conviction.

Each of them took hold of a gold handle and pulled, and the doors — for all the massy opulence of their glistening blue gemstone and gleaming gold — swung open effortlessly on their hinges, without sound, as if they were no heavier than silk draperies. And what they disclosed was, at first, almost nothing. Directly beyond the aperture all that was immediately visible was a wall of what appeared to be thick mist. But for one or two lighter eddies in the otherwise uniform gray, it might have appeared perfectly solid.

"How should we . . . ?" Michael began but stopped as the bird darted between him and Oriens and through the gate, its flapping wings leaving behind two cloudy spirals in the mist as it disappeared from view. Oriens smiled bracingly at Michael, passed through the gate as well, and was just as quickly swallowed up. Taking his courage from the feeling of strength that the waters from the pool had imparted to him, Michael followed.

It was not a very dense mist, it turned out, and it was wholly impalpable. Only a few steps, and Michael had emerged on the other side. The prospect that met his eyes, however, seemed scarcely more concrete. He was no longer in a subterranean chamber, at least as far as his senses could tell. Instead, he was surveying an open woodland. But it was a woodland that appeared to have been drained of all color and reduced to only its barest lineaments. He realized, of course, that by all rights he should have been utterly astonished simply at finding himself under an open sky, and surely a bit unsettled at finding himself in a place so morbidly drab. But at first all he really felt was relief. As he stood there beside Oriens, following the flight of the white bird some distance ahead, flickering like a spinning prism against a pale twilight of silver and leaden gray — ever so faintly haunted, perhaps, by repressed violets and blues — he was merely glad that what he saw was nothing like the traditional images of the Land of Hel. Somewhere in his mind, he had obviously still been harboring the fear that he would discover a realm of leaping flame and enveloping night, jagged escarpments and burning trenches, mephitic smoke and streams of molten iron, machines of torture and fields of blood, souls twisting and screaming in torment, demonic fays swarming in ruined skies.

Instead, the overwhelming impression of this place was one of simple dreariness and melancholy, as well as of an unfinished quality, as if it were only the draft of a landscape that some artist had sketched onto a canvas and then abandoned before applying pigments, or perhaps an intentionally nightmarish evocation of a landscape in chiaroscuro pastels and grisaille washes. They were overlooking a wooded valley, much of it dark and indistinct, as if evening were falling over it — though Michael felt certain that here evening was always falling. Near at hand, there were trees, or at least the shadowy shapes of trees in black and charcoal gray; they stood at the edge of a leafless forest of bent trunks and warped branches that stretched away like dim, petrified coils of smoke against the monochrome sky. Everything was silent except for an occasional soft pattering at the roots of the nearest trees, and after a moment Michael could see that the treetops were dripping with water, not it seemed from any recent rainfall — though he could not be sure of this, since the air here had absolutely no fragrance — but rather from a thin fog that was continuously sliding between their branches. Underfoot the earth was also colorless, like ash, and so insubstantial that Michael could scarcely feel it beneath him. Nothing possessed any very precise detail: no obvious bark on the trees, no clearly defined granules in the soil. Directly before them a path gently sloped away downward. A low ridge rising up on the valley's opposite side formed the horizon. And there, fitfully visible between floating scarves of mist, stood the only visible object that seemed fully physically real in this whole scene, softly aglow with actual full colors: a lone building that looked like an ancient temple, white marble with gilt embellishments, foursquare, a low roof supported on ornate columns and overshadowing an inner court. But in this crepuscular light distances were hard to assess, and so the size of the structure was impossible to discern.

"I believe that is where we must go," remarked Oriens.

As he said this, the bright glint of its wings above the valley announced that the bird was returning. Before it arrived, Michael glanced backward and saw that the wall of mist behind them seemed to rise up immeasurably until it merged with the dazzlingly vacant sheen of the sky. When he looked forward again, the bird had already stationed itself before them in midair.

"Is she there?" asked Oriens.

"Yes," the bird replied. "She sleeps in its inner shrine."

Oriens lowered his head for a moment and Michael could see a tremor of emotion run through his neck and shoulders. Then, looking up again, he asked, "Is there anyone else there — anyone barring our way?"

"No. The living cannot long abide here without being driven mad and the dead are powerless."

"Have you seen any sign of my father?" asked Michael.

"No," said the bird, "but I can sense that he is near."

"Where?"

"Near."

THEY DESCENDED INTO THE VALLEY, WHICH WAS IN fact quite shallow to judge by the downward angle of the path. Between the enlivening effects of the water from the pool and the almost velvety tenuousness of the earth underfoot, Michael felt as if he were being wafted through the forest. The bird now soared in leisurely arcs, before them and behind them, onward toward the opposite ridge, backward toward the gate. As they went down into the deeper shade, the perpetual gloaming overhead seemed to become starker. And still there was no sound but the faint dripping of water from branches.

They had been walking for five minutes or so when the first ghost appeared. It was a moment before Michael was sure what he was seeing — merely a dim, eerily diaphanous shape floating across their way, emerging from the trees on one side of the path maybe twenty yards ahead, which he might almost have mistaken for a shred of fog had it not visibly paused for a moment to stare in their direction before disappearing into the trees on the other side. He drew his breath in sharply through his teeth, but somehow — again, perhaps, because of the waters of the magic pool — he felt no fear at the sight. Then, a moment later, he saw another: this time nearer, gray and largely transparent, clearly a woman wearing what looked like a simple flounced dress of the sort one saw in pictures of the last century, standing below the boughs of the trees to the left side of the path with her gaze seemingly fixed on them; and as they passed her by Michael fancied for a moment that he could almost make out an expression of curiosity, though her features were barely more distinct than shadows on glass.

It was another fifteen minutes at most before they reached the bottom of the valley. Along the way, they saw at least two dozen other specters, wandering the verges of the wood, scarcely taking notice of them. Some were of men, some of women, and a few were of children; all were variously clad in garments modern, old, or (in two cases) quite ancient. Occasionally Michael also thought he could see faint faces among the trees, staring at them as they walked by, but making no sound.

At the very bottom of the valley, they came upon a fairly open grove of smaller trees, four or five feet tall, of a lighter, almost vaporous gray, and with more delicate branches. These too were leafless, but hanging from their branches — weightlessly, it seemed, since none of them was bent down by the burden — were fruit, roughly the size of apples, though less defined and with a vague tincture of purple. An extremely shallow stream, perhaps three feet wide, ran through the middle of the grove, no doubt in the valley's lowest trough, its slow, wan currents reflecting the empty luster of the sky and babbling quietly as they wound around hazily half-formed stones. Oriens and Michael leapt across easily.

Not long after they had emerged from the grove and begun the ascent of the valley's other side, they came upon another ghost, this time of a woman. Though he could still see through her, well enough still to discern the vague outlines of trees, Michael could tell that she was garbed in a simple full-length robe from another age, with a plain cloth wound around her head, from beneath which her hair spilled down over her shoulders. She was not wandering aimlessly like the others, but rather was seated on a small boulder, the only one Michael had seen along the way. As they came near, she turned her eyes directly to them. As far as Michael could tell, hers was a young face, perhaps even lovely; and she seemed to be inspecting them more keenly than any of the others had. Before they could pass by, she raised a translucent hand, clearly bidding them to stop. They came to a halt a couple yards from where she sat. Then she spoke — and now Michael did feel a kind of chill in his body, not so much out of fear as out of the sheer uncanniness of her voice. Her words were audible, but they seemed to be coming not from her lips, but from a far greater distance; the tone was high and thin, almost like the cry of a bat, or like a breeze whistling though a crack in a wall; a ghost of a voice: *Who are you?*

Oriens took a step toward her and, with great gentleness, said, "I am Oriens. This is Michael Ambrosius."

The ghost turned her eyes to Michael and then back to Oriens. *You are so bright. You shine.*

Michael looked down at his hands and noticed nothing but their normal color. Then again, he realized, by contrast to this world of shadows, that color must seem positively effulgent.

You are so bright. The ghost lifted her hands before her face and seemed to be examining them. *I do not shine as you do.*

Oriens looked at her for a moment, and even in profile Michael could see the pity in his expression. "You shine in my eyes," said Oriens.

The ghost looked at him, quizzically turning her eyes slightly to the side. *Can you tell me who I am?*

Oriens lowered his gaze. "I cannot, no."

After a moment: *I so wish that you could. I had a name, I believe. I had a name. Do you know perhaps if I had a child? I remember a child, I think.*

"I do not," replied Oriens, looking up again. "I am sorry. But I am here to find someone who may know the answers to all such questions."

The ghost said nothing, but merely looked at her hands again.

All at once, it occurred to Michael that he had been unconsciously assuming that he must keep his silence in this place, not out of any sense of caution, but on account of an unreflective feeling that sound was somehow improper here. Now he realized he could have been calling out to his father all along the way. He gritted his teeth angrily at himself and then spoke to the ghost: "Please, can you tell us, have you seen another like us? Another who . . . who *shines* like us?"

The ghost lifted her eyes to him and appeared to be striving to recall something. *Another . . . who shines . . . ? Yes, there is another.*

"Do you know where he is? Where we can find him?"

There is another who shines like you, yes, she told them again. Then, after another moment of apparent contemplation, she raised a hand and pointed along the path ahead of them. *He is there sometimes. Sometimes he is not. I have seen him. There is a place up there where we cannot go. I have seen him there, beyond the trees. He shines. Do you . . . do you know my name?*

"No," said Michael, "I'm afraid I don't. I. . . ."

Just then, however, the bird swung down from the facing tree line, out of the silvery sky, calling, "Come! You must not tarry!"

BY THE TIME THEY HAD LEFT HER, THE GHOST HAD already apparently forgotten them. At the sound of the bird's voice, she had looked away and upward; and then her gaze had wandered idly downward to the trees along the path ahead, at which she had continued to stare without further word.

Now, as they proceeded up the valley's opposite side, Michael discovered that it cost him no greater effort to go uphill than it had to go down. The water of the ancient spring, it seemed, was still sustaining him, or this place was too insubstantial to detain him very much, or both. None of the other phantoms they passed along the way — a dozen more perhaps — paid them any particular heed, even though Michael now had begun calling out "Father!" and "It's Michael!" at regular intervals, somewhat quietly at first but soon with considerable energy. The trees here did not, as those in the forests of Oreiotopia would have done, ring out with his cries. In fact, they seemed to deaden sound, and Michael could not tell if his voice had travelled any distance at all. But he continued shouting while the bird circled overhead, looking for some sign of Mr. Ambrosius.

It was only when they were nearing the end of the forest, beyond which a field of sere, ashen grass — or sketchings of grass — sloped gently upward another hundred yards or so to the top of the ridge, that his call was answered. At first, he heard only an indistinct word cried out from somewhere ahead, but clearly in the voice of a living man. And then, even before he could react, he heard his own name shouted out. Immediately, he saw the bird dropping out of the sky like a flare and soaring down toward the edge of the woods, where the path ended. Lowering his gaze he saw, maybe forty feet ahead, the figure of a living man in shapeless gray prisoner's garb practically staggering out of the shadows of the trees to the right, one shaking hand outstretched, and he instantly knew his father, and ran to him.

The bird was flying in close rings only a few feet over Mr. Ambrosius's head when Michael reached him. Michael tried to speak, but his voice broke. Instead, he wrapped his arms around his father's ribs, and then realized after a few seconds that his father was too weak for so robust an embrace.

"Michael, son," Mr. Ambrosius said when he had steadied himself and Michael had somewhat loosened his grip, "How. . . ? Why. . . ?" He held Michael's face in his hands and peered at it from squinting eyes. "Is that really you?"

"Your spectacles . . ." Michael said.

"Oh, they broke them," said Mr. Ambrosius distractedly, still staring with all his might. "They've imprisoned you here too?" he asked, a tone of anguish entering his voice. "Oh, Michael. . . ."

"No, oh no," said Michael. "No. We've come for you . . . and for . . . for *her*. We've opened the gate."

"What?" Mr. Ambrosius's brow furrowed and his eyes narrowed even further. "We . . . ?" He cast a watery glance over Michael's head at the approaching form of Oriens. "Is that . . . is that . . . ?" He relaxed his hold on Michael's face and sank down on one knee. "Son, I'm. . . . Do you have anything to drink with you? I'm so thirsty."

"Yes, yes," said Michael, hurriedly pulling the flask from his jacket pocket and unscrewing its cap. "I do. Here, drink this. It'll make you. . . ."

Michael did not need to finish. Mr. Ambrosius closed his shaking hands around the flask almost brutally, brought it to his lips, and drank deeply. As he did so, Michael looked at the lines in his father's face, which had deepened since his arrest, and at his disheveled hair and more than usually unkempt beard; but then Michael also saw how quickly the water seemed to be reviving him, causing him to straighten his back, stilling the trembling in his body. When he took the flask from his lips again, having apparently more than half emptied it, he breathed deeply and said, "It's the water from that pool, isn't it?" He gave the flask back to Michael and rose easily to his feet. "It's marvelous. Oh, yes . . . I feel quite alive again."

"The water has healing virtues," said Oriens, who had just arrived at Michael's side.

Mr. Ambrosius stared at Oriens, his lips parted, an expression of wonder in his eyes. "Yes, I know. I can . . . I can see you quite clearly now," he said softly.

"That too is because of the water," remarked Oriens.

"Yes, I know," said Mr. Ambrosius, speaking in something of a daze. "The few sips I had before coming here had that effect for a while. But, you" — he lifted his hand and half extended it toward Oriens, then let it fall to his side again — "you're the one, aren't you? The one we've waited for? I didn't know if you were really coming, but. . . ." He paused, staring intently. "What very extraordinary eyes you have."

"Father," said Michael, feeling a very familiar amusement beginning to stir within him, and then an overwhelming surge of affection, "we've come for you."

Mr. Ambrosius looked at Michael, still with an expression of astonishment but also with a burgeoning smile. "So you said, son. So you said. But how? How did you do it?" He looked away in the direction of the far off gate, and then at Oriens, and then at Michael again. "I can't believe it. I'd thought I'd never. . . ."

But then the bird's voice broke out just above their heads, with a distinct note of impatience: "We must not tarry here! There will be time for questions later. Come!"

Mr. Ambrosius took a deep breath, winced drolly, shook his head, and said, "Quite right." Then, though, he arched a single eyebrow and took hold of Michael's cravat between a thumb and forefinger. "Why in the names of the heavens are you dressed like that?"

VI

THEY REACHED THE TOP OF THE SLOPE, THE GRASS making no more noise beneath their feet than smoke would have done, and halted before the edifice they had seen from across the valley. Just as Michael had thought when seeing it from a distance, it was in the form of an ancient temple: a single raised floor open on all sides, a stately but not excessively lofty roof, a long anterior gable, elegantly tapering columns with florid capitals, a few steps leading up to the encompassing porches, a forecourt, and—wrapped in shadows—an inner shrine with a narrow entrance and a low roof of its own. The gold embellishments that wound about the pillars and sprawled along the eaves—vines and leaves and flowers—glowed sullenly against a delicate blush of rose in the white of the marble. There were no doors anywhere. Beyond the building's far side there was only another wall of glistening gray vapor. There really was nothing more to this entire little land, Michael reflected, this fabled nether-world that was the object of so much pious terror and so many nonsensical dogmas, than this single structure, the grim, haunted, dreamlike draft of a valley lying under the low dome of an empty sky, and the dreary curtain of mist that encircled the whole of it.

"I've entered twice," Mr. Ambrosius remarked quietly. All along the way up from the forest's end, he had kept his hand on Michael's shoulder without speaking, but now he let his arm drop. "I've seen her. I didn't try to wake her. I didn't know if I should."

"You would not have been able," said Oriens. "But she knows my voice. It will raise her from her sleep. This is the last day that she will sleep here."

They resumed walking, and the bird darted in ahead of them, the flashing of its wings diminished but not extinguished by the shadows beneath the roof, and came to rest on one of the gold vines creeping along the lintel above the shrine's entrance. Oriens hurried up the steps and across the smooth marble floor, making no sound as he did so. Michael and Mr. Ambrosius followed, moving at a more measured pace and sending quiet echoes whispering through the porch and forecourt. Oriens paused briefly at the shrine's entrance, glanced once at the bird, and then entered. Michael also paused before going in, staring for a moment at the subdued red glow inside; but then, able to make nothing else out, he went in as well, his father directly behind him.

It took a few seconds for Michael's eyes to adjust to the darkness. The interior was of relatively modest size: perhaps ten yards wide and twenty long. Hanging in the spaces between the walls' engaged columns were dark red tapestries with brocaded images of flowering vines, fruit-bearing trees, jetting fountains, and birds with brilliant plumage. The ceiling, which rose little more than twenty feet above the floor, was bordered by elaborate gold moldings in a regular pattern of diamonds and circles. And all the marble surfaces — above, below, on all sides — were dyed a rich porphyry red by the burning lanterns at the back of the shrine: five large urns of ruby glass enveloped in webs of finely spun gold, arranged along a high altar carved from the same marble as the rest of the temple and garlanded in the same vegetal gold. Stretching above the altar and down behind it was a balda-chin of what appeared to be blue — or perhaps purple — silk, suspended on a willowy golden frame and emblazoned with a large image of the sun. The vast antiquity of the place was almost palpable, and its stillness had a gloomily inviolable quality to it. It felt to Michael as if the silence here had never before been broken, and as if no breeze had ever blown in through the porches. And yet the air was filled with a delightful fragrance and a sort of cool freshness, like the mingled scents of blossoming trees after a spring shower has passed.

Michael took all of it in quickly, but just as quickly turned his attention to the very middle of the shrine. There, on an elevated bed — or, rather, on an oblong of polished marble with beveled edges, which might just as well have been taken for a funeral catafalque — lay the Princess Aurora, her head resting on a silken crimson cushion and her hands folded on her breast; and standing beside her, lost in contemplation of her sleeping face, was her brother. Michael held his breath for a second, reached back to touch his father's arm, and then slowly approached, coming to a halt opposite Oriens.

They were alike in beauty, Oriens and his sister, but unlike in coloring. The great image of her above the gate, while very accurate, had given no indication of the difference. As extremely fair as he was, she was just as extremely dark, like a girl from the Southern Islands, with a complex-ion like burnt umber and as smooth as satin; and, while his hair shone brightly gold, hers was gorgeously, glossily black, the sheen of its loosely curling tresses almost amethyst in the lanterns' glow as they flowed over the edges of her pillow and spilled onto the marble. She was also clearly the younger of the two, by (to all appearances) at least two years. And the loveliness of her features was, Michael thought, utterly captivating in its childish gracefulness. Just as in the sculpture, she wore a splendid gown, richly beribboned and embroidered, and small slippers tied with slender silk bows, and as far as Michael could tell in this light all the fabric was of a rich indigo hue. And, resting among the locks of her hair, there was a circlet of tiny flowers, probably white but perhaps pink. Ever so slightly, her folded hands were rising and falling with her breathing.

"She's so beautiful," said Michael in a hushed voice.

Mr. Ambrosius was now at his shoulder. "Yes, indeed," he said, almost reverently.

"She is," said Oriens, bending slightly forward as if to drink her features in. "I had almost forgot how beautiful."

The bird now appeared, and in a moment was hovering a few feet above her head. "Speak to her, my prince," it said.

Oriens looked at the bird. "Perhaps I should try to rouse her gently, by degrees."

"Until she hears your voice calling her, she will not wake at all."

Oriens looked down at his sister again, laid one of his hands on hers, hesitated for only a few seconds, and then said, quietly but clearly, "Aurora, little sister, wake up now." He placed his other hand lightly on her brow. "Sweet sister, wake. Leave your dreams behind. It is I, Oriens, your brother."

She did not stir.

He lowered his head, breathed deeply, then looked at her and spoke again, no less tenderly but now more insistently: "Wake up, little one. The time for dreaming is over. The dawn is past. The hour is come to rise from sleep."

A soft sigh parted her lips.

Oriens smiled eagerly and his voice became even more urgent. "Yes, you heard me. Wake up. Morning has come. At once, little one." He took one of her hands in both of his and raised it to his lips. "Beloved sister, arise."

Again she sighed, more deeply this time, and a smile appeared on her lips. Michael caught his breath at its loveliness.

"Good," said Oriens, "very good. Open your eyes."

But now her smile became less pronounced, and then faded away, as if she were sinking down again into her dreams.

"No," said Oriens, "you must not go back to sleep. Aurora!"

Her lips parted again, and this time she spoke: "Oh, Oriens . . ." Her voice was barely more than a breath, but even so it was sweetly musical, with an almost crystalline note of happiness in it.

"Yes," her brother said, growing excited, "yes, it is Oriens. Aurora, wake up. Open your eyes."

She sighed again, and the smile reappeared on her face. And then, once again, it began to fade. "Leave me for a little longer," she murmured.

"Look at me, Aurora," Oriens persisted. "Open your eyes for me. Look and see."

Something like a very small laugh rose to her lips, but nothing else. "Aurora! Sister!"

"Yes?" She asked drowsily. "What do you want?"

"Look. Look at me. Aurora, open your eyes."

And then, slowly, her long dark lashes flickering once or twice, she did. For a moment, she simply stared upward at the ceiling above her; but then she turned her head and gazed fully into her brother's face. Her eyes were the same unearthly sapphire as his, and seemed to shine with a light of their own, one that easily pierced the dim, narcotic red of the lamps. Her smile widened. This nearly forced Michael to look away; its delicate beauty was almost too perfect to bear. Mr. Ambrosius was also clearly affected; he caught Michael's shoulder in a firm grip and whispered, "Oh, how extraordinary."

Then — something Michael had heard before only once or twice, and never with such richness — Oriens laughed. The sound had a glorious purity to it. A young god's laughter, Michael immediately thought to himself.

Still purer, however, and just as joyous, was the sound of Aurora's delighted voice: "Oh, hello, Oriens."

Oriens released his breath. "Hello, Aurora," he said, his voice faltering at the brink of tears.

She breathed deeply and, waking more completely, stretched out her arms to either side. "What a very curious dream I've had," she said in a voice full of contentment.

A moan of unalloyed joy escaped Oriens lips and, a second later, he took his sister by the shoulders and drew her up into his arms. All of his usual composure had dissolved. At first, Michael was startled at the sight, but he soon found himself relishing it. And, when he saw Oriens's embrace grow more fervent, he could not suppress a laugh of his own.

"Now, now," said Aurora in a fondly scolding tone, gently detaching her brother from herself and pushing him a few inches away, "not so forceful.

Oh . . . " — she sat up, arched her back, turned her head from side to side several times, stretched her arms again, and finally swung her legs slowly around and over the edge of her bed — " . . . I had such a deep, deep rest." She smoothed the long sleeves of her gown and adjusted the lace cuffs. "But I'm quite awake now. You don't need to drag me out of bed."

"That was not my intention," said Oriens, still gazing at her with an expression of desperate happiness. "It was simply joy." He took her hands in his. "Aurora, there is so much I need to tell you, and very little time. Listen to me carefully. We are not in our own home here. We are somewhere we should not be. You have been taken prisoner by a very evil. . . ."

"Oh, yes, I know all that," she interrupted. Then she laughed, and her laughter was even more splendidly otherworldly than her brother's. "Really, Oriens, you must think me very foolish."

"You know?" said Oriens, leaning his head back with a perplexed look. "How? What do you know?"

"Why, all of it, of course. I'm the one who dreamed it, after all." Then she turned and looked at Michael and Mr. Ambrosius. "Hello, Michael. Hello, Valentine. I've been very worried about the two of you. I'm so pleased to see you here."

Michael fought briefly for words, in part out of his amazement at being addressed like an old acquaintance, and in part out of rapt fascination with how astonishingly pretty her face was now that she was fully awake. But he finally managed to say, "You know us?"

"Well, of course," she said with another laugh. "Why wouldn't I?"

Michael felt his own smile broaden, certain that it must look quite stupid just at the moment, but too enthralled to do anything about it.

"How big you've grown," she suddenly added. "You've become quite handsome."

"I . . . " But he could think of no apt reply. "Thank-you."

"Yes, yes, Aurora," said Oriens, still obviously mystified, "but this has not all been only a dream. Understand, little one, it is also a dark spell that was cast over you. The sorcerer who brought you here made you his captive, and it has been a very long time since. . . ."

"Oh, I know that too," she said, turning back to Oriens. "Honestly. I know how he tricked me, and how he played on my innocence. It was *extremely* wicked, and I'm *very* displeased with him. But I've learned a great deal while I've been asleep. I know better now."

"You do?"

357

She shook her head sadly, as if nonplussed by the sluggishness of her brother's wits.

"Aurora . . ." Oriens began.

"Oh, help me down, then," she said, almost imperiously. "It's time we were getting home. This . . . this body is so clumsy."

Oriens stared at her with candid affection for a few seconds; then he wrapped his arms around her, told her to place hers around his neck, and eased her down to the floor. Before removing her arms from him, she kissed him on the cheek. Then she straightened her skirt and stood up straight. She was perhaps four inches shorter than her brother. And this made it seem a little absurd, albeit in an entirely charming way, when she looked around at each of them in turn with a firm, purposeful expression on her face — her brother first, then Michael, then Mr. Ambrosius, and finally the bird — and said, in the casually peremptory manner of a governess calling children in from play, "Come along, everyone. This way."

"Well," remarked Mr. Ambrosius as she strode resolutely out through the shrine's entrance, "I suppose we'd best obey our mother."

LIKE ORIENS, AURORA WALKED WITH SEEMINGLY unnatural gracefulness, and so the sight of her small, determined, lavishly attired form briskly descending the slope into the valley, followed closely by her brother and attended by the low circling flight of the bird, scarcely gave indication of how swiftly she was moving. Yet Michael soon discovered that he and his father had to hasten to keep pace with her. And so also his first assumption—once she had entered the forest shade and had begun periodically calling out, "Come along, everyone, come with me!"—was that she was merely exhorting the two of them to catch up. It was only when the small grove of fruit-trees and the palely glimmering stream in the valley's basin came into view that he began to realize that she was in fact issuing a much more general summons, and it occurred to him to look back.

So much had changed in the past weeks, Michael realized, so many seemingly impossible things had happened, that nothing now affected him as it would have done only a month or so before. What he now saw would once, not long ago, have terrified him, but instead it filled him with a quiet exhilaration. Behind him and his father, following as silently as a rolling cloud of fog, was a great and constantly swelling procession of ghosts. They were floating continuously out from among the dark trees and into the pathway, silvery and transparent. It was already a multitude. The nearest of them were perhaps a dozen or so feet away, but their company stretched back innumerably all the way up to the grassy slope, and more were joining it — hundreds, thousands — every second. The few faces that Michael could almost make out at the very front of their ranks appeared to be staring ahead with little or no expression on them, but it was very difficult to tell for certain. He pulled on his father's sleeve and pointed backward at them. But Mr. Ambrosius simply nodded: "Yes, I've already seen."

"You too, Roxana and Sohrab!" Aurora called out, and Michael looked forward again to see her waving a beckoning hand to her left, where two diminutive phantoms, a boy and a girl in the sort of clothes once worn in Persis, were idly watching from the edge of the grove. "No dallying," Aurora added in a voice that would brook no recalcitrance, clapping her hands twice, and the two small figures immediately drifted across the grove and into the spectral parade.

Aurora and Oriens leapt effortlessly across the stream, as if executing a dance-step. Michael cleared it with only slightly more effort. Mr. Ambrosius's left foot splashed at its edge. As the party ascended the other side of the valley, Aurora continued to call out, and ghosts continued to pour from the forest and into the path behind them. The phantom of the woman to whom Oriens and Michael had spoken was still seated upon the boulder where they had left her. "And you also, Philomela," said Aurora as she walked past. "It's time to go. Your daughter's already with us." And, at once, the ghost rose to her feet, and this time Michael could definitely see the expression of rapture on her face as she glided from the wayside and into the great procession.

Thereafter, Michael did not look back again, and soon he began to find it a somewhat eerie feeling to know that so enormous a crowd was following at his back in such absolute silence. Only when, however, he finally reached the wall of mist again did he turn around. All the way along the path, extending out of sight below but also visible in a long argent line stretching up again on the other side of the valley, were all the legions of the dead. But now they had ceased to advance, and were clearly waiting for Aurora's next command.

"Michael, Valentine," she said, "if you two would go through first, I'll just make sure no one's been left behind."

Michael met her eyes but then, trying not to become too dazzled to speak coherently, he concentrated instead on the little constellation of white blossoms strewn among her raven locks. "All of them? All of them are coming?"

Her smile became positively radiant. "Of course. What did you imagine?"

Michael looked at Oriens questioningly.

"As I predicted," said Oriens. "The dreamer has awakened."

Michael turned his eyes back to what was now a great river of phantom figures. And now he saw that the very foremost among them were no longer gray and silver and transparent, but had become softly golden, and somewhat more clearly defined. Their faces were more distinct, at any rate, and so also were their expressions of profound peacefulness. Then in two of them, a man and a young girl — and then in two or three more, and then another, and so on — small brilliant gleams of a purer, more brilliant gold began to appear, and grow brighter, like sparks or torches shining in their breasts. Michael felt his skin tingling in a quick succession of pulsing waves, running from his scalp to the soles of his feet. And yet still it was not fear that he was feeling, but only wonder. "Father, look!' he said.

"I'm looking," replied Mr. Ambrosius.

As the golden lights burning in the breasts of the ghosts at the front of the procession grew brighter, and seemed to kindle similar lights in those behind them, and as the same warm glow began visibly to spread back through the assembled multitude, the first two figures seemed simply to melt away — as then did two more of them, and then another, and then several others — their spectral bodies vanishing so that only the lights that had been burning within them were left, now floating in air, even brighter and purer and more richly golden.

"But do be quick," Aurora chided Michael. "There's still so far to go."

MICHAEL AND HIS FATHER FOUND THEIR WAY PAST the mist and through the open gate without difficulty. As they emerged again into the great rotunda, however, no one there at first took any notice of them. The Magians were some thirty yards beyond the pool, Mrs. Magian and Laura with their backs turned and Mr. Magian striding vigorously back and forth in the open, excitedly announcing, "I tell you, Eve, it's entirely healed. My goodness me, I'm like a new man."

"Well, still, Basil," Mrs. Magian replied, "don't overexert yourself. You're always too eager to leap right back into things."

"Yes, dear, I know you think so," Mr. Magian answered, "but you really needn't worry. I tell you . . . ." As he was saying this, he turned to his wife, and in doing so saw Michael and Mr. Ambrosius. "Oh, my goodness!" he cried. "Valentine, my dear old fellow!"

Laura and Mrs. Magian spun about and both emitted small, jubilant cries. Laura had reached Michael before he had even succeeded in making it all the way around the edge of the pool and enclosed his ribs in yet another of what had become her very frequent and ferocious embraces. He noticed that her face no longer bore any sign of Lord Theoplast's blow. Mr. and Mrs. Magian reached Mr. Ambrosius a moment later, the former clapping him on the back, the latter throwing her arms around his neck, kissing both his cheeks, and then pressing one of them against her own.

"That was quick," said Laura as she released Michael, obvious relief in her voice. "Where's Oriens?"

"He's not far behind," said Michael.

"What's he doing?"

"Well, I think you'd be better off waiting to . . . ." He paused. "What do you mean when you say 'quick?' How long have we been gone?"

Laura shrugged. "Maybe twenty minutes."

"Oh, no," said Michael. "Surely it was much longer than that."

Laura frowned and shook her head. "No," she said simply. Then she looked toward the gate. "How long will it take Oriens to get back?"

"Oh," said Michael, turning about to watch with her, "they should all be here any moment."

"All?" asked Laura.

"Yes," said Michael, "definitely *all.*"

The white bird glided out from between the open sapphire doors and into the room, circling the pool once and then coming to rest at the same place on its rim as before. Then came Oriens, looking for a moment — as he emerged from the gray mist in his white suit — like a bright alabaster statue brought to life. But before anyone could react with more than an incipient salutation (a happy gasp from Mrs. Magian, an ecstatic but otherwise unintelligible syllable breaking from Laura's lips, a quickly curtailed "My . . ." from Mr. Magian) Aurora came through the gate as well, and everyone at once fell silent. For a few moments, she stood before the open doors surveying them all with her hands on her hips. Michael looked at Laura and saw the expression of fascinated wonder on her face; then he looked at her parents and saw much the same there. But none of them moved. Mr. Ambrosius smiled knowingly, Oriens enigmatically.

"You look so very lovely, Laura," said Aurora suddenly with another of her musical laughs. "We're going to be such good friends!"

"Oh!" Laura practically squealed in her shock, and then began rather ineptly to smooth her hair and brush the dust from the bodice of her dress and say, in a more tempered tone, "I . . . You know. . . . I'm . . . ." She cast a quick, fretful glance toward Michael as if beseeching him to come to her assistance.

"I'm so glad to see you, Basil and Eve," added Aurora.

The Magians both opened their mouths, but neither of them succeeded in saying anything.

"It's all right," Mr. Ambrosius told them.

Mr. Magian looked briefly at his friend, then back at Aurora, and said in a barely audible voice, "Goodness gracious, should we kneel?"

Aurora stared at him with a mild, pensive scowl. "No, that would be very silly of you. Anyway, we haven't time. If you'll all excuse me for just a moment. . . ." She walked to the edge of the pool, turned around to face the gate, and called out, "Come along, my dears. Come along."

A moment later, the veil of mist inside the gate began to turn from gray to yellow, and then to a deeper, more luminous gold, and then all at once — radiant and clear and unspeakably beautiful against the dark glittering blue of the sapphire doors — all the golden lights that had once worn the shapes of phantoms came pouring out soundlessly into the room, an absolute cataract of gemlike sparks, thousands upon thousands, but flowing upward, into the gulf of the ceiling's vault, bathing everything in its splendor. The pool shone like molten gold, and the translucent white of its rim shone like a thin, flickering ring of flame. Now Laura and her parents did move, falling back several yards, and even Michael and his father retreated a few feet. Oriens and the bird remained where they were, however, seeming to bask in the fiery light flooding over them and into the heights above, where — at least, so it seemed to Michael — the sparks simply continued to rise unbated, passing through the ceiling as though there were nothing there. And all the while the small figure of Aurora, silhouetted against the coursing streams of blazing glory, continued to wave her hands beckoningly.

"My gracious," said Mr. Magian, his voice nervously loud, "what's happening?"

"All the wanderers are returning home," replied Aurora without looking back at him. "All the glory that was spilled out into the Emptiness when the vessels were broken. All the lost children. All."

Just then, an immense noise, like the long wordless lament of an unbelievably deep voice, forlorn and angry, seemed to well up all around of them, out of the earth below but somehow also from overhead and from every side. It was as if the whole world were giving voice to an overwhelming convulsion of grief. It persisted for only a few seconds, but it was horribly oppressive all the same. As it faded, Mrs. Magian took hold of her husband's arm while he looked about with wide eyes, Laura drew her breath in between her teeth with a slightly shrill whistle, and Michael looked to his father, who looked back with an expression of uncertainty.

"And now he knows it's happening," said Aurora, dropping her hands and turning to the others. "That's quite vexing."

"Who knows?" asked Mrs. Magian.

"Oh, *him*," Aurora replied with a touch of exasperation, fluttering impatient fingertips in the direction of the colossus of the Great Artisan. "And he'll try to stop it. He'll try to stop all of us. I know it. He's *very* stubborn that way." She went to Oriens and took his hand, looked at him gravely, looked again at the golden lights spilling through the gate, and said, "Well, we'll have to help them escape — help everyone, ourselves included — won't we? There are more doors yet to open."

"Yes, there are," said Oriens somewhat gravely. "Quite a few, in fact. Seven celestial doors to open, seven souls to shed. These spirits have escaped their phantasmal forms, true, but that is only the beginning. Their psychical sheathes will hold them unless we can open the way. And then, of course, there is everyone else." He held out his hands to either side, palms upturned, as if to indicate the entire world.

"Then we should be going," she said with a particularly resolute inflection. "It's time this nonsense were ended."

"My goodness!" exclaimed Mr. Magian.

"Come on, everyone," said Aurora, looking around at all of them. "No time to waste." She began crossing the rotunda in the direction of the glowing wall of crystal. "Michael, Laura, you two ought to come with me."

"She certainly is very . . . *royal*," Laura discreetly remarked as she and Michael hastened to follow.

"Yes," said Michael. "But, you know, it's hardly the first time I've had to get used to being ordered around by a girl."

Laura was too preoccupied just then to strike him sharply on the shoulder, as normally she would have done.

PART EIGHT
Pleroma

The land of Maishan, where the merchants traded
   Beside the placid sea, below me spread.
The brilliance of the lantern had now faded,
   Its song died on the wind. I turned my head
And saw twin treasurers, who brought to me
   My robe of glory, which the court had sent
From far Hyrcania down to Maishan's sea,
   And in my eyes the veil of day was rent:

I had forgot its beauty, how it glowed —
   So many days and years had come to pass —
I gazed and gazed; its crystal colors flowed,
   Till all at once it was as clearest glass
In which I saw myself as though another:
   I was two men with but a single form,
My garment was my spirit's secret brother
   From whom it had in ages past been torn.

The envoys of the king, though two, were shaped
   Each like the other, with one face. They brought
Me riches, and my shining robe they draped
   About me, now a cope of jewels, all wrought
With gold and beryls and green chrysolite,
   Bedizened by the image of the king,
Adorned with sapphires; and to my delight
   It had a voice, and it began to sing.

It sang of ancient times, and it embraced
   My body as I donned it, and my soul;
I clutched its seams with silver thread enlaced,

Its clasps of adamant; and then, made whole,
I and my spirit's twin became as one,
The robe's song wove about me on the air:
"For this I was raised up, my father's son —
To bring him treasure from the dragon's lair."

— from "The Hymn of the Pearl"

I

WHEN THE BIRD HAD ASSURED AURORA, Michael, and Laura that none of the Lupine Brethren were still waiting on the other side of the crystal wall, and Laura had unlocked and opened the door, and all three had confirmed for themselves that the way was now clear, Aurora gathered everyone together by the pool and enjoined them to drink deeply. Michael filled the flask again. The Magians made a few attempts to ask questions of Michael or Mr. Ambrosius or Oriens, but each time the bird interrupted them with a protest of "No time for that now!"

"Do you know where we need to go?" Aurora asked her brother.

"My ship is . . ." he began to reply. But just at that moment the stream of golden lights reached its end, spiraling away into the vault of the ceiling, until the last of the sparks vanished into the softly scintillating stone like a whirlwind disappearing into the sky. Everyone watched, saying nothing. A few seconds afterward, Oriens resumed his sentence, as if nothing of any moment had occurred: "My ship is still waiting for us, anchored in the upper aerial sphere near the lowest of the planetary gates. But to reach it we must return to the mountains in the west, up a long river and far away. It is many days from here."

"I see," said Aurora, pondering.

"Not . . . not if we fly," said Laura hesitantly.

No one spoke for a moment. Michael looked at her, raising a single eyebrow dubiously. She looked back at him and shrugged.

"Fly?" asked Oriens. "Can we do that?"

"Well, there are all those aerial cars up . . . there . . ." She pointed imprecisely toward the ceiling. "And my father used to be a pilot."

"That's very true," said Mr. Ambrosius. "He was. Quite an accomplished one, in fact."

"Oh, but . . ." began Mrs. Magian.

"Good of you to remember," said Mr. Magian.

"Oh, but it's been ages," said Mrs. Magian to her daughter. "Before you

367

were even born. Really, darling, your father's very out of practice. And the way you are with heights . . ."

"Oh, good gracious, dear," said Mr. Magian, obviously enjoying the emboldening effects of the water from the pool, "I'm more than capable of flying any sort of aerial transport."

"Basil, you're not a young man anymore."

"Really, Eve, I'm not done for yet. My heavens, you make me sound feeble."

"Basil. . . ."

"Now, now, Eve," said Aurora in a mildly admonishing tone, "you *do* tend to worry so. You weren't at all like that when you were a child."

Mrs. Magian paused, obviously all at once diverted from her train of thought. "I wasn't. . . ?" She stared at Aurora for a moment, with the expression of someone trying very hard to recall some painfully elusive memory. "No." She shook her head distractedly and looked down. "No, but I've had so much. . . ." Her voice trailed away.

"I know," said Aurora, her voice growing more tender. "But that's in the past. And right now we mustn't be guided by fear. There's simply no time."

MICHAEL HAD NO IDEA HOW LONG THE MAGIC OF THE pool's water would continue to fortify their bodies and minds, but he could see its quite conspicuous effects in the energy and confidence with which everyone now moved. Mr. and Mrs. Magian had exhibited some momentary alarm at the sight of the large chasm and of the slender bronze bridge spanning it, and Mr. Ambrosius had cleared his throat in a way that suggested misgivings. But, when the bird soared to the other side of the fissure and Aurora strode out onto the bridge and began to cross it in a gliding gait and without sound, never bothering to use the handrails, and then Laura followed without the least visible reluctance, holding to the railing but walking with ringing and defiant rapidity, Mr. Magian uttered an "Ah, ha!" of paternal pride and he and his wife ventured out as well with fairly buoyant steps. Michael went next, followed by his father, with Oriens coming last. Now Michael felt no real fear at all, finding the convex span under his feet much less daunting than before, and not sensing the chill in the air; he was even able to look over the edge as he walked without feeling as though he might plummet into the abyss. He had very nearly reached the opposite ledge without any difficulty when a sound like a distant peal of thunder descended through the high ceiling and everything—especially the bridge — shook once, not violently but ominously. He ran the remaining two yards or so to solid ground, his father and Oriens close behind, and then the sound broke out again overhead and a second, more jarring tremor elicited a raucous blare of grinding metal from the bridge's posts. A few fragments of stone fell from the ceiling, and then a cloud of fine dust blossomed downward, sparkling in the light from the wall.

"How predictable," remarked Aurora in a displeased tone. "It would be just like him to knock everything over rather than lose the game he's playing." She shook her head somberly. "He'd tear down the sky and trample the mountains underfoot if he thought it would prevent us from getting away."

"All the more reason to make haste," the bird remarked as it shot out of sight down the granite corridor.

They moved through the series of empty chambers much more quickly than Michael, Laura, and Oriens had done earlier, when they had been burdened by fatigue and depressed by magic and uncertain of the way. The whole party sped through the great circular chamber of rough-hewn stone with the two gently splashing springs, then through each of the softly glowing chambers of polished marbles — sea-green, sea-gray, cinnabar flecked with pink, black, twilight purple, pale sky-blue, deep wine-red, tawny gold, dark malachite green, smoky amber — until at last they came to the smaller room of deep blue and reached the gold elevator door. They fitted rather closely into the car, but were soon rising on the ringing column of water in the metal shaft below. Once, Mr. Magian remarked on how long the journey upward was, and on two occasions, a minute apart, a new rumbling shock sent vibrations through the car, making it shudder and creak. After the second, Aurora sighed. "It's like one of those tantrums you sometimes threw when you were little, Laura," she observed.

At the look of mortification that appeared on Laura's face, Michael could not help but laugh, though he quickly attempted to cloak the sound beneath a fabricated cough. Laura set her jaw, narrowed her stare, and lifted a threatening hand.

"None of that, now," said Aurora calmly, "from either of you. That's not at all appropriate behavior."

Mr. Ambrosius, for his part, made no effort at all to hide the dry laugh that this provoked from him.

Michael, however, merely nodded at the reprimand, soberly and acquiescently, though secretly he was thinking how bizarre it was that the smallest child in their company was (with the exception of her brother) the oldest person among them and (not excepting her brother) the most punctiliously parental.

At last, the elevator reached the top of its ascent and they emerged into the large semicircular foyer of black marble. No one was there to stop them. To judge from the distant clamor reaching them from the other end of the long, sporadically lit hallway, everyone was too engrossed in a general panic: frantic shouts, two or three piercing whistles sounding at once, an alarm bell tolling again, another whistle, the racket of large men running in heavy boots — and, when yet another tremor shook the entire building, all of it in suddenly even greater and shriller volume. Then came the unmistakable crash of real thunder outside, breaking directly above the great dome.

"My goodness," said Mr. Magian, though with considerably more good humor than seemed fitting, as if he were slightly inebriated.

"Are you quite all right, Basil?" asked Mr. Ambrosius.

"Never better," replied Mr. Magian. "Not a trace of rheumatism. First time in ages."

"Make haste!" the bird cried out, circling the room twice with remarkable velocity and then plunging into the shadows of the corridor.

With Aurora still in the lead, they proceeded down the long, echoing, dimly illuminated hallway of porphyry and rose marble and coolly coruscating agate. As they went, the sounds of disorder and terror grew louder and gradually more distinct, and were soon supplemented by the noise of rushing and moaning wind. Another burst of thunder broke overhead and reverberated down the corridor like a receding cannon fusillade. After a while, a broad rectangle of daylight, appearing some distance ahead, told Michael that the copper door to the enormous loggia beneath the dome was standing wide open. When the doorway was only about sixty feet away, a tall figure appeared in it, framed against the light beyond, obviously wearing the uniform of the security service and holding a rifle against his chest. But, though he briefly watched them approaching, he looked away again before they could even come to a halt, as if utterly indifferent to them, and ran off in another direction.

When Aurora reached the open door, she paused and peered out, and Michael, Laura, and Oriens ranged themselves around her, peering out as well. There were any number of figures in hectic motion, to left and right, but there was no one near at hand. This was still Lord Theoplast's private entrance, it seemed, and the various security and police agents in their uniforms and the priests and postulants in their cassocks or fustian frock coats were too absorbed in their own predicament to think to keep a watch on it. Michael could see two aerial cars — one in the murky green of the security service, the other in the sleek black and dark blue of the police — already in flight away from the Central Ministry; and from the distant roar and drone of numerous rotary thrust engines he knew that other cars were also taking off. These and the wind, now howling through the columns of the great peristyle, all but drowned out the general outcry and the whistles and the tolling claxon. Another powerful tremor shook the building, and then a streak of bright white and violet lightning flashed out above the suddenly very gray city, immediately followed by what sounded like the sky itself shattering. Dense, cobalt-gray clouds overshadowed everything now, and far off in the distance, beyond the city, below an immense bank of looming thunderheads, the great bay had turned the color of lead. Michael looked toward the platform where Lord Theoplast's car had landed earlier in the day and, to his great relief, the long black sedan with its winding coils of silver trim was still there.

"Shall we go then?" Aurora asked, raising her voice enough to be heard over the gale, but without the least hint of anxiety in it.

They made their way to the platform at something of a sprint and began ascending its three steps. As Laura's parents and his father were going up before him, Michael paused briefly and looked away, past the copper door and along the bending length of the loggia; and at the farthest point still in his line of sight, just before the curvature of the building hid the rest from view, he saw a lone figure, tall and lean and dressed in a black suit and hat, staring directly back at him. He and Mr. Lucius recognized one another at more or less the same moment, it seemed. The latter took two or three steps forward, as if trying to assure himself of what he was seeing, and even at this distance an expression of almost deranged hatred was visible on his face; then he turned his head to yell something over his shoulder while vigorously waving his arm to someone Michael could not see.

"Quick, quick!" Michael shouted, dashing up the stairs. "We've been seen!"

There were no locks on the car's doors it appeared, or at least none that anyone had troubled to use, and so the whole party was soon inside, under its canopy of blue adamantine crystal. Mr. Magian sat at the center of the front seat, behind the controls and wheel, with Oriens to his left, Aurora to his right, and the bird perched atop his headrest; Mr. Ambrosius and Mrs. Magian sat right behind them on the first red leather passenger seat, facing backward, with Michael and Laura sitting opposite and facing forward.

Everyone hurriedly strapped on their seat harnesses. When Michael allowed himself to look out the window he saw Mr. Lucius, accompanied by three other of the Brethren, running toward the platform. But, the moment Mr. Magian pressed the ignition switch and the rotary thrust engines began to pulse and thrum, Mr. Lucius stopped, signaling the others with outspread arms to do the same, and all four turned about to run back the way they had come.

"They're going to follow us!" Michael shouted.

"My gracious, not so loud, please," Mr. Magian replied as the car rose from the platform and started forward with something of a lurch.

"Basil!" Mrs. Magian exclaimed, her voice becoming shrill.

"Nothing to worry about, Eve," Mr. Magian called back. "Everyone check your harnesses. Not ideal conditions for flying just. . . ." He was interrupted by the grinding screech of the car scraping against one of the columns between which it was passing.

"Basil!" Mrs. Magian repeated in precisely the same tone as before, while Laura impulsively clutched Michael's shoulder.

But Mr. Magian simply laughed as the car swung smoothly away from the great dome and out over the immense gorge of the city center below. Then a particularly violent gust of wind caused the car to veer sharply to the left and downward. Michael saw Mrs. Magian close her eyes and clench her fists in her lap, then saw his father breathing deeply, clearly attempting to compose himself.

"A bit of turbulence," yelled Mr. Magian, as the car began to race upward and away from the Ministry at an unexpectedly steep angle. "Best get away from these buildings. Now, let's see, which way is west?"

Laura's grip tightened on Michael's shoulder, and Michael reached across his chest and closed his hand on hers almost as tightly.

Lightning flashed again, with almost blinding intensity, like steel blazing white and blue in a forge, and so near overhead that it seemed as if the car might run into it; the thunder that instantly followed was so loud that Michael felt it as a shooting pain in his teeth and jaws, and when he briefly closed his eyes a vivid pink impression of the bolt remained like a torn seam across the darkness. Then a blast of wind caused the car to flounder up and down forcibly enough to lift the passengers momentarily from their seats. The rotary engines could be heard shuddering in their mounts. Laura emitted a small cry of dismay. Michael would have done the same had he not been struggling with a momentary dizziness that forced him to tighten his jaws; so he looked anxiously out through his window instead. Drops of rain were beginning to strike the glass and run along it in writhing horizontal streaks. Even the highest of the buildings were several hundred feet below them now, and fleeting wisps of cloud were interposed between them and the car.

"A little sedan like this isn't really made for this kind of weather," Mr. Magian remarked, almost casually. "Now, the old heavy transport barges I used to pilot," he added a moment later, looking back and forth from Oriens to Aurora, "my goodness, those you could fly right through the heart of a hurricane without much more than a few minor shakes and shivers. Like flying fortresses those were." His voice was becoming almost cheerful.

Mrs. Magian opened her eyes and parted her lips as if to utter a rebuke, but then wilted back into her posture of tense silence. Mr. Ambrosius looked as if his entire will was engaged in controlling his breathing. Michael's shoulder was beginning to ache.

"Could you just . . . ." he said mildly as he detached Laura's fingertips from himself and changed the hand with which he held hers. "It's just that. . . ."

"Yes, sorry," said Laura.

Another powerful gust briefly but sharply forced the car sideways. And, at this, Aurora laughed so sweetly and musically that for a moment Michael became strangely calm. Mr. Magian's reaction was to laugh as well.

Laura, however, was clearly not at all amused. "What's got into him?" she whispered angrily. "How much of the water did he drink?"

Michael looked through his window again and, after a moment, realized that the gleaming pewter gray far below, visible in glimpses between passing tatters of cloud, was the great harbor. "We're out of the city," he announced loudly.

"Quite," replied Mr. Magian almost jovially. "Gracious me. Now let's see if we can get above the storm. I know I said it's a little sedan, but it's obviously quite sturdy, and I have to imagine an official conveyance like this can take more than the average car can."

"Oh, Basil," said Mrs. Magian in a tone perilously close to a whimper. "He's usually not like this," she added apologetically, for some reason looking at Michael.

"He'll be fine," remarked Mr. Ambrosius, smoothing his beard with exaggerated strokes but without much conviction in his voice. "I mean, I'd be more worried if he were nervous."

Rain was now beating down and swirling back along the car's canopy and windows. Nothing but eddying gray clouds was visible above and below and on every side.

"Fuliginous," Mr. Ambrosius said suddenly.

Michael looked at his father. "What?"

"Fuliginous," repeated Mr. Ambrosius, attempting a frail smile. "In case you were looking for a good word for the appearance of the sky just now."

"Oh." Michael tried to smile back. "Thanks."

Laura sighed loudly. Michael looked at her only to be met with an expression of knowing exasperation. "That's very important," she muttered. But she did not release his hand.

They flew on for twenty minutes or so more, driven from side to side and up and down, swaying and dipping and bounding, but also plunging persistently westward through the gloom. At some point, flakes of ice began to tap sharply on the blue glass overhead. In the hearts of the clouds all about them, the lightning was flashing constantly, turned pale purple and smoky blue by the brume and rain, and the thunder was becoming a continuous rumbling punctuated by occasional crashes, like the sound of breaking ocean waves. Soon the wind seemed to be buffeting the car principally from ahead, causing it to swerve now one way and now the other as Mr. Magian fought to keep it on course. The most disheartening moment came when a particularly violent stretch of turbulence shook the car for several seconds, ending with a final jarring pitch downward, and once again the throbbing motors protested loudly in their mountings. Michael tightened his grip on Laura's hand and noticed that his father and Mrs. Magian were leaning toward one another so that their shoulders touched; and both had their eyes firmly closed. "Hold on," he said to Laura, or to himself by way of Laura.

"I'm all right," she replied in a strained voice.

But then Aurora laughed again. "Such a temper he has," she said. "It's really very silly."

"I think it's clearing ahead," called out Mr. Magian, still seemingly imperturbable. "Just a bit farther."

Michael looked forward, through the windscreen. At first, he could see nothing to confirm Mr. Magian's assertion, but after several seconds he began to see that the clouds ahead were in fact thinning, admitting more light from beyond, and then noticed that the rain was striking the crystal canopy overhead much more gently now. The next gust of wind that shook the car was far weaker than the previous one, or any before that. The clouds ahead began to take on a pale magenta and then light golden color, and a moment later began to separate into varying layers, darker yielding to brighter, with edges thinly glazed in amber. Then, all at once, the darkness had parted and the distinct shape of a massive cumulus cloud appeared before them, set off against a blue sky, like a snow-covered mountain with dazzling white slopes and folds of soft violet shadow. Michael had never flown at such an altitude and certainly had never seen the vastness of such a cloud from so near. The majesty of it momentarily purged every other thought from his mind.

"Mother, look!" said Laura.

Both Mrs. Magian and Mr. Ambrosius opened their eyes, glanced up at the sunlight pouring in through the blue glass of the canopy, and then turned their heads to look forward.

"Basil," said Mr. Ambrosius in a tone of wonder, "I had no idea it was like this."

"Oh, goodness, yes," replied Mr. Magian, his voice almost serene. "Up this high, it's another world. It's why I miss flying the large barges so much."

Mrs. Magian reached forward and laid a hand on her husband's shoulder, and he briefly placed his own hand upon hers.

That was when the first artillery shell exploded, far off to the left of the car and much too high. The small burst of fire and smoke was unimpressive at such a distance, and the dull report that followed a couple moments later sounded like a single dull beat from a slackened drumhead. Still, everyone in the back seats reacted with some sort of inarticulate sound of alarm. Michael and Laura both tried to turn around, then struggled free of their harnesses and rose up in kneeling positions to stare back, over three more rows of seats, through the broad rear windscreen.

"Basil," Mrs. Magian cried, "we're being shot at!"

Michael saw that at least four vehicles had emerged into the sunlight from the billowing, flaring field of gray behind.

"Nothing to fret about, Eve," replied Mr. Magian calmly. "Can anyone see who's following us?"

"What do you mean 'nothing?'" replied Mrs. Magian indignantly.

"I can see two police vehicles," Michael called out, "and one Security Services barge . . . and one that's just black . . . but not very large, I think."

Another shell detonated off to the right, even farther away. The sound of it did not even reach them.

"What I mean, dear — " Mr. Magian began, "Thank-you, Michael — What

I mean, dear, is that they can't hit anything firing away like that. It would be like trying to hit a fly with a needle from across a large room. Those guns —" He turned the front of the car suddenly downward and somewhat to the left, smoothly but precipitately enough to make Michael and Laura slip back into their seats and begin strapping their harnesses on again. "Excuse me, everyone. As I was saying, those guns are from the barge and they're for firing on targets on the ground, from a stationary position. They're meant for spreading terror below, and for . . . well, the occasional massacre." He inclined the car a little more steeply downward. "They're useless for aerial battle. Whoever it is who's firing is just trying to scare us. Still, we should get down below the wind. Their vehicles are better suited to high altitudes."

Then Oriens spoke for the first time since the departure from the Ministry building: "Can you continue to elude them until we reach my ship?"

"Ah, well," said Mr. Magian, beginning to bring the car back up from its angle of descent, "goodness, that's hard to say." The car was level now. "But I can assure you that they won't catch us easily. I know a trick or two."

Michael looked upward through the car's canopy and saw the great cloud far above, gradually passing by, and beyond its furthest limit only the bright empty blue — deepened by the tint of the crystal — of a perfectly clear sky. Then he leaned over and peered out his window again. The terrain below was fully visible now, and closer than Michael had expected it to be. He immediately recognized the broad, brightly glittering Phlegethon, and the dry yellow grain-fields and fallow grassy flats of the lowlands, and the narrow, gleaming canals among them. He could also make out a number of fishing boats drawn up into the river's shallows, no doubt because of the storm to the east, and even a few minuscule human figures moving upon their decks or on the land nearby. Everything was awash in sunlight. Then he caught sight of a small, drastically fluctuating shape dashing westward along the southern shore and some distance back, and a moment later realized that it was the shadow cast by their car. As he was watching it, a sudden trail of bluish smoke appeared midair, two hundred feet or more below, and terminated in another pointless and inaudible detonation.

Michael unstrapped his harness for a second time and turned about in his seat, again kneeling and looking through the rear windscreen. All four of the vehicles he had seen were still in pursuit, the enormous green barge leading the way; and now a fifth, fairly small vehicle — another uniformly black car — was just discernible as well, a little farther back. He looked past them for a moment, away to where the dark clouds of the storm were still brooding over Kenopolis, and realized that even at this distance the faint outline of the city was minutely discernible, a kind of irregular serration of the horizon, watery gray against watery silver. But there was something else in his line of vision as well, a soft golden haze in the air somewhere between that remote prospect and the sunlit sky through which the car was now flying. For some reason, his eyes could not quite situate it, or even tell whether it was far away or relatively near; it seemed to waver between something substantial and a mere trick of the light, perhaps like a rainbow or like the sun's reflection in the lower western sky just after dusk. So, after a few seconds more, he simply called out, "They're still with us," and resumed his seat.

"Well, yes," said Mr. Magian, "they would be. We can't outpace them. But when we get to the woodlands in the higher elevations, then we may show them something."

"Do you really think so?" asked Laura earnestly.

"Yes, my goodness, yes. This little car is quite a nimble bit of machinery. Once we're up there among the trees and scarps and rifts and valleys . . . well, you just see if they can follow the course your old father will set them."

Mrs. Magian took a deep, despondent breath, then assumed an expression perfectly poised between a grin and a grimace. "He really was a very celebrated pilot, dear," she told Laura. "I'm sure your father can do . . . things. . . ."

"Eve, my love," said Mr. Magian with an unusually effervescent tone of confidence, "I can do things you can't imagine. I once sped for over a hundred miles in the jungles of Aequidialia *below* the canopy, back when I was stationed down there. Mind you, that was a little one-man shuttle. . . ."

"Oh, Basil," Mrs. Magian interrupted, "that was so long. . . ." But then she stopped and shook her head at herself. "Never mind. I trust you, dear," she said. "Just don't . . . talk about it, please."

"Why did you ever stop flying?" asked Oriens.

"Oh, ah, well . . . you see . . ." Mr. Magian's voice became more subdued, though it remained audible to everyone in the car. "That was before I . . . . I was serving evil men in those days, you see, and didn't know it. I hadn't had my spiritual awakening . . . if you take my meaning."

"Really, brother," said Aurora, "it's not at all polite to ask such things."

No one said anything more for some time. Michael looked out his window again, down at the still river and the flowing terrain, for several minutes.

As he watched, the cultivated lowlands gradually gave way to the high waving grasses of the foothills, and the car began to rise at a very moderate angle. Later, he looked out again, and saw that they were still flying over the hills, the car's shadow rapidly flickering and slithering through the bracken and small twisting trees and outcroppings of rock. Still later, he rose up in his seat and turned around again. The vehicles chasing them scarcely made any impression on him this time. He was looking for that haze of gold that he had seen before, and he did not have to look long. It was now a clearly perceptible and lovely splendor in the air, not far behind the rearmost of their pursuers, shining with a fiery radiance of its own. In a moment, Michael knew that he was looking at those countless golden sparks that Aurora had freed from their ghostly forms. They were following as well, all of them together in a great host, leaving the city behind — leaving the world. He opened his lips to say something.

But then a voice spoke from the sky.

II

I T WAS A DEEP AND MELODIOUS VOICE, SEDUCTIVE but powerful, soothing but vibrant, breaking out with perfect clarity through or above the noise of the motors and the air rushing by—a voice, in fact, of so pure a tone and timbre that Michael could not at first tell whether it was coming from without or was instead rising up within his own mind. It seemed not so much to fill the car's interior as suddenly to invade and permeate his senses and thoughts. It was only as he saw everyone else react to it as well that he was certain it was a physical sound:

My child, where are you fleeing?

Mr. Magian flinched so violently that the car skipped abruptly upward. "My lord!" he nearly shouted, steadying their course again. Mrs. Magian grabbed frantically at the edge of her seat. Mr. Ambrosius looked about with a stunned expression. Michael looked at Laura and found his own shock mirrored in her wide eyes and opened mouth.

Why are you wandering so far from home, daughter? Come back, my love.

"What's . . . ?" Mrs. Magian began. "Who . . . ?" Then, unable to say anything more, she leaned across the space separating the seats and placed a hand on Laura's leg.

"She is not your daughter," said Oriens loudly, turning his head side to side and up and down, clearly uncertain where to direct his words.

"Oh, pay him no mind," Aurora said, almost peevishly. "That's just his *persuasive* way of talking."

Who has roused you from your lovely dreams, my child? Close your eyes again. Sleep.

"It's his way," she added.

Have you forgotten that this very night there are to be festivities? You must make yourself ready. Already the torches are being lit, the musicians strike their lyres and lift their flutes to their lips. The guests are arriving and taking their seats below the branches of the garden's trees, and in its sighing arbors. Goblets and plates are being laid, and baskets of fresh fruit and vases full of flowers are being set upon the tables. And all will dance tonight, under the stars and in the moons' light.

Michael was all at once aware that he himself was finding the silky sonorousness of the voice intoxicating. His eyelids even began to droop, and he might have drifted off into a light sleep if his father had not leaned toward him and shaken him by the shoulder.

"Do not listen to him, my princess," said the bird, deftly slipping from Mr. Magian's headrest and onto Aurora's shoulder. "He is casting a spell. He wishes to enchant you again."

"Oh, I know that," said Aurora. But her voice was becoming quieter. "I know."

"Sister," said Oriens, "stay awake."

"You worry so," Aurora replied.

Have we not played such delightful games together? Will you leave me now, all alone, when the day is little more than halfway spent, and when the revels of the evening still await?

Michael looked at Laura again, but she was staring ahead with a vacant expression. Then he looked at his father and Mrs. Magian, both of whom were quite alert and obviously dismayed. The latter leaned forward again and clapped her hands a few inches from Laura's face, and Laura immediately stirred, breathed deeply, and shook her head to dispel her drowsiness.

But first a nap, my dear, in the shade of a flowering tree. And a lullaby played on a harp or a lute.

"You are powerless here," said Oriens, again in every direction and none.

"It's no use telling him," said Aurora, and then she lightly wagged her head from side to side, as if attempting not to yawn or close her eyes.

The car's upward inclination became somewhat steeper. Michael looked out through his window and saw that they had reached the end of the foothills and were now flying above the lower elevations of the mountains, where the long grasses gave way to stony meadows and furze and jutting rocks, and where scree filled the deep creases in the gradient earth. Then he looked forward, through the windscreen, and saw the great wooded mountains rising up ahead of them, the nearest green and russet and ochre, those farther off a soft, lambent, unbroken blue. And just above the more distant mountains, seeming to rest upon the highest summits, was another immense bank of clouds, like a still higher and more imposing mountain range, brilliantly white where it rose to the roof of the sky, meltingly lazuline where it touched the peaks below. "How long before we reach the forest?" he called out.

"Some way yet, I'm afraid," said Mr. Magian, clearly no longer in an ebullient mood. "And many hours more to Oreiotopia."

There is nowhere to go, my child. You are already home. The time has come to return to your house, to rest, to prepare for the evening's entertainments.

"This is not her home," pronounced Oriens in a coldly defiant voice.

All of this is yours. All of it is ours. I made it all for you — for us.

"How very, very silly," said Aurora, but this time her intonation was mild and detached, even dreamy.

"Aurora," said Oriens, almost severely.

"Wake, my princess," said the bird, speaking directly into her ear.

Aurora laughed, again in a lazily removed way. "I'm awake," she said, but her voice sounded already half asleep.

There is nowhere else to go. There is no other world. Do not be deceived. Do not listen to fables and foolish tales.

"Aurora," said Oriens curtly, "do not listen to him. And open your eyes."

"Really, brother, you needn't be such a scold." She seemed to be speaking from somewhere far away now.

"Can we fly no faster?" Oriens asked Mr. Magian.

"Goodness, no," said Mr. Magian with an emphatic shake of his head. "We're putting as much strain on our rotors as they can bear."

The bird took hold of Aurora's earlobe in its beak and pulled at it sharply. But at this she only laughed again. "That's very silly," she said in a contented murmur.

"My prince," said the bird, turning to look at Oriens, "she is succumbing to his spell again."

"Little sister, please," said Oriens, "try to remain awake."

"Oh, yes, yes, I know," she replied, her voice attenuating into a sigh. "You always want me to get up."

There was a time before all worlds, before even the dream of worlds. No sun blazed in the firmament, no moons or stars shone upon the breast of night. I was alone and you had not yet come forth from the darkness. So I made these heavens and this earth, and all that is in them. And then I called you out of the darkness to be my only daughter, my most precious child.

"These are lies," said Oriens, a note of desperation rising in his voice. "Do not listen."

All this I made and gave to you. Then you danced before me, and were all my joy, and the stars sang for you.

"Do not listen."

You know me, my child. You know I love you. You know that I am your God, the maker of all that is, and that beside me there is no other. O, my dear daughter, remember all that we have done together, all that I have shared with you, all the joys we have shared between us.

Michael looked from his father to Mrs. Magian to Laura, and each of them looked back with an expression of helpless disquiet.

This is no time to tire of our merriments. Neither is it time to despair of yet greater joys, or to attempt to flee to worlds that are not real. You need but rest an hour.

"Do not listen," said Oriens again, more urgently.

I am your creator. I am your father. There is no other whom you should seek — no other whom you should love.

"Lies!" Oriens now shouted.

This is your home. Have we not played such charming games in its gardens and courtyards?

A sudden inspiration seized Michael. "The light from the gems," he said, "surely that could break the spell."

"Yes, perhaps," said Oriens. "But I have only the one left, and should we use it too soon, its effect may not last until we reach our destination."

Return now. Sleep in the bower I have made for you, my child. The breeze is delectable, the air is filled with the fragrances of flowers, the birds are singing on the swaying boughs. The warmth of the day is sweet, the cool of the evening is still to come.

Aurora sighed again, but this time no words followed.

Our play is not at an end. The dream is deep. The dance goes on. The song of the stars has not been silenced.

"She is sleeping," said the bird. "She is beginning again to dream."

"But if we wait too long," said Michael, "won't it be too late by the time we get there?"

There, my child. Good. Dream for an hour. Let the breeze kiss your brow and lips and cheeks. Sleep.

"I do not know," said Oriens. Then he yelled to his sister: "Wake! Aurora, wake up!"

"She hears you," the bird remarked, "but once again only as a voice within a dream."

Another of the ridiculous cannon shells exploded well off to the car's right, at the periphery of Michael's vision and again too far away to be heard. Michael looked down from his window once more and saw that the first of the tall forest trees were now appearing below, in a few isolated copses and a few meandering lines that broadened as they crawled up towards the lowest slopes. He turned and looked forward to Oriens again. "Won't her sleep get deeper the longer we wait?"

"It will," said the bird.

Oriens lowered his head for a moment. Even half concealed by his head-rest, the bearing of his head and shoulders was eloquent of agonizing inde-cision. Then he looked up again, gritted his teeth between slightly parted lips, and finally said, "I suppose we must not delay any further." He lifted his hand and unfastened the topmost button of his shirt. "I will. . . ."

Just then, however, the great voice poured over everything, much louder than before and now wholly devoid of the dulcet and sedative intonations of a few moments earlier:

Enough of this! She is mine. Cease your flight.

"Oh, my, my, my!" Mr. Magian suddenly cried out in a miserably braying voice, shifting the car drastically to the left as if trying to avoid a collision. Michael felt himself leaning far to his right, and saw everyone else leaning in the same direction. He was able to push himself back up into a sitting position only with considerable effort, moreover, inasmuch as the car unex-pectedly continued turning and turning. Just as it had achieved a right angle from its original course, one of those supposedly futile artillery shells did in fact explode close enough to its left flank — a few yards below, a few feet behind — that the nearest motor was shaken out of its mounting altogether, whining and grating and then breaking off. The car began spinning and floundering and sinking all at once.

For a moment, Michael could scarcely breathe, and he felt as if he might faint from dizziness. Mrs. Magian cried out "Basil!" again, but this time in a tone of despair. At almost the same moment, Mr. Ambrosius yelled, "Son!" and Laura grabbed Michael's arm, attempting to pull herself upright.

"Hold on, everyone!" Mr. Magian called out. "Just let me correct. . . ." And then the car sprang upward slightly, veered right, then left, then right, and then ceased its rapid spinning and began instead simply to turn in a very gradual spiral, swaying gently from side to side as it did so, almost like a leaf falling on the breeze. The sound of the motors dropped in tone to a deeper, softer drone. "I'm afraid I've cut back the thrust and put us on a safe landing setting."

"We cannot go on?" asked Oriens.

"I'm sorry," said Mr. Magian. "It was that . . . that. . . ." He breathed deeply. "I'm sorry. Everyone, strap in. It's . . . there may be some roughness when we hit the ground."

"What happened?" asked Mrs. Magian.

"Didn't you see?" asked Mr. Magian. "There was a . . . it was an eye.

383

A human eye, but it filled the whole sky ahead. And it was all . . . like fire . . . burning. . . . I thought it would swallow us up."

Michael looked from side to side, trying to tell where westward now lay. After a moment, he saw the nearer ridges of the mountains listlessly swinging by, filling more of the skyline than they had a few minutes before, but nothing else in that direction.

"I swear . . ." Mr. Magian added, but then abandoned the sentence. "Get ready now," he suddenly said as the motors changed tone and became louder again. "Grab hold of something. I'll try to make a soft landing, but it's difficult. Just. . . ."

At that moment, Michael saw the entire turning landscape — trees, a meadow strewn with rocks and wiry brush, tussocks of grass, boulders, the low slope of the earth — welling up on every side. He had not realized they were so close to the ground and he felt about hurriedly for Laura, taking hold of her hand just as she took hold of his and just as the car struck the earth. A violent jolt threw him forward in his harness and then backward into his seat again. Every part of the car rattled and shook and whined. The motors on the right side positively screeched when they were driven into the rocky soil and then dragged through it as the car continued to rotate, repeatedly hammering the ground, sliding down the slope; then the motors that remained on the car's left side also struck the earth and their turbines began to shriek. Grass, soil, dust, and pebbles were flung up on every side and clashed against the metal and glass. Then all of the motors ceased firing at once, the car rattled a few more times as it came at last to a juddering halt, and a final concussive shock sent everyone reeling momentarily sideways in their harnesses. Then there was stillness in the car for several seconds, with no sounds but those of held breath being released. Michael, quietly struggling against small convulsions of shock, looked at his father's and Mrs. Magian's faces, both of which seemed inordinately drawn. Then he turned to Laura, who met his gaze with an expression that appeared to have been emptied of every emotion. He questioned her with his eyes; she answered with hers, accompanied by a slight encouraging tilt of her head. He was not perfectly sure what either he or she had said, but he found the exchange comforting.

"Is everyone all right?" Mr. Magian asked.

They all professed themselves uninjured, in a combination of half-formed words and reassuring mutters, though Mr. Ambrosius pressed a hand to his ribs where one of the harness straps had evidently caused him some pain.

"The princess Aurora sleeps," said the bird, still firmly perched on her shoulder.

"We must waken her quickly," said Oriens.

The car's doors all seemed undamaged, though the moderate incline of the ground here made it more convenient for everyone to leave by those on the downward side, to the left. As Aurora had been to Mr. Magian's right, he was obliged to lift her from her seat, ease her gently into his lap, and then hand her out feet-first to Mr. Ambrosius, who cradled her in his arms, flinching slightly at a twinge from his sore rib as he straightened himself. The clearing was not very large, and there was little level ground, but Mr. Ambrosius carried her to an even patch of grass largely uncluttered by stones or bracken, about twenty yards away, and laid her there on her back, brushing her hair from her cheeks and eyes as he rose again. Oriens knelt down beside her and placed a hand on her forehead. Laura walked half the distance to their position and then stopped, watching them silently.

Michael, however, remained near the car, which was for the most part still intact. The adamantine glass had proved as irrefrangible as reputed; neither windows nor canopy bore a single fracture. The rear mounting where the damaged motor had broken free was twisted at its neck and its rim was broken; but the rest of the car's chassis was largely unharmed, apart from considerable scoring of its paint. The swirling tentacles of silver trim, however, had at various places come away from the body, and some were hanging raggedly aslant. No phosphoric vapors were pouring from the engine. Michael turned his back to the wreck and looked eastward.

At the bottom of the clearing, he saw that there was, no more than fifty yards away, a line of widely spaced trees, some of their yellow and crimson leaves still clinging to their branches, the rest lying beneath them in a bright motley carpet. Beyond the trees, forming a shallow dell, was a lower, larger, and flatter meadow, and it was here that the vehicles that had been pursuing them began landing amid the whirring roar of their motors, sending up plumes and billows of dust and grass as they came close to the ground. Michael watched for a few moments, resigned to whatever would come next, shaking somewhat and feeling weak in all his limbs. He glanced away to his left, northward, through another and thinner line of trees, and saw the huge, placidly fluctuating sheen of the Phlegethon on the far side of an adjacent field, and beyond that a strip of pebbled shoreline, and then a retreating vista of trees and boulders and brush. He removed the flask from his pocket, opened it, and took a swallow of the magical water. It coursed through him in a lovely cool wave of vitality. He took the flask to Laura and she, having drunk from it herself, took it to her mother and father and Mr. Ambrosius. Michael looked again toward the lower meadow. The last of the five vehicles — the second of the two black aerial cars — was coming to rest. The large green barge was the first to turn off its engines, but the turbines of all the other motors soon fell silent as well; and then, after a moment of suspense, doors began opening; from the deck of the barge, still rather high off the ground, four extendable latticed steel stairways were lowered.

He looked away again, toward Oriens and Aurora and the pulsating glitter of the bird as it hovered a few feet above the two of them. All three Magians and Mr. Ambrosius were gathered together at a respectful distance. Oriens was speaking to his sister, too quietly to hear from where Michael stood, and as he was doing so he was also lifting the purse out of the opened top of his shirt, slipping its suddenly glinting cord over his head and drawing it out of invisibility. Michael saw Mr. Magian point at the apparition in surprise while Mrs. Magian and Mr. Ambrosius acknowledged the marvel with an "Oh!" from the former and an "Ah!" from the latter. Oriens opened the mouth of the purse and emptied out its last jewel into his open hand. At once, even through the full afternoon sunlight, the marvelous, otherworldly radiance, with all its richly blended but elusive hues, poured over the clearing and everything in it. And, as in the past, a deep feeling of peacefulness flooded through Michael. Oriens laid the purse aside, leaned over Aurora more closely, placed the gem on the center of her forehead, and held it there.

Michael turned his attention yet again to the lower meadow and now saw a large company approaching, gradually but relentlessly moving toward the sparse line of trees. There were perhaps fifteen security officers in their green uniforms, most carrying aeroballistic rifles, two or three holding pistols. There were nearly as many police agents in their black uniforms with blue piping, all of them with pistols drawn. And, unarmed but of course most dangerous of all, there were perhaps a dozen of the Brethren in their spruce black suits and hats, foremost among them — in fact, leading the entire party of pursuers — the tall, lean, broad-shouldered, utterly unmistakable figure of Mr. Lucius, walking with long lissome strides and positively emanating his usual sinister elegance. But, between the lingering effects of the water and the influence of the gem's light, Michael had apparently been rendered incapable of fear once again. He simply watched, more curious than terrified, wondering almost idly what would happen next.

Then, from behind, he heard Aurora's voice, shedding its sleepiness as she spoke: "Yes, yes, thank-you, Oriens. I'm awake now. Yes, I know. He fooled me again. How silly of me." Michael turned to look. She was sitting up and Oriens had removed his hands from her, but the gem was still blazing on her brow, as though it were set in a chaplet. She was — Michael could think of no other word — glorious. And, when she had risen to her feet with her brother's assistance, and the Magians and Mr. Ambrosius reverently backed somewhat away, she became all the more so. Her lavish gown of deep blue, her garland of delicate white flowers, her dark skin and gleaming black hair and eyes of luminous sapphire — all of it was strikingly beautiful in the enveloping, shimmering nimbus of splendor flowing from her brow. Truly a divine child, Michael thought to himself. Truly a goddess. He wanted to worship her. Then her eyes met his across the distance. "Don't gape so, Michael," she said with the irrepressible laugh of an amused little girl. "You look just like a fish." This broke the spell. He coughed, swallowed, cleared his throat, closed his mouth, and attempted a dignified smile. Then, still not knowing what to say, he returned his attention to the approaching pursuers.

They had all already mounted up the small rise from the lower meadow and were now spread out among the trees, their buffed boots and polished shoes rustling dryly among the fallen leaves. But they were advancing very slowly, very warily. Michael could see that every one of them was staring apprehensively right past him and at Aurora. The light of the gem had clearly weakened their resolve. Many had lowered their guns, in fact, so that the barrels were pointing toward the ground.

And then something else caught Michael's eye: a sudden, warm, blossoming brightness in the air, beyond and above the crowns of the trees. The golden sparks — in their hundreds and hundreds of thousands — were descending from the shining blue of the sky, first as the distant haze Michael had seen earlier and then, within moments, as a vast throng of lights, almost liquid in their clarity but burning brightly. In a moment, they were filling the branches of the trees, or drifting below or soaring over or floating past them, and then were encircling the clearing in a constantly swelling cloud. The treetops soon looked as if they were saturated by fire but without being consumed. The air was faceted with a glassy brilliancy. The security officers and police agents and Brethren had all ceased moving forward, most of them looking up and about frantically at the sparks. A few of them uttered some wordless noises of dismay. Three of the Brethren at the back of the company, already crouching low and staring upward, briefly assumed their lupine forms and then almost immediately resumed their human shapes, as if the transformation were a nervous reflex. A small spasm of elation stirred somewhere in Michael, although he was not sure precisely why. And the lights kept flowing down from the eastern sky.

It was Mr. Lucius who first broke the silence. He too had been staring about with lowered shoulders and upturned eyes; but, after several seconds of this, Michael saw him slowly draw himself up, drop his gaze, scowl angrily, and stare malevolently in the direction of Aurora and Oriens. "It's a trick!" He shouted. "Wake up, all of you!" He glanced back at his men. "It's nothing but an illusion! Do you think some pretty lights can harm you?"

Many of the company looked at him, many continued looking about in bewilderment, but all continued to stand where they were, stupefied or perhaps slightly hypnotized.

"Cheap magic tricks!" he yelled. "Theatrical flummery! Shake yourselves out of it!"

Still, none of them resumed their advance.

"You're bound by the will of God!" he cried, his fury breaking the reins of his customary composure. "There's nothing to fear! Fireflies . . . toy sparklers . . . fireworks for a birthday party!"

Michael turned to Aurora, and opened his mouth to suggest that they should all start fleeing while their enemies were unable to move. But, before he could speak, he saw that the light of the gem was waning in the air around her. A second later, it had quite vanished, and the jewel had disappeared from her brow with a last delicate fading shimmer.

"You see?" Mr. Lucius cried triumphantly. "You see? Pull yourselves together!"

The disappearance of the gem's radiance had clearly released them from their stupor, and now his words did rouse them. The security officer with the most resplendently tasseled epaulets, the most impressive conglomerations of gold braid on his uniform, and a bright yellow cockade on his cap shook his head, stood up very straight, squared his shoulders, thrust out his chest and chin, brought the bill of his cap low over his eyes, affected a menacing glare, and cried, "Come on, men! It's obviously up to us Green Tunics to take this lot in hand — *as always.*" At this, apparently not to be outdone, the sole police agent wearing an officer's tricorn hat and tall purple plume cleared his throat dramatically and yelled, in a high penetrating shriek of a voice, "Quite enough of this procrastination now! Forward, men, on the double quick and not half fast and with heroic dispatch and superbly fearsome alacrity!"

Mr. Lucius rolled his eyes, grimaced, and heaved a sigh. "Come on, men," he said. The look of smoldering hatred on his face had yielded to one of icy resolve. The whole company began moving forward again, out from among the trees and into the clearing, with slow but regular strides. The countless floating lights hovered over and around them — swirled, eddied, rose, fell — but clearly could no longer distract them.

Now Michael's enchanted equanimity was beginning to desert him. The immediate prospect of being engulfed in this small flood of large violent men, and the sudden sense of helplessness that came with it, had dispelled whatever emotional effects remained from the enchanted water or the gem's otherworldly light. Everything seemed at once quite concrete, mundane, and dangerous. The whole line of men was scarcely more than thirty feet away from him now. He took two steps backward. Mr. Lucius, a particularly malicious smile appearing on his face, said, "There's nowhere to run, my esculent. And I and my brothers are famished." The smile widened until it was utterly hideous.

Then, in an instant, it vanished entirely and was replaced by a look of sheer, unreserved terror, of a sort Michael would have thought impossible on those gaunt, cruel, sallow features. Mr. Lucius was no longer paying attention to Michael at all, but was instead staring with wide eyes at something much higher up and farther away, his mouth hanging open, his body halted in mid-stride and visibly shaking. And all his companions were staring in the same direction, with similar wildly horrified expressions, and they too had ceased walking. A few had thrown their arms up before their faces, but still could not avert their eyes from what they saw. A strangled moan escaped Mr. Lucius's throat and he dropped to his knees, actually cowering and swaying forward and backward, clasping his hands together and pressing them against his chest; and a moment later all of the security officers and police agents and Brethren were also on their knees, except for three or four who had fallen entirely prostrate with their arms outstretched on the ground, their faces pressed into the leaves and soil. Michael realized that the daylight had changed. Both the ordinary shining of the sun and the richer glow of the golden sparks had been all at once overwhelmed and vitiated by a drearier, brittler, more arid light, pale yellow but somehow also freezing. And then at his back he heard Laura utter an unrestrained scream, like no sound he had ever heard from her before, followed by his own father shouting "Oh my God!" in an astonishingly panicked voice and both Mr. and Mrs. Magian crying out in obvious dread.

Now Michael was genuinely, deeply, namelessly afraid. He did not want to look. His body was trembling, his mouth felt suddenly dry, he was not sure he was breathing. Even so, slowly, with his head at first bent down, he turned around, then cautiously raised his eyes enough to see his father and the Magians — not kneeling down or abasing themselves, but on the ground even so, as if unable to stand, seated close together, supporting themselves on their arms with palms pressed to the earth. Only Oriens and Aurora were still on their feet, facing westward, the white bird on the former's shoulder, all three illuminated by the beams of this strange new light and staring up into its source. Summoning all his strength of will, Michael turned his gaze upward, in the same direction as theirs, and a moment later felt himself stagger as if he were being physically beaten down; he was vaguely aware of sinking to the ground, and only at the last moment extended his arms to prevent himself from falling flat on the earth. It had been a long day of one unimaginable terror after another, following days and weeks of almost unrelieved fear; but nothing had prepared him for the kind of dread he felt now — the feeling that he was less than a particle of dust, or that he was nothing at all. His breath burst from him in a torrent. The world seemed to rock one way and then the other, and he thought for a moment he might lose consciousness. He stared down at the scant, wiry grass beneath him till he regained his equilibrium and then raised his eyes again, very gradually, trying to breathe evenly, and at last looked directly into the inconceivably gigantic, terrible, and beautiful face that filled the entire western sky, vastly overtopping the mountains' summits, rising higher than the rapidly parting clouds, hiding the disc of the sun from sight.

III

A YOUNG FACE—AN AGELESS FACE. A MALE COUN-
tenance of extraordinary but somehow uninviting—even unbearable—beauty. All gold—skin, hair, eyes—not rich, glowing,
and warm, like the gold of the floating sparks, but cold, hard, metallic,
gloriously dreadful. Ideal features in perfect proportion, strong cheekbones,
firm, straight, beardless jawlines, luxuriant hair massed in thick curls and
flowing around the ears down to a powerful neck and to broad, bare, muscular shoulders that spanned the whole western horizon. Neither love nor
mirth nor wrath on the burnished gold of the lips or in the fiery gold of
the eyes. Neither benevolence nor malevolence, neither kindness nor cruelty.
An expression without affect: sublime, remote, austere, divinely impassive.
Gazing down, seeing everything, looking at nothing. And incomprehensibly
immense, reaching high into the vault of the lowest heaven and far down
to the rim of the world. Michael tried to lean far backward so as to see it
in some kind of sane perspective, but he could not look high enough, let
alone draw back and take the whole of it in, even when he was nearly supine,
and his attempt to do so merely induced a feeling of vertigo.

He sat forward again, looked down at the ground once more, and
resolved to join his father and friends even if he had to go on his hands
and knees — which is precisely what he began to do, ignoring as best he
could the small, sharp stones over which he was obliged to crawl, as well
as the exaggerated effort required of him in his shocked and tremulous
state. He had crossed less than half the distance, however, when discomfort
forced him to rise into a low crouch and to cover the remaining ground at
an awkward sprint. No one else, as far as he could sense around him, was
moving; all were apparently fixed in awe or horror or (perhaps) adoration.
But he kept his eyes turned downward, taking in nothing of the prodigy
above except the bleak, blanching light that was washing over and soaking
into everything. Even when he knelt beside his father, just behind Laura,
he kept his eyes down for several minutes, until the stillness and the silence
and the etiolating glow had begun to give him the eerie feeling that time

itself had ceased, and that nothing might ever happen again. Then he tilted his head slightly upward and to his left and looked at Oriens and Aurora in the hope of finding some answer in their expressions. They, however, seemed simply to be waiting; their faces betrayed neither fear nor confidence. So he waited, gazing at them gazing at the great face in the sky.

And then, quite unexpectedly, Aurora laughed one of her musical, child-like laughs, and her lips parted in a mirthful grin. "Oh, Oriens, it's just so *absurd*."

Oriens looked at his sister with obvious affection, but also with surprise. "Do you think so, little one?"

"He's trying to impress us into thinking he can control us," she said. "But I'm awake now, and he knows it."

Without losing its mildness, Oriens's expression grew graver. "We are far from my ship," he said, "and far from the gates of the heavens above us."

"Oh, but we don't need any of that," Aurora replied. "I should have realized before. Nothing here is real — certainly nothing that can hold us back. It's all an illusion, all magic . . . a dream. My dream. I'm the only gate you need for escaping this world."

"You?" said Oriens.

But then the voice from the sky spoke again, louder and clearer than before, pervading and enveloping everything and everyone, ringing among the trees and stones on every side and up along the slope above the clearing:

No.

On hearing this, Michael could no longer keep his eyes averted. He turned and looked up into the unfathomably vast countenance above. It was the utter coldness of its beauty that now struck him most forcibly. The blazing eyes were too enormous and widely spaced for him to perceive them as directed toward any specific object; and yet he knew that they were fixed on Oriens and Aurora.

"You see," said Aurora, clearly still speaking to Oriens, "it's all just . . . oh, what would you call it? It's spectacle — that's it — spectacle, meant to scare us into surrender."

Go no farther.

The lips on the gigantic face moved as it spoke, but in a way that Michael found distinctly unpleasant to look at, and more than a little unnatural. The mouth parted and closed again, but without any other discernible alteration of features. It did not even seem to be forming the words it uttered. It was more like the movement of a mechanical doll or stage puppet, with its lower jaw on a hinge, than of a living person. All at once, everything majestic and terrifying about the face seemed also supremely lifeless, or perhaps too weirdly sublime to seem alive. It stirred an odd revulsion in Michael that gave his fear a sickly quality.

"But this is my world, really," said Aurora, "though it's not what I would have wanted it to be like. I made it. I can shatter it if I have to."

The lips of the great face moved again and the huge voice broke out even more loudly, now with a hint of anger in it.

I am the creator of this world, and of all that is above or below it. I am your God and your Lord. There is none higher than I, nor any other alongside me. Worship me, and obey.

"Oh, that's simply not true!" said Aurora in irritation, clearly now directly addressing the face in the sky. "Don't give yourself airs!"

"Aurora," said Oriens, "have a care."

"You're just a fantasy, really," she continued. "You're the kind of God an angry child would imagine if he wanted to worship someone like himself — or wanted to be worshipped."

"Aurora . . ." Oriens began in a cautioning voice.

I alone create this world. I alone sustain it.

"Oh, Oriens, he knows it isn't true. And he knows that there's nothing in this world that can really harm me or hold on to me. I'm . . . I'm its breath and life."

Michael felt his father's hand coming to rest on his shoulder. He in turn reached out and laid a hand on Laura's shoulder. A moment later, she placed her hand upon his. But all the while he continued to stare upward at the awful beauty of the great face.

I am the light that shines upon this world. Look to me and I will bring you safely to your rest.

"You're nothing of the sort!" Aurora retorted sternly. "I'm the only light that shines on everything here, if anyone is. Really, I *am* everything here, one way or another. It all came from me, and I brought everything into this world from what I had with me up above. You simply can't keep speaking such nonsense. Just look around — it's all my dream. I'm in everything and everyone here. Pick up one of these stones, and you'll find me there. Split any of these pieces of wood, and there I am." Her voice became quieter as she spoke to Oriens again. "Can't you tell he's terrified?"

After a second's hesitation, Oriens answered, "I cannot."

"Well, he is." There was a touch of petulance in her voice.

Now it seemed to Michael as if the face's burning eyes narrowed slightly. But he also realized that not once had he seen them blink.

My child, you are deluded. You are weary from your long journey. It is time to sleep again.

"I'm not in the least tired," Aurora replied, raising her voice again. "That simply won't work this time."

But see, my child: the night is come.

For the briefest moment, Michael was mystified. The sun was well past its meridian, but nowhere near setting. But no sooner had the last echo of the voice from the sky rolled away toward the distant peaks than there was a sudden noise from above and from every side, not unbearably loud but nonetheless distinctly and unmistakably mechanical — the whirring of cogged wheels, the shifting of gears and levers, cables straining to turn refractory pulleys, a clattering of chains, pistons knocking in their gaskets, a series of metallic clicks and hollow reverberations — and as all of this was happening the sunlight shifted, rapidly and continuously, the angle of its rays altering from oblique to lateral in a matter of seconds, flickering and flashing hectically through trees and off of stones and over grass and brush, as the sphere of Hyperion all at once wheeled swiftly westward. It took only moments for the glow of the sky around the great face's neck and shoulders to change to a pallid green, and then a fiery orange and pink, and then a bright crimson, and then at last a deep crystal blue as the sun sank below the western horizon. And all the other heavens turned with it. The sky overhead had become dark. The stars were out and shining in the firmament. Aurea and Argentea sprang up from the east, each sphere rotating on its own axis, until they had reached their heights. Cerulea glinted like a tiny, intensely blue jewel just beyond the halo of the higher moon.

There were gasps and small cries of alarm all around Michael, including one of each from his own lips. His father's grip on his shoulder tightened, as did his on Laura's. She, for her part, took her hand away from his and reached out to her parents, one to either side. Far behind him, he heard terrified jabberings from the security men and police and Brethren, as well as one piercing, helpless outcry of "Oh, please, please, please!" Then the mechanical noises ceased, and the turning machinery of the many heavens slowed and once more resumed the normal, indiscernible pace of the planets' changeless orbits. All was again at rest. Now it was simply a cloudless night, full of stars, illuminated by moons two-thirds full and at their zeniths. And the great face continued to look down, just as impassive and terrible, more vividly and starkly golden against the dark velvety blue of the sunless sky. Everything — trees, grass, rocks, rising slopes — was still awash in the dry, lifeless glow pouring from it. The warmer, more liquidly radiant gold of the floating lights, surrounding the clearing like curtains of gems or drifting over it in slowly swirling currents, seemed to be shining through a thin, all but invisible film of icy vapor. The luminaries in their heavens also, for all their brilliancy, appeared slightly muted by that cold, vacant radiance. Everything was visible, as on the clearest of moonlit nights, but with a strange and disquieting severity. Michael, feeling lightheaded, realized that this was because he had been painfully holding his breath. He released it in a sudden, convulsive exhalation.

Sleep now, my child. Let the night's breezes caress your brow. Sleep.

"That's not at all impressive," said Aurora pertly.

Michael prized his gaze from the great face and turned again toward Oriens and Aurora. The former was looking down at the latter, pensively but calmly. The latter was staring upward at her gigantic interlocutor defiantly, with lips pursed in obvious displeasure.

"Can you really free us from this place?" asked Oriens gently.

"It's all just a mechanical toy," said Aurora without altering the direction of her gaze. "You just saw that. All he did was turn the gears more forcibly than normal. And it's not even all that well made. Why, there's even a cracked gearwheel between the two spheres of those moons, and two more between the spheres of the red and yellow planets. And there are all kinds of emergency fixes in its springs and such. That's because he didn't properly measure...."

My child, these are mad musings. You must . . .

"And that's quite enough of that!" Aurora interrupted, stamping her foot, suddenly every bit an angry little girl — though no other little girl's foot would have roused (as hers did) a sound like thunder in the distance, coming from every side, and caused the ground to vibrate gently. "I'm not your child. If anything, you're mine."

I love you.

"Then let all of us go, and without any more . . . oh, any more *pouting*." Aurora folded her arms before her and began tapping her toe impatiently.

My child . . . my mother, if you wish . . .

The voice had changed, Michael noticed. It was no longer quite so magnificent and imposing. He turned his eyes to the great face again. Now it seemed as if its stiff features had acquired some kind of expressiveness, however limited — sad, perhaps, or perhaps somewhat hurt.

Would you leave me now? Would you leave me all alone? Why must you go?

Michael drew his breath in. This sudden note of pathos was somehow more astonishing to him than all the sublime remoteness of a moment before. A God proudly proclaiming his glory from on high, it seemed, accorded with his sense of propriety; but a God who spoke with such plain, vulnerable, and perhaps volatile intimacy was weirdly disturbing.

If I have made you angry, I am sorry. But you must not abandon me now.

"Oh," said Aurora, sounding at once both compassionate and frustrated, "don't try to make me feel sorry for you. It's all so silly. This is all just a game for you, and it's time to end it."

And this time Michael clearly saw the face assume a definite, if still quite subtle, expression: one of melancholy, of regret, of wistful incredulity.

Yes, it is a game. One you and I have played together until now. One that we devised between us. One that has given us both great happiness. But it is not the only game we might play.

"Do not listen to him," said Oriens.

"Don't fret so, brother," replied Aurora. "I won't be tricked again."

No trick, my child . . . my friend of many ages . . . no trick. Yes, you are right, this world is only a toy, the diversion of an idle hour. A clever plaything, filled with other clever playthings. If you have wearied of this invention, we can craft another for our entertainment. This whole Kenocosm is only a bright bauble, a shining glass bead upon a potentially endless string of such beads. Other beads — other worlds — might be strung in its place now, if we desire it. We can choose another.

"No," said Aurora firmly. "All these games must end. They're not very nice games at all, and it's time we left them behind."

But wait, if only for a little while. Give me time to convince you.

Michael was certain that those blazing eyes had grown even sadder now, and perhaps — though he was less sure of this — somewhat anxious.

You must not despair of our play only because its diversions have ceased to amuse you. I can dash this world to pieces, if you like, take all these toys apart, cast all these puppets and masks upon the fire, and start anew. There is nothing here that need be spared, nothing that cannot be broken and made into something else, nothing you desire that I cannot provide you. Only do not go. Do not leave me here all alone.

Aurora sighed in a way that suggested that her patience had been exhausted.

Would you like that? Only say as much, and I will sweep it all away. Only ask, and it is done. All these tiresome trifles will be gone. All these tedious romps and frolics ended. Only ask and . . .

"But what of *us?*"

It was a cry of unadulterated despair, coming from somewhere well behind Michael's back. He turned about on his knees, as did his father, and heard Laura do so as well. All the security men and police agents and Brethren were still kneeling or lying face down just this side of the line of trees, except for Mr. Lucius, who was standing farther out in the clearing, his hands still clasped before him and his shoulders somewhat drawn in, but otherwise quite erect. He was staring up into the great face above, and his own expression was one of disbelief and anguish.

"What is to become of *us?*" he cried out. The note of turmoil in his voice was almost excruciating to hear. "My Lord . . . my God . . . will you destroy us as well?" He looked back at his companions and then up again at the celestial countenance. His expression had become even more miserable. "We . . . I have always served you . . . always loved you. My entire life I've sought only your favor. What will you do with us, my . . . my precious Lord?" He lowered his eyes and took two hesitant steps forward, and Michael could see how violently he was trembling. "What of us?" he asked again, his voice now weak and desperate.

For a long moment, there was silence; and this Michael found ominous. Slowly, he turned his eyes to the great face above. Its expression was once again utterly cold, utterly detached — except perhaps for a faint but vindictive hooding of its eyes.

Who reproaches his maker? Who would dare?

"My Lord . . ." Mr. Lucius was clearly attempting to moderate his tone, and after a few seconds he was able to recover a somewhat strained version of his voice's normal suavity. "My gracious Lord, it is only I, the humblest of your servants. I would never dare to reproach my maker. I ask only that he graciously remember his faithful servants, and especially these his most devoted children, the Lupine Brethren, the hounds of God, who have labored century upon century to work his will among. . . . "

But that was the last word he was able to speak. The great face's eyes had narrowed further as Mr. Lucius was speaking, and the corners of its lips had curled in distaste, and now it opened its mouth and spoke.

Enough of this. I have no further need of you. Become nothing.

And instantly a broad, vertical fan of light, whiter and colder and more severe than the light already falling from above, flashed downward at a slightly acute angle to the southern boundary of the clearing and began sweeping northward. Michael turned his eyes in time to see its rays strike the first of the security men, kneeling with eyes cast down, and then each of the other kneeling or prostrate figures in turn; and every one of them simply dissolved into nothingness as the light touched him, like a shadow disappearing in a torch's beams. In the last moment before it reached him, Mr. Lucius drew himself up straight with squared shoulders, his mouth firmly closed, his wide eyes emptily intent on the face of his God. And Michael had to admit to himself that, in that last vanishing fraction of a second, those baleful features seemed to lose their look of betrayed, devastated incredulity and to assume one instead of desolate dignity — even, perhaps, of contempt. Then Mr. Lucius had disappeared. A moment later, so had the last of his companions. As it reached the northern boundary of the clearing, the fan of light simply dissipated in the air. Michael stared briefly toward the trees at the bottom of the clearing, still brightly aglow with the thousands upon thousands of golden sparks floating around and through them. Then he turned his eyes to Oriens and Aurora.

Do you see how easily it is done? I can put all these toys away and make others in their place.

"That was very cruel," said Aurora, her face now quite angry. "You didn't need to do that."

"It was also rather foolish," remarked Oriens quietly to his sister.

"Indeed," said the bird. "We were quite defenseless against them."

Aurora glanced at the both of them and shook her head disapprovingly. "You still don't understand," she said. Then she looked up at the great face again. "We'll be going now," she announced, "and you aren't going to stop us."

Your brother may stay with us, if you wish. Stay with me, the both of you, in the garden we shall make together — stay, my gentle children, my beautiful children, so fair and so dark, son of daylight, daughter of night. Stay.

"And I'm taking everyone with us," Aurora continued: "*everyone*. Even the captives in the celestial dungeons up above."

There was a long silence, and even without seeing the expression on the great face Michael could sense that the mood of the moment had changed.

You shall not go! I forbid it!

The tone was one of candid rage — and one whose inflection Michael found oddly familiar, as if he had heard it before. He looked again to the sky. Now those gigantic features were anything but inexpressive. The eyes blazed from beneath lowered brows, the lips were set in a vicious frown; and yet also, he thought, it looked like a face on the verge of tears.

You shall take nothing! I am master here! I am the God of this world, and I alone say who comes and who goes!

Mr. Ambrosius now had both of Michael's shoulders in his hands, and Michael tightened his grip on Laura's shoulder. And then Aurora laughed, loudly and merrily and quite without care. Michael looked at her again. Her eyes were closed, her whole body was shaking with mirth, and she was plainly attempting to compose herself. "Oh, how absurd you are!" she finally managed to say. She continued laughing a few moments longer, then breathed deeply, gained control of herself, and opened her eyes again. "Come along, everyone!" she called out, looking about. "Everyone everywhere!"

Michael felt something happening to himself, though he had no word for whatever it was. An instantaneous excitement and lightness and sense of release — or, rather, something like and unlike and more exhilarating than any of these things — surged into and filled him. He looked again to the great face, but now with almost no apprehension; and what he saw there was no longer an expression of fury but one of weakness, mortification, and astonished dread.

Please, my child . . . please, Mother . . . I beg you. Do not go. Do not leave me. Do not take it all away from me. Everything I have done, everything I have made, it is all here.

"You understand, brother," Aurora said, "it was only my dreaming that held this reality together. Don't you see? And now that I'm no longer dreaming it's all now overthrown. The moment I woke, it was vanquished. I've conquered this cosmos already. Our kingdom has already triumphed. It's all around us now, spread out over this whole world, and we don't see it only because that's the last spell he has to cast. You only have to see what really is, and we're free. We're all free."

Please . . .

But then the great face was shrinking away, withdrawing into the distance, fading against the night sky, its cold metallic gold growing more and more transparent before the glittering stars.

No, I implore you . . . Mother . . .

The voice had become a distant echo, then a murmur, then nothing at all. The bleak light was gone, the face had melted into the darkness. The night sky above the purple crests of the mountains was only an endless field of stars, shining in every hue. And yet even they looked different — clearer, and somehow nearer at hand.

"It's just a broken toy now," Aurora continued. "It's a dead thing, a piece

399

of ruined machinery, with no . . . no life, no power to hold it together. You can destroy this illusion . . . this false world with one hand."

"I?" said Oriens.

Aurora laughed again. "Why, of course. That's why you came, isn't it?"

"I had not thought so. The way was so long and difficult, I would not have thought it possible."

"But only because I was asleep. Only because the dark magic was still strong. It's easy now. Just reach out with one hand, and the heavens will open for you. I promise."

To Michael, it seemed that her words were infusing his own body and will with a new strength as well. Everything was changing, he was certain; everything was becoming greater, himself included. He looked at Oriens and Aurora one last time and saw that indeed everything *had* changed. Every perspective had shifted, every dimension had been altered, nothing was in its usual proportion. Oriens and Aurora and the white bird were no longer small figures under the vast vault of the heavens. Somehow they had grown to fill the sky, or it had shrunk to their height. It hardly mattered which. They were giants in this world, it seemed, larger even than the great face above the mountains had been. And everything around them looked minuscule, very much like a collection of little toys. Michael could not even tell from what vantage he himself was seeing it now — from above or below or some other place altogether. He reached out with his free hand and found his father's arm, then gave both Mr. Ambrosius and Laura a shake.

"I see it," said Mr. Ambrosius calmly.

"I'm right here," said Laura just as calmly.

Oriens and Aurora towered over everything, looking all about and upward with delighted expressions. The bird was soaring around them on vast, outspread wings. And everywhere the golden sparks were burning, as brightly as the stars — more brightly, in fact — and their number was swelling. Michael could see more and more flowing in from every direction, rising up in cascades and torrents, countless multitudes of them on all sides, flooding over an encircling horizon that had grown so close that he wondered whether he himself might be able to stretch out his arms and take hold of the world's edges. He could even see Kenopolis from here, no longer under a pall of storm-clouds, but ringed by the mild aqueous shimmer of the moonlit harbor and bay and sea; now, though, it all looked poignantly diminutive, like a chaotically turreted sandcastle among shallow tidal pools, waiting for the rising surf to break it down, or like a frayed cardboard diorama in a neglected corner of the nursery. Why, he mused, had they ever felt it necessary to flee from something so quaint and ephemeral?

"Just one hand?" asked Oriens, and his voice rang out over the whole earth.

"Yes, brother," said Aurora, her voice ringing out just as mightily, but more sweetly too.

Oriens lifted his eyes to the sky, and Michael saw that it had become like a dome of delicate glass, composed in a succession of brittle layers. Aurea and Argentea were quite small beside the glorious and titanic forms of the two divine children. The flight of the bird encompassed the whole cosmos above in its gyres. The stars looked like tiny glimmering flakes of tinsel. Gears and springs and bolted fixtures were obscurely visible here and there in the darkened crystalline spheres.

"It's nothing," Michael whispered to himself. "Nothing at all."

Oriens looked down at his sister with an almost doting smile. She looked up at him with an expression of affection and encouragement. Then, lifting his eyes again, he raised one open hand high above his head, as if reaching for something just beyond the fragile surface of the sky. And all the heavens shattered.

IV

TIME AND DISTANCE COULD NOT BE MEASURED. Near and far were indistinguishable. Michael looked for his father and Laura, and knew they were there with him, but all he saw at first were the golden sparks, surging around him like ocean waves. For a moment, when he looked downward, he seemed to see himself lying on his back in the grass, eyes wide open to the sky; but then he decided that it was not himself he was seeing at all, but only a poor, coarse, mechanical effigy of himself, toward which he felt not the least attachment; and, as the sparks seemed to draw him along with themselves, up and away, it swiftly shrank to something small and remote and unimportant, far below, and was soon swallowed up in an impenetrable darkness. He and the sparks, he knew, as well as all things living, were ascending, through the disintegrating spheres, past the vanishing worlds.

And then he heard the voice of Aurora, though he could not say where it came from. "Don't be surprised if some terrible visions meet us on the way," she was saying to everyone. "Just know that they're nothing but visions, meant to confuse and frighten you. If you pay them no mind, you'll know what to do when they come."

Somehow, though, Michael had already known this, and he felt no fear. So he looked up.

And there, in the sphere of Aurea, he saw golden chariots charging toward him, warriors in panoplies of gold and horses in gold caparisons. He saw legions of golden-armored soldiers bearing golden spears and golden shields, advancing under golden ensigns. They were tall, resplendent in their armor, but seemed to move as lightly as floating rain. He saw a field of battle that shone with the color of candle-flames, below mountains of golden quartz and a sky like pale honey. All of it, however, was dissolving before it could touch him. Then great ships of gold and shining amber were foundering in the seas of heavenly aether. Tempests were driving and bearing them away into nothingness. And Michael found that he was wrapped in a garment of glowing, wavering golden light, which he could tell was the outermost garment of many. He removed it and laid it aside, and it sank away toward the darkness below.

In the sphere of Argentea, he saw armies in silver and silver-clad knights on silver-draped palfreys advancing across plains of gleaming silvery grass, under a sky that was bright like a polished mirror and clouds the color of rime on white sea-cliffs. The soldiers had diaphanous wings, like dragonflies, and a few of them hovered above the moving ranks, urging them on. Their spears and swords and shields and armor were as dazzling as ice breaking apart in mountain rivers under the fierce brilliance of the morning sun. Silver horns sang out in the emptiness, silver gongs tolled. The silver ships whose fleets rode the aether's crystal swells were like prisms of cut and spangled glass. But all of it was already fading, already melting into mist. And Michael removed the wan, glimmering robe of silver he now found upon himself, and also let it fall, to disappear in the well of night beneath him.

In the sphere of Hyperion, blazingly bright, titanic figures with wings of fire, bearing swords of white and yellow flame, soared forward with cries of rage and bellows of battle-frenzy, but their cries quickly came to sound meager and absurd in the encroaching void. Vast mountains of fire, oceans of molten ore, searingly incandescent skies — all of it was quickly growing dim and fading against the darkness. The fiery ships that sailed the aethers were already like dying tapers in the night, feebly flickering out. Flakes of fire fell upon aetherial combers to be extinguished in their cold, vitreous dimness. The garment Michael found himself wearing now was one of burning, radiant white, fringed by flames of rippling limpid blue; and this too he removed and flung into the abyss.

In the sphere of Cerulea, nearly naked giants, as much stone as flesh, with bright blue skin, hoarfrost beards, bright fangs, and eyes of flashing aquamarine advanced from a landscape of glaciated peaks and azure skies, amid the pounding of war-drums, with huge bludgeons and spears and axes fashioned from dark blue metal clutched in their massive fists, roaring with the ecstasy of combat and the thirst for blood — but all their clamor was already becoming like the noise of insects in distant trees, and all their ferocity like the ingenuous antics of tiny, boisterous children. And they soon vanished. The blue, gem-bright vessels that thronged the aetherial flood, cyan and topaz and turquoise, dissolved into fragments and then dust and then also vanished. Here the garment that Michael removed was one of deep, rich, glistening sapphire blue; and it too he abandoned to the darkness below.

In the sphere of Viridiana, there were giants again. Some were vegetal and green, striding forward through the shadows of deep emerald forests like walking trees, with sinews like thick vines and beards like great masses of leaves; others were covered in scintillating scales of bice and jade and were emerging from emerald seas, wrapped in clinging seaweeds the color of beryl or agate or moss. They all bore pikes and clubs, either of fire-hardened wood or of petrified coral, and their voices, as they cried out to one another, were like storm-winds rushing along wooded mountain ridges or like the crashing of great waves on a steep shore. They merged in a vast army marching over a measureless, grassy battlefield of rolling knolls and hollows, but soon their ranks melted like fog blown apart by a countervailing wind. A huge flotilla of ships that seemed to be fashioned from translucent peridot rose and fell on the aether's tormented billows, but soon all the vessels were scattered and overwhelmed. Michael now found himself to be wearing a robe of garnet green, far more lustrous than silk, and he removed it and let it fall and it was quickly lost in the lower darkness.

In the sphere of Rudescens, he saw warriors of horrible aspect and monstrous shape, whose only armor was their thick, squamous, scarlet hide, striped in ochre and black. Curving tusks rose up from their lower jaws and curled past their small, blunt ears. Short, sharp horns crowned their narrow skulls. Their eyes were crimson. They rode in chariots of dark copper drawn by what looked like small red dragons. They bore great bows of horn and wore quivers filled with huge, coarsely fletched arrows. The severed heads of vanquished enemies hung from their thick belts alongside their swords' scabbards. They thundered across a plain the color of blood under a sky the color of flame, their chariots raising clouds of vermilion dust, snarling and snorting and howling amid the dissonant blare of crudely fashioned trumpets and the hammering of large, deep drums. But they soon dispersed and vanished like sparks gusting from a dying fire. Ruby ships were beaten to fragments by the violence of the aethereal winds and then carried down into the aether's deepest fathoms. Michael's garment here was a deep and brilliant red, and he removed it and dropped it into the great well of darkness.

In the sphere of Flavescens, there were armies again, but the figures that composed them were tall and slender and delicate in form, like men who had been bizarrely stretched out of shape, gracefully striding on lean, elongated legs, looking almost like walking candle-flames. Their hair and beards were flaxen, their skin the color of butter, their eyes like yellow jasper. They wore chitons or kirtles of light fabric, cream and saffron and primrose, and the only weapons they bore were thin, flexible javelins of some smooth, lightly tawny wood. Their field of war was a meadow lavishly covered in yellow flowers. Their war music was played on tuned lyres and well-tempered flutes. They sang a lovely melody in rich harmony as they advanced. But they soon floated and shimmered away, exquisitely, into nothingness. The bright yellow armadas of their slim ships, bristling with thin pikes, broke apart on the aetherial tides and were carried off like flower petals on the surface of a stream. Here Michael removed the last of his robes, which was yellow like the sunlight of late afternoon, and watched it glide down into the void.

In the sphere of the fixed stars, which were only so many colored lanterns fastened in place by brackets in a changeless firmament, he found that there were no more celestial garments wrapped about him; but still he was surrounded by a kind of faint sheathe of pearly light, colorless and lifeless and clinging like spiders' gossamer, and this he realized belonged wholly to this astral realm. He pulled it away from himself, gently, and sent it drifting away in viscid clouds of torn and twisting filaments. Then the aether of this final heaven parted before him like a thin haze.

He passed through the sphere of the Great Engine scarcely noticing its heaps of wrecked machinery, its ruined clockwork, its sagging gantries, its slackened and broken chains, its uncoiled springs and bent rods, its cold and silent furnaces, its flawed and fractured glass. The outermost crystal wall parted before him and then folded away to either side as he approached it, as if it were water.

There was a wide and level bridge, luminous and milky white and stretching out like an immense frozen beam of light over a boundless darkness and toward some faraway place that he could not see. He did not hesitate, but crossed it at once, perhaps walking, perhaps running, perhaps flying over the abyss. Nothing now required any effort from him and, despite the vast distance, scarcely any time seemed to have elapsed when he reached the bridge's end. Then he saw the darkness ahead parting — or, rather, falling apart in fragments and splinters. Before him now, only light was visible, the same mysteriously serene, opulent, and gorgeous light that he had seen shining from the jewels that Oriens had brought from his father's treasure house; and, as he advanced toward it, two figures emerged from the splendor to meet him. They had the shapes of men, tall and dressed in flowing robes, but their forms seemed to be composed from nothing but light, even brighter and purer than the encompassing brilliance from which they had issued. They brought with them another robe, far more beautiful than those he had shed, and held it out toward him, silently inviting him to take it. All the colors of the rainbow shone and streamed and poured through its fabric and radiated from it in a fluent nimbus, but as he reached for it he saw that it was also a mirror, and that he could see his own reflection rising up in its opaline depths, and all at once he knew himself as he never had before — the same and yet inconceivably different, glorious beyond words, beyond thoughts. He donned the robe, draping it over his shoulders and drawing it about himself, and a bliss he could never have imagined coursed through him and caught him up and drew him forward. Now the light that lay before him was no longer simply dazzling and impenetrable. He could see, through and beyond it, the world from which it came — the world into which, borne onward by the ecstasy welling up in him, he now entered.

V

THE YOUNG GODS IN THEIR MULTITUDES WALKED the lushly flowered meadows, through the long grasses undulating with silvery blue and golden green, or wandered in the shade of the trees at the edge of the great forest, or rested beside the sparkling lake on sands like powdered alabaster, or ranged the high mountain ridges. Wherever they went, their shining forms cast their radiance on everything around them. The air was full of floating lights of every color, the breezes were cool and filled with delectable perfumes, and entrancing music sometimes dropped lightly from the sky. Birds with magnificently glittering plumage and beautiful voices soared and darted and sang. Butterflies drifted from blossom to blossom on wings that shimmered like the dust of gems. Beasts of every kind, but lovelier and sleeker and more splendid than Michael had ever seen them before, roamed everywhere, mingling together without distinction of kind, doing one another no harm.

ON ONE OF THEIR FIRST DAYS HERE, NOT LONG AFTER the court envoys who had greeted the returning exiles had departed to bring word back to the royal city, Michael stood surveying the ruins of the great citadel that had once been the Kenocosm. Already it was being swallowed up on one side in swaying grasses, drowned on another in the waters of a gleaming mere, and covered everywhere by flowering vines. The rest of the dark city—its razed walls and fallen houses—was already hidden in the overgrowth or below the water's surface. "From the story you told us," he said to Oriens, "I had expected an arid wasteland. I remember perfectly how you described it: the Emptiness, and beyond that the great western desert, and beyond that the barrens, and beyond that the fallows, and then the Forest of Dreams, and on the forest's far side the city of Pleroma. But instead"—he looked all about him—"there's all of this—this fertility and life and beauty . . . ."

"It has been changed," said Oriens. "These meadows, this forest, these mountains — none of it was here before. It is as if all the life and beauty that the sorcerer stole from my world and imprisoned in his machine continued to grow there, as though within an enclosed garden, and when the garden's walls fell all of it spilled out again, in even greater abundance than before. Strange. The destruction of his false world has brought increase to the true world. I had never imagined such a thing. But it cannot be denied. Everything is altered. My guide has flown to the city and back, and he tells me that nothing now remains of the desert or barrens or fallows, and even the Forest of Dreams is much changed."

"Is all of this still Kenogaia, then?" Michael asked.

"Everything that was beautiful and alive, I suppose — everything that was spirit, every spiritual body enclosed in coarse bodies of soul and flesh, animal or vegetal or mineral — everything that had been held captive in Kenogaia — all of it has now returned to its true home."

Michael look around again. "This part reminds me of Oreiotopia."

"Yes," said Oriens. "So I thought too. But I am sure that more awaits. I cannot say what we would find if we were to go on from here, deeper into the west, or to the north or south. Someday, no doubt, we shall. All I can say is that to me it seems nothing has been lost, and much has been gained."

WHEN FIRST HE HAD SEEN HIS FATHER HERE, GLORI-ously transfigured and yet immediately recognizable to him, Michael had been unable to contain his joy. He had rushed across the open field. And when their hands had met Michael had discovered for the first time what Oriens had meant when he had spoken of the bliss that passed between the living spirits of this world when they touched one another, without the encumbrances of mortal flesh. Before he could react to this sudden flow of delight, however, he saw that his mother was there as well, by his father's side, and he cried out with an exhilaration so acute it was almost painful. How long the three of them had then embraced he could not afterwards have guessed. Time here was too fluid, too gracious in its patience. He remembered only the rapture of their reunion, the brightness of her beauty, the tenderness of her tears and laughs, the happiness he had never really seen in his father before this moment.

Much the same joy had flooded through him when he found Laura again, that same day, and they too had embraced. Then she had brought him to where her mother and father were; and there he had met her brother Raphael for the first time.

SOFT RAINS SOMETIMES FELL, GLAZING EVERYTHING with gentle brilliancies. At night, the stars above—brighter and more beautiful than those that had shone down from Kenogaia's artificial heaven—pursued their stately dance across the deep blue of the sky. Seven moons in seven hues hung shining in the heavens. The music that came in the wind was different after dark, just as enchanting but in another way.

"YOU SAY THAT WE ARE ALL CHILDREN NOW," SAID Michael to Aurora one day. "But we seem to be of every age. I see children, but I also see men and women."

"Oh, yes, I noticed that," replied Aurora. "Don't worry. For now, I suppose that everyone is still marked by the last lives they led, back when they were confined there." She pointed toward the ruins. "Or at least by one of their more recent lives. I met someone yesterday who had been a frog on numerous occasions. But I don't know if the frogs one sees and hears around here now are actually gods like us as well. I'm not sure how it works. They might just be ordinary divine frogs that *he* abducted when he built his machine. Some of them are very wonderful, though. I do so love frogs. And there was the most delightful squirrel that I felt sure was . . . well, I don't know. But, anyway, everyone here is changing too — though it's not always easy to say how. It's all very new. It will sort itself out by the time we reach the city, I imagine. At least, I think it will. Or maybe afterward."

"What will we become?"

"I'm not sure." She folded her arms before her. "As I just said. Really, it's pointless to worry about it. Some of you will not change *very* much. Others will have to change a very great deal before they're even able to make the journey. And maybe the city will have to change as well, to make room for all these infant spirits who've already traveled so far beyond the city and are also ancient themselves now. I mean, they know so much, but they don't really know much of anything. It will be . . . very new."

Michael hesitated before asking his next question, listening for a moment to a particularly exquisite strain of the music sifting down from the sky. "Those who must change a very great deal," he said at last, "will they be left behind to find their own way to the city? Or will we wait for them?"

"I've been wondering about that," said Aurora. "Pondering it very seriously. It's a very difficult question, I suppose, but I think I should like to wait till everyone is ready. In fact, I'm sure I will, whatever Oriens and the rest of you do. I want to see that none of them gets lost."

"Perhaps we should all wait, then."

"It would be easier for me to keep my eye on all of you."

"You really do feel like our mother, don't you?" said Michael.

"Yes, maybe," she said. "But, really, it's just that most of you are still so very, very *stupid*."

MICHAEL REALIZED ONE LONG AFTERNOON THAT HE already knew everyone here, though he did not know how or why he knew them. But no one he encountered was a stranger, though everyone he encountered was a new discovery.

"One day, perhaps," Oriens had remarked when Michael mentioned the matter to him, "all of these spirits will recall everyone and everything they have ever been, and every life they have ever lived. For now, however, I believe it would be more than they could bear or comprehend. As yet, they are still babes learning to walk."

ONLY MICHAEL EVER APPROACHED THE RUINS OF THE dark city. The others seemed indifferent to them altogether, or perhaps unwilling to revive unpleasant memories. So it was he who one day noticed something small and dully golden protruding from a tussock not far from the edge of the mere. Drawing close, he found that it was the arm of a puppet; and, on extracting the entire puppet from the tangles of grass, he found that its face was the very image that had filled the western sky during the last moments of Kenogaia's existence. It even had a movable jaw on a hinge, as well as a few tiny levers at the back of its head that allowed for alterations in the shapes and angles of its eyes and lips. Except for its mask, which was made from something fairly pliant, it was fashioned principally from wood, coated with an opaque metallic pigment, and it had curled and varnished straw for hair and beads of amber glass for eyes. He contemplated it for a little while, amused at its absurdity, and then set it down again, propped against one of the toppled stones from the city's walls that lay scattered about in the grass and among the vines and beside the water.

ON ANOTHER DAY, MICHAEL CAME UPON A GODDESS
whose radiance was especially pristine in its brightness, like the sparkling
of white diamonds, and whose loveliness was of a particularly delicate kind.
He knew her at once.

"Paichnidia!" he cried elatedly. "I wasn't sure I'd find you here. . . ."
Then it occurred to him that this was probably a discourteous remark.
Lowering his voice, he said, much more decorously, "I'm so extremely
pleased to see you."

"Michael, my darling!" she cried out in turn, and her voice was exquisitely pretty. She leant forward and kissed him on each cheek and then on
his brow and then stood up straight before him, looking him over. "How
wonderful to find you," she said. "Oh, but you mustn't call me by that awful
name. It's a little demeaning, you know. Not that I mean to be proud. But
it was given to me as a sort of cruel joke, I think, as a mark of my captivity."
Then she laughed. "I really was so ridiculous, wasn't I?"

"Not really," said Michael. "No. I think I was, though. I mean, it wouldn't
have hurt me to call you 'Mother' now and then."

Her smile took on a melting gentleness. "Yes, I think it *would* have hurt
you, and I was too foolish back then to understand. But you were always
a great source of happiness to me, even so. And now all of us belong to
one family anyway."

He lowered his eyes slightly, both pleased and somewhat abashed. "What
should I call you, then?"

She raised a slender, elegant finger to her lips thoughtfully and then
said, "Perhaps we'll choose a name together, you and I. I'm very fond of
you, after all, and trust you. Would you be willing?'

"Yes," said Michael, meeting her gaze again, "I would. Gladly."

She clapped her hands in delight. "Perfect! We'll both put our minds to it."

"Yes," said Michael. "Oh, but please, come and see my father and mother.
Join us."

"Your . . . yes," she said, as if only now recalling something. "Yes, yes.
Valentine and Helena. Of course. Yes, I'll come. That would be *lovely*."

ON ANOTHER DAY, AS HE WAS WALKING ABOUT THE
periphery of the ruined city, Michael paused and glanced up at a steeply
angled ledge high on the nearest of the mountains. For only a moment, he
caught sight of a figure standing there. It was a man, at least in shape; but,

whoever the man was, he did not shine brightly like one of the spirits of this world. There was a glow hovering around him, but it was pale, colorless, strangely indistinct. He was robed in dark gray, and a hood covered his head and hid his face. He was too far away for Michael to make out more than this; and, as Michael began to walk in the direction of the ridge, the figure started in alarm, turned, and quickly disappeared.

MICHAEL THOUGHT NOTHING MORE OF IT. AS THE days glided by, many spirits remained in the open fields, others sought out streams and lakes to explore, others ventured for pleasure into the woods and mountains; but there were others also who went farther off, retreating deep into the forests or seeking out remote places high among the mountains. Aurora told Michael that they needed to be alone for a time, to go apart to places where they could not be found until they had completely shed the burdens of their former lives. Many, she said, had become complicit in great evils—or, as she put it, had been "very, very wicked indeed"—and, even if their transgressions had often been committed in ignorance or delusion, still they had consented to them somewhere within themselves, and now needed to be set free, and restored to innocence.

"WHEN YOU SEE THE LIVING ANCESTORS OF THE TREES that you called marmoreans during your life inside the machine," said Oriens to him one day, "or see the chrysastra blossoms as they grow here, your heart will leap up in joy. I long to see them again myself. Just as I long to see the towers and houses of my city once more."

"It shouldn't be long now," said Michael. "And surely it's not very far."

"No," replied Oriens, "it is not. Even so, I shall not depart for home until my sister does."

NOT MANY DAYS BEFORE THE GREAT DEPARTURE began, Aurora called Michael to her side. "Good," she said when he had joined her. "There's someone who wants to speak to you, and then to Laura, and to your parents, and. . . well, to a great many here. But to you first."

"Did he say why?" asked Michael.

"Oh, I already know why," said Aurora. "He didn't have to say. He wants your forgiveness."

"Why?" asked Michael. "What did he do? Who is he?"

"In Kenogaia, you knew him by the name of Lucius."

THE TIME FOR DEPARTURE CAME AT LAST. MANY DAYS or many ages—a distinction, it seemed, of no meaning here—had passed, and all those spirits who had been absent for a time had returned from their many journeys, some from a very great distance indeed. The royal road that had originally been built to span the fallow and barren and desert lands, whose paving stones were sapphire and ruby and emerald and jasper, lay stretched out before them like a huge ceremonial carpet, unrolled through the fields and valleys and woods. Oriens and Aurora led the great procession, and they asked Michael and Laura to walk by their sides. A journey of many days followed, through an ever changing landscape that none of them had ever seen before—at least, not like this. The white bird continuously flew back and forth overhead, all along the immense columns of spirits.

THEY CAME ON THE NEXT TO LAST DAY OF THEIR JOUR-ney to the edge of the Forest of Dreams. They had passed through many deep woodlands already, but none so deep as this. Neither to this point had they seen trees as tall as these, or heard the wind whispering and singing through so vast a leafy canopy. And here Michael caught sight of the figure in gray again, hiding—or attempting to do so—in the ink-blue shade of an enormous copse, some distance off to the left of the road. He was peering from behind the trunk of a particularly large tree at the approaching procession, seemingly unaware that the wan glow that hung about him was visible even amid the closely clustered boles and under the thickly overhanging branches where he stood. Aurora saw him too and pointed him out to Oriens, shaking her head in consternation at the ineptitude with which he was concealing himself. A moment later, seeing that she had noticed him, he slinked away into the forest's darkness.

"It's so silly," remarked Aurora, in a tone that seemed as much wearily affectionate as exasperated. "He can't bear to see us go, but he can't bring himself to join us. I suppose I should just leave him to sulk, but I'm going to have a talk with him."

413

"Sister," said Oriens, "you must not."

"Oh, don't fret," she replied. "I'll be back soon enough. Just you go on ahead. I'll catch up with you before it gets dark."

"No," said Oriens, plainly growing anxious. "I forbid it. It is too dangerous. He has ensnared you before by tempting you to wander off."

"Yes," said Aurora impatiently, "I *can* recall. But I'm not going to make that mistake again. Look here"— she reached out and took Michael by the hand—"you and Laura keep everyone moving onward. Remember, I've been here before. I know exactly where he's going and I know a path that will bring me around to you before nightfall. I'll meet you near a stream where there's a lovely old silver bridge. I'll take Michael with me now and he can help me stay awake if necessary."

"Sister, please," said Oriens, "this is folly."

Aurora scowled at him obstinately. "It's past time you stopped treating me as a little child."

"But you are . . ." Oriens paused and gazed at her pensively. "Yes, I know. You are right, of course," He drew a deep breath. "Be careful, little one. Please." He looked at Michael. "Be vigilant, my friend. Do not let her be beguiled again. Do not let yourself be enchanted."

"I . . . I won't," Michael said.

"I shall look for you both before dark," said Oriens, "and will come to find you if you have not found us by then." He looked at Laura and asked, "Shall we proceed?"

"Yes," said Laura, "let's." Then to Michael she said, "If you're not back before night, we'll *both* come looking for you. And I'll be angry."

"I should hope so," said Michael. "I'd be disappointed if you weren't. There are some things I wouldn't want to change, even here."

"AS I SAID, I KNOW JUST WHERE TO FIND HIM," AURORA told Michael when they had walked together some way deep into the woods along a narrow path, soft with green moss and red ivy. "He forgets how well I know him."

Golden-green sunlight and golden-blue shadows streamed and quivered and flickered and danced about them. The breeze was cool and filled with the fragrances of new blossoms and fresh foliage. And there were voices, murmuring and whispering, for the most part fleeting and faint, coming from somewhere just beyond the closest trees, or occasionally from somewhere farther away. Michael could make out almost none of the words distinctly, but the sound was curiously soothing. "Are you sure?" he asked. "It seems one could easily get lost here."

"I know where we are," Aurora replied. "He thinks I won't remember, but it's where everything began."

"Can you tell me what the voices are saying?" Michael asked a little while later.

"No," she replied. "They're clearer at night. But the forest is just waking up again, I think. Or falling asleep again. I'm not sure what the best way of saying it is. But it's coming alive again in any case, in a new way. The great king of the forest is walking here again, somewhere. You never see him, of course, but he sees you."

Not long after that, they reached the path's end in a small glade, blanketed in creeping ivies and evergreen groundcover and lying under the brow of a humble granite escarpment in which there was a cave. Its entrance was not high, although it looked rather impressive beneath the boldly projecting shelf of rock just above it, thickly matted with leafy vines. A few small boulders streaked with white quartz lay before the cave's mouth. A stony brook glittered and babbled on the clearing's other side.

"Well, come out, then," Aurora called aloud. "I know you're in there."

At first, there was no response. But Aurora folded her arms, began tapping the toe of her slipper, and stared into the cave's mouth with an expression of impatience.

"Well?" she called out again after several moments. "I'm not going away until you come out."

Another few seconds elapsed in silence, but then a man's voice, heavy with resignation, came quietly echoing out of the darkness. "All right, I'm coming. I can see you won't leave me in peace." After another second, a pale glow spilled weakly out of the cave's mouth, and then a tall figure with thick, unkempt white hair and a full white beard, shod in simple straw sandals and tightly wrapped in a dark gray cloak, emerged from the shadows. His gait was slow, reluctant, but he bore himself stiffly upright with an air of dignity.

"You?" said Michael. "You're the . . . the sorcerer?"

The question elicited only a cold glare of contempt.

"Lord Theoplast?" Michael added. "I suppose I already knew, really."

The sorcerer continued to stare at him, then his expression resolved into one of sardonic fatigue. "Yes, well, not exactly," he said. "Yes and no, no and yes. That was certainly my principal emanation in your world . . . my world, rather." He clenched his jaw, struggling to contain a shudder of grief. "You didn't have to ruin it all," he said with a peevish snarl, looking directly at Aurora. "You didn't have to destroy everything."

"Yes, we did," said Aurora. "You know we did. It was a cruel world you made."

The sorcerer sighed and lowered his eyes. "That's your view of the matter, not mine." He looked about, then seated himself on one of the small boulders, arranged the skirt of his cloak around his feet, and looked at Aurora again. "It was a singular invention, though. That much you must admit." He turned to Michael. "Wouldn't you agree, boy?"

"It was . . . very ingenious," Michael said. "I mean, I suppose it was."

"You could have done better," said Aurora. "Much better."

"Again," said the sorcerer, "your view and mine do not agree. I found it much to my liking. It certainly fulfilled my designs."

Michael glanced at Aurora, then looked at the sorcerer again. "But what was it for?"

The sorcerer sneered, shook his head, and turned his eyes toward the stream. "If that's something I must explain to you, you'd never understand. Let's just say it pleased me. It was mine — all mine. The work of my own hands. That's what is was for."

"But it wasn't just your work alone," said Aurora crossly. "Not entirely. You needed my dreams, and you needed the golden sparks of life, and you had to put all of us in a cage, and deceive us, and hurt us . . . hurt them, all my . . . all my children, I suppose."

The sorcerer's head sank to his breast. "Oh, must I listen to this? Please leave me in peace. You've taken everything away. What more do you want from me?"

"Well, isn't that obvious?" asked Aurora. "I want you to come back with us. Come to the city. There's no point in slouching away and hiding here, throwing a tantrum and resenting everyone and pitying yourself. And, after all, everything really nice in the world you made came along with us, and it's even made many things ever so much better. So come back now and join us, and learn to be happy with us. Everyone will forgive you."

"Forgive?" he turned his eyes to her. "Forgive? For what? For having the will to become my own God? For having the will to create something of my own?"

"For having harmed so many."

"You forget," he said: "I am the stuff of deep, unspoken dreams. That is the light that lives in me and sustains me. I am not one of those sparks your people gather from the Sea of Spirits."

"That's no matter," said Aurora. "We can fan it into flame. I'm the keeper of the vessels, and I know it can be done."

"And then what?" asked the sorcerer. "Shall I then become another servant of the High and Hidden King? Shall I pledge my fealty and honor to the Queen Beyond the Veil? What do they do there, anyway, far off in the inaccessible north? Why do they never condescend to depart from their shining towers and glorious bastions to walk the streets of their own kingdom? Why don't you go and convince your father to leave his impregnable stronghold and join you in that wretched city of fools where you live?" He shook his head. "No, I don't want to come with you. Leave me here. Leave me the comfort of my solitude, at least."

"Now, really. . . ."

"Leave me here, little girl." He looked up at her, and now his expression was merely hapless and imploring. "Leave me, Mother, please."

Aurora stared at him ruefully for a time, saying nothing, simply thinking. "Very well," she said at last. "You want to pity yourself, so go ahead. But I'll come back, when you've had time to think. And then as often as it takes. I have no intention of forgetting about you." She turned to Michael, taking his hand again. "Come along," she said, "We're not going to convince him today."

Just as she and Michael had set their feet on the path again, however, the sorcerer called out, "I'll build it again, you know. I also have no intention of giving up. I'll build another machine, a better one."

Aurora stopped and turned around, still holding onto Michael. "Don't be absurd," she said with gentle firmness. "You don't have the resources. We know all about you now. I know you, maybe better than you know yourself. As you said, I'm your mother."

"A figure of speech only," answered the sorcerer, turning away again. "I am my own father and my own mother. I am my own God as well. And I assure you that my magic will not remain dormant forever. I'll regather my strength, however long it takes. You won't be so easily rid of me, you lords and ladies of Pleroma. And you wouldn't want to be. Do you really think I wasn't doing what all of you wanted me to do, somewhere deep within yourselves? You won't be rid of me because then you'd have to be rid of yourselves as well."

Aurora pondered this. "We've changed," she said after a few moments.

The sorcerer laughed bitterly, but continued staring away. "Tell yourselves that if you must. But I know your secret desires. I dwell within all of you, in small corners of yourselves you rarely ever notice, and never ever visit. I hide in shadows in your dreams. Believe me, I have only begun my war upon the gods. I'll regather my power."

After a moment of silence, Michael quietly asked Aurora, "Can he do that?"

"No," said Aurora in a whisper, shaking her head. "No, but he can't admit it to himself yet." Then she raised her voice again. "No, you won't get your power back. Certainly not from us — not from our dreams. I simply won't have it." And she turned about quickly on her heels and strode away, practically dragging Michael along with her.

"YOU SEE," SAID AURORA SOME TIME LATER, AS SHE and Michael were nearing the royal road again, "nothing can really be as it was before. And there really is no saying what will happen next. There are so many new and unlikely things to make sense of. But we can know some things. I mean, just look at us. I know we'll be quite happy. It will be very wonderful for me and my brother to have you and Laura as friends. And who knows? Perhaps when we're all quite grown, you and your friend Laura will be married."

Genuinely taken aback, Michael looked at Aurora out of the corner of his eye, with one eyebrow raised and swallowing awkwardly; but he said nothing.

"Or, conversely," she continued, not noticing his reaction, "perhaps my brother will marry Laura and I shall marry you, and you two can become royal consorts. I've no idea what royal consorts do, of course, but I'm sure we would all have a marvelous time together. But who knows? Maybe none of that will happen, and maybe we'll all be wed to others, or some of us to no one. But we shall remain friends, whatever comes."

"Yes," said Michael, "I know that's true."

"And, whether *he* likes it or not, he has nowhere to go. Sooner or later, I'll bring him home too."

"I believe you will," said Michael.

Just ahead of them, the road lay on the other side of a thinning line of trees, under the pearl-pink twilight that was visible through the swaying branches and rustling leaves. The voluble and happy voices of the great procession were now audible, moreover, not very far away. As the two of them stepped out from the trees and onto the paving stones, the white bird soared toward them. Aurora held up her arm to receive it, and it perched on her wrist, and she laughed in pleasure. A few moments later, Oriens and Laura appeared, still at the head of the great company of spirits, and Aurora and Michael rejoined them. Oriens was plainly relieved to see his sister and friend safely returned. Laura professed her amazement that Michael had been able to find the way back, even with help.

Not long thereafter, they reached the silver bridge of which Aurora had spoken earlier, a superbly intricate and airy structure spanning a narrow, slowly flowing stream, and she and Oriens decided that the procession should pause before crossing it, and delay their arrival at the city for one night longer. If they resumed their journey just after dawn, Oriens told Michael and Laura, they would reach their destination a little before noon. For it seemed best to him — and Aurora delightedly agreed — that all these lost spirits, having wandered so far and having endured so long an exile, should be granted their first sight of the home that awaited them only in the full light of day.

At last I came where nobles greeted me,
Before the Princes' gate, and bade me bring
My gift into the court. There I would see
The throne I would ascend, and to my king
Yield up the Pearl that glimmered like a star.
"Here ends," they said, "thine ancient quest,
The journey that had carried thee so far.
Now enter. Here is Fullness. Find thy rest."

— from "The Hymn of the Pearl"

Made in the USA
Monee, IL
19 November 2024

70608362R10256